THE IRON KNIGHT OF
MALTA

The Iron Knight Of
MALTA

Jean de la Valette, 49th GRAND MASTER.

SHIELD OF EUROPE & SCOURGE OF AFRICA AND ASIA

The fight between the Cross and the Crescent Moon

JOE L CARUANA MBE

AuthorHouse™ UK Ltd.
1663 Liberty Drive
Bloomington, IN 47403 USA
www.authorhouse.co.uk
Phone: 0800.197.4150

© 2013 by Joe L Caruana MBE. All rights reserved.

No part of this book may be reproduced, stored in a retrieval system, or transmitted by any means without the written permission of the author.

Published by AuthorHouse   08/20/2013

ISBN: 978-1-4817-8845-8 (sc)
ISBN: 978-1-4817-8846-5 (hc)
ISBN: 978-1-4817-8844-1 (e)

Any people depicted in stock imagery provided by Thinkstock are models, and such images are being used for illustrative purposes only.
Certain stock imagery © Thinkstock.

This book is printed on acid-free paper.

Because of the dynamic nature of the Internet, any web addresses or links contained in this book may have changed since publication and may no longer be valid. The views expressed in this work are solely those of the author and do not necessarily reflect the views of the publisher, and the publisher hereby disclaims any responsibility for them.

DEDICATION

To my dear wife, Anne-Elizabeth, who patiently waited for me to when I often said, "Just a minute, I'm finishing this last line."

To the memory of my beloved friend and brother, the late Carolus (Charles) Caruana, CBE, former Bishop of Gibraltar, appointed Commander of the Order of St. John of Jerusalem by HRH Prince Philip, Duke of Edinburgh; also Prelate of Honour to His Holiness, Blessed John Paul II; and also Grand Prior to the Order of the Knights of the Holy Sepulchre.

Bishop Charles Caruana was a historian and writer, I therefore shudder to think what he would make of my rendering of this historical fiction novel; a subject that, I know, was close to his heart. The first time I heard about the Siege of Malta and the Battle of Lepanto was from his lips. Since then I have been fascinated by the story of the land of my ancestors, Malta, where we still have relatives, from the Caruana, Azzopardi, and Galea family lines.

My first book, *Spirit of the Phoenician*, deals with the story of how the Caruanas came to be in Gibraltar. After a long voyage from Port Said, on completion of the building of the Suez Canal, my great grandfather Anthony decided to leave Port Said to find work as a naval pilot in Gibraltar. My grandfather Guiseppi was rather young, about 17 years old, and had left behind his even younger girl friend Conchetta, in Port Said. When she became of age he returned to Port Said to pick up and marry. They went to Malta and married in St. Andrew's Church Valetta. Then they sailed west and decided to settle in Gibraltar.

I also dedicate this novel to the brave and proud people of Malta, the land of my ancestors.

During my visit to Malta I visited the Cathedral of Mdina and I was pleasantly amazed to see, amongst the hundreds of colourful marble tomb stones underfoot, a few large slabs bearing my family name of Caruana, all of them, of course, were ecclesiastical personages.

In honour to all of them, whether they were close relatives or not I also dedicate this novel.

Acknowledgment and Thanks

To my daughter Suzanne for the proof-reading of the final draft. Forever grateful.

AND . . .

The Author thanks the Minister for Culture, The Honourable Steven Linares MP, for providing a part-grant to assist with the publication of this book.

Contents

Chronology of Events xiii

Protocollum I — **Sultan Suleiman the Magnificent** 1
    Miraculous Defeat of the Ottomans at Rhodes 2
    Ottoman Council of War 3
    Dragut the Pirate Speaks.. 4
    Reports from Muslim Spies on Malta 7

Contextus I — **Worthy of Eternal Honour**............................. 11
    The Viaticum of a Grand Master 11
    The Last Disposition.. 14
    A Divine and Blessed Death................................. 16

Contextus II — **The Young La Valette** 20
    Children Crusaders.. 21
    Preparation for Military School 23
    The Holy City of Jerusalem 28
    The Competition for the Holy City 32
    The Start of Islam 33

Contextus III — **Knighthood at Provence** 49
    The Initiation 49
    The Call to Arms.. 54
    The Order Takes over Rhodes............................... 55
    The Turks Prepare for War 60

Contextus IV — The Galley slave 65
  La Valette, Prisoner of Barbary Pirates 65
  La Valette Meets Barbarossa the Pirate 73
  The Second Defense of Rhodes 78
  Planning the Escape 84
  Safe Haven 87
  Great Mutiny on the Black Moon 93

Contextus V — In Search of the Holy Cross 103
  The Hurricane 103
  The Wrath of Nature 104
  Plans to Recover the Holy Cross 106
  The Undercover Operation 114
  Secret Landing at Rhodes 115
  The Forbidden Love 120
  The Turks Attack the Island of Rhodes 128
  The East Gate of the City of Rhodes 132
  The Hidden Passage 137
  Makarios the Healer 155
  The Maiden in the Garden 160
  Return to Malta 168

Contextus VI — The Scourge of Africa 174
  Naval Commander of the Order 174
  The Barbarossa Clan 178
  Dragut Reis—The Sword Of Islam 183
  The Harbour of Algiers 187

Contextus VII — The Battle for Survival 205
  The Greatest Grand Master 205
  Order in the Order 210
  The Battle—The Cross and the Koran 217
  The Spies 220
  Arrival of the Turks 225

Contextus VIII — Shield of Europe 239
  The Fight for St. Elmo 239
  A Surprise Counter-Attack 243

	The Fall of St. Elmo 249
	Dragut Is Killed 253
	Confusion and Reinforcements from Sicily? 259
	The Turkish Defector 262
	The Attack on Senglea and Fort St. Michael......... 265
	Attack on the Castile Fortification 273
	Surprise Attack from Mdina 274
	La Valette Leads the Attack 279
	The Resistance of Fort St. Angelo 281
	Arrival of Troops from Sicily 284
	Mustapha Pasha Withdraws His Forces 285
	Invicta—Vittoriosa—Island of Heroes 288
Appendix A —	**Tradition of the Holy Lance**...........................297
	Saint Longinus.. 297
Appendix B —	**Traditional Story of the Holy Relic of the Cross** 298
Author's Notes —	**True and Fictional Events** 303
About the Author —	**Joe Louis Caruana, MBE**............................307

CHRONOLOGY OF EVENTS

1494—Jean de la Valette born in Quency, Gascony, France.

1514—Valette knighted into the Order of St. John of Jerusalem.

1516—Meets Ana Celeste on the island of Rhodes*

1522—Rhodes taken by Sultan Suleiman, Vallete's age 28.

—Order has no fixed headquarters.

1530—Order settles in Malta, aged 36. Tripoli given to the order.

1534—Continues as Captain of Knight's Galleasse, aged 43.

1541—Valette helped Admiral Juan de la Gorda, aged 47.

1541—Valette captured and enslaved.

1542—Escapes and returns with Saracen galley, aged 48*.

1546—Valette commander and governor of Tripoli, aged 52.

1547—Mission to search for the Holy Cross*.

1549—La Villier takes over Tripoli from Valette.

1551—Grand Master de Homedes defeated and loses Tripoli.

1554—Valette promoted to General of the Fleet, aged 60.

1555—Valette promoted to bailiff of prior of St. Jailles and grand commander of the Langue province, aged 61.

1557—Promoted as lieutenant commander to Senegel.

1558—Valette unanimously elected Grand Master, aged 64.

1565—The Great Siege of Malta, aged 70.

Different Names of Personalities

The Sultan's name is found in different books, spelled in different ways: Soliman or Sulyman or Suleiman.

The Turkish corsair Dragut's name has also been spelled as Torghud.

Protocollum I

Sultan Suleiman the Magnificent

Sultan of the Imperium Ottomanus

Never was a title so well deserved. The many names given to the Sultan of the Ottoman Empire unfolded like a roll of drums and flowed like an unfinished symphony. He was known as Allah's Deputy on Earth; Lord of Lords of this World; King of Believers and Unbelievers; King of Kings; Emperor of the East and of the West; Prince and Lord of the Most Happy Constellation; Majestic Caesar; Seal of Victory; Refuge of All the People of the Whole World; the Shadow of the Almighty Dispensing Quiet in the Earth; and the Lawgiver.

He ruled North Africa's Mediterranean coastal countries, Algiers, Morocco, Greece, Macedonia, Persia, Arabia, Anatolia and Egypt. Not since Alexander the Great and Holy Emperor Constantine had there been such a powerful, ambitious, and sometimes ruthless leader.

In 1522, at age of twenty-seven years he was at the height of his conquering career and the head of a vast fleet and large army that had driven the Knights of St. John of Jerusalem from their island fortress of Rhodes. Contrary to his habitual practice of completely annihilating his enemies by executing them, he spared the valiant Christian knights because they put up such a heroic fight. He felt an uncharacteristic compassion for the Christians, especially their leader, seventy-year-old Grand Master Villiers de L'Isle Adams.

Among them a young knight he would regret not having beheaded on the spot:, one Jean Parisot de la Valette. But because of his great admiration for the chivalrous old Grand Master L'Isle Adams, he allowed the Christian knights to embark with the remnant of the army, most of who were injured, with their weapons and belongings, allowed them to depart in their own ships. Indeed a great gesture on the part of the Sultan.

His passive countenance did not betray his wrong decision of allowing the Christian knights to leave the island of Rhodes after he had forced an armistice. The Christian knights, on the other hand, who were great believers in miraculous interventions by the Almighty, considered this decision a supernatural intervention.

Years later, the Christians had regrouped and recovered their strength, harassing Turkish shipping. Since moving to Malta, the Christians had created a great seafaring fleet of superb and powerful galleys and galleons, with La Valette at its head. They roamed the Mediterranean Sea from Gibraltar all the way to Alexandria and to the doorstep of Constantinople itself. The maritime ports of the West, Venice, Genoa, Sicily, Cataluña, and Spain had all prospered as a consequence.

The Sultan was now under great pressure from his Council to correct a situation that had got out of control.

MIRACULOUS DEFEAT OF THE OTTOMANS AT RHODES

The Sultan's predecessor, Sultan Mehmet the Conqueror, had attempted to take the island of Rhodes from these fierce Christians known as the Knights of the Order of St. John of Jerusalem.

Mehmet had accumulated many great victories in the course of his career and had therefore built a very strong reputation.

But in 1482, Mehmet met his match. With a vast fleet and an army of 100,000 men, he assaulted Rhodes and its citadel, where the knights' garrison was ensconced. They built a bridge with a makeshift structure of boats and pontoons, which collapsed. A second attack was more successful, and some of the Ottoman troops succeeded in raising the Sultan's standard on the walls of the Christian fortress. After a three-month siege, a lesser force of five hundred knights and two thousand foot soldiers defeated the Ottomans again. The Turks were forced to retreat and give up. No fewer than ten thousand men and a score of vessels were lost in the assault. What was the reason for this unexpected defeat?

Before the Ottoman army attacked, the knights had raised banners carrying the cross and images of Christ, the Virgin Mary, and St. John the Baptist along the walls of the citadel. The fighting was at its height, and the Turks thought the victory was theirs, there suddenly appeared a golden cross in the clear sky and a miraculous image of the Virgin Mary carrying a spear and a shield. Next to her, a man in shining white clothing stood before a great host of "warriors of light". To the Muslims it appeared like a heavenly army in the sky above the citadel. When the Ottoman soldiers saw this apparition, they ceased fighting, paralyzed with fear. The knights took advantage of their hesitation and cut them down, driving them back.

Mehmet met defeat and perhaps it was coincidence that Mehmet died that same year.

Ottoman Council of War

In the year 1564, Sultan Suleiman the Magnificent was seventy years old. The wise old Sultan had called an emergency war council at the urging of his advisors.

The Sultan sat majestically on his throne on the raised dais in the opulent council chamber of the emperor's palace; he was attired in his splendid robes of silk with gold stitching, and enormous jewels and pearls adorning his grand turban. The chamber was decorated with tasteful and comfortable couches with an assortment of colourful silk cushion. Great silver lamp holders adorned every pillar and corner of the chamber. Tapestries of damask depicted hunting scenes with Arabic script along the borders praising Allah and his great prophet Mohamed.

Around the dais stood all the Sultan's chief advisers. He kept them standing and did not invite them to sit.

For the military: Mustapha Pasha; for the Maritime, Reis Ali Piali; the head imam of the principal mosque was present. Behind these stood the top generals and their chief assistants. The Sultan had also invited his trusted corsair friend, Dragut Reis, owner of a large fleet of gallleys, and particularly. His knowledge of the Mediterranean Sea, for there was no island, cove or bay that Dragut had not visited in his many years of pirating the seas, and because he had attacked the island of Melita on seven occasions, made him an indispensable expert in this particular war council, his advice now would be crucial.

Suleiman the Magnificent raised an arm, his palm facing upward, and pointing towards Dragut as if to beckon him to open the session. This gesture in itself was highly complementary for Dragut, and was understood by everyone present as the Sultan's means of choosing a special advisor.

The fact that they were received and remained standing was a good omen; it meant that the council would be brief and to the point it also meant that the Sultan was not in the mood for pleasantries.

Dragut the Pirate Speaks

Bowing before his Lord the Sultan, Dragut said, "My Sovereign Lord, and Allah's favoured son, so long as Malta remains in the hands of the Christian knights, so long will every relief from Constantinople to Tripoli run the danger of being taken or destroyed. This cursed rock that we call Melita is like a barrier interposed between us and our possessions.

My spies inform me that the infidels are building their fortifications, and that the maritime traffic from Sicily and Venice is growing. If you do not act, it will, in a short time, interrupt further all communications between Africa and Asia and all the islands of the Archipelago. The Christian fleet is fast and powerful and has become a nuisance to us throughout the region. Not one day goes by that our shipping is not attacked."

Dragut continued, "Our spies on the island tell us that this year alone the Spanish king has gifted the Christians with two new vessels. We also know that their leader has built another great warship, which he has funded himself, and this has twelve heavy guns; also their previous leader, Claude de Sengle had another warship built before he died last year. This adds four powerful battleships to their present fleet. My Lord, this island of Melita is not like Rhodes. Rhodes was only forty miles from our own shores, and we could control their movement, but now the Christian galleys have made their presence felt to the captains of Your Highness's warships and merchantmen. They have succeeded in interfering with trade in the Levant between Alexandria and Constantinople. Its distance from our area of operation is such that we have difficulty spying on their movement.

"Furthermore, my Lord, the island's position in the heart of the Mediterranean gives it the command of the east-west trade routes. Everything that passes through the channel between Sicily, Malta, and North Africa is at the mercy of the Maltese galleys. They let few opportunities slip through their fingers. They make unexpected lightning attacks on our ships and then disappear."

Of course, the Sultan knew all of this, but still he listened in silence, taking in every word that came from the most notorious of the Barbary corsairs in his service.

Although he was a pirate, Dragut had the respect and ear of the Sultan. Like the Sultan, he was a fighter and an opportunist. The Sultan heeded him more than he did his own Admiral Reis Pasha Piali, because the Sultan knew that Dragut was the finest and greatest of the Mohammedan seamen of his time. He knew better than anyone else the irritant the knights' fleet had been and recognized what powerful and fearless fighters they were. That is why he told the Sultan, "Until you have smoked out this nest of vipers from that island, you can do no good anywhere else."

Admiral of the fleet Reis Piali listened intently to the corsair, looking through the visor of his bushy eyebrows and walrus moustache and beard. And then, without movement, he looked at the Sultan in an attempt to detect the Sultan's reaction to this insolent opinion. Surely the Conqueror of the East and the West must be annoyed at hearing this undermining of his power; he knew that this matter amounted to an irritant, a small pebble in the Sultan's sandal.

For over four centuries the aggravating nuisance of the Christian knights remained. For over four centuries the Great Ottoman Nation had expelled them gradually from the sacred lands of Palestine and then from Rhodes. The fearless Dragut continued, hand on hip, whilst holding a sort of map drawn on velum in the other hand. "Allow me, Most Preferred One of Allah, with all due respects, Gracious Lord and General of our Armies, these accursed Christians, assisted by the Spanish Emperor Phillip's fleet, attacked and took from us the port of Rock de la Gomera, in the North African coast, in the area of the Rif, which used to be one of my favourite ports. They also successfully attacked some of your ports on the Greek coast and got away."

The imam of the Great Mosque interjected and addressed the Sultan, "Most favoured of Allah, Malta is swollen with slaves, true believers, and followers of the Prophet. Also among these slaves is held for ransom the venerable Sanjak of Alexandria, and the old nurse of Your Majesty's own daughter."

Dragut interrupted the imam and added, "Yet their biggest provocation was a few years ago when they captured one of our great merchant ships between the islands of Zante and Cephallonia. This ship belonged to Kustir-Aga, and was captured by three Maltese galleys led by the greatest sailor of the Christians of the Cross, a Spaniard named Romegas, and assisted by another insolent Christian, a Frenchman called La Valette. The ship was bringing valuable luxuries and merchandise from Venice to Constantinople. As the imam has said, true believers are being kept in the dungeons of the knights and are suffering flogging like dogs at the oars of the very galleys that are raiding the empire's shipping. This fellow La Valette escaped us once before when we had him as a slave, and he commandeered Kust-Ali's ship the *Black Moon*. He is indeed a crafty fellow."

The Sultan spoke. "But this Christian knight you speak about is no longer a corsair in their fleet. He has since been elevated to the position of grand master and governor of the island of Melita. Surely he is someone to approach with respect."

"Yes, my Lord, his insolence has exceeded his prudence. We must teach him a lesson. As a young man he was one of those that Your Majesty, in your great generosity and mercy, gave him his freedom, all those years ago at your last victorious battle, when you routed the Christians from Rhodes. He was also commander and governor of Tripoli, which he organized and made ready for our invasion not so long ago. I have personally crossed swords with him on a couple of occasions, and I am not ashamed to say that he took me prisoner during the battle of Rhodes, and later Your Highness liberated me. He is a slippery roach that must be squashed under foot at the first opportunity and I am looking forward to doing this when your Majesty so dictates."

The imam raised his arm in a gesture of asking permission to speak and then pleaded with the Sultan, "It is only thy invincible sword that can shatter the chains of these unfortunates, faithful to Allah, whose cries are reaching heaven to the very ears of the Prophet of God."

Reports from Muslim Spies on Malta

"Your Highness," added Dragut, sensing that the Sultan was being convinced by his contribution. "Your Highness, my spies, and I have sailed close to the island, we have observed and taken notes. I am convinced that those fortifications that the Christians have rushed to build can be taken within a couple of days—provided, of course, that our force is sufficiently large."

"What is the enemy's strength, faithful one?" the Sultan asked Dragut.

"We have estimated the island's strength at no more than twenty thousand, my Lord."

"Even less than that, your Highness, between twelve to fifteen thousand at most," added General Mustapha Pasha.

Reis Ali Piali, the fleet's admiral, added, "Sovereign, we can surround the island and trap all the enemy's ships inside their harbours, and they won't be able to sail to or from the island. We'll thereby cut off their supplies and make them impotent to fight us in the sea. Just as our brother Dragut has said, the island will fall within a few days."

"Surely, then, we must attack and crush the infidel Christians. Their forces seem weak, and our great fleet and brave army can exterminate and crush them underfoot," added many of the other members of the council.

The Sultan raised his hand to beckon silence, then, in his composed and constrained voice, spoke out. "I have painfully carried in my heart all that you have said and what I have heard. It is the Almighty Allah's wish that the army of the Almighty chase and crush these infidels from the territories that the Great Prophet, Mohammed—praise be his blessed name—has given to this humble servant of Allah.

"Those sons of dogs whom I have already conquered, and who were spared only by my clemency at Rhodes forty-three years ago, I say now that for their continual raids and insults, they shall be finally crushed and destroyed!

"Order your generals to prepare our nation for war, forthwith! The Christians at Melita will be eliminated from the face of the earth. Melita must fall! Bring me La Valette's head. This is the Will of Allah! The Will of your King! Your Emperor has spoken!"

BARBAROSSA BROTHERS

SULEIMAN THE MAGNIFICENT

Contextus I

Worthy of Eternal Honour

The Viaticum of a Grand Master

The chamber was not small, but neither was it large. The vaulted ceiling was held by three marble columns, ending with a capital that formed two vaults to the ceiling. There was but one window that reflected light to the ochre-coloured sandstone walls and threw a narrow spotlight of brightness on the marble flooring and the simple bed with its even simpler wooden frame and wool-filled mattress. The chamber was amazingly sparse and stark. In fact, the rest of the chamber was in virtual darkness, lit only by numerous yellow candles stuck in an iron candlestick, and sputtering torches held in black metal sconces along the rough-cut stone walls. The silent whispers of the flames, off the candles and the torches, was the only thing that moved in the room; no one would say there was anything of beauty in the chamber, but there was.

A door-less wardrobe stood against one wall. In it hung several long tunics—some white, some red, and some black. Several tunics with cuirasses, which were no more than over-the-head short capes, that bore eight-pointed crosses on the chest and back areas. The colour of the cross varied with the contrast of the colour of the tunic. The four arms of the cross represented the four virtues: Prudence, Temperance, Fortitude, and Justice. The eight points in the extremities of the arms represented the eight beatitudes: blessed are poor in spirit; blessed are they that mourn; blessed are the meek; blessed those that hunger; blessed are the merciful; blessed are the pure in heart; blessed are the peacemakers; and blessed are they who are persecuted for Jesus's sake.

The Cross was known as the Cross of St. John. In time this cross would become known as the Maltese Cross. The red tunics bore a white cross, the white tunic a red cross, and the black tunic also bore a white cross. Several knee-length tunics bore a long, red cross that went from the neckline to the hem and from shoulder to shoulder.

By the bed stood a small table that held a triple candle holder with short stubs of candle and piles of melted wax on the base of the holder, a much-worn copy of the Holy Bible in the vulgate, and a ceramic drinking vessel with a water jug.

Across the hall, opposite the bed, hung a simple wooden crucifix with a rustic, wooden carved figure of the crucified Christ.

In one corner stood a wooden frame that looked like a skeletal mannequin; it was draped with the pieces of a suit of armour and its accompanying chain-mail vest. Placed on the top was a shining full-head helmet with a closing visor that permitted vision through multiple slots. At the feet of the mannequin were a pair of shin-guards and steel shoe covers. Across a chair lay a simple but much used sword made of the finest steel, and its leather scabbard with two steel rings that would hang from the belt. Next to this hung a long shield with the eight-pointed cross painted in black. On the wall was another magnificent sword, this was undeniably an ornamental sword; new that had never have been used in battle. Its hilt and guard had gold trimmings, and it was encrusted with jewels. This had come all the way from Toledo as a gift from King Phillip of Spain, following La Valette's great victory over the Ottoman Army. After France, Toledo produced the best steel ever produced the fighting swords for the Spanish knights,

Only two days earlier, La Valette had been about his business, agile, erect, and dignified and busy as usual. He was certainly not a man about to die. He had decided to spend the day engaged in his favourite sport, falcon hunting, in the open countryside under the hot Maltese sun, and he had unwisely not protected his head from the sun's heat.

The falcon formed part of his coat of arms, as did a clawing lion that stood on its hind legs. When King Charles II of Spain gave the island of Malta to the Order of St. John, his only demand as payment was a silver coin and a live falcon. For the last thirty five years this payment was faithfully made to the Spanish Crown. La Valette so treasured King Charles's generosity that he made the image of the falcon part of his heraldry. Over and above this he knew that the King too had a passion for the sport of falconry.

But today things had changed dramatically, a truly mortal change. The grand master had come down with severe sunstroke and lay in a state of delirium.

His sunburnt and flushed face was the only give-away that he was in pain, because no complaint or moan left his lips. The fever of the sunstroke had taken its toll. The white scars of a life of battles criss-crossed his pale skin, testimony to his year as a slave and the mortal relics of many battle injuries. At his own request and as his last wish, he lay naked in his bed, his body frail and sinewy, a small loincloth around his midriff. He had prepared to meet his Maker, and he wanted this last moment on earth to be his most glorious moment, his final battle. It had to be a humble one; his wish was to give himself to God, just like Jesus had done, naked and free of all worldly possessions. He had confessed and received Holy Communion and had been anointed, forehead, hands, and feet, with the extreme unction oil.

Around his bare neck he wore his companion of sixty years, his prayer beads, the rosary that his mother had given him as a child. They were made of rolled rose petals that, after so many years, still gave off the fragrance of the red rose from Provence, his home town, which he had left as a young man and had never gone back to visit.

Held tightly in his hand and close to his chest, he held a piece of old wood, about two feet long and four inches wide. It looked like a piece off a tree trunk. When La Valette first obtained this piece of wood, it had been three feet long, but as the years went by, many persons asked for small pieces of this special wood; so piece by piece the wood was reduced to its present size. He clutched the piece of wood as if for dear life, like a drowning sailor clutches a spar from his sunken ship. It was the last relic of the tree—the tree upon which Jesus Christ had been crucified, and which he had recovered from the clutches of the Saracens in a secret raid on Rhodes.

All his trusted friends were around his bed: his confessor the Bishop of the order, Monsignor Carolus Caruana; several priests and servants; a host of knights who had been his comrades-in-arms for many years, leaned on their broadswords, their shining war helmets under arm, their colourful tear-shaped, shields rested against the walls, each painted with its individual heraldry. They stood back in the shadows of the walls.

THE LAST DISPOSITION

Several nuns who had cared for La Valette were there singing Gregorian chants in low voices. His lifelong and loyal comrade and secretary, the last and only remaining English knight, the one-armed Sir Oliver Starkey, stood close by looking down in incredulity at this once indefatigable Titan of a man. There wasn't a dry eye in the room. They had not expected this moment to come about in this way; it was a severe blow. Several sobs broke the silence.

Before the last rites were dispensed again, the grand master's advisors had arranged for him to make his last dispositions. There was much to be done, and his first requests were that arrangements be made for all his household slaves to be set at liberty, and to forgive his enemies. He also granted pardon to the group of knights that had rebelled and not long ago escaped the order's jurisdiction. He appealed to all his knights to live in harmony, peace, and unity and to uphold the ideals of the order he had served so faithfully.

He beckoned Francois de la Valette, his nephew, he drew him close to him; kissed both his cheeks, his forehead and gently caressed his face. With tears in his eyes, he brought Francois's hand to his lips and kissed that, too, gazing with intense love into his nephew's eyes, a tender smile on his lips. He gently pulled Francois towards him and whispered in his ear. Francois raised his head to look at the man on the bed, gave a sigh, and buried his face on the bare chest before him and sobbed, trying to hold back his shaking body. Still in a whisper the old man said, "You knew all along didn't you?"

"Yes Grand Master. I suspected as much. Thank you for telling me yourself." He then kissed the dying man's forehead.

Francois remained kneeling by the bed holding La Valette's other empty hand, kissing it incessantly, and weeping as child, at the age of forty-six. Francois de la Valette had just learnt, in private, that he was the son of the dying man, not his nephew, as he had been told ever since he was a child. But to Francois he had always been uncle Jean, who had taken care of him after the deaths of his parents, whom he had been told had died at the siege of Rhodes. And to Jean he had always been, "petit Francois".

Throughout his life the dying man had declared to everyone that he was the boy's uncle and guardian, but for a few years of his infancy he had never left his uncle's side. After the battle of Rhodes, he had been brought up by his mother's parents on the island of Crete. When the child grew to be a man, he inherited his grandfather's business in Crete dealing in gold. But Francois, too, joined the order as a secular Knight of St. John of Jerusalem and Rhodes, or more popularly, the Knights Hospitellers. He had fought on many occasions in land battles against the Muslims, and sailed the seas side by side with his uncle. His dream was one day to sell his grandfather's gold business and become a full time knight just like his uncle Jean Parisot de la Valette, whom he admired and adored. As La Valette's confessor, the bishop was the only other person in the room who knew about this well-kept secret. With a humble smile, the grand master looked towards the shining light coming in through the open window, and with a small movement of his free hand, as if he wanted to reach for something or touch the misty rays of light, he spoke his last words: "Ana Celeste. Jerusalem, Jerusalem."

A Divine and Blessed Death

Francois's reaction, as if intended to distract the attention of all those present, was eclipsed by something else. La Valette's eyes were transfixed upon the brightness of the window, because there, sun's powerful rays changed to one of sparkling multiple colours, as if filtered through a stained-glass window. But there was no glass window there; the myriad of rays simply travelled through the uninterrupted space of the narrow opening. The light shone upon the naked body of the old warrior, covering the piece of wood held tightly against his chest. The naked body seemed soft with the brightness of the rays; it glowed as if covered in a phosphorescent, sheer silk cloth. The body did not look ugly anymore; rather, there was a translucent beauty to it. Everyone present was spellbound, paralysed with awe and disbelief at this phenomenon. They saw the dancing sparkles forming into what appeared to be a heart travelling slowly up the rays of light. Floating with it was the shining, old piece of wood. Both disappeared into the only cloud that they could see, suspended in what was an unusually clear sky of cerium blue. The bishop stood motionless over the body of the deceased, thinking that La Valette had died he leaned over it intending to close the dead man's eyes. Instead, he stood there in a frozen posture looking towards the window. In a while the body and the piece of wood were no longer there.

Everyone stood motionless and awe. The bed stood empty; only the brilliant light shone on it. Surely he had departed this earth just as he had prayed he would, like Christ, naked and taken up to Heaven to meet his Lord and Saviour.

Though confused, no one was really surprised at this event. They expected no less a spectacular end for such a spectacular and dedicated soldier of Christ, the Forty-Ninth Grand Master of the Order of St. John of Jerusalem, and Grand Commander of the Garrison of Malta, who only two years earlier had defeated the greatest Ottoman army ever assembled. His victory had become a victory for Christendom, and the Ottoman plans of conquering other parts of Europe had thereby been frustrated. La Valette become known as 'The Shield of Europe'. Christians could hold their heads high once again; the Knights of the Order of St. John had become the heroes of Europe, and no doubt many others would now wish to follow their example and continue with the knights' five-century old effort of crusades to retake the Holy City of Jerusalem back from the Muslims.

All those present fell to their knees, bowed their heads, closed their eyes, and prayed fervently, marvelling at this supernatural event happening in their midst. The bishop led the exhortations in a Litany of the Saints and Alleluias. At last, when the name of the last of the saints had been extolled, they stood up, brushing away the dust from their garments and the tears from their eyes, clutching each other in an embrace of brotherhood. When they finally looked at the bed, expecting to find it empty, they instead found, to everyone's surprise, the body of La Valette lying peacefully on the bed, clutching the piece of wood to his chest.

A couple of days later, and in accordance with his wishes, he was laid to rest in the chapel dedicated to the Blessed Virgin, Our Lady of Victory. His demise brought to an end one of the most illustrious epochs of chivalry of the various orders of Christian knights: the Knight Templars, the Teutonic Knights, the Knights of St. Lazarus, Los Caballeros de Santiago, and the Knights of the Orders of Jerusalem, Rhodes, and Malta. This became evident on the faces and behaviour of the silent and weeping crowds that lined the streets and participated in La Valette's funeral procession along the streets of Vittoriosa, which were covered with flower petals, and then across the harbour to the city that now bore his name, Valetta.

Grand Master Jean Parisot De La Valette. 49ᵀᴴ Grand Master of

The Order of St. John of Jerusalem

**LA VALETTE'S COAT OF ARMS
A FALCON AND A LION**

CONTEXTUS II
THE YOUNG LA VALETTE

Jean Parisot de la Valette was born in Quercy in Gascony, France, in 1494. He came from an ancient noble family from Provence, hereditary of counts of Toulouse. Various members had accompanied the Kings of France in the First, Second, Fourth, Fifth and Sixth Crusades. Jean Parisot's grandfather, Bernard de Valette, had been a Knight and King's Orderly, and his father Guillot had been a Chevalier de France. Several of his family members had been chief magistrates in Toulouse, which meant that they governed the province of Provence in the name of the king.

Young Jean grew up with this background and influence. Wherever he turned in his home, he would encounter some relic of one of his knight ancestors, trophies of past battles. The halls of the château were festooned with large embroidered tapestries depicting various battle scenes of the gallant knights in full armour riding fierce-looking war horses, foot soldiers bearing lances, others carrying banners and standards taken in battle, and others of mortally wounded warriors and dead opponents. The walls of the hallways and passages of the château were decorated with an assortment of weapons, swords of various sorts, lances, shields, and body armour.

Invariably, all talk in the household centred on the latest news that came from the western Mediterranean. Breakfast, lunch and dinner were started and ended with a devout prayer, of thanksgiving to the Almighty for all his kindly gifts and favoured protection. At the dinner table the conversation turned to recounting some heroic deed carried out by some family member, or commenting on the latest gossip that had been reported from the royal palace of Versailles.

CHILDREN CRUSADERS

Jean had a fourteen-year-old friend called Oliver Starkey. He came with the latest news. "They say that a shepherd boy named Stephen from Clyes-sur-le-Loir, near Châteaudun in the Vermandois, walked to see the king at Saint-Denis and told the king that he had had a vision of Christ instructing him to lead a crusade to Jerusalem. They say that Stephen embarked on a preaching tour of the countryside and gathered many followers among the youth and children of the area. He promised them that because Christ had called the crusade, He would supply food and water on the march and bring them safely to the Holy Land, and that if they followed Stephen to the south of France, they would find that Christ would part the waters of the Mediterranean to enable them to walk all the way to the Holy Land."

Young Jean listened incredulously, fascinated. "But Oliver, we are in the south of France. How come we never heard of this Stephen and his story?"

"Well, Jean, they also say that around the same time, a German youth named Nicholas of Cologne mobilized a similar pilgrim army in the Rhineland. He called for the liberation of the Holy Sepulchre, and like Stephen, promised that God would part the seas as they made their way to the Holy Land, demonstrating their faith by trusting in His deliverance. Stephen's followers were mainly children and youths, with adults and priests in the company. As they marched through the countryside, young people simply dropped tools, abandoned their flocks, and joined the march. Under Stephen's leadership they headed south until they reached Marseilles. There were as many as thirty thousand of them. Many died of exhaustion, illness, or starvation on the way, and others simply drifted away. Furthermore, the sea did not part for them." Oliver paused for breath.

"You mean to say that the sea did not part like it did for Moses, so they could walk to the Holy Land? If so, this could not be from God. God would not abandon these young children. He would have parted the waters," Jean affirmed with an authoritative look.

Oliver continued. "The story goes that two merchants from the city offered to carry them by ship to the Holy Land, and Stephen embarked with the still sizeable remnant of his followers in seven ships."

"My God, how I wish I could have gone!" Stories like this filled young Jean's imagination with the great desire of becoming a knight, just as some of his ancestors had done before him.

"Wait, Jean. Reports have come back that two ships had been lost in a storm; two others ended up shipwrecked on the North African coast, and survivors were taken as slaves. Some say that these ruthless merchants purposely took all the young people directly to North Africa and sold them there to the Barbary corsairs," added Oliver sadly.

"Then these young men were fools. You don't go on a crusade unless you go in the company of knights. Stupid idiots!" growled Jean, brandishing his wooden sword. "Quick, let's go to the oak tree. I have seen some Saracens spying on us. Be careful; we will give them the surprise of their lives."

His playtime with his friends in the family's huge Château Fleur La Valette and its hundreds of acres of grounds and woods was naturally taken up with imaginary fights between knights and the infidel Muslims. Jean invited many of the young boys in the vicinity to join in those games. They fashioned wooden swords made from the branches of the oak trees and makeshift shields of stiff leather. Some donned gowns upon themselves as crude surcoats, painted with a black cross on the front to imitate the real Crusaders, and some even wrapped white bands of cloth around their heads, pretending they were Saracen turbans. Jean gave all the participants a handful of apples from the château's orchard, so the games were very popular. Many were the occasions when he came back home dirty and scuffled with bloody brow, nose, and scraped knees incurred in the children's make-believe battles in the imaginary fortifications of Jerusalem. The vivid imagination of these children knew no limits.

Preparation for Military School

As Jean grew in age and stature, his days became more structured and disciplined. Not a minute of any day was wasted. His parents engaged the best tutors that money could buy in order to provide Jean the best education possible. A priest came to give Latin and mathematics lessons, subjects he avidly detested.

Jean's real favourite and the one he particularly looked forward to seeing was his elderly mentor and history teacher, Lord Williams, he enjoyed the lessons when they touched upon the military history and tactics of the early Crusaders.

Lord Williams Starkey was a nobleman of English stock who had once borne arms as a Knight of St. John and had also received a knighthood from the king of England, Henry VIII, when the Holy Father had honoured Henry with the title Defender of the Faith. Lord Williams came from a long line of Crusaders that could be traced back to the days of King Richard the Lion heart. He had piercing blue eyes, and was tall and good-looking, with a pointed, meticulously trimmed white beard and mustachio. Lord Williams must have had a powerful build in his younger days. He moved with a proud swagger, and when he stood still, with one hand on his hip and the other resting on the hilt of his sword, his favourite stance, unmistakably showed noble breeding and elegance. He must have been a formidable foe to his enemies. He was the epitome of a classic chevalier, a perfect specimen of chivalry.

He was a permanent guest, in retirement, with former knights and friends of the La Valette family, with whom he had fought years ago in various crusades in Europe, North Africa, and the Levant, defending the Cross. He was accompanied by a young, tall, and handsome nephew of

Jean's own age called Oliver Starkey, who looked strikingly like his uncle, Lord Williams, both in looks and build. He, too, was looked upon as a member of the family.

Lord Williams had become, in fact, the charge and minder of young Jean and Oliver. It was his responsibility to prepare these young men for military service in the tradition of both families.

A middle-aged lady came to teach the youngsters etiquette and even dancing. He detested these two tuition sessions even more.

A cavalry officer came three times a week. Now this he enjoyed in spite of the shouted instructions of the riding master.

Another of Jean's favourite tutors was the master-at-arms and fencing master who came twice a week to teach Jean to fight with the foil, the sabre, the lance, and the crossbow.

Yet another of his favourite tutors was the firearm captain who came once every two weeks to practice with pistols and harquebus's, teaching them to clean, dismantle and repair arms, always working against the clock, impressed upon his mind were Lord William's words: "Your life depends on your reloading speed."

"We will now learn the basic moves of swordsmanship, the elegant part of swordplay, fencing with rapiers. Lord Williams took a rapier and took the stance for fencing. "You stand thus, right leg forward, slightly bent, left foot perpendicular to the right foot, thus, left hand raised and bent at the elbow, this is to retain your body balance, body slightly bent right side forward to present the minimum of body target to your opponent. You then lift your blade vertically in front of you face as if in a salute, which is precisely what you are doing. Then you extend you right hand and blade forward with you weapon's tip pointing up into the air. You are now ready to fence. A tentative touching of blades is normal, but do not be over confident because your opponent may rush you with a thrust.

"If your opponent's blade is aimed to the right you present your sword guard slightly to the right this will deflect his thrust to your right away from your body. If the thrust is to your left you shift your wrist to your left and deflect to the left. At this moment you may have an opportunity to attack yourself by taking a long step forward with your right leg and extending your arm forward to its full extent.

"These are the three basic moves that your fencing master will be practicing with you, guard, parry, thrust and lunge. Guard, parry, thrust and lunge. These are important techniques the difference between a good swordsman or a street fighter.

"Now for some serious pointers with battle swords.

Lord Williams gave the two aspiring knights a real sword since up to now they had been using with heavy practice wooden swords.

"Your sword is an extension of your arm and your shield the extension of your body armour. You will learn to use the shield for both defense and to kill. The edge of your shield is a mortal weapon and its steel, pointed boss can smash an enemy's face. You must learn to use both if you are to survive. First we will learn how to cut with the sword. Here are two branches off a tree which I have planted into the ground. That is your enemy. I have scrapped part of the bark off at about shoulder level. That gentlemen is the area of your opponent's throat. You must aim for that area to cut the throat. Now, let us see you try." Sure of themselves since they had been handling swords since very young they set upon the two-inch thick tree branch. They swung with all their might and to their amazement the branch moved but remained in one piece. "O.K, try once more," said Lord Williams who in his active days had been a fine swordsman. The youngsters put all their strength into the action and the same thing happened, the horizontal sword-strike pushed the branch away. "That is no way to cut. It is not the amount of force that you put behind the sword that counts it is the technique of cutting through and you manage that not by cutting horizontally but by a slight angling of the sword. Let me show you." Lord Williams stepped forward with his right leg and simultaneously made a diagonal cut with the edge of his sword and away came a piece of the branch exactly at the place that had been marked. With a movement of his feet and a backswing with his sword he made another downward diagonal cut and off came the second piece of branch. Fast as lightening he moved his other leg forward and swung the sword in the opposite direction and behold a third piece of branch came off so that three short pieces of the once tall branch laid on the ground. The two youngsters stood there in amazement, the three strokes had been executed in the blink of an eye. "There you are, I hope you were observing the stroke called the diagonal technique, a sure way of cutting the enemy at the neck. I will now leave you with your sword master to practice until you get the stroke perfect, balance, speed. Keeping your eye on your opponent's neck is the secret."

Following the sword exercise they retired to the lecture chamber where a servant waited with a jar of cool lemonade.

"Hear me, gentlemen," shouted Lord Williams at his audience of two, in his gruff voice, as if the room were full of people. "Today we are taking delivery of two new horses that have arrived from the German breeder Conradt von Bremen. These are warhorses, destriers the like of which were ridden in their day by the Teutonic knights; they are not the playful ponies you have been accustomed to ride. The two horses are accompanied by an experienced German horse instructor whose duty it will be to make you two gentlemen proper cavalry officers—I mean warriors. I do not want any horseplay during your instructions; I want you to take this seriously. These horses are fearless, and they can be dangerous, they are trained to kick, push and bite anyone they think is an enemy, so listen carefully to your instructor. He will teach you not only to ride, but also to ride in full armour, and to handle your sword and lance on horseback. A warrior on horseback is a frightening sight to the enemy, and more so if the warrior is a knight. Learn carefully, because your life depends upon it.

"At the end of this season—and only if you are good enough—I can arrange for you to participate in this year's beginners' tournament."

"Have the horses got names?" asked the excited Jean.

"What colours are they?" added Oliver, equally enthused.

"Can we keep the horses forever?" continued Jean.

Raising a hand in a plea for silence, Lord Williams continued, "All in good time, gentlemen, all in good time. These horses have a lifespan of eighteen years, if properly looked after. But now, before we proceed with our history lesson, I have a couple of observations to make on your other training."

He cleared his voice with a polite cough and added, "Oliver, your Latin tutor tells me that you seem to be far away during your lessons. I want to know why?" He stopped and waited for Oliver's answer.

"Well, sir, the reverend Pater Ricard is most kind and patient, but he tends to repeat himself with his lessons on Virgil and his grammar; and I already happen to know what he is teaching. Don't get me wrong, sir, I mean no disrespect to him, sir, but I get bored after a while." The truth was that young Oliver was an excellent Latin student and was an avid reader of the classic Latin scholars; he even kept a journal in the Latin language.

"In that case, Oliver, I want you to tell Pater Ricard exactly what you have told me now so we do not have any further misunderstandings—honesty above all, young man, honesty. There is no justification for wasting time. I am reproaching you for your attitude during the Latin lessons; however, I have to commend you on your diplomacy."

"As for you, young Jean de la Valette, I have been watching you at your firing practice. You are far too slow. Your attempts at reloading have taken twenty-five counts. You would have been dead at the twenty-second mark. If your enemy was thirty paces away, running at you, on your first shot you would not have had time to reload for a second shot, which meant that in a real battle the enemy would have rushed at you and put his lance through you, no doubt leaving you a dead man. Not good enough. Not good enough. Both of you need to practice over and over again until you learn to reload in fifteen counts." Lord Williams said, striking his opened hand fifteen times. "Fifteen counts is all you get for a second shot, and then a third, and so on. It's the only way to survive."

"But that is impossible, sir," said an incredulous Jean.

"No! Nothing is impossible, especially when your life is at stake. It may be impossible for a rifleman, but not impossible for a knight. A knight will do the impossible, and so will you. Practice, practice, and more practice—that is the secret, getting to know your weapon, your powder, and your shot until you can load in your sleep." Lord Williams shook his index finger in the air as if it were a pistol, "You have to become the best, nothing but the best. A knight on his own must strike fear into his enemies, and besides, one well-prepared man can make the difference between victory and defeat, so which side do you want to be on—on the side of victory, or on the side of defeat?

"I have not quite finished. As of tomorrow morning I expect you both to get up at six in the morning, come rain or sunshine, and I expect you to run three times round the estate grounds before breakfast! Any objections? Good, no objections. However, on the following day I want you to increase the run by one round, and increase by one further round on subsequent days until you reach ten rounds around the perimeter. After that, you will run carrying a log of wood, which I will prepare for you. You will continue until I tell you to stop. You think this is tough? You wait till you get to the military school."

Standing erect and solemn, he looked down at his two charges and said, "I want to make knights out of you two, knights that your families and the world will not forget.

"We will now remove ourselves to the study for refreshments and a bite to eat, and after that we will commence our history lessons."

After the repast break, Lord Williams rejoined them.

THE HOLY CITY OF JERUSALEM

"We will start at the beginning. What do you say if we start with the origin of the Order of St. John?"

"That's great, my Lord, but we are also interested to know how the Crusades started," hinted Oliver.

"And also what gave rise to the enmity with the Saracens," added Jean.

"Just bear with me a minute. We have a lot of travelling to do today," answered the tutor, moving towards some upright boards. Stretched on the wooden boards was a map of Europe that included England, France, and the Mediterranean region from Spain to Egypt and up to the Balkans and the Black Sea.

"By its side was another map, an insert of the Levant indicating the principal cities and ports of Italy, Malta, Greece, Rhodes, Cyprus, and Palestine, including sections of the North African coast from Tangiers, Tunis, and Egypt, the Holy Land.

Pointing at the smaller map, and particularly at a spot marked Jerusalem, he said, "This is where it all started, the principal area that concerns us today, the Holy City of Jerusalem and the surrounding land where Jesus our Lord was born and died, and from where Christianity was spread to the whole known world.

"It is essential that you get acquainted with the geography of the territories that we will be dealing with because I have no doubt that you will, in time, travel to these places.

"Here is Jerusalem, and here is Acre, the capital of the Kingdom of Jerusalem, as it was known to the early Crusaders.

"St. James the Elder, one of the twelve apostles, was the first patriarch of Jerusalem, and gave his life there in martyrdom. But this you know from your Bible studies. Then the Christian Church spread to Antioch and thence to Greece and Rome where it was persecuted for its beliefs. Because Christians would not pay homage to the emperors, they were persecuted. The faith of the followers of Christ was so strong that no persecution could eliminate them. For protection they literally went underground in the areas of Ephesus in Anatolia and in Rome, living in subterranean places known as catacombs. Blessed Peter and Blessed Paul both gave their lives for Christ in that city of Rome." Seeing that young Valette had his hand raised, Lord Williams paused and prompted Jean to speak.

"But Lord, when did the persecution of Christians stop to the point where the Christian faith spread throughout the Western world?"

"Good question, young man. Good question. Yes indeed, an act of providence from the Almighty took place—a miracle some would say. In the fourth century, the great Emperor Flavius Valerius Aurelius Constantine had a vision of a shining cross in the sky before a battle. Then in a dream he heard Jesus tell him "With this sign you will conquer". When he later won that battle, he took that vision as a supernatural sign and adopted the cross for his army's symbol, later he converted to Christianity and in an the Edit of Milan A.D. 313 he introduced freedom of religion. He came to embrace the faith in Christ, just as his mother, Empress Helena, had done before him, and who had for many years prayed for his conversion. From then on, all of the Roman Empire converted to Christianity. He built many Basilicas. Constantine split his seat of power between Rome and Byzantium, whose name was changed to Constantinople, named after him. Later it became the capital of Anatolia and of the Ottoman Empire. With the excellent Roman roads and system of travel, the good news of Christianity spread to the known world. The success of Rome's secret had been its system for quick communication, and this system became a blessing for Christianity.

"In those days, the Holy Land became mainly a Christian dependency. Empress Helena, a Christian herself, started building schools, poorhouses, and churches upon holy places that Christ had visited. In particular, a small chapel was built over the site where Christ had been buried, the property of one Joseph of Aramathea, called the Holy Sepulchre which the Emperor himself supported. The place of Christ's crucifixion was not far; it was upon the Hill of the Skull, called *Golgotha* in Aramaic, the language used in the times of Jesus. These sites were identified early and protected.

"Many Christian people from all over Europe, Italy, France, Spain, England, and Germany made pilgrimages, making these places centres of veneration. Many pilgrims fell sick or injured or starved on the way. So in the spirit of the Good Samaritan, some religious people set up houses of refuge for the pilgrims and gave them food and medical help. Shelters for the pilgrims were built along the route, from France, to Italy, to Greece, and all the way to the Holy Land.

"For close to three centuries, since the liberation of Christians by Constantine the Great, Christians visited and lived in the Holy Land in relative harmony with their Arab and Jewish neighbours. In fact, the local population welcomed the visiting Christians because they were a source of commerce."

"But why would people want to travel so far to get to the Holy Land?" asked Jean.

"Simply to *be*, to *touch*, to *walk* in the footsteps of Jesus, and to visit the places where he had lived and died. It is a wonderful and moving experience. I know and as you will find out too."

They heard the pealing of a bell coming from outside from the far end of the château.

"Ah!" exclaimed Lord Williams. "The *angelus*! And the *sect* hour. We better repair to the chapel with the others for our midday prayers. Prayer is as essential to our souls as knowledge is to our minds. How else are we going to retain all that we are learning if not with the power of prayer? You young fellows need a miracle to get all of this into your heads. So let us say the Angelus before we go to pray the sect hour at the chapel."

The three of them recited the angelus in one voice.

"And the angel of the Lord declared unto Mary, 'Hail Mary full of Grace the Lord is with you, and she conceived by the power of the Holy Spirit' *Salve Regina, Mater misericordiae; vita, dulcedo, et spes nostra, salve . . . . et Iesum, benedictum frauctum ventri tui, nobis post hoc exilium ostende. O Clemens, O pia, O dulcis Virgo Maria. Amen.*"

In silence they walked the long corridors of the château towards the chapel to participate in daily sacred office, in the tradition of the Order of St. John of Jerusalem. It was a strict prayer routine. *Matin* was prayed 2:00 a.m., *louds* at 5:00 a.m., *prime* at 6:00 a.m., sect at noon, *nones* at 3:00 p.m., *vespers* at 4:00-5:00 p.m., *terce* at 7:00 p.m., and *compline* before retiring to bed, around 8:00 p.m. Sometimes on a busy day, which was almost every day, *matin* and *louds* were said consecutively, as were *nones* and *vespers*.

Lunch was served after chapel, and later the youngsters had their one-hour Latin lesson, and after that a two-hour fencing lesson, followed by a one-hour lesson of etiquette. In the later part of the afternoon they prepared for *vespers*, which tended to be the longest of the daily prayer sessions before the evening meal was served.

The only free time the youngsters had was the period after the evening meal and bedtime, when the two would retire to their bedroom and read; they would go to bed and talk in low voices about the day's events. They both knew that they had to rest well since they had an early start running around the estate's grounds, a quick wash, breakfast, practice firing lessons and handling guns or fencing, and maybe something else, which could be ordered without notice. Lastly they would continue with the much looked-forward-to history lessons, the next of which was on the subject of how Islam spread to the Holy Land.

The Competition for the Holy City

"Before we start on our history lesson," began Lord Williams, "I would like to comment on this morning's training, because if you two have expectations at becoming knights, you have yet a long way to go. That fencing exhibition I saw this morning was the worst sword handling I have ever seen in my whole life. A street fighter in the streets of Baghdad would have floored you several times over. The secret is to remain calm and collected. Practice your parry more effectively; watch the eyes of your opponent, since his eyes will tell you the direction his sword will be headed; parry-and-thrust, parry-and-thrust, two quick back-steps, watch his eyes, then one quick step forward and thrust; aim for the head since the head moves slower than the body. Your opponent will be ready to move his feet, but not his head. Your attacking motion must have speed and force so that your foe does not have time to see. You must move fast as a bee and then sting! Then withdraw. If you notice some hesitation or weakness in your opponent, you go in fast for the kill. Dazzle the other person with speed and accuracy; he may surrender before you kill him.

"I shall have a word with your instructor tomorrow. I shall order him to make sure you use heavier weapons; the rapier just won't do, and your arms must get stronger! By the way, how many runs around the estate have you done today?"

"Four, sir; it's our fourth day. But we expect to do five rounds tomorrow, sir."

"Well done," Lord Williams continued. "We will now continue with our history journey. Where were we? Ah, yes the appearance of Islam in the Holy Land.

"Since the time of Constantine, everything was developing normally for the Christian population in the Holy Land until, sometime in the sixth century, everything changed—forever. What had been holy pilgrimages of great devotion of heart forcefully became the road to confrontation and blood. Christendom lost its focus on the spiritual significance of the place. Because it was being pushed out from what it considered to be its home, the pilgrims were no longer inspired by the motive of religion. It became a mission of hurt pride and holy vengeance."

The Start of Islam

Lord Williams continued, "Let us try, then, first of all, to get some idea of these men of the East, the Mohammedans, the followers of Mohammed, or Saracens, whom we had to face, and who have managed to keep Europe in a state of constant turmoil for upward of five centuries. To do that, we must go back to the latter years of the sixth century after

Christ. Here starts our account of who and what motivated the Muslims. At least, this is the Christian side of the story.

"About fifty miles from the shores of the Red Sea stands the city of Mecca, one of the few important towns found on the fringe of the great sandy desert of Arabia. Mecca had been visited by pilgrims because embedded in the walls of the sacred building known as the Kaaba was the 'pure black stone,' said to have fallen from heaven on the day that Adam and Eve took their sorrowful leave from the gates of Paradise. The Arabs of those early days were closely connected with their neighbours, the Jews of Palestine, and claimed the same descent from Abraham through Ishmael, his illegitimate son.

They bowed down before the 'pure black stone' in the Kaaba. The *jinn* inhabited the whole realm of nature—oceans, rivers, mountains, and caves—with spirits good and evil, called *jinn* or *genii*, made not of clay, like mortal men, but of pure flames of fire.

"Hence there arose superstition, black magic, false prophecies, evil omens, and all such things as had in them the germ of truth, but had been misunderstood and misapplied. From the midst of this imaginative and nature-worshipping people there arose a prophet.

"In the year AD 570, in the city of Mecca, a boy child came to be.

Tradition has been active regarding the cradle of this child, the young Mohammed.

"For the first five years of his life, according to Arabian custom, the child was sent to a foster mother in the mountains that he might grow up sturdy and healthy. His mother died, and he was left to the care of his uncle, *Abu Talib*, a wealthy trader, who was so fond and proud of his nephew that he let the boy accompany him on many of his long caravan journeys to Yemen or Syria.

"He had no books, but he was an eager listener to the poems recited by the story-tellers in the marketplace of each great town. Moreover, since his own home was at Mecca, the 'fair of all Arabia', the centre of trade for

India, Syria, Egypt, and Italy, the boy had plenty of chances to acquire their knowledge.

"Mohammed grew up a silent, thoughtful youth, loved and respected by his companions, who named him *El Amin*, the 'Faithful One.'

"In vain did Mohammed call together the members of his tribe, saying unto them, 'Never has an Arab offered to his people such precious things as I now present to you—happiness in this life, and joys forever in the next. Allah has bidden me call men to Him—Who will join me in the sacred work and become my brothers?' Deep silence followed this appeal, broken only by the high, childish voice of little Ali, who cried out, 'I, Prophet of Allah; I will join you!'

"A spirit of active opposition arose among the men of Mecca. The enemies of Mohammed would lie in wait for the pilgrims going up to the Kaaba and warn them to beware of a dangerous magician, whose charms sowed discord in the household, dividing husband and wife, and parent and child. Meantime, Mohammed himself was the object of open insult in the streets of Mecca, as well as of actual violence. The tide of persecution, however, was not stayed, and at length Mohammed, unable to protect his followers, persuaded them to take refuge in Abyssinia under the protection of the Christian king.

"But Mohammed was vouchsafed a marvellous vision or dream. 'Awake, thou that sleepest!' cried a voice like a silver trumpet, and there appeared to him an angel of wonderful brightness, who bade him mount the winged steed, *Borak the Lightning*, and ascend to the temple at Jerusalem. Thence by a ladder of light, Mohammed rose to the first heaven, made of pure silver, and lighted by stars suspended by chains of gold. And so it came to pass that many others followed the Prophet. And now, we find ourselves fighting against his descendants. Their battle cry, which binds them together, has always been *Allahu Akbar*.

"He and his followers preached the message that there was only one God, something, of course, that Christians and Jews always believed, but the Mohammedans said that Allah was his name, and that his commandments, those given to Mohammed in a vision, were to be observed and no other. Anyone who did not believe in Allah was an unbeliever and an infidel to God.

"Mohammed reportedly died in Jerusalem and was taken up to heaven in the area where Solomon's temple once stood. With the death of Mohammed, Jerusalem also became the Holy City of Islam and was soon conquered and ruled by the Islamic forces.

"Naturally, the Christians and the Jews resented this, and though there were many quarrels, the Muslims tolerated the Christians and Jews because of their inferior numbers. For a while both Christian and Jews lived there under sufferance of the Muslim."

Jean raised his hand to ask a question.

Pausing to give way, Lord Williams leaned on the table and beckoned. Jean asked, "Sir, what was the reaction to all this by the Christian side?"

"A Benedictine monk, Brother Gérard, initiated the action; but five names played a leading part in what became known as 'THE JUST WAR'. These men were Emperor Alexius II, Pope Urban II, Bohemond, Prince of Antioch and blessed Raymond de Puy who justified the bearing of arms by some of the religious members.

"From then on, in the year 1095, the monk warriors assaulted Jerusalem, easily defeating the Saracens in the name of Christianity, and created four Christian territories in the Holy Land.

"The Saracens had one thing that our people did not have. They had a powerful purpose. They had an objective. Their call to arms was not only religious, but also intended to impose that religion. Their holy book, the Koran, contained a call to *jihad*, a fight to the death for their beliefs. Our side did not have this strong motivation at the beginning, so no one set out at first to fight or impose anything. The purpose was to defend. The spirit of peace and love, and the beatitudes as set out by Jesus called for forgiveness of your enemies, for humility, for turning the other cheek. Violence was alien to the gospel of Jesus. The motivation of a Christian was a passive and defensive one. This contrasting difference in objectives, between the new religion of Islam and the Judaeo-Christian ideals was not apparent to our people. For a few hundred years Christians took a beating from the Muslims in our own territory. We needed a Christian type of call like the call to jihad so as to defend our rightful place in the Holy Land. The type of calling that came out of it was called a *Crusade* because we took up the Cross.

"But the situation in the Holy Land went from bad to worse. Of course, our stand was that the Holy Land was holy to the Jewish and the Christian faiths long before the Muslims came, with Jesus Christ himself a Jew who preached, taught and died in the city of Jerusalem.

"Our settlers were few so the Holy Father had no alternative but to send out preachers throughout Europe to tell the people what was happening in the Holy Land, and about the slaughter of Christians there. Encouraged by many religious preachers throughout Europe the rallying point being the Cross, the sign of the Crusades. There were no Christian knights as yet, only Christian warriors.

"Many of those who took up the Cross came from noble houses in Europe, Italy, France, Spain, England, and Germany, they were able to establish a considerable and powerful force. The fight was in effect a religious one, with the intent to preserve the Christian faith, and at the same time to help the sick and the poor victims in the Holy Land.

"The French called these territories *Outremer*, or 'Land beyond the Sea.' The Christian Kingdom of Jerusalem was thus created and defended with sporadic attacks. These were divided into the states of Jerusalem, Tyre, Acre, Beirut, and the counties of Tripoli, Edessa, and Antioch.

"Before and after this, Islamic expansion had continued throughout the Mediterranean. Muslims invaded Spain through a landing in Gibraltar in the year AD 711."

"Was this Brother Gérard the person who started the Order of St. John?" asked Oliver.

"Good question again, yes. During the reign of Emperor Constantine his mother Helena established houses of rest in Jerusalem. In the year AD 600, Pope Gregory, hearing of the large numbers of pilgrims travelling to the Holy Land and of the hardships they endured, expanded this service and commissioned that a hospital be built in Jerusalem to treat and care for the Christian pilgrims. Later, in AD 800, *Charlemange,* emperor of the Holy Roman Empire, enlarged the hospital and added a library to it.

"But in the year AD 1005, *Calipha Al Ho Kim* attacked Jerusalem and destroyed the hospital and three thousand other Christian buildings of that city.

"By the year AD 1023 another Caliph, one *Aza-Zahir* of Egypt seeing that Christian merchants from Amalfi and Salermo came to do trade with them, gave them permission to rebuild the hospital. The hospital had been on the site of the monastery of St. John the Baptist and was served by Benedictine monks. The guest house was situated on the other side of the road of the Church of the *Holy Sepulchre.* It was very big, as it was always occupied by numerous pilgrims because pilgrims arrived in Jerusalem exhausted or sick."

"But sir, weren't the people informed what conditions were like, and about the perils they would face in the Holy Land once they got there?" Oliver enquired again.

"Yes they were, but still they came, in large numbers. Therefore the needs grew and grew, and the guest house of St. Maria Latina became more a hospital and hotel than a church. This church was then commonly known as the Hospital of Jerusalem. It attended the sick and abandoned children, fed the starving, clothed the needy, and cared for discharged prisoners.

"The Benedictine monk Gerard was considered so saintly that he became known as Blessed Gérard. This community is the historical root of the Hospitallers Order of St. John. In fact, the *statutes of the Benedictine order* is the basis of the Brotherhood of St. John of Jerusalem, and these statutes rule our order. Its spirituality goes back to the Benedictine principle of hospitality, expressed in chapter 53 of the *Rule of St. Benedict,* which reads: 'All guests who present themselves are to be welcomed as Christ, for He Himself said: "I was a stranger and you welcomed me." (Matthew 25:35) Proper honour must be shown to all, especially to those who share our faith (Galatians 6:10) and to pilgrims.' And that is exactly what the hospital of Jerusalem and its brotherhood did.

"Blessed Gérard and his successors called the sick 'the poor of Christ', indicating that they were to be welcomed as Christ. Members of the hospital order made the promise 'to be servants and slaves *to our lords, the sick*'. They considered it a favour to have the honour of serving the poor and needy, and thus receive the grace of being close to Christ."

"How we wish we could serve the people in that way," added Jean.

"Sir, but don't you think that that spirit has gone with the times and with the brutality that has existed in between?" asked Oliver.

"You are right, young man" interjected Lord Williams, "Such an attitude is still a contradiction to the spirit of our times. But let us not deviate from the trajectory of our lesson. The hospital was actually regarded as a spiritual community, and the sick were not only cared for bodily, but also benefited from the spiritual care with the application of the sacraments, Bible reading, and prayer time, with frequent Masses and benedictions. You must always remember that the *Rule of the Order of St. John* reads, in chapter 17: 'When a sick [person] comes to the house, . . . he may be received as follows: After he has first faithfully confessed his sins to a priest, he may receive Holy Communion, and afterwards he may be carried to a bed and may be lovingly fed every day, according to the possibilities of the house, even before the brothers have their meal. And the reading and the gospel may be read in the hospital on all Sundays, and the sick may be sprinkled with holy water during the procession.' This is primarily the first and true mission of the order. The military side was something that was imposed upon us by circumstances outside our control. The hospital was considered a community of saints, a church building, and a community hall. The ward was a big room with an altar inside, so that all the sick could participate in Holy Mass without having to leave their beds. The Holy Book says 'Whenever you did this for

"Wait a moment before you go; I have a piece of news for you. Soon you will be entering the priory. I have already made the necessary arrangement for your admittance into the order sometime next month."

The two young men jumped up with joy at this news, and they embraced and slapped each other on the back whilst Lord Williams looked upon this demonstration of joy with much satisfaction. The priory was where knights of the order were truly made.

Map of the Mediterranean-1556

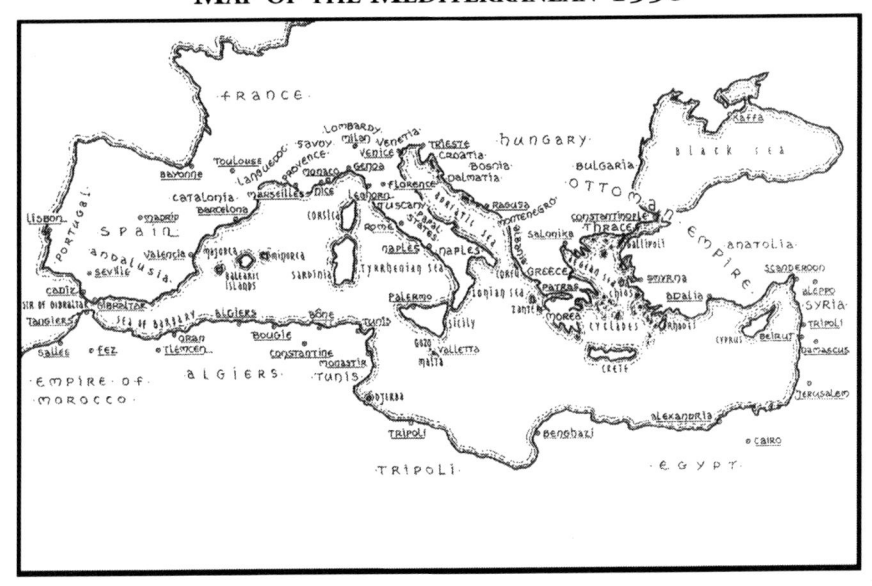

BLESSED ST. GERARD

ARTIST'S IMPRESSION OF THE FORTRESS IN THE
ISLAND OF RHODES

LA VALETTE. IN SURCOAT

GRAND MASTER JEAN PARISOT DE LA VALETTE.
49ᵀᴴ GRAND MASTER OF
THE ORDER OF ST. JOHN OF JERUSALEM

CREST OF THE ORDER OF ST. JOHN

Contextus III

Knighthood at Provence

The Initiation

Ten men lay prostrate, arms stretched out in front of them, on the floor of the main altar of the principal chapel of the knights' priory. The chapel's hall was full of visitors, but with few knights, since these were stationed abroad. The hall was musty with smoke and the smell of incense.

The Grand Master of the Order of the Provence Langue towered over them, as did the chapter's priests and bishop. The walls of the chapel and the hanging candelabras were full of burning candles that spewed black smoke to the ceiling and flickering light onto the postulants.

The grand master made the postulants repeat the age-old spiritual vows of chastity, poverty, and obedience in the tradition of the Order of St. Benedict. Very solemnly, the grand master declared upon them, "Your very posture on the floor is a gesture of humility and surrender in obedience to the will of God and the Order of Knights Hospitallers of St. John of Jerusalem, because first and foremost you are joining a religious brotherhood whose aim is to care for the sick and the poor, in the tradition of the Blessed Gérard, following the example of Christ. You shall observe always the prayers of the hours and the sacraments."

Afterwards they presented themselves most respectfully before the person performing the ceremony, and requested to be received into the company of brothers, and into the Order of the Hospitaller of Jerusalem.

He proceeded to point out that the engagement they were to enter into was one of perfect obedience, and the severity of the rules, which would no longer permit them to act for themselves, which obliged them absolutely to renounce their own will and pleasure, and implicitly to comply with that of their superiors, so that if ever they felt an inclination to do one thing, they were compelled by their vow of obedience to do another.

He next asked each candidate whether he found himself disposed to submit to all these obligations. He was asked whether he had ever before taken the vows in any other order; whether he had ever been married; if his marriage had been consummated; if he owed any considerable sums; and if he were a slave. Because if, after having taken the vows, it were discovered that he had been in the last-mentioned situations, he would immediately be stripped of his habit with disgrace as a deceiver, and be given up to the master to whom he formerly belonged.

The postulant was presented with an open missal, on which he placed both his hands, and having answered all the above questions, made his profession in the following terms, in Latin:

"I do vow and promise to Almighty God, to the holy eternal Virgin Mary, mother of God, and to St. John the Baptist, to render, henceforward, by the grace of God, perfect obedience to the superior placed over me, to live without personal property, and to preserve my chastity."

Having taken his hands from the book, the brother who received him said: "We acknowledge you as the servant of the poor and sick, and as having consecrated yourself to the defense of the Catholic Church."

To which he answered: "I acknowledge myself as such." He then kissed the missal placed it on the altar.

The brother took the black mantle, and showing the postulant the white cross upon it, addressed him: "Do you believe, my brother, that this is the symbol of that Holy Cross to which Jesus Christ was fastened, and on which he died for our sins?"

"Yes, I do verily believe it."

Then he added: "Then we command you to wear it constantly." The new brother then kissed the cross; and the other threw the mantle over his shoulder in such a manner that the cross was placed on his left breast.

The brother who had received him then kissed him, saying. "Take this sign in the name of the Holy Trinity. We place this cross on your breast, my brother, that you may love it with all your heart; and may your right hand ever fight in its defense, and for its preservation! Should it ever happen that in combating for Jesus Christ against the enemies of the faith, you should retreat, desert the standard of the cross, and take to flight in so just a war, you will be stripped of this truly holy sign, as having broken the vow you have just taken."

They took their vows of obedience to the Church's supreme leader, the Holy Father, Pope Julius II.

This first part of the ceremony was the spiritual ritual.

The vow of chastity was necessary for a knight because had no time to care for a family. Should a married man choose to become a knight, he would have to relinquish his family following the words of Christ, *"There is no one who has given up home, brothers or sisters, mother or father, children or property, for me and for the gospel who will not receive in this present age brothers and sisters, mothers, children and property—and persecution besides—and in the age to come everlasting life."* (Mark 10:29)

A knight had no time to serve anyone else except God and the work of the order.

Likewise, a knight had to relinquish all earthly goods and live in accordance with the rules of the order, which did not cater for the comforts or the finer things in life. Knights lived in community, sharing everything with his brethren knights, and so made vows of poverty, as practiced by the early Christians according the Acts of the Apostles.

Following the constant fighting and confrontations with the Muslims, the order that once catered only for the bodily and spiritual needs of the sick, had of necessity become warrior monks, the first of whom had been Blessed Raymund du Puy, who succeeded St. Gérard.

They were told that the origin of the term *knight* derived from the Anglo-Saxon word *cniht*, meaning "boy", or "page boy", since the steps to knighthood started as a boy. His early upbringing would therefore be governed by his family's ambition.

The ten men dressed in plain grey, hooded in floor-length tunics, in the fashion of the Benedictine monks, were asked to kneel on their left knee, in a row of ten kneelers.

The grand master of the Provence Langue, George Clairvaux, pronounced in his booming voice, "I, George Clairvaux, grand master of the Most Holy Order of the Knights Hospitaller of St. John Of Jerusalem, and of the Langue of Provence, hereby knight you as brethren into this majestic order, to defend the Catholic faith, and to always honour and obey the commands and wishes of the Holy Father and your grand master, present or to come."

The grand master stood in front of the kneelers Jean's named was called first, since he had acquired the position of principal recruit. The grand master raised an elaborate golden sword and tapped Jean twice first on the right and then on the left shoulder saying, "By the power vested upon me as grand master I hereby name you, Sir Jean Parisot de la Valette, Knight of the Order of Hospitallers of St. John of Jerusalem. Arise! Sir Jean Parisot de la Valette!"

Jean, with tears in his eyes, rose and took the white surcoat with the red cross. He gave this to his squire, who, with much difficulty, placed it over him, the tunic reaching down to below Jean's knees. Then he put the black mantle on the new brother, tied it with strings round his neck, allowing the white eight-pointed cross to fall on his right shoulder, and said: "Receive the yoke of the Lord, for it is easy and light, with it you shall find rest for your soul. We promise you nothing but bread and water, a simple habit of little worth. We give you and your parents and relations a share in the good works performed by our order, and by our brothers, both now and hereafter, throughout the world."

In reply, the newly professed knight answered, "Amen," which means "So be it."

The bishop came forward bearing a small crucifix, which he lifted and placed on his lips, the new knight inclined forward, kissed the crucifix, and made the sign of the cross on his chest.

Jean's father, his uncle, his elderly grandfather, and Lord Williams, his mentor; all sat at the back of the chapel. They were a few of the fortunate knights who had returned to their homes unharmed from the Crusades. They knew better than most the perils that confronted the young man.

There was much handshaking and back-slapping at the end of the ceremony. But now the handshake was different. It was, in fact, a warrior's arm lock in the Roman style. All the new knights were attired in their full dress, with swords and scabbards hanging on their sword belts, and shining helmets with movable visors held under their arms.

Two items distinguished Jean from the others. His sword was not shining new; rather, it was old and simple, in fact totally plain. Also, La Valette had endured the ceremony leaning on a homemade crutch the result of a fall off a horse.

La Valette's sword was a fighting sword, an heirloom handed down the La Valette family line, the sword his father and grandfather and his great-grandfather before him had worn in battles in the Crusades. It had no fancy gold braid on the handle. Rather, the handle was a plain cross as the hilt or guard, and in order to deflect a sword thrust, it had two rings cast on the underside of the guard so that swords would not lock and catch. The handgrip was circular, and the knob on the top of the handle was a simple knurled sphere. There were no jewels, gold, or silver on this sword. A sword that had seen much action.

THE CALL TO ARMS

An unexpected attack by the Ottoman forces had provoked a need for another papal call to arms to strengthen the garrison on the island of Rhodes. So Rhodes, it appeared, was to be the destination of the new knights.

Years earlier when the Crusaders were driven from Acre, the last Christian stronghold in the Holy Land, they made their way to nearby Cyprus, but the Christian king of Cyprus, fearing retaliation from the Ottoman Turks, asked them to move on. The order's grand master had his eye on the beautiful island of Rhodes, *the garden of the Mediterranean,* a perfect spot to create a maritime fighting force. The order was intent on starting a maritime force to fight at sea rather than on land.

Enormous confusion resulted when knights who spoke many languages fought in battle but could not understand each other. It had been like Babel when they were building the famous tower. Consequently there were many casualties and even battles lost.

The grand master of the day created eight different divisions, calling them *Langues*, or languages. From France, Auvergne, Provençal, England, Aragon, Castile, from Spain. Later one each from Germany and Italy were added. The new arrangement was a great improvement, making it possible for some harmony and cohesion in the knights' army.

The three-year training period Jean and Oliver had endured had been tough and relentless. They came to appreciate all the hard work that Lord Williams had prepared them for. Their new instructors were veteran knights who had lived in many difficult situations in several crusades.

Induction into the gunnery division was something new to Jean and Oliver. They had to join in the handling and movement of cannons of all sizes. The *basilisk*, a titan of a gun, was named after the legendary monster. Its power and accuracy were fatal. It could fire cannonballs of up to two hundred pounds in weight, and lived up to its name; its roar and the flame that spouted from its mouth were truly monstrous. Its handling required two huge oxen. It could be moved up or down only with the use of long, iron levering bars.

The *culverin* was another type of cannon—very long barrel, for long-rage firing, luckily it was not as heavy or awkward to use as the *basilisk*.

Mock charges on destriers were a daily thing, as was sword-play with heavy broadswords, which also helped to strengthen their arms and shoulder muscles.

Physically, Jean had grown into a strong young man. Powerful, and serious in character, he had acquired the reputation of being fearless in all the challenges presented to him.

Whilst other knights of his age engaged in all the things that young men do—going out to drink, gamble, and occasionally, secretly going to taverns where ladies of ill repute practiced the oldest of the professions—Jean did not; he took his vows of temperance and chastity very seriously. As soon as he laid down his weapon or finished his war games, he would set himself apart with his Bible to pray and contemplate. He was a stickler for keeping to his prayer times five times a day.

Oliver was by far a more intellectual individual, and excelled above everyone else in his company in the Latin and Greek languages. His knowledge of the classics was extensive. Yet he, too, was a physically powerful young man and an excellent swordsman and strategist.

THE ORDER TAKES OVER RHODES

Veteran knight Jacques Vidal had participated in many engagements with the Saracens, in particular in the first raid by the Turkish leader Mehmet II of the island of Rhodes, with his considerably large army. Vidal had been assigned to the guidance and the training of recently knighted young men.

Whenever the opportunity presented itself, he recounted his experiences in minute and explicit details. Though his stories as to how the knights resisted that first invasion of Rhodes were somewhat embellished.

He told the story, one that had been handed down to him by another valiant knight, of how one hundred years earlier, Grand Master Foulques de Villaret was able to sail from Cyprus to take over possession of Rhodes because he thought that this would restore the order's standing and would enable them to continue the fight against the Muslims. He had been forced to move to Cyprus, itself a Christian protectorate. Now the king of Cyprus wanted the knights off the island.

Grand Master de Villaret had his eye on Rhodes as an ideal base on which to settle the order's remaining forces. There was a big problem though. The beautiful island was controlled by Christians—Greek Orthodox Catholics, separated from the Roman Catholic Church through schism (a difference as to the headship and leadership of the Christian Church), but nonetheless it was Christian in every other respect of faith.

There was a very clear, specific standing order in a papal edict that no order—including the Order of St. John of Jerusalem—should attack another Christian community. Obviously, this edict covered Greek Orthodox Christians. In so doing Grand Master de Villaret was breaking this papal edict. The order's ethos was bound up with the struggle against Islamic power and not with attacks on Greek Orthodox Christians. Even though this went against all their principles, Grand Master de Villaret went ahead. The pope did not wish additional animosity with the Catholic Greek Orthodox hierarchy.

Villaret's pride and hope was that of one day they would re-take possession of the Holy Land. Rhodes would be the ideal platform to try to open their missions for helping distressed pilgrims while harassing the Muslims at the same time.

For many years, Rhodes had established itself as something of a pirate's haven. Rhodes itself remained in a state of permanent alarm.

The low number of knights and soldiers now available to the Christian side was alarming, and this made land battles impossible against the massive and still growing Turkish forces. The idea came about that the Hospitallers could do much better if they turned their tactics from land battles to sea warfare. The archipelagos of Rhodes was an ideal mass of islands in which to hide, resupply, and attack the enemy of Christianity.

Apart from Cyprus, the only larger islands left were Chios and Rhodes, which were made up of twelve islands. Agathonisi, Astypalaia, Halki and Kalimnos. The latter island was barren rock, golden beaches, and tiny green valleys, and owed its fame to its celebrated sponge fishing. There were also Karpathos, Kasso, Kastelorizo and Kos, the island that gave the world Hippocrates, the father of medicine. The island looks like a huge floating garden. From the very first moment that Christians lived in Rhodes, they acquired the hope that God, the saints, and the angels would bestow them protection. The capital of the Ottoman Empire, Anatolia, was a mere thirty miles away!

Once the Knights of St. John of Jerusalem took over, the Greek inhabitants of Rhodes became vassals of the order, and for a long time, resented their presence. The order, if the truth be told, was not very magnanimous with local populations.

However, Grand Master Villaret, disregarding the papal edict, immediately started on a programme of repairing and enlarging the fortifications of the city and constructing no less than twelve lookout towers. A grand new hospital was built where the sick and injured were given assistance. The city of Rhodes had been created within the wall of a very long line of fortification walls difficult to defend with few troops.

Knight Vidal told the young knights the story about a servant of the Hospitallers in Rhodes who was actually an enemy spy, passing himself off as a Christian. It was said that when he reached out and touched a venerated holy relic, the skeletal hand of the saint, *"grabbed the traitor, and wouldn't let go."* the traitor recognized his crime and confessed his treasonable intentions.

From Rhodes, the few Hospitallers' war ships waged a constant war against the Turks, which was "as violent as it was just."

The knight Hospitallers had to adapt their medieval military system to a naval one. The male population they conquered were compelled to participate in what came to be known as *servitudo marina*, marine service and were conscripted to work on the Hospitallers' vessels. Ironically, in the east, the Kingdom of Cyprus asked them to organize raids on Mameluk, Egypt.

It had fertile lands, good climate, and an abundance of water, as well as exotic and rich orange and lemon groves, and olive fields. Vineyards produced excellent wine. Well-protected coves and bays for sheltering vessels made it an outstanding naval base from which to continue to harass Turkish shipping.

The two young knights listened intently to Knight Vidal's tales with astonishment. At the end of one of these sessions they were hastily called to the main hall.

Rumours had gone around the convent that an illustrious knight, an admiral of the fleet in the Mediterranean, had arrived at Provence, and that he would be staying at the convent. All kinds of speculation went around among those preparing to become warriors. All the new recruits, knights, and servants-at-arms were assembled in the main hall to be addressed by the visiting admiral. Everyone sat silently and expectantly, wondering what an admiral had to say to a company of warriors trained for field battles, fighting on horseback, and firing the biggest cannons imaginable.

Spellbound, they heard him say, "As you men already know, the rules of our order require that you do a caravan of one year at sea doing galley service." He continued, "I am fully aware," as if he had read their thoughts, "that you men have been trained for land warfare, on solid ground. But I have news for you. Soon you will be boarding the order's vessels in the coastal port. And during the month-and-a-half long trip it is my intention to make sailors out of you men. The order's tactics have changed drastically, and for obvious reasons, we are no longer in a position to take on our enemy the Saracens on land, so we have proceeded to take them on at sea. Gentlemen, I wish to inform you that we are being very successful with this policy. We are harassing the enemy's commerce by disrupting it. We sink and kill more of the enemy in the waters than we do on land and at much less cost to us. They fear our ships and turn tail when they see us coming.

"When possible, and we are able to, we take prisoners, making them slaves for our own fleet, and workers for the fortifications. On several occasions we have commandeered their vessels and made them our own, thereby increasing the strength of our fleet. So what we require most, at the moment, are men with sea capabilities, sailors, captains, and admirals. Your home, at least for now, will be a galley, and not a comfortable room in some auberge or convent. I am afraid you have no choice in the matter. You have taken vows of obedience, and this requirement you must strictly observe. I wish you God speed, and I look forward to seeing you aboard when the time comes soon. We sail for Rhodes in four days time."

The sea voyage was painfully slow for Jean, but not totally uneventful. The challenge of getting over seasickness came first. The galleys were not known for their stability, and it was unwise to sail in bad weather. It was wiser to find shelter in the lee side of an island and wait for the heavy seas to subside and then take off with a favourable wind abeam. Sailing from west to east was not as easy as sailing from east to west because the prevailing winds in the Mediterranean tended to come from the Levant. But the route had been wisely planned to navigate from island to island close to the friendly coastal countries. Barring a few bad days of cruel weather, the trip progressed as planned.

The other new experience for Valette was living in such close contact with so many other crew members. Another thing to get used to was the quality and quantity of food, as was the issue of personal hygiene.

All the new knights on board were made to drill on weapons and to learn the handling of the rigging and sails. There was time off only for sleep, eating and personal needs.

THE TURKS PREPARE FOR WAR

Veteran knight Vidal was accompanying this contingent on their trip to the east. When the day's chores had come to an end, most of the crew found a place where to sit or lie down on the deck. On this particular night, with calm seas and a fair wind, when visibility was excellent, the *galleass* making good time, with most of the crew sitting around on the deck chatting, Vidal was prompted to tell them one of his historical stories. He soon warmed up and started with how the Muslims were incensed with the order's move to Rhodes.

By1440 far too many of his merchant ships had fallen prey to the Christians, and the wealth and loss was mounting. From Rhodes, the Hospitallers had become masters of the Mediterranean Sea. The Sultan was desperate to counter-attack.

Cunningly, they also had a network of spies behind the enemy's lines who provided secret information about the Ottoman forces and their intended plans.

The Sultan sent a fleet aimed at destroying the knight vessels in the port of Rhodes, but the Hospitallers, with information received from spies, reacted before the Sultan's fleet arrived and sent out their own fleet to intercept them as they went through a narrow channel. The Hospitallers surprised and out maneuvered the Egyptian fleet and inflicted heavy losses on the Mameluk forces.

The Egyptian Sultan again sent a huge force to attack Rhodes. A mass of no less than eighteen thousand troops succeeded in disembarking and setting siege, putting the city under heavy bombardment, and breaching its defenses. This lasted for two years, but fortunately, a Christian naval force, arrived in time for the Christian forces to organize and form up for a battle in the open fields. The knights won a decisive victory.

This victory by the Christians aroused great interest in other parts of Europe, and many started to travel to Rhodes to join the naval fleet.

Veteran Vidal said that the Turks had a tremendous advantage in this campaign over their Christian adversaries, who were fighting against impossible odds. The Turks' advantage was that they were fighting close to their mainland making it easy for supplies and reinforcements to get to them promptly.

Vidal assured his captive audience that, "This happened only fifty years ago. But now, gentlemen, we are coming, and I can assure you that one Christian knight is worth two hundred Muslim fighters, and our arrival is feared. However, information coming from our spies is that the Ottoman Turks are preparing to attack Rhodes again, and it is only a question of time before they launch, what we consider will be a fierce attack."

CHARLES V OF SPAIN

KNIGHT IN HALF ARMOUR

KNIGHTS VENERATING THE HOLY CROSS

CONTEXTUS IV

THE GALLEY SLAVE

LA VALETTE, PRISONER OF BARBARY PIRATES

The last thing La Valette remembered was this huge Turkish corsair, bare-chested and hairy, wielding a scimitar in one hand and a dagger in the other. The corsair had thrown himself upon him with a murderous wild look in his face. La Valette's own sword had been dislodged from his grip as he simultaneously defended himself from some other adversary with a lance that had scraped his side superficially along his ribcage. He had fallen, his half-helmet having slipped off his head during the great commotion. The deck was slippery with a thick slick of blood and water with entrails sloughing about; even body parts slid back and forth with the reeling of the vessel. The weight of the unfortunate big Saracen corsair had hit La Valette and unbalanced his body with such momentum that it forced him onto the deck, where he hit his head on the edge of a crate, knocking him out cold and dislocating his shoulder at the same time. His motionless body sprawled on the wooden deck looked grotesque and unnatural. For a moment he had seen death staring him in the face. His final thought was the image of Christ and his inner voice saying, "Thank you, Lord." It was all he could think of saying, the end had finally come, and death was at the door.

In the confusion and turmoil of the cross-fire taking place between the two decks, luckily a bullet hit the big Turk smack in the head, going through his colourful turban and bursting his head open like a watermelon. Blood and brain showered upon La Valette. Men were screaming in anger, rage, and fear. They jumped about the deck like monkeys in a cage, slashing with swords and piercing with lances. The noise was unbearable; the scene was one of pandemonium. In a flash, the thought of that two-day storm crossed his mind. The ships were still in convoy formation when the storm came upon them from the land. The *San Giovanni*, La Valette's flagship, had been tossed and heaved about on the sea like a piece of cork in the water. It swung this way and that, up, down, and sideways, with the men tied to the deck for dear life. The deck was continuously awash with the insane and terrifyingly angry sea. La Valette had donned a waterproof canvas storm coat with a hood over his body that was bare, except for his breeches, since he had been called on deck by the alarm raised by the watch.

In a daze of pain he could hear the loud noise and the hand-to-hand fighting continuing around him, and he wished he could get up and continue to defend the *San Giovanni*, but he was unable to move his arm to pull himself up straight; he was pinned between the main mast, and a heavy barrel full of water that had rolled unto him. He recalled how, as the storm trailed away, he took off the canvas coat, only to see the enemy ships around the *San Giovanni*. He laid facing down, unconscious. He did not know how long he had lain there, but now he heard cheering and jubilant voices screaming in victory: "Allah is great! Allah has given us victory!"

"Great is our leader Abdu-Radman Kust-Ali, victory to him! Curse to the infidels!"

Through misty eyes and a fuzzy head he heard cunning Abdu-Radman Kust-Ali, fleet commander of this Turkish squadron, order, "Throw the dead overboard, and put the prisoners in iron." By Kust-Ali's side stood the most fearsome pirate of them all, Aroudj Barbarossa. Barbarossa walked to the man facing down on the deck. He kicked the half-naked man in the ribs, and with his foot, he turned him around to face the sky to determine if he was dead or alive. Barbarossa knelt down and touched the man's throat to feel for a pulse. "This one is alive. This one will fetch a fair ransom; by the trim of his beard I can tell he must be important.

You men—take him and put him in the single cell down below. Get the infirmary to care for his shoulder and head wound. Quick! Don't chain him yet."

La Valette was lifted onto his feet, and a bucket of seawater was thrown onto his face to bring him out of his semi-consciousness. La Valette responded promptly to this harsh remedy and shook his head several times, like a dog that shakes the water off its back after fetching a stick from the sea. The sailors handled La Valette roughly as they propped him up and shoved him to one side against a wooden wall. His face scraped against the planking in the rough handling, and Barbarossa gave the sailor responsible a mighty swipe with his closed hand, telling him he did not want this prisoner hurt any further. Before being taken to the cell, a Greek medic came and treated La Valette's head wound, covering his head with a long piece of linen. He manipulated La Valette's shoulder into place and provided him with an arm sling made of canvas. With his good hand, La Valette reached up tentatively to touch the lump on his scalp.

As had been ordered, they placed him in a single cell surrounded by iron bars below deck. The door was locked, and La Valette sat down to recover from the blow to his head and his dislocated shoulder. Slowly and painfully he came about and started to look around, taking note of his surroundings. He noted that there were as many as four larger cells, all cramped with men, with standing room only. Some were wounded severely, with cuts in several places. But they all made a brave and superhuman effort to appear to be good merchandise, because the alternative was a brutal dive over the side of the vessel.

La Valette looked frantically about searching for his friend Oliver, fearing that he may have perished in the fight and had been thrown overboard. There were so many men cramped into each cell that he could not see him. He stood on tiptoes and moved this way and that trying to catch a glimpse of his friend's distinguishable straw-coloured hair. He finally caught sight of what looked like the reflection of something lighter over the heads of the other men who were either bold or black-haired. "Oliver! Oliver Starkey! Over here, Oliver; it's La Valette," shouted Jean across the passage. Oliver was slumped against the hull, attempting to sit down, but unable to do so on account of the overcrowded cell. He seemed to be badly injured. On seeing this, La Valette forced himself up and started to shout in an attempt to call the attention of a crew member.

After a while one of the guards appeared, a barrel-chested individual with a bullwhip in hand, wearing loose Turkish pantaloons held up with a wide leather belt. La Valette addressed him in Arabic. "Hey, you there, send for the doctor immediately." The guard gave him a blank look, then opened his hands and shrugged his shoulders indicating that he did not understand. La Valette was surprised because the fellow looked like a Saracen. Then he addressed him in Greek, and to his amazement he replied in Greek. This guard must have been one of the thousands of Christian renegades that had converted to Islam and joined the services of the Sultan, accepting Islam at an advanced age, even to the point of having to be painfully circumcised as an adult.

"Listen to me, you idiot. Don't just stand there. Get hold of my shoulder and push it into place." The Greek obeyed and with a loud crack the shoulder fell into place. "There are men over there that need to be attended by a surgeon. Call the crew's medics to come down quickly. And tell the captain I want to speak with him immediately. I am responsible for these men, so be quick about it."

"The medics are treating our own crew members first, so you will have to wait your turn," replied the guard. He looked at La Valette, gave him a half-smile, laughed, and disappeared up the companionway. Those able-bodied prisoners who witnessed the command from their admiral shouted back to La Valette, "Well done, sir. This one here is dying, and that one there, your friend, is bleeding to death and will soon die if not helped quickly."

With a sigh of resignation, La Valette despaired. Here he found himself, the "shining knight" of the Order of Hospitallers of Jerusalem, trained to give medical help to anyone, now a prisoner of his hated enemies, the Muslim Turks, known to be cruel and ruthless masters, worse than the Moors, Algerians, Arabs, and Syrians. These people had no compassion whatsoever, and here he was, unable to offer medical help to his own people. If the Saracens found out who he was, he was surely going to be beheaded and fed to the sharks. He decided he needed to speak to his men.

"Listen to me, men. If these infidels find out who I am, they will behead me. But if I live, I promise you I will find a way of getting you all out of this mess. We will simply tell them that I am just the captain of our ship and give another name. No mention of knights being on board. Is that clear men?"

La Valette continued. "We are now in for a tough time. Our lives as slaves won't be easy. We will be treated harshly; we may even be sold as slaves if we are surplus to their requirements. But pray to God for strength and be brave. You did very well today. It was the fault of that dreadful Spaniard Garcia de Toledo who got us into this mess by not following my advice. We were supposed to have gone directly to take possession of the old Spanish territory of Velez de la Gomera, on the North African coast. I advised him that we should sail directly there, since there were reports that Kust-Ali and Barbarossa were reported to be in the area. If we had done that, we would have been well ahead of the storm that got us. As it was, when the two-day storm was over, we found ourselves alone, separated from our squadron, and surrounded by Kust-Ali and Barbarossa."

La Valette sat down on his bunk and pondered how fate had turned against them in a matter of days. He found it strange that Aroudj Barbarossa should be on another's ship, because usually his campaigns of terror had been either on his own ship or on land, where he had terrorized the Algerians and Moors. He had in fact conquered the Maghreb for the Ottoman Turks.

La Valette sailed from Provence at the age of twenty and had been based in Rhodes, where the knights' fleet was stationed, and where he joined a captain of a galley sailing with the knights' fleet, which consisted of 150 ships of various types.

His early days in the order's marine section had been an interesting experience. He became fascinated by ships and the art of sailing. He learned how to navigate at night using the stars as a guide. He found out about the vagaries of the winds and the unpredictability of the ocean, and learned to respect the sea. As his fascination with ships grew, he read that the Phoenicians had built the first ocean-going *biremes* and *triremes*, about how the Greeks had improved upon these, and how the Romans, though at first not a seafaring nation, had perfected the war galleys. By his day, ship construction had improved by leaps and bounds. The Spaniards, Portuguese, and Venetians had built fine ships that had sailed the unknown seas with great success. On the other hand, the shipbuilders of Genoa had also built a reputation for themselves with a different class of merchant vessels that was used widely in the Mediterranean for trading.

He remembered how impressed he had been with the construction of the *tartana*, a beautiful, streamlined galley of eight oars on each side, bearing two main masts and one short sail on the stern. Then there was the *vascolo*, with two gun decks of six per side and a high stern, a predecessor of the *man-of-war* of the seventeenth century. But the vessel that had filled Jean with awe was the largest and most feared vessel, the great *carrack* of Rhodes, which was swift, agile, and easy to handle. Incredibly, it had eight decks. It was so large it could carry a galley on board deck. It was said that nothing could sink it, and that no one ever got sick in it. It could stay at sea for six months without requiring re-watering for that whole period. It carried a large oven that could bake several hundred loafs at a time, to provide fresh bread every day, so there was no need to take hard biscuits. Its hull was metal sheathed, it could take on board five hundred men, and was said to carry fifty cannon.

There were the normal *galleys*, propelled by oars and one sail to take advantage of favourable winds. A galley could reach a speed of three knots an hour. Then came the *galleass*, bearing ten guns, a large galley with three masts, intended to sail by wind-power. But it also had sixteen oars should the wind fail, or to help in maneuvering during battle or moving inside a port. Also, there was the "hyena of the sea", the *galliot*, which worked in a group of several vessels, hence its appellation, harassing the enemy from every side. It was smaller than the *galleass*, highly maneuverable, and carried a couple of small cannon. Together they could do a lot of damage to a lonely vessel found out at sea. They were never far from one of the larger war ships.

It was a pack of these hyenas that had found La Valette's galley, the *San Giovanni*. Not far away, in sight, close to the horizon, was Abdu-Radman Kust-Ali's flagship approaching fast, with a fair wind astern, to finish the work done by the six galliots.

Before La Valette was taken below, he looked around in an arc of 360 degrees, sweeping the horizon with his eyes, but there was no sign of Admiral Garcia de Toledo's other vessels that could come to his rescue.

It took two days before the ship's medics came down to the hold to render medical treatment to the injured prisoners. They came escorted by four guards, one of them holding a bunch of chains and buckles. La Valette said he was a doctor and offered to help the ship's medics. They made the men line up in the narrow confines of the hold and started to separate the injured from the healthy. One group, the healthy ones, was placed in one of the cells, and the other, the injured, relocated in other cells. A couple of dead bodies were dragged up the companionway, and a few minutes later everyone heard several sonorous splashes announcing the unceremonious sea burial of their late comrades.

Several of the worst-injured were treated first. One of these was Oliver. Luckily, Oliver too had dispensed with his knight's tunic. He had received a sword slash across the back that left a wide-open cut where bone and tissue were visible. He had lost a lot of blood and was ghastly pale. The Greek medic soon stitched up and bandaged his side, back, and chest, and gave him a drink of water. Another of the injured had a broken leg, so the medic soon sandwiched his whole leg, encased by three wooden planks. The fourth man had a broken arm and a four-inch wound in his abdomen, both of which were treated with great dexterity by the much-experienced Greek medic. Jean helped the medic in his rounds, comforting his men as they visited. The treated patients were moved to share Jean's cell, which made Jean believe that they were being kept apart because, for the moment, they were useless as oarsmen in the galley. All the others, including some with slight head and body wounds, had been treated but moved in with the healthy members, in preparation to send them to the rowing benches.

A guard ordered the healthy men to line up. Each in turn was chained, his wrists held with manacles, and his ankles encased by a bracelet. Another man made each prisoner lift his foot on an anvil and hammered home a rivet that made sure the bracelet was securely in place and would not come off. One by one, they were moved up the companionway to the rowers' level. There were many galley slaves seated at the oars, all of them leaning upon their oars, resting, or taking advantage to sleep whilst they could. All looked despondent. But it was clear that the ship had lost many oarsmen; there were many gaps in the benches. The Christian captives would fill these gaps. They were pushed, punched, shoved, and directed to specific seats. Once seated, a long, continuous chain was threaded through a ring in their ankle bracelets, and the end of the chain was secured to one of the wooden beams. The rowers were tethered to their places with little possibility of movement.

Someone came down into the hold carrying a large woven basket filled with pieces of broken bread. Another came with a large clay pot full of water and a bronze ladle. Both were placed in the narrow walkway of the hold, where two guards, with their dirty and calloused hands, started to distribute the bread. Each of the guards held a bronze ladle filled with water from the clay pot, and placed it in each oarsman's mouth to drink.

Men who had formerly been soldiers and sailors were now mere slaves, awaiting one of the most gruelling tasks a man could face—to row all day with virtually no rest except at night. Their saviours were bad weather and dark moonless nights, for in bad weather and in moonless nights, the galleys needed to find shelter so as not to hit unseen reefs or rocks. In bad weather particularly, they had to wait for the passing of the storm's fury and heavy seas, since galleys were not very stable vessels.

"How in heaven's name do we sleep in this place?" asked one of the new prisoners.

"There is no heaven in this place, *mon ami*. This is the real hell. You sleep where you are, however you can," said one of the old-timers.

Another of the old-timers answered, "Unless, of course, the captain decides to find a deserted bay and beaches the galley there. Then, hopefully, he will allow us on land, and we can sleep on relatively firm and dry land. As for your bodily needs, you pee where you are and you can defecate when we stop rowing, not before. In such a case we all share the perfume of shit. This is why this ship is known as the *Black Moon*. You can count yourself lucky that we have other four-legged crew members who help clean up the rats and the cockroaches. So don't worry when you see them, they are on our side and they have a task to do—to clean up after us."

La Valette Meets Barbarossa the Pirate

A couple of weeks later, when La Valette and Oliver had recovered from their injuries, they were taken up to the captain's enclosed space, an excuse for a cabin. La Valette observed that the facilities in the knights' galleys were superior to this one. It was obvious that Kust-Ali was not high in the Muslims' naval hierarchy. The two men were ordered to stand in front of Kust-Ali and Aroudj Barbarossa. Barbarossa looked at them both with a clinical eye; he went as far as touching both men's beards. Once on deck, La Valette glanced around, scanning the horizon for signs of landmarks that he might recognize in order to get an idea as to where they were. He did not see land but he did see another larger galley close by that flew a skull and crossbones and another red pendant with a green half-moon. It was not Kust-Ali who spoke to them first, but Barbarossa, who stood by Kust-Ali's side. His left arm was missing, and a folded empty sleeve hung loose. His good arm held the hilt of his scimitar. "What is your name?" he said, pointing and addressing La Valette. "And what is your title?" La Valette had resolved to keep his identity hidden; since he knew very well that the ransom money, if asked for—as it surely would be, would increase with the importance of the captor's title, as had always been the case. But if Barbarossa recognized who he was, he could even be beheaded, since La Valette had once been responsible for Barbarossa's imprisonment in Rhodes many years before.

"My name is Jean Baguette, and I am captain of that ship you have taken. What is the name of this vessel?"

"To answer your question, you insolent Christian, this ship is under the command of His Excellency Abdu-Radman Kust-Ali, and the vessel's name is the *Black Moon*. Now let me ask you a question. Your face is familiar," grunted Barbarossa, eyeing him with a suspicious look. "Have we met before, somewhere? Do you know who I am?"

La Valette looked at the man over and said disdainfully, "I would say, from the colour of your hair and your missing arm, that you might be the one known as Barbarossa the pirate. And further, I do not believe I have had the displeasure of meeting you before now, otherwise I would have had the pleasure of killing you."

Barbarossa found La Valette's reply cheeky, insolent, and yet funny. He laughed out loud in a roar, and looking at Kust-Ali said, "No, Kust, I will not take him as I thought I would. I will leave him with you, since you are shorthanded. But I will take his ship as part of my booty. So farewell, my friend. I will take off now for my ship. We will rendezvous as we have planned in one month's time. May Allah accompany you in your journey, and may he provide you with more fortune and even more infidels. Farewell, my brother."

With this he embraced Kust-Ali and kissed him on both cheeks. Before bowing, turning around, and looking once again in the direction of La Valette and Oliver, he shook his head in a quizzical grimace, smiled, then climbed down to the small boat waiting by the side. His men rowed him to his own waiting galley. With a sigh of relief, at seeing the back of Barbarossa go, La Valette and Oliver turned and sorrowfully watched as their ship, the *San Giovanni*, was towed away. They both wondered if they would ever see the *San Giovanni* again, the ship on which they had served for so many years. The corsair Barbarossa had made a very lucrative catch when he chose to take the *San Giovanni*.

"Do you think he recognized you Jean?" asked Oliver.

La Valette replied with relief, "It is possible. For a moment I thought he recognised me, but it has been such a long time since last we met. Besides, look at the sight of me. I look like a deckhand. He knew me when I was young and I was dressed in my full knight's armour. But look at me now—half naked, unshaved, dishevelled, bandaged, and dirty. No, I don't think he did. Thank God for that. He would have cut my throat here and now if he had remembered that he was once my prisoner. I hope that the penny doesn't drop, that he doesn't recall me later. If he does, he is quite capable of sending a message to Kust-Ali to behead us on the spot."

With this, La Valette and Oliver were shown to the rowing deck and ordered to sit. Luckily, they were not separated and remained seated side by side. The rowing master, bullwhip in hand, came and shoved them in place, and another slave arrived to shackle them in place on the chain that held the other rowers. There were five to each seat, and he estimated about fifteen rows of seats.

"You there," ordered the rowing master, pointing with his whip to the slave who had handled the chains. "Show them what to do." The slave sat beside La Valette and gripped the wooden handgrip pegged to the side of the massive oar shaft.

"Have you ever rowed before?" he asked the newcomers.

"Yes and no," replied La Valette. "Yes, I have rowed, and no, I have not rowed like this before."

"Then watch everything I do. I will not repeat this." He placed his right foot on the edge of the bench in front of him, emphasising the movement and expecting them to do the same. "Now take a stroke!" They placed their right foot on the edge as instructed. La Valette and Oliver and the other three struggled to push the loom of the sweep away from them. Pulling on the oar, they involuntarily came to a standing position with the effort, and then fell back with all their weight onto the goatskin covered bench. The huge oar didn't stir the vessel one single inch. "Once again, you useless human beings. Do it once again and do it right this time," shouted the rowing master, taking a flying swipe with his whip that reached the back of both of them with the tails of the thongs. They cringed with the sting. Very slowly, the oars started to sweep into the water, and even more slowly, the vessel started to move. "Pull again, you lazy bastards. Pull again. Pull on water, not on air, dump-shits."

The rowing master finished his instructions and now gave a signal to a huge Turk, also handling a whip, and who, they found out, turned out to be the timekeeper. This fellow put a whistle to his lips and blew a single blast. All the oarsmen bent forward, still seated on the bench, arms extended, pushing the oar handles in a low arc ahead of them. The whistle sounded again, and in unison the oarsmen stood up and pulled, raising their arms so that the blades of the oars dipped into the sea. A third blast and the oarsmen flung themselves backward, dragging the blades through the water as they fell back on the padded benches. Scarcely had they regained their seat when the timekeeper's whistle signalled them to repeat the movement. A drummer, alongside the timekeeper, struck the first beat of a slow, steady tempo as the vessel gathered way.

And so the tedious and hard work as a galley slave began for La Valette and Oliver, and for those other survivors of the *San Giovanni*. La Valette's active mind immediately started to think about survival and escaping. He recalled what Cervantes he had written when they had liberated some Christian slaves. *"The Christian galley slaves on-board were so badly and cruelly treated that no sooner had they caught sight of us than they jumped up, seized the Saracen captain, and dragged him along the full length of the ship, administering so many blows to him that his soul departed for hell; so much hatred had he inspired among them."*

La Valette wondered if he would ever get the opportunity to do something similar, where in the confusion of the heat of battle, he might free himself from his chains and swim to a friendly ship, or perhaps the ship itself might be captured by friendly forces, or even strike a reef enabling them to escape. Or perhaps they might even mutiny and take over the vessel.

La Valette was familiar with Cervantes' account when he had been a slave. Cervantes wrote, *"I was kept a slave in Algiers for five years."* Accompanied by a few companions, he overcame a guard that had been detailed to escort them, but the fugitive didn't get far before they were recaptured. As punishment, the Spaniard was sentenced to work in a quarry, crushing stones and transporting them to where the port's fortifications were being rebuilt. His next escape involved conspiring with a mysterious intermediary who arranged for a brigantine to arrive off a certain part of the coast. But the brigantine was ambushed, and Cervantes and his fellows were captured again hiding in a cave. After this attempt he spent five months chained in a dungeon before being bought by Hassan Pasha of Algiers. His fellow fugitives were not so fortunate, being hanged or impaled, whilst the janissaries, who had negligently allowed them to escape, were also executed. In the fourth year of his captivity, he managed to escape once again, accompanied by a renegade known as Abdurrahman or, in a previous life, Giron, a native of Granada. This Giron persuaded Cervantes to return to Spain. A Valencian merchant arranged the escape, but a defrocked priest, Blanco de Paz, betrayed them and alerted Hassan of the attempted escape.

Five years as a slave? Never! Said La Valette to himself. *Never! I'll get out of here long before that.*

There was little time or energy to talk. It took all the slaves' concentration to keep the rhythm of each stroke. Lack of concentration would result in a "crab" that could lead to the injury of the other rowers on the line, or even to an oar breaking, either of which would be fatal to the culprit; a severe flogging on the spot would be the result. The other consequence would be that it would take the effort of the remaining four rowers to do the work of the suffering rower.

The flogging and privation of food and water was continuous. Several oarsmen had been unchained, taken up on deck, and thrown overboard as punishment for some small infringement or for just being sick. The whole rowing crew and even others on aboard would have mutinied if it had been possible, but it wasn't. La Valette was a good judge of his men so he and Oliver prayed out aloud, in the hope that the Christian slaves would join in. Prayers of intercession to the Virgin Mary were repeated over and over again.

La Valette encouraged his men to employ the rowing as exercise, not as toil and punishment; exercise to gain physical strength, rather than giving in to despondency and defeat. "Grow strong, men. One day we will regain our freedom. Then we will need all the strength we can muster to fight this scourge of humanity." In a whisper to the men close to him he said, "Listen to me men. If any of you happen to see any sharp metal item like a nail, get it and pass it on to me. Don't let those Turks see you. Pass this message on to the others." In whispers, the word went around all the oarsmen.

La Valette's hopeful intimation of an escape did not go unnoticed by his fellow prisoners, and the mood of the slaves was uplifted with optimism and encouraging. The hardships were now bearable; their leader had a plan.

The only other possible exercise was the exercise of the mind, thought, prayers, thinking of the past, and looking towards the future, of what had been, of what could have been, of what could come, of hope—hope in things to come.

La Valette, in the rhythmic and monotonous motion of rowing, remembered his history tutor, Lord Williams, recounting how, after two hundred years, the knights had been evicted from Acre and had settled in Cyprus, but only for a while. The stay in Cyprus was not happy and short-lived, so they decided to take over possession of Rhodes. The order had embarked on building proper fortifications and defences in Rhodes, expecting, sooner or later, an attack by the Turks, especially since they had waged a determined sea war against the Muslim fleet, and this was tickling the underbelly of the Ottoman Empire, with their constant disruption of Turkish shipping, as well as the frequent raids on Anatolia's coastal towns.

THE SECOND DEFENSE OF RHODES

As the team of oarsmen went forward, dug their oars, and pulled, La Valette's mind drifted to his first encounter with the pirate Barbarossa. It happened when the Turks attacked Rhodes and were trying to take it away from the Knights of St. John of Jerusalem.

The last straw had come when the Sultan heard news that Muslims on the island were being ostensibly persecuted, so the Sultan sent a large Muslim fleet, reportedly carrying between seventy thousand and one hundred thousand soldiers with artillery and siege weapons. This turned up off the coast of Rhodes. This fleet was a combination of Dragut's corsairs and Barbarossa's pirate fleets, since both had joined forces with the Ottoman fleet.

The garrison of Rhodes was under the leadership of the colourful and chivalrous Grand Master Pierre d'Aubusson, who had just received a contingent of two thousand foot soldiers and five hundred knights from France. D'Aubusson had been vigilant and had prepared well against a possible attack, building up substantial supplies and military equipment. Close to d'Aubusson was the young knight Jean Parisot de la Valette, recently arrived from France, eager to engage in battle with the Saracen forces.

The long-awaited allied Ottoman fleet and army finally attacked Rhodes. The odds were totally against the Christian fortress, but through a miracle and fierce fighting, the knights held the Ottomans back until they withdrew and gave up in their siege, but waited at anchor undecided as to what to do. A couple of the Barbary vessels, more daring than the Ottoman fleet, made a brave landing on the island. Close to one hundred men landed in the darkness of the night, approaching from the eastern end of the island, which was not as well defended as the western end of the island, where the main attack had taken place. Barbarossa the pirate led this sortie. He managed to find a place to land, and climbed over a short wall close to the Eastern Tower. His aim was for a few men to go over the wall undetected, and try to open the Eastern Tower's gate for the waiting force to enter and attack from the rear.

Grand Master d'Aubusson had placed young La Valette in charge of guarding the Eastern Tower. La Valette did the rounds around the walls at all hours of the day and night, encouraging the guards to keep vigilant. His rigorous discipline paid off. In the stillness of the night, one of La Valette's lookouts heard and spotted the attackers and raised the alarm. He fired a warning shot that woke up the rest of the knights' contingent. They lit bundles of hay soaked in oil and threw them over the wall. The hay set fire to a whole lot of hay and brush that had been purposely laid at the foot of the external walls of the tower to illuminate the surrounding area when the enemy attacked. The silhouette of the attackers flitting here and there in the darkness immediately became visible to the guards on the walls, who promptly aimed their crossbows and shot their arrows into them. Others discharged their firearms into the stealthy enemy. Many fell before they even attempted to climb over the wall. La Valette took a look over the wall, and judged that this was not a large force. He formed a war party numbering some two hundred men of his own. They opened the gate and charged the attacking pirates head-on. A bloody combat followed. During the fierce hand to hand fighting, with La Valette leading them, they managed to overpower the motley invaders:of Barbary pirates of mixed races, Muslims, and even renegade Christian sailors.

Leading them was Aroudj Barbarossa, distinguishable by his missing arm and long, red beard. When La Valette and Barbarossa crossed swords, La Valette proved to be the more accomplished swordsman. Barbarossa was a strong and brutal fighter, and wielded and struck hard with a long sword, but La Valette was not intimidated by his brutal strikes and wild swings, tactics that would be acceptable in a seafaring and boarding situation, but not under the present circumstances. La Valette carried two swords: his long sword in his right hand, and a medium-length one in his left. He parried every thrust that Barbarossa made, and countered by launching at him now and again and cutting Barbarossa's body in several places. The larger Christian force overwhelmed the pirate attackers, and Barbarossa and a couple of others were the only ones left still fighting when La Valette finally yelled at Barbarossa. "Put your weapon down, red-beard, or get killed! You are surrounded—look around you!" By then ten of La Valette's foot-soldiers were surrounding and pointing their swords and firearms at Barbarossa. They were waiting for the knight to give the next order, to kill him or take him prisoner. When Barbarossa looked around and behind, he immediately saw his dreadful predicament and dropped his weapon while at the same time raising his one arm and the stump of the other. Close to forty of the invading force had been killed, and only six of the Christian force had been injured. The rest of the pirates had made haste back to the waiting vessel.

Jean de la Valette had the prisoners tied and taken into a dungeon. He ordered six guards to accompany him, and took Barbarossa to the grand master, who immediately imprisoned him in a top security cell.

A message was immediately sent to the Muslim leader, Commander Palaeologos Pasha, saying "Your pirate friend Barbarossa is a prisoner of the Knights of Rhodes." He intended this to be a demoralising message, since Barbarossa, until then, had a reputation of being invincible.

The message was in fact not needed The Ottoman army had already withdrawn. Since La Valette was stationed in the far end of the city fortress, he did not know about the Ottoman withdrawal. Why had the Ottoman army and its fleet withdrawn from the battle and departed? Being a man of faith, he could only think that an act of God could have produced this withdrawal. Rhodes was saved, and on top of that, they had the bonus of capturing the notorious Barbarossa. La Valette and his guards guided Barbarossa, now in chains, to the secure prison cell. He instructed the jailers to provide the prisoner with water and food.

La Valette—the slave—pulled on his oar with the usual monotony of motion, his mind once again going back twenty-four years before that encounter, and recalled when he had seen Barbarossa for the second time. That had been a sadder occasion, when Sultan Suleiman the Magnificent attacked Rhodes yet again in a second attempt at a siege of Rhodes.

The order was now under the command of Grand Master Phillip L'Isle-Adam, who had sent out desperate appeals to Christian countries for reinforcements, but except for a small contingent from Crete and Venice, the order received no great help.

The Turks launched a concerted attack on a section of the town wall defended by knights from Aragon and England. The Turks started an incessant artillery attack, but unknown to the knights, they had started to dig tunnels under the fortification walls. They persisted with digging for over a month. Tunnelling was a very effective siege manoeuvre that the Muslims had learned. They dug tunnels underground from far away, starting behind the front line in their camp, the entrance hidden under large tents. They dug until they reached the foundations of the walls of the fortification, and carried away earth and rocks on a system of trolleys on wheels pulled to the entrance of the tunnel by hundreds of slaves. Once they dug and reached the foundations of the walls, they dug deeper and wider, until they undermined the foundations of the fortress's walls.

The enemy was invisible. The defenders were totally unaware of what was happening, even though the defending Christians put their ears to the ground close to the walls, listening for noise underground, so they could be ready should the enemy break through. But the idea of the tunnelling was not to break through. With a hollow chamber underground, the wall of the fortress had no support below the foundations. The idea was that the heavy wall would suddenly collapse under its own weight into the empty chamber below. In this instance, forty feet of wall collapsed. The English-Spanish bastion toppled over, taking men and masonry with it. Immediately, the waiting Ottoman army rushed in, gaining entry through the breach that had opened up.

La Valette had observed the concentration of the enemy on the other side of the wall at a vital point of the fortification and informed the grand master. The Grand Master Phillip L'Isle, La Valette, Oliver, and Nicholas Hussey, together with their fearless company of knights, ordered a shield formation of foot soldiers and a company of heavy cavalry behind. They waited for the enemy to climb the rubble. They did not have to wait for long. They charged the attacking invaders, fighting them on the breach before they were able to get a hold inside the fortification. They forced them back the same way they had come. After receiving heavy losses the Ottoman commanders made a wise decision and ordered a strategic retreat.

It did not take long before the Ottoman army increased its numbers with newcomers and with siege engines, composed mainly of janissaries, and attacked. This time they spread east and west to the bastions of Italy, Provence, and Spain. Twice in one day the Ottomans captured the Spanish bastion, and twice it was retaken by the Hospitallers, with La Valette, Hussey, and Oliver's company of mounted knights charging back and forth, clearing the area of the ever-advancing Turks. The more enemy they slaughtered, the more enemy came forward. There was no end to the advancing army of frantic and suicidal Muslims. A trumpet was heard in the distance. Could it be that the Turks were retreating, again? "They're moving back! To me, men; to me and regroup!" shouted the brave Grand Master L'Isle to his men on either side of him.

When Sultan Suleiman, who was further away upon an observation tower, saw the retreat of his army, he became furious. From the top of the observation tower, he screamed and ordered the execution of the army's commander, General Mustafa Pasha, because he had failed to take the city despite his vast numerical advantage. However, he was persuaded to spare Mustafa because he was advised this would demoralize his men. Nevertheless, he replaced him with Ahmed Pasha. They withdrew to regroup.

A month later the Ottomans reorganized their army and launched another powerful attack, but again this was driven back.

By then the knights and townspeople were close to exhaustion and running short on provisions; yet they continued to drive back the Turks. Grand Master Phillip L'Isle had to face reality; neither his knights nor his foot soldiers or the townspeople could go on any further. The Turks, on the other hand, received daily reinforcements; the small Christian army was at a great disadvantage and in peril.

After another attack and another successful repulsion of the Turkish forces, the grand master took advantage of their success and requested peace terms from the Sultan. Terms were given, but the people were not happy with the terms and refused the Sultan's counter-offer, so the Sultan ordered that bombardment of the city should commence again.

The Spanish Bastion was taken at this point, and the knights were convinced that their fate was sealed. But Grand Master L'Isle-Adam requested another truce. This time the Sultan agreed and a treaty of peace was agreed to, under which the knights and the islanders could depart the island with their weapons within twelve days. Suleiman was so impressed with the fight put up by the knights and the courage of the noble Grand Master L'Isle-Adam that the Sultan was quoted as saying, "It gives me no pleasure to force this fearless old man from his home."

The grand master invited the Sultan to enter the city. The Sultan, to the alarm of his advisors, dismissed his guards on entering, saying that his safety was not in question because it had been guaranteed by the honourable grand master of the Hospitallers. As he rode in, he was heard to say, "This is worth more than all the world's armies." Such was the chivalry and respect that the Grand Master of the Knights Hospitallers commanded from his enemy. While the unruly file of evacuees was riding out of the fortress of Rhodes for the last time, La Valette's horse slid on the blood-covered slippery cobblestones and faltered in front of a company of enemy warriors who stood watching them go by. Amongst them was a one-armed man with a red beard, wearing a shining pointed helmet and in full armour. The red-bearded, one-armed man took off his helmet to wipe the sweat off his brow, his gaze fixed on La Valette. It was not a hostile look; rather it was a face full of admiration. Barbarossa again did not recognize the knight as the young knight who had taken him prisoner one night many years before. The pirate's admiration was due to the fact that La Valette had the remains of two arrows visibly embedded in his body, one on his thigh and the other to the back of his left shoulder. The knight raised his hand to his helmet's visor and made a smooth salute in Barbarossa's direction. Barbarossa looked in amazement and returned the salute, but he was immediately called away. La Valette was not surprised to see Barbarossa there since he had heard on the grapevine that Grand Master d'Aubusson had received a hefty ransom from the Sultan for the release of Barbarossa a few years earlier.

While the vessel rolled and the oarsmen laboured at the oars, in his thoughts, La Valette recalled the great tribute that was paid to the Knights Hospitallers, a tribute that came from no other than Roman Emperor Charles V, who declared: "Nothing in the world was ever so well lost as Rhodes."

Planning the Escape

La Valetta's ruminations were broken when the whistle blew, signaling the oars to stop. All the oarsmen stopped lowering the ends of the oars down to the level of their knees, which brought the wide ends of the oars, on the seaside, to an upward-diagonal position out of the water. It was an opportunity for the oar-men to give their backsides a rest. The man next to La Valetta, one of his own sailors, nudged him with his elbow. "Here, sir; hide these. These have been passed on for you—two big nails and a sharp piece of iron one from a man in the front and another from the back found these." La Valetta smiled at the man in gratitude and stealthily hid the items under the goatskin seat-covering. He in turn nudged Oliver and winked at him.

Except for some coughing, breaking of wind, and some groaning from someone in pain, there was comparative silence in the hold. "What do you intend to do, Jean?" Whispered Oliver.

La Valette answered, "You see that iron ring in the post to my right, almost in front of me?" He indicated with his head. "I have been studying this chaining system, and I think that if I were to work on that wooden beam and loosen the bolt there, it would be possible to get the chain off. I have noticed that the chain is continuous, and if we were to get that bolt off the beam, we could thread the loose chain off every man in this damn hole. Then we would be left just with the manacles and the foot bracelets, but all that would simply be jeweler on us. We would nevertheless be able to move and fight with free hands and feet."

"What about the slaves on the deck below?" murmured one of the men who was listening on the bench behind La Valette.

"We cannot help them until we ourselves are free. But as soon as we are free, a few of us will go to set them free as well," Replied La Valette.

There was a shout from behind. "You there, shut up, in the front—keep quiet or I'll come there and sock you one," came a gruff voice from the companionway. The kicking, slapping, punching, and whipping were the order of the day.

"But we have no weapons to fight with. How can we . . ." whispered Oliver between clenched teeth.

"Shh . . . You see those horizontal poles tied to the hull on either side of the ship? Those are spare oars. The moment we have our hands free we take care of the whistle-blower and his drummer-boy, we get hold of the oars, break them into short lengths, and use them as weapons. We stay down here, remaining as quiet as possible until we are ready. Then we can break into the armoury, which is right there, behind that partition ahead of us. When we were on deck I saw a sailor open a hatch and bring out a musket from there. The armoury's position is exactly behind that wall in front. We might be able to create a diversion inside the armoury by setting it on fire, but I am not sure of that yet. There is probably some gunpowder in there, which could be dangerous. We will have to wait and see. Pass the word to those close to the partition so that they can take care of breaking into the armoury from this side, as soon as I have the ring off that beam."

"Jean, if we set fire to the ship, how are we going to escape?" whispered an incredulous Oliver. "Good question, Oliver, but when we take action we will either be close to land or close to a friendly galley."

The *Black Moon* seemed to be standing by, waiting for something to happen. After a pause of about five minutes, Jean looked back to make sure there was no guard close by and continued, "It may take some time before the opportunity presents itself for us to act, but we will wait, because sooner or later this vessel is going to meet and engage a Christian galley, and that is when we will act, mutiny and take over the ship. The confusion above when they are preparing for battle will give us an excellent opportunity and more time. They cannot disregard an approaching enemy ship to check on us, especially when they think we are in chains. They will know that something is wrong when they see that the oars are no longer moving, so we have to be fast. We have to act quickly and be ready by then."

Oliver sat back and sighed, not believing what he was hearing. If he had not known La Valette the way he did, he would think that he was crazy. But he knew La Valette well, and he also knew that if anyone could pull a stunt like this one, it would be him. La Valette, the quiet, unpretentious, unassuming, fearless knight was a calculating genius. When he went into action, he struck like a cobra—fast and deadly. He was not at all surprised that Jean would think something so unexpected, because thanks to La Valette's capabilities, tactical mind, and intrepid bravery, they had on several occasions saved Christian ships, capturing many corsairs' vessels, adding to the order's fleet of galleys. La Valette waited for night-time, when the vessel was at anchor and when everyone would be asleep, before starting to work on the iron ring that was the weak link in the chain.

The days and the weeks went by, and La Valette noticed that the oarsmen were growing stronger and fitter every day. So he reinforced this strength by giving them a pep talk, while their oar master went on deck. "The time will soon come when we will show these Saracens what kind of stuff we Christians are made of. My old teacher used to tell us that one Christian soldier was worth two hundred infidels, and we are going to prove it to them."

"Quiet down there! This minute!" came a voice through the hatch's opening.

The *Black Moon* had been engaged in a few sorties on peaceful and harmless coastal villages, plundering and taking innocent villagers prisoners—the cowardly action of barbaric corsairs. So far, they had not engaged in any serious sea battle. On a few occasions they entered a small port and unloaded surplus slaves for sale to some North African tribes of the interior. At the same time, they took on board fresh water, live animals, and fruit to replenish the vessel's stock to feed the corsair crew and the slaves. La Valette noted that there were six other galleys in Kust-Ali's fleet. All the vessels received provisions from the villages.

SAFE HAVEN

On other occasions, the *Black Moon* and the other six vessels moored in a secluded bay that was totally hidden from passing ships.

On arrival, the slaves were manhandled and ordered to clean the lower decks of the vessel. La Valette ensured that he went back to his own area so that no one would notice the work he had started around the iron ring on the upright beam. Luckily, the wood work he had done was on the side and not the front of the beam, which was more difficult to see by someone coming down the companionway. There was no sign of wood splinters since these had been distributed throughout the oarsmen one by one. He had always taken the precaution of finding some dirt and muck on the deck's floor to smear over the freshly cut wood in order to disguise his work in progress. On one occasion he used some human excrement to cover the handy work. However delicately he tried to do the cover-up job, it took him a couple of hours before being able to remove the smell from his finger. It was only when the drinking water was brought that he managed to spit some of it and wipe it against the underside of the bench.

When they had finished the work below deck and were ordered to move up and away they passed by an opened hatch that led to one of the holds below. As if uninterested in their surroundings, La Valette and Oliver, seeming oblivious, glanced down. They saw sailors carrying goods down into the hold: big amphorae filled with wine or spices; large packages of pottery; plates bound in rawhide and straw and protected with layers of bark. There below, in that hold, they got a glimpse of weapons, axes, swords, shields, javelins, and handguns.

Several seamen with ropes were hauling up other cargo. "Careful, men, with that cargo; that's gunpowder you are handling," Kust-Ali warned his men.

"Perfect!" whispered La Valette to Oliver when they were out of earshot, walking down the gangplank. "That hold is just where we thought it would be, right in front of us."

The men were made to clean their surroundings, scraping with iron pallet knives and hard-bristle brushes, sloshing saltwater this way and that. When the cleaning work was done, a couple of trap doors were opened to reveal the bilge on the underside of the lower deck. They formed a chain in a single line passing wooden buckets, and the work of emptying the bilge area started. It was dark below decks and cramped. In time the men got accustomed to the darkness. Once in a while one of the overseers came down with a lit torch and provided some light at the bilge hold entrance. At the commencement of this operation, two men lowered themselves into the bilge and stood knee-deep in the filthy water, rank with smell of urine, vomit, and other human waste. It took over six hours before the bilge was emptied and refilled with fresh saltwater and then emptied again, and filled once again for the sea water to act as ballast.

After this nauseating operation, the whole crew was made to step ashore, taking all the smelly slaves with them. The slaves were released from the chains and buckled instead with leather ties on their waists and around their necks, joined to each other with a rope like prayer beads.

The gigantic Turk who was the oar master stood on the beach as they unloaded. He ordered them all to get into the water. All the slaves from all the vessels were disembarked and made to enter the water along the long sandy beach. They were allowed to wash themselves as best they could. They played and splashed each other like little kids. The cool seawater felt good. This was one of the rare occasions when they were able to scrub themselves clean with the beach sand and flush away the vermin that clang to their hair and bodies as well as the crust of filth that had stuck to their bodies. It was said that head lice could be got rid of by submerging your head and holding your breath for as long as possible. The lice would drown and loosen their grip and float away, or so they said. The prisoners were watched by a line of guards, they were allowed a long time for this welcome scrubbing and ablution break.

Eventually they were led to a crude barricaded compound made of cane and palm branches, separated like cattle corrals. The whole perimeter of the enclosure was covered with a palm-leaf roof for shade. The slaves shuffled through and were tied to the trunks of date palm trees. Young boys from the nearby villages appeared carrying baskets full of fruit and unleavened bread, whilst others carried goatskins full of water. They had obviously done this before.

It was an opportunity for most of the men to sit in a row, one behind the other, and each in turn shaved the other's heads to a shiny scalp, and then trimmed each other's beards. Shaving their hair was the best protection against hair vermin, lice, nits, and other human parasites. Shaved hair was thrown onto a fire. All of this was done under supervision of several guards who had handed them the sharp daggers.

Although La Valette did not have a clue where they were, he noted that they had been brought to this base on at least three other occasions. For future reference, he glanced round the land and made a mental note of the coastline and the hills and mountains in the backdrop, for he thought that one day, when he was free and in command of his own ship, he would make sure to return and somehow repay Kust-Ali and his people for their hospitality. He also noted that every time they came here, captain Kust-Ali took off in a small ketch with a few men and rounded the coast, out of sight. He had no doubts that this secret bay was Kust-Ali's hidden base, and that his trip down the coast had to be to visit some nearby port where he would meet with some of his fellow corsairs to exchange the latest news. Maybe, thought La Valette apprehensively, when Kust-Ali met with Barbarossa, this fellow might have remembered where he had last seen the Christian prisoner who called himself captain Baguette.

When morning came, the prisoner slaves were kicked awake and shuffled on board. Back on the clean vessel, in their customary seats, refreshed, rested and nourished, they resumed rowing to the command of the whistle and the beat of the monotonous drum. When they were ordered to stop rowing, they heard the commotion that accompanied the preparation of hoisting the sails. The sailors pulled the main mast upright from the bow end into position. Once the mast was up, they hoisted the cross-beam ensuring this was secure, untied the sail, and unfurled it. A slight wind filled the white sails of the *Black Moon*, which rolled and shivered until the vessel was carried forward to the lapping of the displaced water on the sides. Since there was a fair wind, the slaves were ordered to pull-in the oars, and were grateful for the power of wind and for the opportunity to rest and move ahead without effort.

La Valette continued to lead the men in prayers and some Christian songs and this gave courage to the men. With the North African coast to his right and the position of the sun, he knew that they were travelling east. From his calculations he reckoned they had been captive now for well over ten months, and yet they had not encountered a single Christian war ship. It was obvious that Kust-Ali was avoiding making contact with the enemy. He earnestly hoped that if the vessel continued to sail east to Algiers, it would be intercepted accidentally by one of the large knights' fleets that roamed that area of Northern Africa.

That night the *Black Moon* anchored again in a protected bay. Someone had heard that they were somewhere close to Algiers, the principal port for the pirates and the Ottoman Fleet. La Valette had guessed correctly. The vessel dropped anchor for the night together with several scores of other vessels. His intuition hinted that this convoy of ships was preparing for a battle. This could only mean that there was a Christian fleet nearby. The slaves were given the usual piece of unleavened, flat bread, water, and behold!—A whole pomegranate each.

In the gentle rolling motion of the small swell, La Valette pretended to sleep like everyone else, but in fact he was fully awake and aware of all the movements around him. In the loud silence, broken only by snoring and the monotonous groaning of the vessel's hulk, and when he was confident and satisfied that all the guards had gone to the open deck above to sleep in the cool night air, and after hearing the hammering of the wedge that secured the hatch of the hold they were in, only then did he lean forward at full arm's length with the sharp and pointed piece of iron and start to chip away furiously to pry loose the remaining wood around the large iron ring through which the long chain had been threaded. He had a premonition that their time for action and escape would come sooner rather than later. It was time to prepare their escape.

La Valette worked around and around the ring, carving out a splinter of wood at a time. He picked up the splinters of wood and gave them to Oliver, who in turn slipped them to the men around and through a gap in the floorboards of the bilge area underfoot where the stagnant, filthy, and smelly bilge water sledged back and forth. When he was satisfied that he had pried enough wood off, he left a minimum of wood that needed only a strong tug to pull the bolt free. Luckily, the long chain placed no strain on the bolt; the chain lay loose and lazy on the deck floor. He had whispered a message to the rowers on the bench closest to the forward partition, where he hoped the armoury stood, principally based upon what they had seen before and on his knowledge of his own galleys.

A couple of men on the forward bench stretched to their limit to finger and test the wooden wall in front of them. Only two of them could do this at a time without overstretching the chain that bound them together. One of the men passed the message that there was one joint between two of the planks in the construction of the wall, which presented a slight gap that offered some possibility of separating. He said that they needed a strong tool to use as a lever. They looked around and passed the word to the rest of the oarsmen.

Soon someone hissed and whispered to a forward bench that he had a loose floorboard underfoot that intersected with the hull proper, meaning that that end of the plank would be beveled and present a chisel-type end that could possibly be introduced in the slight gap in the partition.

La Valette passed the message to the man who had discovered the loose plank. "Make sure you have it ready to pass forward to the front bench when the time comes. We must be fast and coordinated. When I give the order, the chain is to be threaded through the rings in total silence, whilst we row so that our escape from our chains is not detected until we are all free. The chain must not scrape or rattle when passing through the iron ring. As the chain is being passed, you men close to the hull side will pass the loose plank to the front bench. Because they are at the end of the chain, that bench will be the last to be free, so if they get the plank quickly, two of them can introduce the plank and lever into that gap. The other three on that bench will soon be free from the chain to join the other two men in the front to put all their weight behind the lever and work the boards on the partition free. We must be disciplined and time our every move. The five on the front bench will be the first to enter the armoury and will start passing the weapons back through the line to the rest of us. Oliver and I will be the only others to leave our benches and enter the armoury. Our mission will be to locate arms or pistols and gunpowder. Since we are trained weapons officers, we will try to quickly load a few weapons and pass these along. We hope we can do all of this in record time."

The next few days were tedious as usual: rowing, eating, rowing, praying, rowing and sleeping. La Valette had given a slight pull on the chain and observed that the ring on the upright beam moved slightly. It was ready to come off; next time he pulled it would be with some force and the thing would come loose.

La Valette thought of nothing else but of escaping and rejoining his own forces to fight against the Ottoman navy backed by Barbarossa's own corsair fleet, now sponsored by Sultan Suleiman the Magnificent. His mind went over old battles and the political situation. He recalled how the order had many of the best sailors in the Mediterranean from Spain, Portugal, Genoa, Venice, and France. These were experienced navigators, the greatest of which was Admiral Romegas, who knew all the ports and the smallest secret bays in the Mediterranean. At his private expense, La Valette had written to his father back in Provence, who had sponsored the construction of two galleys to add to the knights' fleet. His action had been an example to other wealthy commanders who had done the same. The knights' fleet was superior to the Muslims'. The class of vessel constructed in the west, the more modern weapons, better firing power, as well as the quality of its sailors all combined to make the Christian navy a formidable opponent. He could not wait to join them again.

La Valette also knew that the advent of a new Ottoman Turkish Empire in Anatolia had changed things dramatically. The balance of power had shifted, and it marked the beginning of a new phase in the age-old struggle—one of outright conquest. Turkish expansion had been slow and patient, but it ushered in colonization, a new order, the imposition of the Muslim religion, and a new way of subjecting a conquered people to total domination. The Muslims did this in Anatolia, Greece, the Balkans, and Persia. The Turks could not countenance a sea ruled by the *Ferengi*, or Franks—the Christian European.

Great Mutiny on the *Black Moon*

One calm morning, just before sunrise, when it was still very dark, in the full splendour of a Mediterranean summer, almost a year to the day after La Valette had been taken prisoner with the others by the Turks, the peace and calm was broken by much commotion above deck. They had rowed out of the bay where they had spent the night, and now stood about two miles off the coast. They could hear the crew shouting excitedly and cannons being moved and rolled into place, with orders being given right and left. The whistle and the drum beat furiously, like at no other time.

With the intuition of an experienced warrior and the foresight of a seasoned sailor, La Valette had suspected during the night that the morrow would not be like other days. As they had picked up anchor, there was expectation and excitement in the air. In the twilight of the day the crew was nervous and was rushing around preparing for something—it seemed to him for war. Sail had been set, and the vessel was moving by wind-power, so the oars had all been picked up, and the oars-master and drummer had gone up to the deck level to perform some other duty. The slaves tried to look through the tiny gaps in the hull from where the oars protruded. The excitement was contagious; all the slaves were caught in it. All the oarsmen were pressing and climbing over each other trying to see through the oar-holes, but the only things they saw were the beach, the shoreline, and many other galleys anchored in the same place. To the port and the starboard side, the report from La Valette's men was the same. Galleys, galliots, brigantines, and all sorts of other ships were around them. Everyone seemed very busy and in a hurry.

This is surely it, thought La Valette, *the Ottoman fleet is getting ready for battle.* The fight, surely, had to be with Christian forces. But La Valette reckoned that the *Black Moon* was not heavy enough to be in a front-line battle and would, therefore, not be one of those joining the initial fight. *Somehow*, he thought, *he would take over the vessel and put her out of action.*

In the quiet of the early morning, and with the noise going on above them, La Valette gave a hefty pull at the bolt, and the chain came loose. He signaled to the men to start pulling the chain through the rings in their individual foot bracelets. At the same time, the row behind passed the lose plank to the front row, lost no time in prying the sections of the partition apart; it was easier than they had thought. In no time the men were stretching and flexing their legs and arms. In less time than that, the men in the forward row pulled at the lever and pried open a gap wide enough to get through; they started passing back weapons of all sorts: axes, swords, shields, and javelins. Several of the men went to the companionway to intercept the guard should he try to come down. They hid in the shadows and waited for La Valette's order. Meanwhile, La Valette and Oliver had entered the hold's armoury and located the handguns and the gun powder, powder horns, lead balls, and flints.

Another man came with them and told La Valette, "With your permission, sir—I'm a gun expert, sir. Can I help you load, sir?"

"Good man. Take care of those over there," said La Valette, pointing at some harquebuses. In less than five minutes the three of them had loaded a score of handguns and harquebuses.

The rest of the prisoners were now set, cutlasses, swords, shields, and handguns at the ready. La Valette and Oliver moved forward. Since the galley was presently moving under sail, the lack of movement from the oars was not a problem. "We need to get hold of that brute of a Turk who has the key. Bang on the hold's door, and as soon as someone opens and shows his face, grab him and pull him down. Then wedge the trapdoor from the inside so they can't lock us in."

They could hear the firing of distant cannon; the battle had started! Through the trapdoor La Valette heard some words exchanged between two Turkish sailors, and since La Valette had managed to pick up some Turkish words during his year of confinement, he was able to decipher the words.

"It's the infidel Christian fleet!" he heard someone shout from above deck.

"Right men, this is our chance. We are going to take over this ship, so we need to surprise the captain and the crew. Knock on the door now, and be ready to drag the fellow in." Day had broken and the yellow sun was rising in the horizon. Two men stood at the ready close to the door. One of them banged. The men were counting on the likelihood that whoever opened the door, hopefully their oar master, would not suspect freed fighting slaves, and that the light from the outside would blind him for a moment so he wouldn't be able to see for the second or two that it would take to pull him into the hold.

"Who banged down there?" was all the man had time to say in the moment it took him to open the trap door and lean into the hold to peer but with the speed of a cobra two pairs of hands gripped the fellow by the shirt and belt and dragged him down head first; a simultaneous cross-cut with a cutlass cut the Turk's throat and silenced him forever. A prisoner cut the cord that held the keys strung around the oar master's waist. He took the keys and jumped the stairs to the door that led to the other lower level. They found a guard sitting there. Before the guard had time to react, he was traversed through the stomach with a sword the freed slave carried. The other slaves were soon let loose with the acquired key, and most of them were provided with a variety of weapons. Those without weapons untied the idle oars and broke them in shorter pieces to be used as clubs.

All of this had taken less than one minute. La Valette and Oliver had waited till they received word that all the prisoners were loose. With a few other prisoners they jumped out of the hold like lightning. Crouching low La Valette waited a split second, and when he reckoned sufficient men had climbed up on the main deck, they attacked the closest members of the crew, catching them totally unaware from behind.

Some of the escaped prisoners went right and some went left. It was a fearsome sight to behold; men crawling out of the hold like naked animals let loose from their cage now prowling the deck and the rigging. Those like La Valette and Oliver, who each carried two double-barreled pistols, fired almost at point-blank range. La Valette held back one of his pistols and unsheathed a sword from its scabbard, and with Oliver by his side and a few other prisoners, dashed for the covered area in the stern, screaming and shouting fiercely, scaring the surprised crew who turned to look back to find out what was happening. It was not surprise in their faces; it was fear—pure, unadulterated fear. Where had these jackals come from, and how? The hundred or so avenging prisoners, fearless with their sense of new-found freedom, cut down, shot, or lanced through the surprised and flabbergasted sailors and the vessel's company of soldiers.

Some did not wait to find out what was happening. The pandemonium was enough to encourage them to dive overboard into the sea.

La Valette and his chosen team surrounded Kust-Ali, the helmsman, and a couple of other fakirs, who stood there with elaborate turbans and fancy weapons by their side. "Take a rope and tie this one up," ordered La Valette indicating Kust-Ali. "Throw those two overboard. We have no time to take prisoners or watch over our backs."

"Oliver, take the helm and steer towards that big knights' ship; it has our flag." The ship was one of the grand carracks of Rhodes belonging to the Christian fleet. He noticed the order's special flag that signified that the grand master was on board; it was the flag of Grand Master D'Omedes.

Turning upon Kust-Ali, and roughly placing the point of his sharp sword on Kust-Ali's throat, La Valette shouted at him, "Where's your bag of flags, you scum? Quick, I don't have all day, man!" Mouth wide opened and apparently still in his catatonic condition of surprise, Kust-Ali pointed to a cabinet behind La Valette.

La Valette pulled out a canvas bag and emptied it on the deck's floor. There was a host of different flags, but he could not find what he was looking for, a white flag. He looked around and ordered one of the Turkish prisoners who was about to be thrown overboard by two of the former slaves to remove his white blouse. He took it, tearing it along the seams to open the blouse in a wide, square piece. He tied it on the hanging lanyard that dropped from the very top of the stern mast by knotting the sleeves. He lowered the Turkish red flag with the white half-moon and white star in the middle and raised the white blouse so that the breeze would allow it to flutter in the wind.

Whilst all of this was happening, the sound of cannon cross-fire had increased to a deafening level. The sea battle and the exchange of fire was taking place further up the line, between some of the heavier warships. The grand carrack and its escort, two Venetian galleasses, were out maneuvering and out-gunning four Turkish men-of-war. The *Black Moon* had either arrived late to the rendezvous, or had not been assigned a prominent place in the battle plan.

The grand carrack was a formidable opponent. It carried thirty young knights doing the regulation six-month tour of duty, as well as a full company of soldiers. It was powered by two large blood-red sails of incredible length; the crosspieces bearing sail were so long that they bent over at the far ends. It also had two levels of twenty-four oars each level and on either side of the vessel. As soon as the quarry was within cannon-shot and the battle started the red sails had been quickly furled. The huge black flag with the eight-pointed cross gallantly flew from the stern flag pole and another, slightly smaller flag flattered, from the top of the main mast. The oars had taken over and had positioned the vessel for battle. To turn the vessel around quickly, one row of oars were pulled whilst the opposite row pushed on the oars, thereby turning the vessel almost on a pivot. It had three decks of cannons of tremendous size that would devastate the enemy on impact. It also carried a couple of catapults that would sling away "Greek fire", a large earthenware pot full of oil and flammable liquid. The pot was fitted with a burning wick so that when the pot hit the vessel and broke it would spill the oil and liquid and the burning wick would set the oil on fire; it was a deadly weapon at sea.

Two Turkish vessels were already on fire. La Valette could see men jumping overboard. The range of the large and long carrack cannons was far-reaching so that from their stationary position they could aim at vessels whose gun range was half as long and their power miniscule in comparison.

La Valette was glad to see that there were two grand carracks in this fleet. He ordered the acting helmsman, Oliver, to steer toward the one bearing the grand master's flag. This was strange because it was very rare for the grand master to go out to battle at sea. However, unless there had been a change in command during the year of his imprisonment, he suspected that Grand Master Juan or Giovanni D'Omedes, the Spaniard from Aragon, would be on board.

The mutinied *Black Moon* slowly approached the grand carrack, and La Valette could see its guns bearing on him. He also saw a whole crowd of people gathered at the stern looking at them in amazement. "Jump up and down, men. Wave! Jump! Before they fire at us. Let them know we are friendly, or else they will blow us out of the water," shouted Oliver. All the men started jumping, screaming, and waving at the same time. All the crew followed suit; in joy and ecstasy they shouted in Italian, English, French, and Portuguese.

The battle seemed to be over. Part of the knights' fleet was taking captives and captured vessels. Other Turkish vessels were making a strategic retreat, heading home while they could.

The grand carrack's port door was opened, and a catwalk was laid. Valette went over to Kust-Ali, roughly took him by the scruff of his tunic, and peering into his face he asked, "Do you know who I am?"

"You are Captain Jean Baguette, are you not?" replied a subdued Kust-Ali.

"No! I'm not! If you ever see that murderous scoundrel Barbarossa, you tell him that I am Jean Parisot de la Valette, Knight of the Order of St. John of Jerusalem, in the service of the Cross of Jesus Christ. Tell him that I fooled him, and that I was the one who took him prisoner in Rhodes. But I do not think you will see him for a very long time, because I will make sure you spend the rest of your life below deck, on the oars, gathering calluses on your soft backside."

The freed prisoners on the *Black Moon* boarded the grand carrack, and a prize crew jumped from the big ship onto the galley to sail it back to base.

The untidy, half-dressed, starving, stinking group of men was taken to see the captain and the grand master. They grinned, looking very relieved and happy. La Valette was at the front, a sinewy disheveled specimen, naked except for a filthy loincloth.

"Who in heaven's name are you men?" asked the grand master.

"My Lord, you took your time to get here, didn't you?" Obviously the grand master had not yet recognized the much transformed La Valette and Starkey with overgrown hair and scraggly beards and skeletal bodies. "What do you mean, we took our time? Who are you anyway?"

"My Lord, at your service and at the service of the Order of St. John of Jerusalem, I am your Brother Jean Parisot de la Valette, and this is Brother Sir Oliver Starkey, of the same order," he explained, bending over and sweeping his arm in a mocking bow.

"At your humble service, my Lord," added Oliver, bowing his head also.

"By my oath, it's impossible, it's incredible, *No me lo creo. Dios.* God, I can't believe it. La Valette? Starkey? *Dios mio.* My God. God Almighty, man, we had given you up for dead. *Bendita la madre de Dios.* Blessed mother of God. La Valette and Starkey indeed. What a pleasant, glorious sight for these sore eyes. Captain! Please take care of Sir Jean's men immediately. They will need scrubbing and cleaning before they mix with our crew and infect the rest of them with vermin. Give them clean clothes and feed them well. Don't spare any of the luxuries on your ship, Captain; these men deserve nothing but the best. Gosh, La Valette you look terrible, honestly, really terrible. Come you two, you can clean up in my cabin, and then we will celebrate today's victory and our most miraculous reunion. You can tell me all about your adventure. It's been almost a year since you disappeared, hasn't it?"

"No, Grand Master, it's been twelve months, two weeks and five days."

BROTHER OF THE ORDER IN RAMSON NEGOTIATIONS WITH THE SARACENS

BARBAROSSA BROTHERS—BARBARY PIRATES

CONTEXTUS V

IN SEARCH OF THE HOLY CROSS

THE HURRICANE

As they sat in D'Omedes cabin in the great carrack drinking a cup of refreshing light red wine, recounting the new arrivals' recent adventure and their daring escape La Valette recalled the first time he had encountered the current grand master. This had been on the occasion of an emergency Council meeting.

Around the circular table sat the twelve senior Knights of the Order of St. John of Jerusalem and Rhodes, Jean de la Valette being the youngest sitting with them.

Malta's current grand master was Pierre del Ponte, and under discussion so far, was the performance of the lieutenant to the grand master, Juan D'Omedes, a Spaniard from Aragon. D'Omedes had been accused by the Hospitallers of being more interested in local politics and restoring rights to the native Maltese, by suggesting the setting of a *universita* in Birgu, a form of local government, rather than concentrating on the defenses of the island as ordered. D'Omedes's weak point had been that he was a Spaniard, and since the French tended to have a more powerful official lobby than the Spaniards, there was much rivalry between the French and the Spaniard. Even war on the main-land existed between Spain and

France. Influence in the order seemed to go against D'Omedes. Secondly, D'Omedes had suffered a humiliating defeat at the hands of the Turks in Tripoli, North Africa, and defeat was viewed dismally by the order.'

Bu now he found himself sitting across the table celebrating his escape with D'Omedes, now promoted to Grand Master. D'Omedes had embarked on this sea-faring adventure in an attempt to regain and restore further his tarnished reputation. He was now old and reaching the sunset of his career as a knight.

The Wrath of Nature

Sitting next to the grand master, at the grand Council meeting, was forty-three-year-old Jean de la Valette, who, ten years after his return from slavery, had been appointed Governor and Commander of Tripoli in North Africa.

Of the other eleven knights present, one belonged to the Langue of Castile, who was the seneschal, and ran the administration of the order locally; another from the Langue of Aragon; two from the German Langue, one of whom was the military marshal of the order; four from the Italian Langue; three from the Langue of Provence; and one from the Langue of Auvergne. The Italian Langue had a larger representation because they actually had a larger number of knights based on the island at that particular time.

Since their common language was Latin Sir Oliver Starkey was taking notes in Latin. He was the intellectual, the only knight of the English Langue because King Henry VIII had closed all Roman Catholic monasteries, convents, and religious orders in England, including those of the Knights of St. John of Jerusalem, following his separation from the Catholic Church's seat at Rome.

The grand master began: "Brethren, the second item on our agenda today concerns three other pressing matters. The first urgent item is the horrendous battering that our island has suffered during the last couple of days by several hurricanes that have swept the island as never experienced in any part of the Mediterranean. The effect has been catastrophic. Luckily, we managed to move most of our fleet from its path, ahead of the hurricane, to a more sheltered position on the lee of the island. Regrettably, in the process of moving, we have lost four galleys and several brigantines. Most of the vessels that survived have suffered considerable damage that will take many, many months to repair. This will be our opportunity to modernize our fleet and renew our fortifications. As the saying goes, 'every cloud has a silver lining'.

"Worst of all, two of our brethren and six hundred men have drowned mostly slaves and sailors. Their bodies have been found along the rocky coastline and on beaches.

"Thousands of buildings, homes, warehouses, and homesteads have been completely destroyed.

"There are tens of thousands of people homeless out there who will be starving before long. We will have our slaves help with clean-up and moving the rubble, and later with building.

"For this reason we have sent off messages of appeal this very day to all our European friends for funds for the restoration that we will need to do with the greatest of haste. We hope that food and clothing will come quickly from Sicily and from Brother Valette's fortress in Tripoli. I need not tell you that we are acutely vulnerable to an attack from the Ottoman Turks should they hear of our predicament. We do not expect to hear from many of our friends for a month or two; we hope relief from Sicily and Tripoli arrive within two weeks,

"The other item on our agenda concerns our Fleet. We are hopeful that King Philip as well as His Holiness the Pope will donate us several of the latest war ships at their disposal. I am commissioning the building of a vessel from the order's treasury, and Brother Jean de la Valette, here, has kindly offered to donate another galley, on behalf of his dear father. We already had a gift of two vessels from the prior of Saint Jailles, to add to our fleet, and these are being built in Genoa. We have also written to the prior of France, and we expect that under these serious and lamentable circumstances he will also donate two vessels. We will embark immediately upon the repair of our own damaged fleet.

"The other item is that of the island's fortifications. As far as the fortifications are concerned, I move that we do not delay to build on the peninsula of Senglea a much needed new fort, Fort St. Michael. Because of its proximity across the harbour from Birgu, we need to make special plans for this fortification. We will construct an iron chain to close the harbour entrance to the port between Birgu and St. Michael, and a larger chain that will close the entrance to the big harbour of the Sciberras peninsula area, from Fort St. Elmo to Gallows Point. The layout of our coastal fortifications is such that we need to anticipate that any of these forts can fall in the hands of our enemies, and we must plan to prevent them from being used against us should this were to happen. The Italian engineer has already been instructed to start drafting plans for this fortification."

Two of the engineers, the Italian and the Maltese, took notes on the last instructions.

Plans to Recover the Holy Cross

The grand master took a drink of water, coughed gently into his hand, and said, "And now the next and final item on the agenda, which is the reason why Brother Jean de la Valette has been called from his duties in Tripoli to attend this meeting. Unfortunately, or fortunately for us, he was caught up in this terrible hurricane and has lived this nightmare with us. Brother Jean has written to me previously on this matter, and I wholeheartedly agree with his plan.

"We sincerely believe that what our order needs, or rather, what our Christian Europe needs, is a new moral victory! A victory that will restore the people's faith in our order as guardians of the faith, and at the same time restore faith in God and our holy cause. We need a victory like no other victory before. A bloodless victory against the Ottoman Empire and Suleiman, the so-called Magnificent."

Several of the knights around the table sat back with puzzled looks and shrugged in amazement. "But Lord, what kind of victory can be won without the shedding of blood? Surely the only kind of victory that we have known has been won by the sword with much blood spilled." Comments like this one dominated the incredulous noisy mutterings that came from those around the table.

"Please, gentlemen, Brother Jean will explain. Please go ahead, Brother Jean. You are the best person to explain this plan; after all it's your idea anyway," added the grand master, nodding and pointing to La Valette, begging him to start.

La Valette gave a soft cough, cleared his voice, and his opening words produced a stunning silence. You could hear a pin drop in the large grand master's chamber. "Brethren! Not only a bloodless victory, as the grand master has said, but also a warless victory! It will involve no more than six individuals. Our mission, Brethren will be to steal or better still, to take back, recover the relic of the piece of the Holy Cross on which Christ died from the hands of the Turks! A Cross that is rightly ours! Yes, we will take it from under the noses of the Saracens at Rhodes." The momentary hush was deafening, but this was followed by an excited cross-fire of questions, everyone talking at the same time.

"The Holy Cross?" "But that is impossible!" "You must be crazy." "The island of Rhodes is in the control of the Ottoman Turks, in a well-guarded fortress, no doubt. There must be at least twenty thousand soldiers on the island at the present time. How could we steal the holy relic from under their noses?" Remarks of that kind came from the other ten incredulous brethren.

Jean de la Valette raised his hands asking for silence. With both hands raised above his head, he patiently waited for the rumblings to subside. "Please, gentlemen; please hear me out. Let me tell you what amounts to a fascinating story.

"Down in Tripoli, we have been busy preparing our fortifications for another possible siege by the Sultan's fleet. The days there are long and drawn-out, which means that I have time to go on my daily exercise walk along the beach, mostly accompanied by a couple of brethren and companions-in-arms. One of them is here with me today, Brother Oliver, who as you can see is there busy taking notes of what is being said." Oliver looked up and smiled at the rest of the company; he raised his free hand and greeted them all without lifting the quill from the parchment.

"One day," continued La Valette, "Brother Starkey and a couple of other brethren and I were walking along the beach when we came upon a small fishing boat that had not been there the day before. The boat had been washed ashore and was holed and looked pretty bitten up, obviously the victim of a cruel sea. We stopped and looked inside the boat. To our surprise, there was a man inside the boat, face down; he looked very dead to us. He was in a ghastly condition. He lay there bruised and bloody. True to our vows, and in the spirit of the Good Samaritan, we lifted him out of the boat and laid him on the sand. I was about to order that a hole be dug wherein to bury him, when out of some instinct, I went down and placed a finger on the side of his throat to feel for his artery and a pulse. Lo and behold, I felt a beat! 'This man is still alive! Let's see if we can revive him.'

"'But Commander,' said one of the brethren. 'Can't you see that he is a Saracen, a Muslim?'

"I replied, 'Of course I can see that, but Brother, you are forgetting one of the first vows of the Order of the Hospitallers, which is charity—charity on whoever it might be. Even our founder, Blessed Brother Gérard, took Muslims into our Hospital in Jerusalem, although he kept the Muslims separate from the Christians, of course, but he nonetheless succoured our enemies. Our duty is to help the sick, the injured, and the needy.' And that is precisely what we did."

"Hear, hear!" came a few voices from around the table.

"Oliver here," continued La Valette, pointing at Oliver, "Brother Oliver carried a water-skin with him and poured some water into the poor man's mouth. The water did not go down. It just flowed out of his mouth. Brother Oliver and the other brothers laid the fellow down flat on the beach, facing upward, and they twice pushed down heavily on the man's chest and tried again to give him water, this time filling his mouth. The reaction of the almost dead man was immediate revival; the poor fellow did not want either to drown or choke on dry land after having survived a storm at sea. He splattered the water all over us like a runaway whale. No sooner had he done this than he asked for water. Oliver gave him some more, this time more slowly, and this time he drank a few mouthfuls before Oliver took the skin away. Then a brother fetched some seawater and poured this over the fellow's head and face to cool him down and bring him about. He had sunburn blisters on his cheeks, and his lips were dry and cracked. We lifted him up and placed him in the shade. I asked the brethren to go to the fort and fetch some help. The fellow was cared for, fed, and clothed by our people in the infirmary. I went to see him every day in order to follow his progress.

"I need to add that one of the thoughts recurring in my mind during my daily walks along the beach was the unfortunate loss of the relic of the Holy Cross, which our order, regretfully, was forced to leave behind when we left Rhodes. At the time I wanted to go back and fetch the relics, but as you know, my Lord, since you were there," said La Valette looking towards the grand master, "I was on horseback with the rest of the men were ready to leave the fortress of Rhodes, but I still had part of two enemy arrows embedded in me—one on my thigh, and the other in my left shoulder; and besides, the Turks were pressing us to leave the island.

"Fortunately, Sultan Suleiman was merciful to us, in so far as he let us go free with our lives; this was because our order had put up such a brave defense of the island. In fact, the Sultan admired our late grand master, Phillip L'Isle-Adam, for his bravery and chivalry. On previous occasions, in the Holy Land, when the Sultan had overpowered our forces, he would not spare *anyone*; he beheaded all Christian survivors, including women and children. After beheading them, he would then crucify the bodies and place the heads on poles for everyone to see.

"However, on this occasion he spared our lives and allowed us to take our personal possessions, we had no time to go back to pick up our sacred things, including the holy relics. The piece of the Holy Cross was one of them, something that we had zealously guarded for centuries, because it had been handed down to us from the times of the apostles, in particular St. James the Elder, who was the first bishop of Jerusalem, and who was martyred by the Jews, some say on an upside down cross on the walls of Jerusalem, and others say that he was boiled alive. Nevertheless, since Brother Oliver Starkey is an expert on this subject, he will give you an account of the other holy relics that we kept at Rhodes. Brother Oliver, please proceed, if you don't mind," concluded La Valette, and resumed his seat.

Brother Oliver Starkey stood up and took over. "As Brother La Valette has already said, the relic of the Holy Cross is not the only holy relic we left behind. In the two hundred years that our order had resided in Rhodes, we had accumulated a collection of some of the most precious holy manuscripts of the earliest bibles written in Greek. These relics came from Antioch, Jerusalem, Damascus, Acre, and other former Christian cities. For example, we had an illuminated manuscript, a copy of the gospel of St. Mathew in its complete form, dating to the second century after Christ. We also kept in our library some of the illustrated teachings of St. John the Evangelist and St. Prochorus. We had a homily on the assumption of the Virgin Mary, dated the year 380, by Pope Damasus, from the church of St. Andrews in Jerusalem. There was another manuscript on the life of St. Basil the Great. And from the oldest monastery in Christendom, St. Catherine's monastery, we kept homilies on meekness by St. Athanasius and what is believed to be an early version of St. Mark's gospel in Greek. I have seen and handled all of these holy relics. All these are irreplaceable treasures of our faith that are now lost to us. However, we do know that they were kept in storage in one of our houses in Rhodes, and they will remain lost to us unless we retrieve them."

Everyone in the room looked and listened, spellbound, as Brother Oliver sat down and the grand master asked, "Does anyone have any further questions?"

"Yes, Brother Jean," said Brother Fidelio Lombardo, one of the Italian knights. "Most fascinating and interesting, but many of us already know this, even though we have given all those relics up as lost. For all we know, they may even have been destroyed by now, and if they have not been destroyed by the Saracens, they are surely well kept out of reach and under guard, in a safe place, by the Muslims there. So how do you propose to get your hands on them?

La Valette explained: "Good question, Brother Fidelio. This is why providence placed this poor fisherman in our path. I am convinced that finding this fisherman was no accident; rather, I am convinced that it was an act of God—providential, you might say. The relics have not been destroyed, and we have a good idea where they are kept. I have spoken a lot to this fisherman, and he is so grateful to us for saving his life that he is willing to do anything to repay us, even with his life, he said, and I believe him.

"I mentioned to him that I had lived as a very young man in Rhodes, before its capture by the Turks. We exchanged ideas, and I shared my recollection of the city, the market place, and the docks, the gardens, the fortifications, and the fortress. He told me that he lives at walking distance from the fort, in fact, close to the Eastern Gate, and that he goes there to sell his fish, so he is very well known and knows everyone, including the rich and well-to-do people.

"When I mentioned that we had a library with holy things in them, he said knew the library and had been in it. 'How come a fisherman like you knows the library inside the citadel? Surely you do not read or write, and have no business inside the citadel, so how come?' I asked.

"'No, I don't know how to read or write.' He replied. 'But many years ago, while I was not fishing on account of very bad weather, a cousin of mine, who happens to be a guard inside the fortress, employed me and my brother to move some heavy crates from the library to a cellar. My brother, my cousin, and I, with two other men, moved seven heavy wooden crates and some lighter items to a cell two levels down some stairs.'

"Brothers, imagine my surprise and temporary confusion. Was I hearing correctly, or was it my imagination playing tricks on me? The fisherman I was talking to, the castaway we had brought back to life, knew the exact location of our Christian treasure! Including, I should imagine, the relic of the Holy Cross, about which I had been contemplating whilst walking on the beach only moments before finding this half-dead man. It appeared that this man had the key to fulfilling my desire. And he was prepared to do anything for us in return for saving his life. This was too much of a coincidence; surely God had played a hand in this.

"I waited for the right moment to broach the question to Said Tafur-Ali, for that was the fisherman's name. One day I asked Tafur-Ali if he thought about his family, and if he wanted to return to his home sometime soon. He replied, 'Yes, Lord, I would dearly like to go back home to my family, my wife, and five children, because they must think me drowned. But Lord, how can I return? My boat is broken and not seaworthy. Besides, the distance is too great for sailing and rowing. I was blown to this place by a storm that lasted several days, but to return from Tripoli in North Africa to Rhodes on the Greek coastline is almost impossible. I could not navigate this route, Lord.' He was right, of course; he had a long diagonal journey to steer. The pattern of the stars to navigate by and this region was unknown to him.

"I told him, 'Do not worry, Tafur-Ali; it is possible, I have a plan that may help you. I can take you home in my own ship. And on top of that, I would get your boat repaired, plus I would give you a purse of silver coins.'

"'Why would you do that my Lord? It is I who owe you, not a bag of silver, but a bag of gold, and my own life too. Truly Lord, I need to repay you in whatever and whichever way I can. I am indebted to you beyond words. Your Christian kindness and charity have impressed me more than I can say. Lord, I have seen you at prayer five times a day, and at the same hours that I do my prayers; you must be a servant of Allah like I am. I always heard and was taught as a child that Christians kill all Muslims on sight, and that they burnt them alive, and even eat our young children. Obviously this cannot be true. There is surely something wrong about our quarrel,' said the fisherman philosophically. I realized that sometimes wisdom comes from the mouth of the simple at heart.

"'Yes indeed, my friend Tafur-Ali. You are absolutely right; there is something very wrong in the quarrel between our nations and our religions. For example, my friend, just assume for a moment that the black stone was stolen from the Kaaba in Mecca. What would you be prepared to do to recover the holy black stone?'

"'My Lord, that is unthinkable! I, or for that matter any other good Muslim, would go to any length, any sacrifice, go anywhere that I would need to go, even to the end of the world if needs be to get back the holiest of holy objects,' said Tafur-Ali in a very passionate manner, gesturing energetically with his arms. 'Anything and anywhere,' he added.

"'You speak from the heart Tafur-Ali; well said. But you see—I have a serious problem.'

"'What is your problem my Lord? Your problem is my problem, and I will do anything within my power to assist you in whatever way I can,' added Tafur-Ali with sincere bravado.

"'My problem, my friend, is that just as you would do anything to recover your holy black stone of Mecca, should it be stolen, I too would like to recover several holy items that are kept in those crates that you moved from the library to that cellar. You see, my friend, those things are ours and are very holy to us, and mean the world to us Christians. Is there any way in which you can help me recover them?'

"'My Lord, after what you have done for me—healing me, giving me back my life, and now offering to take me back home to my family, I pledge to help you reclaim those holy things that are rightly yours. Besides, they are of no value whatsoever to my faith, they are kept in a forsaken dungeon in the island, yet they mean so much to you. Tell me what I have to do, my Lord, and I shall do it.' continued Tafur-Ali.

"'It could be very, very dangerous for you, Tafur-Ali, should they catch you helping a Christian steal from the Sultan.'

"'But my Lord, I am prepared to give my life at your service. Besides, the kingdom of Rhodes does not belong to the Turks or the Arabs. It belongs to the Greeks. I happen to be of Greek origin whose family was forced to convert to Islam. My father once had a Greek name. He said it used to be Dimitri Popodopulous, but it was changed to Tafur-Ali. I am proud to belong to Islam, and follow the ways of Allah. But first and foremost, I have Greek blood flowing through my veins, and there are many times when I resent being under the control of a Colonial power.'"

"Brothers," said La Valette, looking around the table, "I knew then that I had an ally—not only someone who felt he owed me his life, but an ally who did not care for the present rulers of his homeland, the island of Rhodes.

"Tafur-Ali has come to Malta in my ship, and as soon as we organize our undercover operation, we will set off for Rhodes to recover the cross.

THE UNDERCOVER OPERATION

"Now I will tell you our plan. We will take a fleet of ten vessels, one of them the large Venetian gallcass, and nine others galleys and brigantines. We will take the fisherman's craft, which we brought with us from Tripoli for repairs here, on the deck of the galleass. We will make the small craft seaworthy, and we will leave some of the surface damage unrepaired. We will fit a new sail just for the approach, but will replace it with the old and torn sail when we get to Rhodes. We do not wish to create any suspicion from anyone curious enough to look closely at the fishing boat.

"Tafur-Ali's boat will go unnoticed when we land there under cover of darkness, and we will land very close to Tafur-Ali's village. The rest of the fleet is for escort protection. But we will aim to sail south of the island, beyond the horizon out of sight of land, under cover of darkness. The galleass will release us there, and we will sail from there, in the fishing boat, for Tafur-Ali's village. It will appear to be a small, local fishing vessel coming in the dark after a day's fishing, and will not draw any attention should someone see the boat beaching.

"Tafur-Ali assures us that he has a perfect hiding place, close at hand and in the hills, for us to hide and use as a base. This cave is used only occasionally by a goat herdsman who is a close relative of Tafur-Ali. The fleet will return to base and then return for us ten days later, to a predetermined spot closer to the island than where it left us, to pick us and the cargo up. They will make a signal to us with a lantern, and we will build a fire on the beach as soon as we see thesignal in the distance.

"Brother Jean, who will accompany you on this mission? You mentioned that it would involve only six men," asked the Marshal.

"Yes, Brother Marshal. Since this is primarily a seafaring adventure, I propose picking six men with sea experience. The military capabilities go without saying, but all those who go on this mission must be veterans of the last Rhodes campaign. Everyone must be familiar with the land, the fortress, and the citadel. Here is the list of the names of the four other candidates that I propose; the two others consist of my companion Knight Oliver Starkey and Tafur-Ali, of course."

The marshal looked at the list and nodded his approval. "Emanuel Viale, Lionelli Bochetti, Pietro del Car, and Joanni Caviglia. All excellent men, Brother Jean. Please look after them, as I am sure you will. I want them back home in one piece."

―――・※・―――

Secret Landing at Rhodes

The south-westerly wind carried the small felucca with its seven occupants closer to the shore. Five of the passengers were lying low, on the floorboards of the small vessel, covered with an old piece of canvas, to minimize the silhouette of figures on board.

There was a moon in a clear night that reflected on the deep-dark blue, calm water. Tafur-Ali pointed ahead, and Jean, following his direction, saw the dark outlines of the low hills of the island of Rhodes and a cluster of small huts, which Tafur-Ali claimed was his village. La Valette felt a twinge of nostalgia remembering those familiar hills. Soon they could hear the breaking of the waves upon the pebbled beach.

Tafur-Ali gathered in the single, new sail. With the help of the others, he submerged the cloth into the water, adding onto it a few of rocks brought for the purpose. Then he pushed it down with the oars. The cloth spread out and slowly disappeared out of sight like a huge manta ray. Jean tied the old, tattered sail in place along the slanting pole. The sail and pole were lowered. Tafur-Ali set out the oars and started to row to bring the boat to the place and position that he had marked out.

As soon as the small boat ground on the pebble shore, they safely beached it and quickly dragged it up well above the water line. Tafur-Ali signalled for the others to follow him. Lionelli Bochetti and Emanuel Viale carried two large, heavy, canvas bags each, obviously the weapons bags. Joanni Caviglia and Pietro del Car carried two other canvas bags containing a couple of day's ration of food. Oliver Starkey carried upon his shoulder a rolled-up bag containing a few waterproofed canvas cases.

With Tafur-Ali in front, they took a zigzagging route uphill on what appeared to be an animal track. Tafur-Ali made sure they kept as far away as possible from the village, though a solitary dog barked once and breaking the silence of the night. Soon they embarked on a sea of sand, where a succession of tall, hard-packed sand dunes extended in all directions, like waves on the surface of an ocean. It was the ideal land cover to hide out of sight of prying eyes. The sand dunes spread out for a couple hundred yards; then suddenly they rejoined the animal track.

Running low in a bent-double position, they climbed the hill, around boulders and olive trees. After about fifteen minutes of climbing, and out of breath, Tafur-Ali called a halt. Relieved, they all threw themselves on the ground, blowing and huffing while stifling their panting. La Valette wiped his brow with his sleeve and asked Tafur-Ali if they had much farther to go.

"No, not far to go. Just over the ridge, to the right. There is an outcrop of rocks up above, and our cave is located there. You, Lord, and the others make yourselves comfortable. I shall go to my house and surprise my family. Do not be surprised if you hear screams of joy, that will be my wife. I shall then find my relative, the goat herd keeper, and tell him to look after you until I return. Tomorrow morning I shall go and look for my cousin, the one that works as a guard for the Mameluke soldiers who are stationed on the island."

The team settled inside the cave with all their gear. Oliver took out a large spread of canvas, and with the aid of long pieces of branches, placed a curtain over the entrance to the cave so the light of the candle they would light would not be seen from the outside. Fortunately for them, there was a grove of orange trees on the hill in front of the cave's entrance, which served as a natural screen. The cave was not large, but it was spacious enough for their immediate needs. They settled in the cave and prepared to have a meal of cheese, bread, and some salted beef, washed down with watered-down wine. In low voices they commenced to go over some of the details they had discussed on board the Venetian galleass during their seven-day trip.

La Valette said, "We are fortunate that this cave and Tafur-Ali's village is on the eastern side of the city and fortress, because Grand Master Phillip L'Isle planned a secret escape route out of the fortress, below the walls of the twelve towers and gates. Pray to God that the Turks have not found these secret passages and blocked them, because it will be very difficult otherwise to leave the fortress with our treasure through the upper gates, which are surely guarded day and night. Can anyone remember where the entrance to the secret tunnels are situated from the inside?"

"I do," replied Emanuel Viale. "During the early days of the Ottoman siege, my company of knights used the secret tunnel to get to the exterior, in disguise, to forage for supplies around the countryside."

"Where is the entrance located?" asked Oliver.

Emanuel continued, "If I remember correctly, it was situated at the very lower level of the East Tower, close to the East Gate. Though if the truth be known all the Gates and Towers have secret underground passages. There is a large hall that was used for storage and sleeping quarters. There are six columns around the inside of this hall. Next to one column immediately opposite the stairs is a wall with a large, rectangular wall-stone. This is, in fact, a secret door to the tunnel that leads to the exterior. About three feet from the ground and six feet from the rectangular wall-stone there is a small stone the size of a brick. This stone comes away if you pry it with the blade of your sword or dagger. When you move this rock out of the way you need to put your hand inside the cavity. There you should find a lever that you turn all the way to the right, and the large rectangular stone should open as a door. The only problem is that you need someone inside to close the door and place the brick-sized stone back into place. We need to arrange for someone to remain behind us to close the secret door." "Brother Oliver—can we have a look at the map of the city again? I think we should study this further to try to time and get acquainted with our surroundings," said La Valette, stretching his hand over to Oliver to get the rolled leather map. Oliver placed this on La Valette's hand. La Valette rolled the map open and placed it on the ground in the middle of the circle now formed by the six men. In front of them was a map that showed the city, fortifications, and the countryside around the city. La Valette pointed his finger to a spot that was close to a cluster of huts by the seashore on the eastern shore of the island.

"We are somewhere near here," murmured La Valette, pointing at a clump of trees and what should have represented some rocks. "Our immediate problems are, first, we must get past the security gate outside the fortification that controls the approach to the city. Second, how do we get into the fortification, and specifically to the East Tower? There are four roads that approach the city from the east and the west on flat terrain. On our route are four windmills, a vineyard, and another olive grove before we get to the Eastern Gate. We do not expect any problems up to that point. But there are twelve main towers around the city's stout walls. In between the towers are other structures used as barracks and storage rooms. Our destination tower is here. This tower and the gate next to it may be guarded during the daytime. Does anyone have any ideas?" asked La Valette.

"Yes, I have a suggestion," replied the knight from Genoa, Joanni Caviglia. "As you say, Brother, the Eastern Gate must be guarded to control the movement in and out of the city. If scrutinised closely, we could stand out as foreigners, so that is a risk we cannot take. Then should we enter the city proper, we will have to make our way to the tower, which means we would surely have to pass by more guards at the entrance to the tower. This doubles our risk. So I suggest we should enter the tower at night by climbing up the wall next to the tower and entering the tower through an entrance on the bastion level, there must be a door there, there always is, and if I recall rightly, there is an entrance there."

"Good suggestion, Brother Joanni. We will need a rope or a ladder to climb up the wall. That wall is about fifteen feet high, so a ladder would be a better solution," observed Brother Pietro Del Car, Knight of the Aragon Langue.

"We brought a rope with us just in case, it is at least thirty feet long. But how do we get such a long piece of rope through the security gate?" asked Brother Lionelli Bochetti, Knight of the Italian Langue.

"Our friend Tafur-Ali will have to go fishing," added La Valette. "If he brings a big catch of fish, he can cart his catch to the Eastern Gate. The coil of rope can be placed on the bottom of his cart beneath the fish. No one will suspect anything sinister if they see a coil of rope in a fisherman's cart. Then he can discretely approach the wall close to our tower and secretly drop the rope in the corner of the tower and the wall for us to fetch later. Therefore, our approach needs to be done at night if we are to bypass the gatehouse, and if we are to climb the wall unseen. This we can do only under cover of darkness.

"But what about the ladder suggestion? We need to wait for Tafur-Ali in order to agree to this plan. He may have some valuable ideas. We also need to find out what kind of information he brings when he returns. Having allies on the inside is our only hope to get to the holy relics without shedding any blood, which we must avoid at all cost. We kill only as a last resort, and only if our lives are in peril. If no one has anything further to add, I suggest we call it a day and rest until Tafur-Ali comes for us in the morning. With your permission, I will read the *compline* prayers before we sleep."

La Valette knelt down and the other Brothers followed. "Heavenly Father, at this hour which marks the end of the day, we come before you again in thankfulness to glorify your name. You have watched over us through the day and now we seek your protection throughout the night.

Forgive us, Lord, for thy dear Son, the ill that we this day have done, that with the world, ourselves, and thee, we, ere we sleep, at peace may be. Send us calm rest to restore our bodies and souls, so that tomorrow's dawn may find us more ready to give glory to the Father, Son, and Holy Spirit.

"We shall take turns guarding our small hide-out fortress. I shall take the first watch, Joanni, please take the second watch, and you, Pietro, the third, Emanuel the fourth, Oliver the fifth. Angel of the Lord watch over us."

Wrapped in their cloaks, cowls over their heads, the men made themselves as comfortable as possible. They had previously picked their weapons, and out of force of habit, each of them slept with his own sword by his side under his cloak.

The fire slowly faded and died as the cave grew colder and darker. The darkness hid the secrets of the morrow, which would soon reveal the dangers they would be facing. They were so close to the holy relics that it seemed like a dream. They needed the protection and guidance from God to pull through this.

Whilst they slept, the fragrance of orange blossoms travelled with the wind secretly invading the cave. Jean's sleepy thoughts drifted in the nothingness of the scented air. His dream was as real as the sword he held closely to his chest as he slept; the strong fragrance drugging his senses.

THE FORBIDDEN LOVE

Jean's *mind traversed the bridge of memory that took* him to a familiar, beautiful garden abounding in flowering shrubs, climbing honey-suckle, and rosebushes, accompanied by the rhythmic and refreshing sound of a playful cascade of a water fountain. Indeed, Rhodes was an island garden full of enchantments. All kinds of fruit trees grew in this garden: peaches, pomegranates, pears, apples, cherries, and several orange and lemon trees whose fragrance he enjoyed. The surrounding countryside was equally fertile and productive. His rides through the hills and country paths, during his stay in Rhodes years ago, were the most beautiful by far that he could remember, even more so than those he had known in beautiful Provence, in the South of France.

He remembered this garden, the place where he had met Ana Celeste. Ana Celeste—the forbidden love of his life.

His early days at the fortress had been rather high-spirited as a young man newly arrived from Provence. On one occasion, when on leave in the city centre, he had gone to a highly recommended tavern known for its good wine. He went with his friends. Unused to and unable to hold his drink, young La Valette got himself into a fight with a customer and knocked the quarrelsome fellow cold. This other side of La Valette was unknown, and surprised all those who knew him well. He was called before the order's council and severely disciplined. On another occasion, a knight from one of the other orders had, La Valette alleged, touched upon his honour, and therefore he called the other knight out to a duel, something that was strictly forbidden in the Order of St. John of Jerusalem. These two events landed him twice in jail and earned him severe reprimands, with the report bearing the remarks in the margin: "Juvenile high spirits". In his sleep he smiled at these distant memories of his arrival at the island of Rhodes shortly after having been made a Knight of the Hospitallers.

In his dream he remembered a lovely spring day in the year 1516, at age twenty-two, when he was strolling through the beautiful garden in his dream. He was enjoying the serene surrounding when he noticed a pretty young girl looking down at the tranquil goldfish swimming lazily in the pond while she fed them with breadcrumbs. He went up to the fountain, and standing just behind her, in a mild tone he said to her, "They are beautiful and carefree, wouldn't you say?" She looked up at him and blushed and turned her back on him, and lifted the tip of her head-cloth to cover her face as if to cut off any chance of a conversation with this stranger. She was wearing a lime-coloured chiffon tunic with a trailing head-cloth with a laced edge, which she promptly picked up to cover her head, and made as if to go.

"Please don't go, miss. Do not be afraid; I mean you no harm. I am new in the city, you see, though I've come to this garden a few times before. I like it here. I like the peace, the smell of the flowers; I also like to look at the fish swimming in there, in the pond. Do you come here often?"

"I come here only on Saturday mornings; it's the only time I can get away on my own. Sorry, but I have to go now, I'm running a little late already. God be with you." She turned to go, but Jean reached out and got her by the arm. She was taken aback and looked at his hand holding her arm in shock.

"Please let me go; you are hurting me. I have to go now," she whispered fearfully, looking at him straight in the eye. "Sorry miss I did not mean to hurt you". Then he asked her. "Please, can I see you again? Perhaps next Saturday?"

"I don't know," she said, still in a whisper, and then left in a hurry, leaving Jean flabbergasted, not at her speedy departure, but at her striking eyes and beauty. He had never seen eyes so green before, so large they were almond shaped and shone like emeralds. The fragrance of her perfume had reached his nostrils and had filled him with desire—and intimacy. It was a new experience for him, being sworn to scorn women. He had noticed she was wearing a cross, so she must be a Christian. He wished he had had more time to get to know her better. How he wished it were Saturday already to be able to see her again. He looked at himself in the reflection in the placid water of the pond to make sure he was looking well dressed and that his hair was tidy and in place. The reflection showed his white tunic with the black cross of the order, his sword in place in its scabbard and the dagger in its silver sheath.

He already knew that the coming week would seem endless. He hoped that the training and manoeuvres and the prayer time would keep his mind busy. Prayer time? *My God*, he thought, *I am vowed to the order to obedience, poverty, and chastity; yes chastity, which means I cannot have a relationship with a woman. It would be a sin and would make a travesty of my vows to the order if I were ever to do that.* His mind was in turmoil. *I live for the order; how can I have time for a woman? I should not, I must not, I will not*, he thought. And with that determination, he attempted to discard the remaining clear picture of her face in his mind. But try as he could, he could not rid himself of that unbelievable portrait of a face.

The week went by, and Jean tried to immerse himself in his training and duties to avoid thinking of the tantalizing girl. Incredibly, the fragrance of her remained with him during the week. He had never known anything as distracting as this. The thought of seeing her again drew him forward like an arrow coming off a crossbow. Like sticky honey, he could not shake off the thought or the smell of that young girl.

When Saturday came, he walked, in deep thought and uncertain, in the direction of the garden. There was still time to turn back. *So what was the problem*? He thought to himself. All he wanted to do was to see the girl and talk to her; that was all. There's no harm in talking, is there? Anyway, the vows of the order did not say, "Thou shall not talk! Thou shall not look at pretty girls!" Surely there is no harm in just looking, so long as you don't touch. The sin would be in the touching and not in the looking, talking, or smelling.

With these confused thoughts, he stepped into the garden and walked through the flower pathway covered with lilac wisteria overhead on one section, and with bougainvilleas above and clinging to the wooden trelliswork. He looked around, but all he saw were mothers with young children running around. He took a seat on one of the benches close to the fountain and from there watched the goldfish swim in their tedious, monotonous, unbroken circle. In his semi-trance he noticed that the smooth surface of the pond was disturbed ever so gently by small ripples, the ripples being formed by the scattering of breadcrumbs on the water. The fish went into an eating frenzy, attacking the feed on the surface of the water. And there she was. The effect was electrifying on Jean. He looked up and saw the girl, like an apparition, standing there feeding the fish. His heart fluttered, and he almost fell over as he rushed to get up and clumsily tried to walk nonchalantly towards her.

"Good morning, miss. I am glad to see you again, and glad, too, that you were able to make it here today."

"Oh! Please, don't think that I have come on account of you. I always come here on Saturday to feed the fish. The fish would miss their meal if I didn't come," the girl replied indifferently, without looking at his face.

"I am so glad you came anyway," said Jean awkwardly, barely able to get the words out. "For a moment I thought I would not see you again. By the way, my name is Jean Parisot de la Valette. I am a Knight of the Order of St. John of Jerusalem. May I ask what your name is?"

"They call me Ana Celeste," she mumbled.

"Very pretty name. Celeste. What does Celeste mean?" asked Jean, sheepishly.

"Fallen from heaven I think. I was named Ana after the mother of the Virgin Mary. I'm sure you knew that."

"Yes I did, but I think, honestly, you must have fallen from heaven because your eyes are angelic," whispered Jean, his voice sounding foolish and strange to himself.

"Don't be silly; my eyes are green."

"Yes I know, but what I really meant was that they are heavenly beautiful, I have never seen eyes so pretty. Are you a witch by any chance?" asked Jean with humour in his voice.

"What, a witch? Me a witch? Why of course not! Why would you say that?"

"I say that because I think you have cast a spell over me. I have been bewitched by you since the moment I caught sight of you. Not only are your eyes fascinating, but that auburn hair of yours is just too much for me. You leave me breathless, miss," said Jean with a glitter in his eyes.

"Flattery will get you nowhere, Jean Parisot de la Valette, simply nowhere," replied the young lady rather coyly and blushing.

"Oh! So you do remember my name. You can call me Jean, if you please. May I call you Ana or Celeste please?" he said, laughing. She was obviously finding this conversation rather amusing.

"You can call me by my name Ana Celeste. If you just called me Celeste, I would not be Ana, would I? And if you called me Ana, I would not be Celeste. Understand?"

"I think we were meant for each other, Ana Celeste," added Jean.

"Why would you say that? I don't follow," replied Ana Celeste.

"Because of your names. Ana means 'gracious', and Celeste means 'sent from heaven'. And my name, Jean, means 'God is gracious'. Can you see the similarity? I don't think that this is coincidence, that you are 'gracious sent from heaven', and 'God being gracious' with me. Voilà!" said an incredulous Jean.

"What does *voilà* mean?" she asked.

"Very simply an affirmation, like: 'There you are.' It is simple and very clear, don't you see?" replied Jean.

Embarrassed, Ana Celeste discretely changed the subject.

"Do you live in the large auberge of the order in the city?" asked the shy girl, with some curiosity. "And may I ask how long have you been living in Rhodes?"

"I arrived in Rhodes only three months ago." replied Jean.

"That isn't very long, is it? I imagine you are beginning to get to know the island. I was born here, and my grandparents came here a few years before the Roman Catholic Christians came and took over the island from us."

"Who do you mean by *us*?" asked Jean curiously.

"*We* refers to the Catholic Greek Orthodox population. This island belongs to us and was taken forcefully by your order. You Christians from Rome attacked and killed many other Christians, which was not a very Christian thing to do. Was it?"

"No it was not. I am sorry that you feel that way. Though that took place long before my time, I can assure you it won't happen again, if I can help it," said Jean apologetically, lowering his head somewhat shamefully. "I hope you will forgive us for such a transgression."

"Well there is nothing anyone can do about this anymore. Like the saying goes, 'You shouldn't cry over spilled milk. So forget it. My grandfather says that one day the Catholic knights will have their day of reckoning with the Ottoman Turks," she replied. "So, there is no need to forgive. Please let us forget the whole unsavoury incident," replied Ana Celeste.

"Does your grandfather believe that the Turks will attack the island of Rhodes? Because if they do attack, we are certainly prepared for them. I can assure you that they shall not take Rhodes. The island of Rhodes is our last stronghold close to the Holy Land, and from here we can harass the Saracen ships. One day we will return to the Holy Land to retake it victoriously for Christianity. Then your grandfather will be very glad that we did take the Holy Land and that we did it from this gracious island." Ana Celeste saw the determination and conviction with which he said it, and could not help but admire her newfound admirer.

Seeing that she was getting fidgety, obviously intending to leave, Jean asked. "Can we meet again next Saturday, here at the same time?"

"We must meet somewhere else. My grandmother is asking me lots of questions. She may suspect that I am seeing someone, and she could send someone to follow me, so I need to be careful."

"Do you ride?" asked Jean.

"I love riding and have my own horse; I live in a large cottage at the far end of the city close to the wall," she added.

"Then that is fantastic. When and where would you like to meet? It needs to be one of the discrete gates from where we can ride into the surrounding countryside. The Western Gate sounds to me the best place; there seems to be fewer people around there. Shall we say next Saturday at this same time?" suggested Jean.

"Yes, fine, by the Western Gate at this hour, then," agreed Ana Celeste.

Jean could hardly wait for the next Saturday to come. When it finally did, he rode there early. He got off his mount and took out a plain tunic from his saddlebag. He changed his tunic and placed his knight's white tunic, with the red cross, inside the saddlebag.

When Ana Celeste arrived on her horse, they took off at a trot down a road in a northerly direction towards the hills.

And so their friendship grew into a tender loving relationship, with them holding hands and laughing at the most trivial things. She told Jean that her father was a merchant and was hardly at home. He would travel to Venice and other cities, particularly to Anatolia, buying and selling. She said he specialized in the commodity of gold, and his trips were long so she hardly ever saw him. That was why she lived with her grandparents and had been brought up by them. Her mother had died of the fever when she was barely six years old, so Ana Celeste had very little recollection of her.

Their meetings in the garden and the rides on horseback continued, and their relationship progressed to the point where they both realised that they were in love. Passion overtook circumstances, and the inevitable fused two young hearts and two bodies in the melting pot of mutual desire. Jean met the grandparents, and they invited him to their house. Yet Jean's situation did not permit a formal celebration of marriage. But with the consent of the grandparents, who had by now witnessed their close relationship, permitted their unofficial in-family union, with a blessing by the local Catholic priest, who was unaware that the groom was a Knight of the Order of St. John. The grandparents provided a room for the newly-wed couple, but Jean rarely spent the night in it.

Jean eventually found out that in his own company there were several knights in the same predicament, and was told that the hierarchy would look the other way and put a blind eye to this kind of situation, provided that it did not interfere with their duties and obligations as knights and did not create a scandal.

Jean recalled the day when Ana Celeste announced that she was pregnant.

His joy had no bounds. He jumped up and down and picked Ana Celeste up off the ground, holding her high in the air, and was promptly reprimanded by an alarmed grandmother, who ordered him to put the frail mother-to-be back on the ground.

Eventually the day of the birth of the baby arrived. A baby boy! They baptised the baby and called him Francois Jean Parisot de la Valette. He became petit Francois to his close family.

The discrete relationship continued and blossomed.

The petit Francois was about three years old when the worst of their fears came to pass.

THE TURKS ATTACK THE ISLAND OF RHODES

It was the second time in fifty years that the Turks had attempted to invade the island. On the first occasion, fifty years earlier, the Hospitallers of the Order of St. John of Jerusalem miraculously defeated an immensely large military and naval force. It was then that the Knights of St. John acquired the name Hospitallers of St. John of Jerusalem and Rhodes.

The second invasion lasted six months. It was a hard, drawn-out siege of attacks, retreats, and victories oscillating, first to the Ottomans, then to the knights. The fortifications were a mass of rubble. It was not until the knights and the townspeople of Rhodes were close to exhaustion and lacking in provisions and ammunition, that they were ready to negotiate terms of peace. As soon as the armistice was called and both parties started to parley, Jean took the opportunity to gallop off to Ana Celeste's cottage.

Jean was wounded. He had the barbs of two broken arrows still embedded in his body. One arrow got him in the thigh of his left leg, and the other on his right shoulder. The pain was unbearable, but he had

had no time to have it treated and removed by the busy surgeons in the order's well-equipped hospital.

He galloped from the other end of the city in a fury, whipping his horse into a lather. From a distance he could see the cottage was not standing up as he had left it, and smoke was rising from what appeared to be ruins. He arrived to a greater pain. The cottage, which was not far from the fortress's wall, had received a round shot that had fallen through the roof, demolishing the cottage. Neighbours informed the knight that Ana Celeste had been inside at the time the shot hit the cottage, and was instantly killed by the shot.

Jean's pain was one of devastation. Utterly broken and stressed with all the amount of killing he had seen and done, he fell to the ground and wept until he fell involuntarily asleep with sorrow and exhaustion.

When he woke the neighbours led the knight to where the grandparents had taken refuge, to his great relief e saw that petit Francois playing in the garden next door.

There was little time for mcuh. The body of Ana Celeste was still unburied. He told them to wait for him, that he would be back to bury his wife and companion.

Jean's duty to the order and his duty to his dead wife, baby, and the grandparents were in conflict, but he thought he should go back to headquarters and find out what kind of outcome the peace talks had produced. If history would be followed, all Christians would be beheaded; no one would be spared. That had been the practice following past victories by the cruel Ottoman Turks. He could have escaped by staying with Ana Celeste's grandparents, and not returning to his unit. But he rode off and went back. Everyone was glad to see him when he arrived at headquarters, because he had been missed, and everyone thought that he might have been killed. He could not believe the good mood everyone seemed to be and could not believe his ears. They told him that Sultan Suleiman had granted a pardon to all of them, and was allowing three days for the knights to leave the island of Rhodes, with their weapons and personal possessions only. They could even leave in their own vessels. Over and above this, the Sultan had given the civilian people of Rhodes six month to leave the island.

Jean did not wait to be seen by the surgeons. He asked permission from his commander for leave, saying he was going to look for some friends in the city.

He rode his tired horse back to Ana Celeste's cottage, and there helped to bury his partner and companion. He gave instructions to the grandparents to look after petit Francois. He could not tell them where the order would be going to, since the order found itself again without a home. He thought that they might end up in Venice, but he was not sure. When Jean finally told them that they, too, had to leave their home and the island, they were heartbroken; they had lived there virtually all their lives. After a while, the grandfather said that the best solution for them was to head for the island of Crete, where Ana Celeste's father had other properties, and he was sure that he would look after them.

Jean picked up petit Francois and held him close, kissing him, as tears streamed uncontrollably down his face. He turned to the grandparents, kissing both of them. "Farewell, my friends. God protect you and keep you safe. If it is God's will I promise you we will meet again," cried Jean, barely able to talk as his heart throbbed.

"Adieu, Papa," whimpered petit Francois, with tears in his eyes, waving his small arm as he held his grandfather's hand.

"Adieu, my son," replied Jean, putting the child down as he kissed his forehead.

"May God be with you, and may your travels be blessed with fine winds and fair skies," replied petit Francois's grandfather.

Jean put the boy down by his grandmother, mounted his horse, and kicked the spurs into the animal's raw stomach; then he galloped away in the direction of the fort to rejoin his company of knights. He rode blinded by his own tears; the ride was a complete burr.

When he arrived, the knights were hastily preparing to leave. The order had been given in haste to move out fast. They did not wish to delay their departure, fearing the Sultan, or someone high in command, would change his mind.

He was informed that the only things they could take were their vestments and the icon of the Madonna of Philermos. Some of the knights hid some of the books from the archives. The rest of their treasures had to be left behind. The Sultan's graciousness had gone to the extent of allowing them to take their vessels without the armaments; the ships had to be unloaded hastily.

The loss of Rhodes placed the order's administration into panic, and dealt a big blow to any vestigial nostalgia for the medieval ideals of chivalry that had been built over the two-hundred-year stay on the island.

For the next seven years, the order was homeless; they had become virtually a boat people. After the loss of Rhodes they spent months on board ships, roaming from one European court to another. The newly constructed carrack St. Anne served as the grand master's headquarters. This floating existence for an order that had for centuries held its own feet on very solid territories made the acquisition of a new base for the order a pressing necessity.

They moved the Hospitallers' convent first to Messina, but their stay there was short-lived. Then they went to Cuma near Naples, because there, in their desire to attend the sick, they knew that they would find natural caves where they could provide hospital care. When they left Rhodes, they had taken with them all the sick and injured. These included plague-stricken victims. Subsequently, they transferred their headquarters to Civitavecchia, thence to Viterbo, Cornetto, Villefrache, and finally Nice.

It was during this unsettling period, when the order found itself displaced, that La Valette made a trip to Crete and located the house of Ana Celeste's father and the grandparents, who had taken charge of petit Francois.

Young Francois was now eight years old. Jean had not seen him for three years. He stayed there a few days and visited the boy every day, remaining with him for the better part of the day. He promised his father-in-law and the grandparents that he would come for the boy when his order found a permanent location from where to operate their activities. He told them that there were rumours that some place was going to be given to the Hospitallers, but he did not know where or when, but as soon as he could, he would come for the boy.

THE EAST GATE OF THE CITY OF RHODES

La Valette and the other knights woke up with a start. They simultaneously jumped onto their feet, swords extended, ready to meet their foe. They had been disturbed by the sound of a voice and the ringing of cowbells.

They threw the canvas flap wide open, and the daylight rushed in to illuminate, the once dark cave, that reflected the light as from a giant lantern.

A comical fellow with a shepherd's crop in his hand stood in the doorway, his head tilted to one side, and a wide, big smile filled his round and unshaven face, showing a toothless grin.

"Good morning, masters. Gracious me, what violence!" the man remarked when he saw the swords pointed at him. "Not to be afraid me friend. I is Andropulous Katriaki, your friendship. Tafur-Ali, my dearest brother, says I find you there—me pardon—here. He sends greetings in the good morning and a gift for you and good." He picked up a large wicker basket from the side of the cave entrance and brought out clothes and parcels of food. "Dees eese for yu. Tafur-Ali says you took dresses off und place thees on yu. Yu might look better liken Rhodians maybe und not blaady strangars, he says."

They opened first the parcels of food, which contained pieces of goat cheese, flat, round loaves of fresh bread, and a jug of goat's milk. Then they went to the parcel of clothing, which they picked from the bundle inside the basket. The garments were old burnouses of various sizes and colours. They were dirty and smelled to high heaven. There were several colourful keffiyehs of the type worn by desert Arabs to wrap around their heads, which would also cover their faces, if need be. Then there was an assortment of sandals, buskins, and cothurni. They tried them on for size, exchanging garments and footwear with each other, attempting to find the right size. The burnouses were extremely important. Tafur-Ali had thought of everything. The burnous was a cloak that reached to the ground and had a hood that also covered the head, so with the combination of the keffiyeh wrapped around the head and the chin, it would be a perfect disguise, assuring them that they might blend in with the locals.

"You like, yes?" said the ever-grinning Andropulous. "Yes, vely shplendid, good, vely good look on you."

"What else did Tafur-Ali tell you, Andropulous? When did he say he would be coming here?" asked Jean.

"Ah! Yes, very wise. I forgot; my mind is very loose, you see. Tafur-Ali said to me to tell to you, on his bee have, to stay here. Tomorrow he come. Said he, first very important, he visit castle and speak with brother Ebu Mehmed. You know Ebu Mehmed? No? Very good man he, Ebu Mehmed very important man, the castle he guard is. He can help very well, like I help very well too. Yes?" Andropulous added with a theatrical play of arms and hands, never losing his toothless grin, of course.

"Andropulous, you mean Tafur-Ali has gone to the fortress to see his cousin Ebu Mehmed the guard, don't you?" asked Oliver, in an attempt to get a clear picture of the message.

"Yeas, vely good, brother-cousin Ebu Mehmed at the castle fortress, Vely good you understand vely much, yes?" Andropulous replied.

"And we are to wait here until he returns sometime tomorrow, right?" asked Pietro del Car.

"No, vely wrong. He not come sometime tomorrow, he come tomorrow vely morning, when before sun comes out. He says not worry, he ready everything when he back here. Yes not worry, please. Tafur-Ali he vely important fish-man. He vely brave, vely clever man. Yes, yes, vely clever." And with that, Andropulous bid them farewell and joined his goat herd outside, and they saw him go, the goats following him closely as he settled at a spot not far from the cave. He turned and waved at them, and with his finger he patted the rim of his eye, indicating to them that he would keep watch.

They changed into their ragged garments, and then they knelt and prayed the morning office. They scrutinised the map of the city and the fortress once again and mulled some ideas around until night came once again. Just before the sun set over the western mountains of the mainland, Andropulous indicated to them that he would be taking the goat herd to the pen, but that he would return.

When Andropulous returned, he came alone with his shepherd dog.

"Dog mine. Rufus he called. Rufus and me we stay the night und guard for yu. Rufus good guard dog, will smell wolves and peoples vely far away. We know when people come. I sleep over that tree." With that he walked over to the tree he had indicated and pulled out the rolled-up blanket he had been carrying on his back. He put the blanket and a bag he was carrying, slung over his shoulder, down by the tree. He sat down and started to eat.

The team watched him and were doubly grateful to Tafur-Ali for taking this precaution. The presence of the shepherd dog and its keeper gave them special comfort because that night no one had to keep watch.

Even before the sun's rays appeared in the eastern sky, Tafur-Ali arrived at the entrance to the cave. Rufus, Andropulous' dog, gave a low bark, not one of alarm, but of recognition, and Andropulous stroked him to stay put as Tafur-Ali approached.

The six knights waited for Tafur-Ali to sit down around the fire they had built inside the cave.

"I bid you good morning, friends, before the sun touches our faces. Allah be praised. I observe you have converted to peasants and Islam. Your tunics are wonderful," said Tafur-Ali jokingly as he greeted his friends.

"Welcome, our friend. What news have you, Tafur-Ali?" asked Jean.

"Good news, Lord. I have not wasted any time. I have made contact with my cousin Ebu Mehmed the guard. I managed to convince him to help us because Ebu Mehmed is a family man and he cannot make ends meet with his soldier's wages. He wondered if you would be gracious enough to consider giving him a loan of a few bezants. He is hard pressed and needs money to pay the doctor for treating his young child. He promises he will pay you back," said Tafur-Ali apologetically and shrugging his shoulders, on a matter over which he had no control. Jean knew very well that this was a form of payment for his services, not quite a bribe, but a perfectly normal custom in the Levant.

"Okay, Tafur-Ali, we will advance your cousin Ebu Mehmed a couple of gold coins. I hope that he can be trusted to help us. What arrangements have you made so far?" The rest waited for Tafur-Ali to resume his report.

"My cousin says that the crates were stored in a room, not in the Eastern Gate, but in the Middle Gate," explained Tafur-Ali.

"I know where the Middle Gate is. Carry on," said Jean impatiently.

"Do we have to climb the wall with a rope to get into the fortress?" interrupted Lionelli Bochetti.

"No we do not. The plan is that I will go to the Middle Gate with my donkey and cart and a load of fish. I will have to make arrangements to buy some fish from one of my friends because I do not have time to go fishing, and of course I will have to pay for the fish," Tafur-Ali said quickly. "But that will only cost a couple of silver rings," he added as an afterthought.

"That's perfectly okay. Carry on, what else?" Jean agreed impatiently.

"After selling the fish, the cart will be left there with a broken wheel. My son will sell the fish whilst we do other things. My cousin, the guard, says the tower was recently repaired, and that there is a long ladder lying on top of the battlement. The ladder can be lowered for you to climb up and hide in the tower." Tafur-Ali's grin of satisfaction at having made all these arrangements showed on his face. "Lord, you happy with plan?" asked Tafur-Ali.

"Perfect, Tafur-Ali, just perfect. There are just a few things we wish to add, which we have discussed here. First, we think that the operation must be done on Friday and at night, when the sun has gone down, and when the Muslims, including the guards, are gathered at the mosque for prayer time. Can we be guaranteed that your cousin will not be at prayer and will be ready to lower the ladder to us?"

"Yes, Lord; Ebu Mehmed is not a very rigid Muslim. Neither am I for this particular mission. He and I will be ready. The offer of your most kind loan to him will ensure his complete faithfulness to your wishes. I have also asked him to have ready for us some torches for us to see in the dark. When we get to the storage room we will climb back to the tower and lower the holy items you pick up to take with you. Will that be all right Lord?"

"No, Tafur-Ali. We have a safer plan that will keep us from having to be into the open after we go inside. But we need your cousin to help us when we leave. Brothers Pierre and Oliver remembered that all the towers had secret underground passages that lead to the outside. These passages were built many, many years ago and were used during the last big siege. We have to plan to take our holy items, as you call them, from the storage place to the basement of the tower. There are two ways we can do this. The first one is risky because it means having to run along the battlement in full view of anyone who may be looking up at the battlement. The other and best way is for us to locate the second entrance to another tunnel that joins one tower to the outside. An underground tunnel interconnected all the towers, and all of them had an access to the exterior. But we need to figure this out when we are there or else find the entrance once we are below the tower."

"You said my cousin should stay behind. How can my cousin help us?" asked Tafur-Ali.

Oliver said, "He needs to stay behind to close the secret doors to the underground passages after we leave because the doors cannot be closed from the outside. Only someone on the inside can open and close the door. That is why we need him to stay whilst we make our escape. Please convey our plans to your cousin so we are all in accord, and then we can get ready for Friday night to make our move. Today is Wednesday, so we have two days to wait. I suggest that in order to get familiar with the area, our team make a couple of trips to the city, going separately, today and tomorrow evenings, to look around the area where we will conduct our operation. Observe the people and the regular guards there and get acquainted with the location. Tafur-Ali, it may be a good idea if you were to go to the wall with your donkey and cart and sell some fish there so that the neighbours won't find it strange that you are at the Middle Gate and not the Eastern Gate."

"Very well, Lord. As you say, it is a good idea. I shall go immediately and hope to find some fish to sell from the evening catch. We will meet here on Friday evening after I leave my cart behind by the Middle Gate," agreed Tafur-Ali.

THE HIDDEN PASSAGE

When Friday morning came, Tafur-Ali plodded with his small, large-wheeled cart, drawn by his donkey, up the winding street, through the upper town, moving cautiously downward towards the city walls. Since he had all the time in the world to spare, he went through the busy outskirts of the city.

Houses were awash with flowers; fully blossomed hanging baskets and wall-mounted pots, others houses were decorated with doors in carved wood and colourful shutters. There were potters' homes with their goods piled high on wooden racks outside; metal workers plying their trade in the open, protected from the heat of the furnaces by leather aprons; and textile workshops with dyed cloth drying on racks outside. Silver-smiths concentrating on the creation of fancy necklaces and broaches. Basket-makers weaving all kinds of ingenious carrying contraptions. Tafur-Ali smelled a combination of hot metal, baking bread, and flowers in the rich scents of trodden animal dung and perfumes, and spices with a hundred other smells he couldn't name. The noise all around was of laughter and complaints, the braying of donkeys, the creaking of the cart's wheels and the leather traces, women's shrill voices, and the calls of peddlers. A cacophony of sounds appropriate to a Greek opera

He, his son, and Andropulous, who Tafur-Ali brought along, with his dog to serve as a lookout and to guard the cart whilst they were inside the fort and could see the walls up close. The walls grew out of the ground at an angle so gradual it seemed possible to climb them, but then straightened up suddenly and soared towards the sky.

Tafur-Ali's cart was laden with fish, and he made his way to the Middle Gate to sell the merchandise. It was brisk business, and by midday Tafur-Ali and his son were surprised that they had sold all the fish on the cart. A couple of the guards approached and received the usual gift of a bunch of fish, they left extremely happy.

Before returning, he surreptitiously loosened the wedge that held the wheel in place and then knocked the big wheel off so that the cart tilted over. He cursed out loud and pretended, for the benefit of other stallholders and other on-lookers around the area, that the cart had broken. He asked a couple of acquaintances there to keep an eye on the cart because he was going home to fetch some tools and would be back before nightfall. He made sure that the couple of grateful soldiers, leaning against the wall, overhead what he said. He had feigned the cart's breakdown just below the battlement close to the Middle Tower, the location where his cousin had said that the ladder lay. Andropulous and the dog stayed behind for a while to ensure that no one came to disturb the cart, which would be needed later to carry the expected heavy loads.

They had calculated the time when most of the faithful would be going into the various mosques for Friday prayer in the vicinity of the Middle Gate, so they set off towards their destination, starting off from different directions, approaching the meeting point separately. They estimated that it would be twilight by the time they met, and with the sun setting in the west at the other side of the city wall, the shadows from the buildings and the walls would be at their longest. Under the cover of the shadows they passed close to the wall in almost total darkness. The Middle Gate, being a minor gate, was not lit by torches on either side of the entrance, and furthermore they were relieved to have seen, on the previous two nights, that this particular gate was closed every night, which meant there would be a minimum of traffic around, and that the surveillance by guards would be at a minimum, if there was any at all.

Since there was no war going on the danger of invasion was nil, the guard system was rather lax and sloppy; routine inspections were careless or even neglected. The situation seemed ideal for their attempt at stealing the holy relics.

As arranged, Tafur-Ali was the first to arrive. He proceeded to fix the wheel in a matter of minutes, but, in case anyone was looking, he made believe it was a big deal. He whistled, and from the semi-darkness above, a black head appeared over the battlement. The head hissed like a snake. Without a word, the head above lowered a long ladder. Its position had been agreed before hand; the ladder would be lowered in place in the corner of the tower and the battlement, where it would be darkest. Tafur-Ali immediately made sure it was secured.

The knights were now close by. The closed gate they were slowly approaching lay in the shadow of the tall round tower, almost twice as high as the wall. The ladder was in place. After this was done, the first of the knights appeared, from the dark, like an apparition. From the shadows came another, and then from the other direction another, until the team of six, plus Tafur-Ali, were all in a group crouched and leaning flat against the dark wall.

No time was lost in climbing the ladder; Jean observed that the ladder was of the kind as used in a siege.

They climbed over the battlement and went down on a crouch. When the seven of them were over the wall, Ebu Mehmed appeared from behind the door in the tower. He hissed and beckoned. They quickly entered the tower and closed the door behind them. Once inside, Ebu Mehmed produced a torch. "For now we light only one torch until we are below. Too much light might be seen from outside," he rightly added.

They carefully climbed down the spiral stairs until they reached the large hall in the basement, which was the location where they knew the secret entrances should be.

La Valette whispered, "There are two entrances, we must first locate the secret exit door. Brothers Pietro, Emanuel, and Lionelli: you three go over there and locate the exit, open it, and leave it wedged open in case we need to make a quick escape. Brothers Oliver Starkey, Joanni Caviglia, and Tafur-Ali, and I will try to locate the entrance to the communicating tunnel."

They lit a couple of extra torches. Lionelli held his torch high, and the three of them—Pietro, Emanuel, and Lionelli—went straight to the big, rectangular, dark grey wall-stone. They had to marvel at the precise work of the masons who had built this tower. Every block of stone fitted perfectly one into the other, even though they were all of different sizes. From the big, rectangular wall-stone they measured the distance they had been given, six feet along and three feet from the ground. Close to that spot they located a stone the size and shape of a brick. Emanuel pulled out his dagger and introduced the point in the side-joint of the stone, and feeling his way around, tried to move the stone. He had to attempt this action several times, but the brick-shaped stone did not move.

It was frustrating, and a couple of them started to sweat in the stifling, almost airless enclosed area. Panic almost set in; they started to believe that the information was not correct. "Brother Oliver, can you give us a hand here? Is this the correct stone? We are having difficulty in prying it open."

Oliver Starkey quickly moved over from the other end of the room and took the torch. He inspected the stone as he measured the distance from the edge of the big grey slab. "This should be it, but by God, this stone won't move," he said in dismay.

"In that case, try the other side of the slab; see if there is a similar stone on the other side. Maybe the hinges on that door open in the other direction," Jean murmured from the other end of the room.

The group moved over to the other side, taking quick measurements, and after a quick inspection, saw there was another brick-sized stone in the same position as the one they had tried unsuccessfully. They used the point of the dagger to clear some dirt from the joint, and then Oliver introduced the point into the space and moved it sideways. The stone slipped a fraction to the front.

"There you are, fellows; it's all yours," said Oliver Starkey as he moved quickly back to the other group and joined them in the search for the position of the other entrance that would connect through a tunnel to where the storage chamber where the holy relics should be kept.

"Ebu Mehmed, please come here, my man. Are we or are we not immediately below the position of the battlement? Is this the centre line of the battlement above?" asked Oliver, pointing above and painting an imaginary line with his finger down the wall from ceiling to floor.

Ebu Mehmed, held his torch up high and looked up and down, to one side and then the other, and back to the wall in front of them. Moving forward he leaned back against the wall, slapped the wall with the back of his hand. "This is the position you are looking for. The battlement is above us here," he assured Oliver, stamping his right foot down on the floor stones for further emphasis.

"Tafur-Ali, try to remember; do you think that this is the place you took the crates from the library?"

"Yes, Master, I am sure that behind that wall is the place where we stored the crates. Though the proper entrance is further along on the other side."

"Good enough then. Now for the secret lock," affirmed an excited La Valette.

With that, they proceeded to look for a large, rectangular stone in the form of a door, similar to the one that backed out to the exterior. But they could not see such a large stone. All of them were looking closely and frantically for such a rectangular stone. None was visible.

"Hold on." Kneeling down and closing in with his torch, La Valette ran his finger over the perimeter of a joint of a stone half the size of the stone on the other side; meanwhile the others had successfully opened the exit door. "Try this brick-size stone here," he said to Oliver, pointing with his finger at a small, rectangular stone. Oliver pushed the point of his dagger in the gap of the brick-sized stone and put some slight pressure on the dagger, penetrating the joint. He jiggled the dagger about, and the stone moved slightly outwards. With the other hand he pulled out the stone, and it fell into Emanuel's hands. Oliver put his hand into the cavity and felt around in the inside. He gave a sigh when he got hold of what must have been the lever that opened the door. He turned the lever clockwise, and the small stone slab moved slightly. He tried again, but the stone would not move. Joanni and Tafur-Ali sat on the ground, and both pushed with their legs on the stone slab. Nothing happened. Then on the third try they pushed simultaneously; the slab shifted, and the opening was revealed.

"Okay, boys, we need to bend double and crawl into this space. The builders were very clever. This is not an entry door, it's a crawling escape exit," observed La Valette.

Tafur-Ali volunteered, "Lord, please let me go in first with my torch and make sure that the way is clear."

La Valette nodded his head in agreement, and with that Tafur-Ali crawled into the opening. After only ten seconds they heard Tafur-Ali let out a scream that sounded like an echo, long-drawn and hollow.

"What is the problem, Tafur-Ali?" asked Oliver.

"Snakes, Lord! Big, bloody snakes. Several of them, Lord," answered the frightened voice of Tafur-Ali.

"Let me get through," said Oliver. He crawled in with a torch in one hand. "Jean, pass me a scimitar," shouted Oliver from the inside. A scimitar was promptly thrown into the opening.

The light from the flames of flickering torches reflected off the shinny skins of a few huge, nervous, fat snakes, giving them a wet look. This place was damp and humid; it was no place to store valuable things. The reptiles were not used to such bright light or being disturbed in their silent lair. They cowered against the walls, frightened. They had their tails coiled, but their bodies were raised and their cheeks blown out flat in a frightening and menacing manner. They hissed and darted forward incessantly. Long, scaly, and brown, they were agitated, obviously disturbed, twisting and sliding from here to there in the flickering light that illuminated the big, fearful eyes in the huge space around the walls and corners of the chamber.

"I don't like snakes, Lord. They seem to be the guardians of the treasure and hell," said Tafur-Ali in a shaky voice.

"My God, they are truly big, these monsters from hell. Tafur-Ali, watch me and do as I do. There is no need to be afraid. All we have to do is force them to withdraw against the wall. If we are lucky, we will force them to find the hole they came in through in the first place. If not, we will have to cut them down. They must be here because there are rats in this place, and they come here to hunt them. Just look how fat they are," said a cautious Oliver.

He placed the torch at arm's length in front of him, took a step forward, and swung his sword this way and that, which made the snakes back up. One of the snakes did find a cavity in the wall and rapidly crept through. The other snakes were more stubborn and stayed, hissing and darting their long bodies at them. Each time one of them sprung forward it received a scathing cut from a sharp falchion or scimitar. In this fashion, several reptiles were severely cut apart, with bloody heads and tails wiggling around the floor.

In confidence, Oliver turned his head slightly sideways and called out, "You can start coming in now, Brothers." In what turned out to be a great mistake, his slight movement to address the team on the other side of the entrance caused Oliver to be distracted for a split second, and the last of the surviving snakes dived forward and managed to reach his forearm, biting deeply into Oliver. Oliver hit it with the sharp edge of his sword. The snake, which was about six feet long, as thick as the upper arm of a grown man, and with a partly severed head hanging by a stretch of skin, dug his two sharp fangs into Oliver's forearm, and clung there. Oliver let out a loud screech and shook the snake about, but it would not come off. Reacting like lightning, Tafur-Ali quickly got hold of the reptile's head that had stubbornly dug its fangs into Oliver's arm, and with great difficulty, completely sliced the huge snake's head off. The headless body of the snake fell and continued to wriggle on the ground, but the severed head would not let go from Oliver's forearm. Instantly, Tafur-Ali drew his dagger and introduced the sharp blade into the snake's mouth and pried its jaws open, pulling the head off with the other hand, until the head and the fangs came off Oliver's forearm. The snapping snake's head fell to the ground as well, and to no avail, Oliver, in a rage, hit it several times with his falchion until the huge snake's mouth stopped snapping.

Oliver held his arm in pain and started to suck for dear life. He sucked his own blood and some of the poison as well, he hoped, for the snake was bound to have injected some poison into his blood system. He spat the thick, red substance out onto the damp floor. "Do you know if this type of snake is poisonous, Tafur-Ali?" asked Oliver, worried, sucking and spitting.

"Master, I am ignorant of such matters. Ask me about fish, because I do not know much about snakes; I pray to Allah that it is not poisonous."

Tafur-Ali came to Oliver and waited for Oliver to suck and spit out more of the ugly mixture of spit and venom. He then wrapped a piece of cloth round the two black spots that looked like two beauty spots on his arm. He wrapped another piece around the bicep area of his upper arm that would serve as a tourniquet to slow down the flow of blood to his heart. A red ring instantaneously started to build up around the two black spots.

"Boy, oh boy!" said Oliver. "Just my luck. Please, Lord, please don't let this snake be a poisonous one."

In the meantime, in the other chamber, La Valette had inspected the exit passage on the other side of the tower. He had quickly walked to the end of the passage, which had a dog-leg to the right, indicating to him that the final exit passage had been constructed to end by the side of the wall. If it followed the pattern and design of other secret passages, it would end in a trap door above them, leading to the outside of the wall, which after so many years would be overgrown with grass, roots, and weeds. His only hope was that no one had placed anything heavy on top of the trap door, which would make it impossible to lift the door open.

Once the snakes had been taken care of, they came against a plain stone wall. It was time to find an another entrance to the other side, which they hoped would be the resting place of the holy relics. This meant that access to the storage area had inadvertently made them pass through two secret entrances.

La Valette and Oliver approached the wall with their torches and looked about. It did not take long for them to find the low slab of stone with hinges and a mechanism visible from their side since the secret door was designed to be opened from the other side. They noticed the mechanism to be rather ingenious. This had been the work of the famous Italian engineer Laparelli Cortona, who had come to Rhodes to design the new fortifications of the fortress city about two hundred years earlier. From this side of the wall they noticed that the hinges and the lever had been heavily greased with animal fat, though at present it was dusty and covered with dirt sticking obstinately to the grease, however it was still functional.

"Well, it's now or never. Now we will know if our information is correct and if our planning has paid off," said a rather animated Pietro del Car.

"We will soon know. *Vigilancia, voluntas Deus*, if it is God's will," replied La Valette. *"Prudencia.* Be watchful." He added. "Ebu Mehmed, you don't go any farther. You stay here and wait for us."

Slowly and silently Tafur-Ali and Joanni Caviglia reached out, got hold of the inside-handle, and pushed in unison in a clockwise motion. The door opened slightly, silently and quickly. To their surprise, the adjacent room was fully lit. They looked through the door gap and saw there were men sitting at a table with their backs to them. They pushed the door open and all stepped into the room, the four guards were playing cards, and judging from the crates in there it was obviously the storage place they were looking for. Since the entrance seemed to be in a corner position, it was difficult for anyone to see them entering. The air was heavy with smoke, and the smell was a pungent herbal smell that the knights recognized as *keefy*, or marijuana, a recreational herb that had been smoked in North Africa and in the Levant for centuries, going back to the days of the pharaohs. The smoke almost made Pietro del Car sneeze, but, holding his nose he held back before giving away their presence.

La Valette stepped forward as if he were entering the parlour to his own house and said in Turkish, "Good evening gentlemen. Sorry to interrupt your game, but we have some business to do in this room. You are all under arrest. Keep your hands on the table."

The four guards looked up as if they had seen an apparition. It was evident that they were not aware of a secret passage down at this level, the light from the lantern on the wall, and more so the four flaming torches that had appeared miraculously through the wall showed clearly the surprise in their faces. Their jaws dropped, the cards in their hands fell face upward on the table,

"I said, keep your hands on the table, gentlemen, and don't attempt to go for your weapons. If you do you will be dead men," ordered Oliver, moving forward to the spears leaning against the wall, which were close to the stairs leading upward. Oliver noticed that the four men at the table were also carrying swords in their scabbards. He cautiously moved closer to the spears and placed them further away from the soldiers. Jean also moved closer, whilst Tafur-Ali covered his head and face with his keffiyeh to avoid recognition.

Turkish soldiers were not known for their cowardice; in fact they were an extremely brave and fearless race, and La Valette suspected that once they had recovered from their surprise they might react, especially since the attire and appearance of the newly arrived visitors was lamentable. They looked like a bunch of ruffians. Little did these Turkish soldiers suspect that they were facing some of the fiercest and most disciplined fighters of the Order of St. John of Jerusalem.

La Valette asked Emanuel if he had brought spare rope with the canvas bags that would be used to carry the holy relics. "Yes, Brother, I do have rope, but I think we may need it for our mission."

"Tie these guys up anyway, Brother."

At that very moment the four guards jumped up together as if in accord and drew their swords and attacked the infiltrators. La Valette parried a strong blow from the guard closest to him, and felt the strength of the man's arm and shoulder bearing down on his own sword. He pushed the guard's swords upward and made a half swirl with his falchion feigning to lunge at his face. The guard lifted his own weapon to parry the stroke, but Jean finished his movement with a reversed swerve of the weapon. He pointed the tip of his sword down and lunged, piercing with his curved sword the guard's open front, cutting through cloth, skin, and his ribcage. The falchion went deep up the hilt of his weapon. With his foot he pushed the body of the guard off his weapon and turned to meet his next adversary.

Oliver Starkey, Emanuel Viale, Lionelli Bochetti, and Joanni Caviglia were all engaged in combat with the other guards. Had the guards known that these assailants, who had disturbed their game, were Christian Knights of the Order of St. John, they would have surrendered at the very beginning. Usually, the savage notoriety of the knights produced nightmares in the minds of Saracen warriors.

By now, Oliver, with his forearm lightly swollen, skewed one of the guards through the neck with a very swift and almost invisible stroke that appeared as if he were writing with the tip of his sword in thin air. The guard stood there with his mouth wide open, wide-eyed, not believing his fate and the rapidity with which his life was about to end.

Emanuel Viale had swirled around with his cloak, throwing it in the air with the agility of a bullfighter over the head of his opponent, blinding him, and then chopping down through the edge of the cloak, cutting through it, and taking off the guard's cheek and ear. The guard dropped his weapon to get hold of his disfigured face and screamed in pain. In the flurry with his cloak, Emanuel had taken a deep wound in the left shoulder, but he continued as if nothing had happened. Tafur-Ali charged the fourth guard with one of the guards' spears, harpooning him with his own lance. Only one guard was alive, the one with half his face missing. It had taken but three minutes to silence the guards.

"Tafur-Ali, see what you can do for the cut on Brother Emanuel's shoulder. We don't want him to bleed to death and have to leave him behind." said La Valette, gesturing to Tafur-Ali.

"I know that we said we would try to keep this a bloodless mission, but this incident changes our intentions. We cannot leave any witness alive. After all, it was not our fault that these guards were taking time off to play cards and neglect their duties," said Pietro del Car.

"Regretfully, I have to agree with you, Brother Pietro; we have no choice. The guards can identify us and also Tafur-Ali, which would be bad for him, his family, and his village. I will not ask any of you to do this regrettable job. I shall do it myself."

La Valette moved to where the injured guard knelt. The man was bleeding profusely and would soon be dead anyway through loss of blood. La Valette went to him and said *"Deus et clemens.* God is forgiving." The others looked away as La Valette quickly pierced the guard's heart to the hilt with his dagger. He made the sign of the cross on himself and added, this time speaking to the dead guard, "*Homini comendare te Allah.* I commend you to your god."

Turning his back to the guard on the floor, he said hurriedly to his men so that all could hear, "Let us look for what we came for, and when we finish our mission, we will clean up this room and the blood and then hide the corpses in the exit tunnel."

They approached the crates, which were stored two crates high, one on top of the other. Oliver brought out two pieces of iron bar from one of the canvas bags and handed these to Joanni Caviglia and Pietro, and asked them to proceed to open the other crates further on. He reached into the canvas bag, fetched another bar, and proceeded to open the crate in front of him. For a while there was a state of frantic industry in the storeroom whilst they loosened and lifted the lids of the crates. Lionelli Bochetti, who was a lover of art and of ancient things, could not contain himself, and took his falchion and proceeded to work on another crate.

Even though there were two torches hanging on the wall brackets, La Valette in the meantime held his torch high while he searched the room with his eyes. He went around the room looking at the other items. The place was more of a cellar than a room, and the air smelled of stored furniture, even though the furniture was restricted to a few chairs and a table.

He came across a long item, about two feet long; it was wrapped all around in thin leather. He took his dagger and cut off a piece of the leather at one end of the item. He had hit metal with the point of his dagger, and then he opened the leather to see that the metal was the tip of a lance. He tore it further and saw the shape, it was indeed the tip of a lance—thin, long, and pear shaped at the end, in the fashion of the ancient roman lance. He drew his breath. "Praise be to God!" he said, "Could this be the lance that belonged to Longinus? God is great, I cannot believe our luck!"

He proceeded to wrap the leather back around the spearhead and leaned it by the exit door. Then he proceeded to look around to see if he could locate a smaller item, perhaps another package, possibly about three feet long, about eight inches wide, and about three inches thick. Though he looked frantically around the place he could not locate such an item.

In the meantime, from inside the crates, Oliver was picking out various books. Some he discarded but others he handed over to one of his colleagues to place aside. As he went from crate to crate, the number of items started to accumulate piling up on the floor, which Pietro del Ponte in turn started to put away into the canvas bags that had been brought for the purpose. When the two bags had been filled to full capacity, La Valette asked, "Where is the Holy Cross? Where is the Cross? Has anyone seen the piece of the Holy Cross anywhere?" The reply was negative.

"Let's start moving out, and let's get this place cleaned up. Brothers Joanni, Emanuel, and Tafur-Ali, start getting this place in order. "Where in heaven's name is the Holy Cross? Please, God, please show us the Cross," prayed an impatient and frantic La Valette in a way that everyone heard and were surprised by it since La Valette was usually calm and collected in the most trying of situations.

After a moment of looking around, he said, "We are running out of time. We must move out from here with what we have. Joanni, Emanuel, Tafur-Ali—please place the lids back on the crates and make the place look as if no one has been here. Brothers Lionelli and Pietro, hide those unfortunate corpses in the tunnel passageway. Brother Oliver, don't lift any weight. Take care of your arm."

La Valette sounded very annoyed as he gave orders. Then unexpectedly, with his right foot he impatiently kicked one of the smaller crates to one side in an attempt to push it into place against the wall, and there on the floor, by the side of some smaller crates, laying against the wall, he could discern a package wrapped in leather that, at a glance, appeared to have the measurement of what he had been looking for—three feet long by six inches wide.

He shouted, "Found it! Found it, the Holy Cross! This must be it!" La Valette cried out joyfully. "*Deus gracia. Deus gracia*," he said out loud as he picked up the parcel and held it close to his chest. "Thanks be to God. Here it is, men! I have found it! The Holy Cross! God is faithful. He has answered our prayers. Praise God. *Deus Gracia, Gracia plena*. Nothing but a pure gift," said the jubilant Valette.

Oh his way out, with the leather parcel under his arm, the ecstatic La Valette picked up the long item leaning against the wall, also wrapped in leather, with his other hand. Crouching down, he crept through the low entrance. Oliver, in spite of his painful arm, insisted on carrying one of the large canvas bags, and Pietro del Ponte the other bag. They appeared to be very heavy and awkward to carry.

Oliver threw the canvas bag with its heavy contents over his shoulder and they all started to move out. The others stayed back to clean the storeroom. Dragging the corpses by the legs, the men laid them side by side on the other side of the secret door in the connecting tunnel. Joanni Caviglia and Emanuel Viale looked about, making sure that everything looked as if it had been undisturbed. They even tidied the cards, placing them on a pile, and set the chairs under the table. They removed the guards' lances and swords and put them by the dead men. All the crate's lids were nailed and then put back in their places. Luckily, the blood on the ground had been soaked up by the earthen floor, but Tafur-Ali scraped up some extra earth from a corner of the room and spread this over the place where the guard had bled profusely. He stamped the area with his sandals and spread further earth until he was satisfied that the floor looked as the original one.

It was done. Anyone coming into the room and looking for the guards would not see anything undue, and would appear as if the guards had never been in the place in the first place. It would take many days before anyone found the corpses, if they ever did. It depended on whether the smell of the rotting flesh permeated through the thick stone walls. Most likely the disappearance of the guards would be thought to be a matter of simple desertion, something not uncommon in the Ottoman army.

The team had reached the end of the secret escape passage, and with their swords they started to prod the ceiling where the exit from the secret passage was supposed to lead them into the open. They prodded again and again until Pietro del Ponte cried out, "Here I've hit wood!"

With that they started to loosen the earth above their heads until the wooden square trap door was revealed in its entirety. "Okay," said Emanuel, the biggest and the strongest member of the team, an ox of a man. He reached up and pushed. Nothing happened. "I need leverage; I need something to stand on, to be able to push with my back."

"I think I saw a stool in a corner in the hall we just left," said Joanni Caviglia.

"Tafur-Ali, please run back to the hall and fetch the stool in the hall beyond. Maybe the stool will help Brother Emanuel and at the same time, please ask your cousin Ebu-Mehmed not to close the secret door until we tell him to do so." Said La Valette, pointing in the direction they had come from.

Tafur-Ali returned in a flash with the stool. Placing it below the wooden trap door, big Emanuel stood on the stool bent over and pushed upward with his shoulders. As he shoved and pushed, small amounts of earth came loose and fell on those below. The more Emanuel pushed, the greater the amount of earth that fell, until with a loud whoosh the whole ceiling fell down covering the three persons immediately below the door with an incredible amount of earth and wood. The wooden trap door fell in as well, almost intact; the edge of this hit Joanni Caviglia on the temple and cut his skin.

The opening was not very high, but the caved-in earth buried the legs of the three who were there up to their knees. It took them a while to dislodge their legs and regain full movement. They now had a dark but starry sky above them. Immediately, they put out all the torches.

La Valette said, "Tafur-Ali. Tell your cousin to follow us and close the exit door and make sure to clean the place up and not leave any evidence of our visit and tell him to go home or whatever, but to leave the place as unobtrusively as possible. We will close the escape hole."

"Yes, Lord, but what does that word mean, the last word you said, Lord? I don't understand."

"Unobtrusively? It means to leave unseen, quietly, in secret, so that no one sees him. Get it?"

"Yes, Lord, very clear now. Anobutrosily," replied a relieved Tafur-Ali.

"Give me a hand," said Emanuel to his nearest companion. Someone in the dark hole placed his hands together and bent down so that Emanuel was able to put a foot on it, and holding to the edge of the opening, lifted himself, while the other person below heaved him up over the edge. He went over the top and then laid flat on the ground and looked around.

He noticed that the position had been perfectly estimated. There behind him and to his left was the tower, and Tafur-Ali's cart was in the shadows in the corner. The silhouette of a man, who seemed to have risen on hearing the sounds coming from below, was standing by the cart. He suspected this must be Andropolous. Emanuel looked up to the top of the battlement to make sure that there was no one peering down at him.

"All is clear," he hissed. "You next, Tafur-Ali, give me your hand." He reached down and a hand gripped his. It was not Tafur-Ali, but La Valette. "Okay, next up." Both Emanuel and La Valette reached down and pulled Tafur-Ali out in one full motion. Tafur-Ali touched ground and immediately ran bent over double to the cart where his cousin, the cart, and the donkey were waiting.

Those remaining in the escape hole started to pass the canvas bags and the bundles to the surface. The last to leave had lifted the trap door, which seemed to be in very poor condition, and closed the hole, with Mehmed holding it up in place. They threw dirt and scrubs over it to hide the escape hole as well as possible, from below Tafur-Ali's cousin had used a lance to hold the trap-door in place.

Then carrying the "treasure", they made it to the cart loading all the items in the cart. They cleaned up as best they could. Tafur-Ali had hitched the donkey to the cart. It was now well past midnight, but in this hot climate it was not unusual for people to move about in the dark.

As soon as everyone was ready, Tafur-Ali and Andropolous urged donkey to move on and rather stubbornly it finally took its first steps forward. The other six in the team followed the cart at a short distance as if accompanying a funeral for the next day's burial—the precise impression they intended to give should anyone see this caravan. To their joy they observed other traffic moving along this road.

They walked away from the closeness of the city walls. Mist lay heavy and grey in the valley. Beyond it the hills were still touched with pink, though the sun was a long way from rising in the sky ahead of them and low clouds were filling the sky. Now that they were alone they could hear no sound but the barking of dogs in the distance and the bleating of sheep and goats in the fields nearby.

The weather had changed from two hours ago. The sky was now overcast, and rain began to fall, slowly at first, then in a torrent. Lightning flashed, and by its light they could see the path ahead.

The rain was not a bad thing because it would discourage others from travelling, no fool would be walking in the open in this wet weather.

La Valette hastened his steps and caught up with Oliver and walked side by side with him. "How's your arm, my friend?"

"It hurts pretty badly. The pain has spread to my shoulder, and I am starting to feel it going to my head. What kind of snakes do you think they were? Blooming big weren't they?" Oliver asked La Valette.

"Yes, they were unusually big; rather well fed, I imagine. But I don't know what kind of snakes they were and neither does Tafur-Ali. But I have asked him if there is a doctor at his village, and he told me that there is a healer there who may be able to help. I pray to God that that is true."

Silently they made it to the hillside and the cave they had been using as the base for the operation.

"Lord!" said Tafur-Ali calling La Valette's attention. "I do not think it is wise for you to keep the things you have recovered with you in the cave. It may not be wise in case the alarm is raised and they start looking for you. In such a case you will not be able to escape with much ease.

You will be impaired by the load. I suggest, my Lord that we take the baggage to another place where no one will think of looking. I have a fishing hut close to the beach, and we can dig a hole in the sand and bury the baggage in there until it is time to leave. At the same time, Lord, I suggest your men come and help, but while they are hiding the bags, we can find my healer friend and treat your friend's snake bite."

"Excellent suggestion, Tafur-Ali. You have truly proved yourself to be a great friend of ours—very brave and very creative. You would make a great warrior," said La Valette, patting him on the back while he complimented the fisherman for his brilliant suggestion.

Tafur-Ali gave some instructions to Andropolous and the others proceeded towards the beach whilst he, La Valette and Oliver went off to find the healer.

Makarios the Healer

About half a mile away from the fishing village they located the healer's hut.

Tafur-Ali went in and explained to the wizened old man, who happened to be of Greek descent, "This is my good neighbour Makarios. He is the best healer on this island." La Valette and Oliver shook hands with Makarios. Tafur-Ali recounted what had happened to Oliver, that a big snake had bitten this poor fellow's arm and as he could see for himself they area of the arm where the bite had taken place was hideously inflamed. He told the old man that these men were a couple of merchants that he had met on the road, and that they had stopped him and asked him for urgent help. The old man invited the visitors to enter his simple shack, which was festooned, roof and walls, with all kinds of drying shrubs and herbs. There were also several animals in different stages of dehydration, including a couple of snakes hanging up to dry, judging by the icon and the lit candle in a corner of his hut the man must be a Greek Orthodox Christian. There were a couple of wooden stools around and he asked them to sit down.

He unwound the old rag off Oliver's forearm and had a close look at the wound in the light of the small fire that was still burning in his stove. He looked, frowned, and pouted. Then he asked, "What did the snake look like?" Was it black, brown, yellowish, greenish? Did it have a white diamond shaped pattern on its back? How big did you say it was?"

Since both Oliver Starkey and La Valette spoke Greekfluently they understood the old man immediately. They answered him in the Greek language, and the old man raised his eyebrows in surprise. They told him that the snake was neither black nor green, and it did not have a white diamond pattern on its back. "The colour was brown with some slight pattern of yellow spots," they informed the old healer.

"You speak very good Greek, my friends. From the look of you, neither of you look like the merchants I know. You look as if you have come from the sea. I do not believe a word you have said. I am disappointed with you, my neighbour Tafur-Ali. You should be truthful with your true and close friend Makarios.

"You said the snake was brown with yellow spots? That sounds to me like the *rat snake*. They are found in humid places, like on the banks of streams and rivers. They hide among the reeds and wild cane plants. Very dangerous for rats, rats are the snake's favourite diet. They are not known to attack humans, but that again depends if they are frightened. Their venom is not mortal; it will not kill you, but it can cause a lot of discomfort and infection.

"The infection is the most worrying side, because if it is not cured promptly, it may lead to having to cut your arm off. But I will prepare for you a poultice to place over the wound, and we will see what happens in a few days time. You were lucky, my friend, it was not a black snake. The black snakes come from the *black mamba* from Africa, and they have cross-bred with the brown snakes. I hope your brown snake does not have mamba blood in it. Some stupid people brought them to the island many years ago, you can find them around in the countryside. Be very careful in the future. Don't play around with the black mamba; it is really not black but a very dark brown. It has no other colour, and they don't grow fat; rather they are sleek and move fast as lightning they say it can outrun a man." "Does your arm hurt here, and here?" asked the healer, touching Oliver's biceps and shoulder areas.

"Yes, it hurt when you touched it."

"Hmm?" was the only thing the healer said, throwing a sly look at La Valette who watched every move he made with great interest as the healer pressed his lips with his index finger as if in doubt about the reply he had just been given.

With that, the old man went around the room picking dried plants hanging from the ceiling and from small jars standing on shelves here and there. He reached out to one of the dried snake skins, cut a thin slice with a sharp knife, and threw this into the mortar with the other ingredients. After a few minutes of pounding and mixing the ingredients in the wooden mortar and pestle, while adding some olive oil, he tore a piece of cloth into a long bandage, and spreading the thick compound on the wound, he wrapped the linen bandage around Oliver's forearm and tied it securely.

He then picked up an elongated, white ceramic bottle adorned with flowers and poured some of its contents into another white ceramic bowl.

"Here, drink this; it will do you good."

"What is this, a special medication?"

"Yes, very special. It is my favourite drink. It's called Ouzo—sweet and smooth aniseed liquor that will warm your inside and give you strength to get back to wherever you are spending the night."

La Valette reached for his pouch and brought out a gold coin and handed this to the healer. "We are most grateful for all your help, Makarios; we thank you from the bottom of our hearts. May Allah be with you."

"Allah my friends? I am a Christian, like you, but not a follower of Rome. Your Greek is very good. You do not learn Greek like that in the shops or streets. You gentlemen are finely bred, and you must have learned Greek at some good school. Am I right?"

"Yes, you are correct, wise Makarios. A very fine school," added La Valette truthfully.

"You are Christian knights, are you not? Your secret is safe with me. Do not be afraid, my lips are sealed."

"We can assure you we are not here on any hostile mission. Our visit is temporary and we are not looking for trouble."

"Be gone now, Christian friends. You better take your friend to rest; and here, take this with you." Makarios picked up the elongated white ceramic bottle with the painted flowers on it and handed it to Oliver. "Don't drink this all in one go or it will give you a headache."

Oliver and La Valette reached the cave and found the other four knights sitting around a fire even though it was now getting light, but they were damp from the rain that had fallen on their journey here.

Tafur-Ali had gone to his home to check that everything was fine with the hut and the location where the bags had been hidden. A hole had been dug and the items hidden in it, and Tafur-Ali's fishing boat had been placed over the hole next to the hut. Andropolous had been charged with staying close to the hut. He sent one of his sons to tend to the herd of goats and had taken them higher up the hill, and told him to keep an eye on any strange movement, especially by soldiers, in the area.

Since they hadn't slept the previous night, the knights had agreed to rest the whole day and meet with Tafur-Ali late that night, the task at the moment was to dry their clothing

There remained two days for the assigned time to rendezvous with their ship. This waiting game would put their patience to the test during the next two days.

The knights diligently kept to their daily office prayers; they petitioned the Almighty to continue to keep them safe and gave thanks at the same time for the fact that no alarm had yet been raised and no search parties were out there looking for suspicious looking characters.

Earlier that night La Valette suggested to Tafur-Ali that he should go to the Middle Gate the following morning with Andropolous to spy and try to find out if any alarm had been given concerning the four guards that must have gone missing or even found dead. He was to send Andropolous back with any information they may get, whether positive or negative.

At midday, in the heat of the hour, Andropolous returned and informed the knights that they could relax. There was no undue panic or commotion in the city, but on the sidewalk outside a tavern they had overheard some soldiers talking about several of their colleagues going absent without leave, that it was most probably a case of desertion.

Andropolous assured the knights they could relax.

On the following day, since they had lots of hours to kill, La Valette told his friends that he was going to take a walk to the city. His brothers objected, and told him he would be taking a risk, adding that if he were questioned, he would have a hard time explaining what he was doing in Rhodes.

La Valette assured them that he would be extremely careful and that he would be perfectly safe. However since they were extremely agitated and could not figure out the madness of this resolve to go to the city, La Valette had no alternative but to tell them his purpose. He told them that the last time he had been in Rhodes was twelve years earlier, when he was twenty-eight years old when the order had been driven out by the Turks. That several friends of his had died on the day of the Turkish invasion, and he wanted to visit the place where they had fallen while he was here; that was all.

They were not convinced that his decision was a wise one, but since he was the senior knight in the team, there was nothing they could do once he had set his mind to it; and they did know that he was a very stubborn man.

The Maiden in the Garden

On the following morning, La Valette bade farewell to his colleagues, and when he stepped out of the cave, he saw Tafur-Ali standing there, as if waiting for his exit.

"Good morning, Lord. How do you find the day today, good yes?"

"Yes indeed, I find it a fine day, Tafur-Ali, but may I ask what you are doing here? We made no arrangement to meet this morning. How come you are here? Is there anything the matter?"

"No, Lord, everything is very good and very well with me and the world. I was about to go to the city and I just thought you might like to take a walk with me," added Tafur-Ali rather coyly.

"Tafur-Ali, who has put you up to this? This must be Brother Oliver and the others. They sent a message to you, didn't they? They don't trust me on my own; they worry I may get lost, is that it?" he said in a very loud voice so those in the cave would hear.

"No, Lord, no disrespect to you, Lord, but it has been many years since you were in the city, and the place has changed very much. There are places you may go and places you may not go, so to avoid any problems it would be better if you had a friend by your side. We never know what could happen, do we?" interjected Tafur-Ali, looking very concerned.

"You people are treating me like a small child; I can't believe it. Okay, let's get going. It might not be a bad idea to have company with me. Let's go, you crafty little half-Greek." Tafur-Ali laughed at this, and the hidden eavesdroppers inside the cave heard his chuckle but were relieved.

"That way, Tafur-Ali, to the Western Gate. I want to go and visit the garden that is located close to the church of St. Catherine, the area where some of the better-class mansions and cottages stood." La Valette pointed in the direction of the Western Gate.

"Lord, the church of St. Catherine's is no longer a church. It is a Muslim mosque now, but I know the district that you mean. Did you know people in that district, Lord?"

"Yes, Tafur-Ali, someone that I knew very well all those years back. It seems so long ago and unreal that I sometimes think that I have made up those memories from a dream—in parts a very good dream, and horrible in other parts," said La Valette, shaking his head as if wishing to shake those thoughts away.

They continued walking towards the Gate in silence, avoiding people and changing directions whenever they saw a group of soldiers on patrol standing by watching the crowds. It was obvious that the Sultan was making sure that peace and order was being enforced, and that a close watch was kept on a population that had once been Greek, but were now converts to Islam.

They went through the Western Gate, avoiding the watchful eyes of the guards there. Everyone seemed relaxed, so La Valette assumed that the disappearance of the four guards had not raised any suspicions in the authorities, but even so the authorities would rather not give too much prominence to the desertion of a handful of soldiers.

They came to a rather well kept property with plenty of land around it and horses grazing in the fields. One of the horses caught La Valette's attention, it had the same colours that Ana Celeste had ridden, and La Valette stopped to look and admire it.

"Nice horse, Lord. I like that one very much. Unfortunately, I cannot afford a horse like that one with the money I make selling fish. All I can afford is a little donkey, but mind you I wouldn't change her for any horse in the world, Lord. I have too many mouths to feed, Lord. I cannot add another mouth," added a rather subdued Tafur-Ali.

"A family I knew lived here, my friend—a very good and dear family. The owner owned a horse exactly like that one. I'll bet that one must be a descendant of her horse." Tafur-Ali immediately raised an eyebrow.

"A girl friend perhaps, Lord? Was she pretty, my Lord?"

"Very," was all La Valette said as he continued to walk. Instinctively, he stopped again when he saw people outside the residence. He looked closely to see if he recognized anyone there, but there was no one he remembered. He knew they must have moved away.

They walked another half a mile and came to the archway that was the entrance to the garden where he had met Ana Celeste, the mother of his child, petit Francois. La Valette told Tafur-Ali to wait for him outside the garden entrance, to keep watch, was his excuse.

This visit was his alone, and he wanted no one else there by his side.

Jean strode slowly to the fountain and stopped. He took in the fragrance of the flowers, and in particular the orange blossom that came from over the hedge. An image of Ana Celeste came to his mind, so vivid that he felt her sheer, lime green, chiffon gown touch his arm. He looked at the empty space beside him and clearly saw her emerald green eyes smiling up at him. He reached out to take her hand.

"Did you finish feeding the goldfish my love?" he whispered, looking at the ripples that the presumed breadcrumbs had created, seeing the goldfishes feeding on them. "They seem to be happy you have not missed their dinner today. They have waited a long time for you to come and visit them. What kept you so long?" Jean murmured, and lifting her hand, he placed it to his lips and kissed it. The fragrance of her perfume filled his nostril with exquisite pleasure. Tears filled his eyes as he kissed the hand again. "My love, how I have missed you. I am so happy to see you again, to touch you, and to smell you so close to me. I have waited so long to come here to meet with you again." He looked at her again, but she said nothing. She stood by his side looking at him, her eyes shining greener than ever, her fragrance sweeter.

Then he fell to his knees, placing his forehead on the ledge of the font, he cried. His sobs tore at his chest. His whole body shook with hurt and an unfeeling pain. She had been his one and only love. He did not regret breaking the order's vows, for with her he had experienced the greatest joy he had ever known. He had since resolved that he would not break them again. Never. He had considered that the tragedy that had befallen him had been nothing more and nothing less than retribution for his act of disobedience, not to the order, but to God himself. He had sworn again, many years ago, after having confessed his sin to his confessor that he would never again talk to another woman. There could never be another woman in his life like Ana Celeste, the beautiful Rhodian Greek girl with the emerald green eyes and that happy and innocent laugh, who had given him a son.

It was Tafur-Ali who, true to his character, never lost sight of his Lord and was keeping watch over him, so when he saw him fall to his knees, he became extremely worried. He ran to La Valette and took him by the shoulders. "Lord, master, what is wrong? Are you sick? Let me help you to the bench. Please come and sit down."

He helped La Valette to the seat, not knowing that this was the seat where his Lord had once sat with Ana Celeste, the same place where they had held hands and exchanged endearments and expressions of unending love.

Jean sat down and placed both his hands palm down on the seat, and was sure he felt the heat of her body rise from the stone seat. His sobs knew no end.

He bent down and placed his elbows on his knees and his hands to his face, and the tears continued to flow like a stream in full flow.

Transgressing the order of protocol, but extending the dearest expression of friendship, Tafur-Ali placed his arm around the senior knight's shoulders and said in a most tender voice. "You must have loved her a lot, my Lord. It grieves me to see you like this. Put on a brave heart, my Lord, for when she died, she went up to paradise and is there with all your angels and saints, waiting for you to come to her. Otherwise, Lord, there is no meaning to life. In your Christian faith, love is the greatest of the virtues, and although I am a Muslim Lord, I do know that in your faith love conquers all. You have shown me, Lord, that you are a person who loves from the heart, that your person is full of faith in God. Yes, Lord, you are a warrior, but your war shield cannot stop the arrow that has pierced your heart. Pray to your God, Lord, for more strength, for whoever your God is, he will give it to you; he will give you strength for who you are and for what you are. One day he will return to you everything that the locust took away." These words from this humble fisherman were a consolation to La Valette.

La Valette dried the tears off his eyes looked at his companion and said, "Love, Tafur-Ali, is a mystery. We embrace it where we can. Usually we do not choose who we love. It just happens. A voice speaks to us in ways the ear cannot hear. We recognize beauty that the eye cannot see. We experience a change in our hearts that no voice can describe. There cannot be evil in love—at least not in a pure and true love."

With a surrealistic feeling that the day's experience in the garden had really happened, La Valette wrapped his Keffiyeh over his head and face and together they walked back to the cave in total silence.

The other brothers looked up and immediately captured La Valette's somber mood; they said nothing. Tafur-Ali left, and within the hour Andropolous appeared carrying a basket. He had brought some food for the knights: cheese, bread, milk, and a flagon of wine. "Tafur-Ali suggested that I should buy this farewell present for you, for tonight is the last night for you with us. Tomorrow night Tafur-Ali says you will sail away to a faraway place."

"This man Tafur-Ali thinks of everything. I have a feeling that we will miss him when we go. He has proved to be a great ally," added Brother Joanni Caviglia.

The following day, as the sun was setting over the western mountains, and the darkness was descending upon the land, for it was a moonless night, the team of knights, with Tafur-Ali and Andropolous, sat by the hut on the beach with Tafur-Ali's fishing boat already at the water's edge loaded with the baggage.

A pile of dry driftwood had been gathered and it was ready to be lit when night had finally set in. The arrangement was that the pickup vessel, no doubt a small galley with a small crew of rowers, would come close to the island and light a lantern as a signal to the team on the shore, who would in turn set the pile of driftwood afire as their counter-signal, acknowledging that they had seen the boat's signal.

Prior to this, La Valette had set Tafur-Ali aside and handed him a leather pouch full of silver coins. "I promised I would bring you back to your home, and that I would also give you a bag of silver if you would help us. You have helped us more than I ever imagined, so here is your silver. Please give Andropolous and your cousin in the Tower what you think is proper; the rest is for you."

"But Lord, one day you saved me and you brought me back to life and back to my family, how could I not help you?"

Tafur-Ali went home, settled with Andropolous, who seemed to be over the moon with joy, and then hid the money.

They were all sitting around the pile of driftwood when La Valette noticed that Tafur-Ali had returned from his home with a rather large bag over his shoulder.

"What have you there, Tafur-Ali? What have you in that bag?"

"These are my belongings, Lord. I have decided to come with you and serve you in whatever way you wish me to. I was hoping you would not mind, Lord. I have come to realize, Lord that I have more to offer than just to go fishing."

"That comes to me as a big, pleasant surprise, Tafur-Ali my friend. You will be most welcome to join my company."

"Sire, there is one more thing I would like to ask of you."

"What else can I do for you? Go ahead and ask."

"When you have the time and you think it convenient, I would like you to talk to me about your God and this Jesus Christ whom you venerate, for I believe that I would like to become a Christian, like my forefathers before me."

"It would be my honour to teach you about Jesus Christ and to bring you into His fold. And I promise to be your godfather on the day of your baptism. I will also teach you the ways of a warrior, you have the courage but lack the skills, Soon, in a fight; you will be as good as any other knight. I promise you. Now we will move over there and talk to Brother Oliver. He seems somewhat off colour."

La Valette moved over to where Oliver Starkey was and sat next to him. "How are you feeling, Brother Oliver?"

"My arm feels very hot and is rather painful; has been all night through," replied Oliver, rubbing his forearm as he spoke. La Valette could see that droplets of perspiration were forming on Oliver's forehead.

"Let me have a look at your arm, can I?" But first he reached out and touched the man's forehead. "You seem to have a fever. It must be the infection." He took Oliver's arm and slowly lifted the edge of the bandage. He saw that his arm was very dark, like a deep purple. In so doing he also caught a whiff of an unpleasant odour. He did not remark but he did not like at all the look or the smell of this wound.

"Soon we will be on board our ship, and I am sure that the medic on board will be able to treat you properly. We have left this for too long, and Makarios's medication has not stopped the infection. Patience my friend; we will soon get a signal from our people."

As if he had been heard from the far dark horizon, Joanni Caviglia and Emanuel Viale both stood up and pointed out to sea. "There is the light. We see the flickering light. Quick, light the fire."

The goatherd Andropolous went for his flint box and wick. He struck the flint twice, and sparks flew lightining the dried coil of wick, Andropolus blew on the wick and produced a small flame, in turn he placed this on the fine palm fibers he had gathered and soon produced some tiny flames. Andropolous added more twigs and small branches to the growing fire, and soon they had a decent fire going.

"There it is again," shouted the others. "They have seen us. Let's move. Into the boat we go. Okay, Tafur-Ali, push your boat out and off we go."

They all pushed at the boat, and one by one they got in. The last to climb in was Andropolous, who was coming with them to bring the boat back to the village.

On the shore stood a small group of people knee-deep in the water, Tafur-Ali's family—his wife and children. They stood there waving and saying goodbye, with tears in their eyes. The smaller children were crying, saying, "Don't go Daddy, don't go; don't leave us behind." Tafur-Ali, also with tears in his eyes, said, "Don't you worry. I am just going for a long fishing trip, but I shall be back for you all." He turned his back on them and looked in the direction of the distant, flickering light. He raised both hands to his face, and with bent head, cried. La Valette felt this to be a most heart-rending moment, so much so that he too had a tear streaming down his cheek and stopping at his beard.

"There is still time for you to change your mind, Tafur-Ali. You can go back with Andropolous."

"No, Lord, thank you. A man must do what a man has to do. I will return one day to my family, and when I do return, I will return as a man with dignity and of substance thanks to you, my Lord."

Holding Tafur-Ali's shoulder and looking down at him, La Valette said, "Are you sure? You can go back if you want to."

Tafur-Ali turned back and blew a kiss in the direction of the group of people on the beach now looking very small, like ants on a hilltop. "Goodbye, my dear family. Goodbye. May God keep you all safe."

Emanuel, the strongest of them, had taken the oars with Andropoloous and pulled away, putting all their strength behind every sweep; and he, too, had to sniffle. On a downward glance he noticed tears running down Andropolous cheeks.

RETURN TO MALTA

La Valette glanced in the direction of Oliver and saw that he was bent double on his seat, obviously in great pain. La Valette's concern grew to one of alarm. He feared the worst for Oliver's arm. He had got a nasty sniff of putrefaction when he was close to Oliver. He had seen many wounds in this condition during his many years as a warrior. It did not look at all good. He suspected that the remedy would have to be a drastic one.

As arranged, the rendezvous was made with a small galley of fourteen oars. All passengers and baggage were transferred to the galley, and the small fishing boat shoved off.

With tears in his eyes Andropolous started to row towards the shore. *Back to my speech-less friends the goats and sheep again, no more excitement.* Thought Andropolus.

The galley's oar crew turned their vessel and started to row. Within two hours they caught sight of the light of the prearranged signal from the Venetian galleass and soon they were all aboard. The galleass's crew started to applaud them and pat them on their backs.

La Valette immediately called for the ship's surgeon and handed Oliver Starkey over to his care. "Please attend to this, doctor Gallopous. Brother Oliver was bitten by a snake about eight days ago. As you can see, he is not feeling very well. Please let me know your opinion after you have examined him. I would appreciate that very much."

Gallopous was one of the best doctors working for the Order of St. John. He was considered one of the best front-line surgeons, and had assisted the order in many of their battles, both at sea and on land.

La Valette and the other knights were shown to their quarters. "Do you want your baggage with you?" asked the captain of the Venetian galleass, the *St. Paulus*.

"Yes please, but we will not open the baggage until Brother Oliver is with us. After all, he is the expert on these antiquities. But we will have a look at the piece of wood, which is the Holy Cross, and that long item," suggested La Valette pointing to the smaller leather wrapped bundle.

Then La Valette turned to the captain again and introduced Tafur-Ali. "Captain this is my good friend Tafur-Ali, whom you met on the outward journey. He is here now as part of our contingent and will form part of my company of soldiers. He will be training as a sergeant in the militia at Tripoli. He has proved to be a hero and a most brave campaigner. If it had not been for him, this mission would not have been possible. Therefore, he is to be given all the courtesy as if he were a member of our order. You have my permission to call him Brother—Brother Peter of the Cross of Rhodes. His father's previous name was Petrus Popodopulous. Soon he will be received into the universal church of Christ and will be baptised and given the name Peter of the Cross of Rhodes. *Peter* after his father, and *Cross* in recognition of his contribution to the retrieving of the holy relic of the Cross."

When La Valette finished, everyone on board cheered and applauded. "Captain, with your permission we will celebrate our successful return and Brother Peter's conversion in the cabin allocated so kindly by you to our team."

The captain gave some orders to his first mate, and the group moved to the cabin. Soon the first mate returned with a couple of stewards who brought with them several plates with bread, cheese, and fruit, as well as a sealed amphora of wine, which they had been told came from Sicily.

They sat around the cabin and ate, drank, and made loud conversation. La Valette leaned over and picked up the long broken lance they had recovered from the dungeon and proceeded to unwrap the leather covering. When all the wrapping had come off, it revealed an ancient spear of the type known to have been used by Roman soldiers. He inspected the metal edge that was stained and obviously needed cleaning and sharpening. He slid the wrapping to the end and looked at it closely. Then he took his dagger from its scabbard and gently scraped the soiled section of the wooden shaft. He blew gently to remove the fine scraping, and then brought the shaft close to his eyes. The shaft was broken close to the metal point and was held together with thin strip of leather.

He stood up and moved to the open window in the stern of the ship and looked again. "Blessed be God. It's what I thought it was. There are some words carved on the shaft. It says 'Centurium Longinus'. Gentlemen, do you know who centurion Longinus was? Centurion Longinus was the name given to the Roman soldier who was ordered to pierce the side of Christ when He hung on the cross, and the lance thrust was intended to ensure that Christ was dead. The Bible tells us that when the side of Christ was pierced, by this lance, water flowed out of His side, instead of blood. And that when Christ died the skies, which had been blue and cloudless all day, darkened with grey clouds that rumbled with lightning and thunder breaking the silence, everyone at the crucifixion looked up in awe. Then Longinus, frightened and in disbelief, is said to have exclaimed, *'Truly this is the son of God.'*

"This lance, gentlemen, has been missing since the order lost the Holy City of Jerusalem over three hundred years ago. Heavens knows how it got to Rhodes.

"When the order was in Jerusalem, in the years before Islam existed as a religion, Brother Aguilers, known as William, Bishop of Orange, had a vision where he was instructed by St. Andrew, the Apostle, that the missing lance was buried in the cathedral of St. Peter's in Antioch. William searched for it and started digging in the cathedral, and after much digging, finally found the lance, which everyone thought had been lost forever.

"Gentlemen, this lance pierced Jesus Christ's side and the centurion who killed Christ was this Longinus, so named because of the long lance he used. His real name was never known. Tradition has it that Longinus became an ardent follower of Christ and evangelist, spreading the good news wherever he went. There is no doubt that someone carved his name on the wooden shaft."

Then La Valette picked the smaller package and also unwrapped the leather covering. La Valette dropped the wrapping to the deck and held the piece of wood, a piece no more than three feet long and about six inches wide by three inches thick. "And this, friends, is a piece of the Holy Cross on which Christ hung and died for our sins."

He fell to his knees and everyone else did the same. He kissed the relic of the cross and raised it over his head. They all bowed their heads and chanted "*Deo gracia, alleluia! Gloria in excelsis Deo.* Cross of Jesus, protect us and our order."

"This is what we came for, the relic of the Holy Cross of Christ," pronounced La Valette, with restrained emotion, and close to tears. "In gratitude for this great honour, we will cut a very small splinter of wood for each of the men who undertook this mission. A holy relic that we can leave as inheritance to future generations."

The door opened at that precise moment and the doctor stepped in and apologized. "Sorry to disturb you gentlemen, I seem to be interrupting something important, but my message is urgent. Brother Jean, Brother Oliver wants to see you. I am sorry, sir, but I had to amputate his right lower arm before the infection spread further. Gangrene had set in already and the arm had no routine cure."

With that La Valette rushed out of the room and ran to the doctor's quarters.

Oliver Starkey lay on a bunk with his eyes closed moaning slightly. His forehead was full of perspiration.

La Valette knelt down by the bunk and said gently, "Oliver, it is I, Jean. I am here by your side. I am sorry, my friend, I really am." He looked at the bloodied, bandaged stump. He picked up a clean cloth from a chair close by and wiped Oliver's sweaty forehead dry.

"Jean, hold my hand my friend. Let me feel the warmth of your hand. I feel safe with you close by. Please don't leave me alone, Jean. I am frightened. I never thought I would ever be frightened. What about the Holy Cross, did we recover it, have you seen it?"

"Yes Oliver, we did recover it, I have seen it. It is beautiful. Our dream has come true. Christianity can now boast of having the Holy Cross that the Saracens stole from us. As soon as you are better I will bring it to you to have a look at it," offered La Valette in an attempt to build courage and hope in Oliver's mind.

"I want to see it now Jean, please; now. I want to touch it with my remaining hand. Jean, what will happen to me now? I won't be able to use a sword. I won't be able to fight and be by your side," he said in a quivering voice and misty eyes.

"Oliver, my friend, you need to rest. Remember that we have overcome many obstacles together; so this is but a small inconvenience to you. We will teach your other arm to swing a sword as efficiently as your right one did, just wait and see.

"However, I have further good news for you. You remember that long item in the leather wraping? Guess what it is? It is as we thought: Centurion Longinus's lance. It has his name carved at the end of the broken pole. Can you imagine our luck? We came for the Holy Cross and we leave with the Holy Cross and the Holy Lance, the lance that pierced Jesus' side.

"But we still have more treasure to uncover. We have two heavy bags to unpack, but these I shall leave until you recover and are well enough to do so, because the privilege of looking over those manuscripts and scrolls is yours and yours alone. Here is a piece of Holy Cross relic for your personal keeping." He offered Oliver the small piece of wood on a square piece of soft leather. Oliver picked it with his good hand and placed it to his lips. "And here is the big piece of the Holy Cross for you to hold. I knew you would want to hold it. Now sleep, my friend. Soon we will be home."

DIVINE GUIDANCE

Contextus VI

The Scourge of Africa

Naval Commander of the Order

The fantastic news of the recovery of the Holy Cross and Longinus's Holy Lance, together with the heroic accounts of La Valette's daring expedition to the island of Rhodes, spread throughout Christendom. It had been a long time since the Christian world had had good news concerning affairs in the Middle East in the struggle against the Muslims.

There were celebrations in all the convents of the Order of St. John of Jerusalem in the eight countries of the different Langues. The name of Jean Parisot de la Valette was on everyone's lips, proclaiming him a hero. The kings of Europe and His Holiness the Pope Paul III showered him with honours. Nevertheless, he took all the praises with silent affability. His reputation said that he was *the rarest of human beings, a completely single-minded man, dedicated to his religion.*

Even though La Valette was known to be a polite, humble and reserved person, dedicated to the order and his duties who never left the convent unless he went somewhere on duty, yet he was reputed to be a fearless fighter who paid back his enemies with the same coin that he received and with double the ferocity.

La Valette stayed close to Oliver Starkey during his recovery. During that time La Valette confined himself to the convent for prayer and contemplation. He also moved about the island of Malta, acquainting himself with the country and visiting the ancient Phoenician and Roman ruins and together with Oliver reviewed the sacred manuscripts. Oliver, the intellectual, explained to La Valette the finer points of those second century manuscripts, which had been in the Church's possession since then. Oliver began to translate some of the manuscript from the Greek into Latin. This served as a great therapeutic exercise for Oliver helping him in his healing.

Now and again La Valette and Oliver would go into the country side with a falcon which he had bought and trained, and spent the day hunting wild hares and partridges.

One day La Valette decided to go and see the Grand Master Giovanni de Homedes concerning his eagerness to return to his post of Governor of Tripoli, in North Africa.

"My dear Fra La Valette." It was the first time that this particular grand master had addressed him with that religious title, *Fra*, short for *Fraile*. Normally that was the Spanish word for a monk, or brother, used to address individuals in the order in its spiritual context on formal occasions. "I am so glad you have come, Fra Jean. I have been meaning to speak with you about an urgent matter, but alas, time has not been gracious to us. I have good news and bad news for you. Would you like to hear the good news and the bad news?" La Valette nodded in the affirmative.

"Yes? Well, The bad news first. I have to inform you, my dear brother that you are not going back to Tripoli." La Valette was taken aback, his disappointment showing in his face.

"However, the good news is that the Council of Elders has decided, and I have agreed, that in view of your experience as a Knight Mariner, and your excellent record at sea that you should be promoted to Captain General of the order's Fleet, with immediate effect, of course. What have you to say to that Fra Jean?"

"But what about my command of Tripoli, Excellency? We were in the process of preparing new defenses. You have taken me by surprise, Grand Master but I am greatly honoured."

"The question of the command of Tripoli has been taken care of, Fra Jean. I have already dispatched Brother Gaspard De Valleir to fill your post as governor of the fortress and of the city of Tripoli. With Brother Nicolas de Villegaignon as second in command. Our spies have sent us urgent information that the Turkish pirate Dragut, together with the murderous Barbarossa and an army of close to ten thousand are preparing to attack Tripoli. We have only one hundred knights and about 620 mercenaries there. Your first mission as General of the Fleet, La Valette, is to proceed forthwith to the North African coast and rendezvous there with Admiral Andrea Doria, who has been sent by Emperor Charles himself. You are to seek both Dragut and Barbarossa and put them out of action. It is imperative we destroy or weaken the fleets of these two corsairs before they join up with the Sultan's maritime forces."

La Valette knew very well that neither of these two foes were easy targets. They were cunning and illusive. After twenty-four years of roaming the Mediterranean, he knew these two scoundrels' hideouts. He would search and destroy them! He looked forward to facing again the scoundrel called or Barbarossa.

Before pulling up anchors, La Valette called a meeting of his top naval officers and all the captains of his fleet.

"You all know that our orders are to seek both the Barbarossa and the Dragut fleets. This is no easy task, because although the Mediterranean Sea is small, it has many shelters where these pirates can hide, but God is on our side. First we rendezvous with Admiral Andrea Doria somewhere close to Tripoli.

"Advance intelligence is the key to our operation, so we will assign our three fattest brigantines to scout and gather information. One brigantine will go directly south-west, another directly ahead of us, and the third will go in a south-easterly direction. On sighting any enemy activity, they are to report back to the flagship. May God be with you all, and may He grant us fair winds and good fortune."

La Valette stood on the high quarterdeck and looked around him with pride, noting how his squadron was following his flagship in precisely the correct formation ordered. He stood on the deck of the *St. Anne*, the biggest of the Maltese grand carracks. It was 132 feet long and forty feet in the beam. Her superstructure rose seventy-five feet above the waterline. She could carry four thousand tons of stores or merchandise and had stowage for six months victuals. Moreover, she had a blacksmith's shop, a bakery, luxurious saloons and cabins, as well as a chapel. Her armament consisted of fifty long range-guns and a number of falconets and demi-cannon. She carried a crew of three hundred, had a full armoury with weapons for five hundred men, because she also carried an additional four hundred light infantry and cavalry.

The *St. Anne's* most important feature was that she was sheathed in lead and brass sheets, and was hence cannon-proof. She was therefore the first-ever armoured war vessel to be built and adapted to resist the projectiles of her own time.

La Valette self-acknowledged that his twenty-six years in the knights' maritime fleet had been momentous and exceedingly successful. He was now commander-in-chief of the order's navy, and he intended to remain so for several more years. He was also lieutenant to the grand master and therefore a most senior knight.

Little did he suspect the momentous development that was taking place.

Despite the decisive defeats he had brought on the Sultan's navy at sea, the Ottoman Empire by means of massive efforts was rebuilding its navy in a very short time, largely by imitating the successful Venetian galleasses. More than 250 ships had been built, including eight of the largest capital ships ever seen in the Mediterranean. La Valette had not yet seen any of these new vessels. With this new fleet the Ottoman Empire was trying to reassert its supremacy in the Eastern Mediterranean but they had La Valette to contend with.

The Barbarossa Clan

The Barbarossa brothers were sons of a former Christian named Jacob. Jacob had been taken prisoner in Albania and converted to Islam. Jacob had four children: Aroudj, Elias, Isaak, and Kheir ed-Din (the pious or "fruit of Islam"). On account of the eldest son Aroudj's red beard they became known as the Barbarossas. All four brothers became corsairs. They were reputed to be as cruel as they were courageous.

The Barbarossas' fierce reputation came about because of their ruthless and bloody sorties and pillaging of defenseless coastal villages.

Now the cunning Barbarossas joined forces with the Sultan's Turkish forces. They became the most notorious of the Barbary pirates, with emirs along the North African coastline succumbing to them.

In alliance with the Sultan's fleet, they fought against the Knights of Rhodes. The Barbarossas' galleys had been acquired by stealth and piracy. Later, when Aroudj's fortune improved, and with the assistance of the Sultan, he built a fleet of superb galleys in the arsenals of Anatolia. Seasoned and hardy men crewed his ships, the majority coming from the Balkans, especially Albania, also many from Genoese or Venetian possessions who had turned renegade.

The Turkish drive along the North African coast was a Holy War, and the expansion of the Empire knew no limits. Reports circulated that somewhere in the Italian coast they had seized two papal galleys, one of them the *Cavalleria*, a Spanish ship bound for Naples that was carrying three hundred soldiers and sixty Aragonese nobles. One report said *"The ship's captain scuttled his ship so that it could be of no use to the corsairs. Another report said that the ship suffered damage in a storm and made fighting impossible and it was cruelly necessary to abandon ship and surrender."*

Stories were told of how Barbarossa attacked the port of Bougie in North Africa. Eight days of bombardment followed and the tower that the Spaniard Pedro Navarro had erected at Bougie was reduced to rubble. As the one-arm Barbarossa watched the onslaught, a Christian round—shot suddenly took off Barbarossa's remaining left arm. He collapsed and died. The Spaniards took his body.

Spain celebrated his death. Festivals, cavalcades, and processions followed one after the other all over the country. The captain who had defeated and killed Barbarossa, Fernandez de la Plaza, was declared a national hero and was ennobled at once. The captain's coat of arms was designed to show the corsair's head, scimitar, and banner. Barbarossa's cape was given to the monastery of Santo Jeronimo at Cordoba. Barbarossa's head was chopped off, exposed in an iron cage, and hung in one of the main gates. His armless body was nailed to the wooden gate in Cordoba, and during the night was illuminated by torches for everyone to see.

If Aroudj's reputation had been notorious his younger brother Kheir ed-Din's was even worse. He outlived his elder brother by twenty-six years. Though he had black hair, he dyed his hair red in memory of his brother Aroudj. Kheir ed-Din achieved legendary notoriety.

Kheir ed-Din was as brave as his brother, but obtained greater powers. He defeated Emperor Charles in a battle off Algiers. The Sultan greatly pleased appointed Barbarossa the governor of the country, and sent troops to assist him. With this aid the corsair made himself supreme along the Barbary Coast, every Turkish and Moorish desperado, from the Straits of Gibraltar to the Levant, swarmed to him to man his fleet. Drawn by the magic of the name and the promise of gaining much wealth pirate captains begged to be able to serve under his flag.

His corsairs ventured past the Straits of Gibraltar snapping up huge galleons sailing home from the Spanish American colonies to mainland Spain, vessels laden with the treasures from the Indies: gold, silver, and precious stones.

Time and again Barbarossa harried the shores along the northern Mediterranean in search of plunder and captives, both of which he took in great abundance.

On one occasion seven Spanish royal galleys were brought into the harbour, including the *Capitana*, the flagship of the Spanish navy.

He took the fort of Algiers made the garrison prisoners, pulled down the fortress, and set thousands of Christian slaves to work to build a breakwater and harbour with the fortress's stones.

He put to sea and attacked Minorca, plundering the town, seizing several rich prizes, and returning to Algiers with six thousand captives and much booty.

He moved further up the African coast to Cherchell and joined his one-time comrade Cara Hassan whom he beheaded soon after.

He later attacked Sicily and the coast of Italy.

The Barbarossas could not have it all to themselves. Soon two Christian leaders would emerge who would thwart the corsairs and Turks of Algiers. Jean de la Valette and Andrea Doria, of Genoese descent, were to chase the Barbarossas relentlessly. Both men were audacious and brave. Though not yet acquainted, each in his own way harassed the quarrelsome Turks and pirates.

A week after the Christian fleet had left Malta to rendezvous with Andrea Doria's own fleet, one of the fast scout brigantines, returned with a valuable report. The brigantine's captain reported to La Valette. "Sir, we were short of provisions and water, so we entered the friendly port Majorca, and the port was alive with the news that Barbarossa had attacked the island, off Formentera in the north of Majorca, only ten days before we arrived and defeated *El Caballero Portundo*, a Basque knight and general-in-chief of Spanish galleys. We were told that Barbarossa captured seven galleys and took Portundo's son and the galley's captains for ransom payment."

"Did they say in which direction they sailed?"

"Yes sir, I specifically asked. They said that they headed south-south-east." La Valette had his map laid out in front of him by his assistant Francois de la Valette. He pointed at the map and with his finger traced a line from the island of Majorca in a south-south-easterly direction. "Here he is, on his way to Bougie on this side of Tunis, one of the pirates' hideouts. We shall sail in that direction and hope he will not stop there; with God's help we may intercept him in this area ahead of Tunis. Well done, Captain Ambrocio. If you need any provisions for your vessel, please ask the purser. If not, I bid you God speed."

La Valette knew that individual piracy had been transformed from being the pastime of a handful of brigands to a full-blown state enterprise, encouraged and financed by the Ottoman Sultan.

An unexpected report came when they met a French merchantman on its way to Algiers. They ferried its master to the flagship and asked for the latest news from his last port of call. "Your Excellency, as we left we could not believe our eyes, but we saw Turkish ships entering Toulon. We know they are allies of the king of France, but we had never seen this before. We also know, Your Excellency, that the Turks land expeditions each month on the Christian coasts, particularly in the kingdoms of Naples, Calabria, and Sicily to take slaves."

This was news to La Valette, though he knew that these were operations of war conducted by entire fleets as part of a comprehensive strategy, for the Ottomans were contemplating conquering the Mediterranean and even invading Italy and regaining Spain.

He immediately sent a report of this news to Emperor Charles V.

Slaves still made a good, tradable commodity. Christians could be sold to Muslims and Muslims could be sold to Christians. It was a lucrative trade. The Ottoman Sultan needed slaves to build his fast expanding Empire but he was going to far.

Even though La Valette's mission was to engage Barbarossa and Dragut and bring them to account, there were other enemies of more celebrated and renowned, captains of adventure, conquerors chasing their fortunes, risking their lives in dangerous expeditions. Others, supported by loyal clans, formed dynasties of their own. They imposed laws and subjugated those they conquered, and lived, for the most part, on the spoils of their raids. The Christian forces and the Fleet of the Knights of the Order of

St. John battled against all these adversaries. La Valette had resolved to put this right.

On the other side of the Mediterranean, Andrea Doria's list of successes grew in leap and bounds. He managed to expel a Turkish fleet that was hounding the area around Provence. He was taken into papal service. Then he went into the service of Francis I of France, who made him Captain General of his navy during France's war with Charles V of Spain.

Andrea Doria left the service of King Francis I because he disagreed with his policies. Instead, Doria went over to the service of Charles V.

La Valette's galleys sailed towards their destination with a fair wind astern and the gentle rhythm of the oars.

Good navigation and timing and the help of the brigantine scout allowed La Valette to locate Andrea Doria's fleet off the African coast. The combined Christian fleet was now something to reckon with, led by the two most popular seamen in the Mediterranean Sea: Their mood was full of positive expectations. They met aboard the Admiral's flagship and discussed their strategy and objectives. With an embrace and a joint blessing by the admiral's chaplain, they parted.

It was not long before the Christian galleys were in action. They sailed to the Ottoman fort that the Spaniards had named *La Corona* (the Crown) and captured it, sacking the city, taking prisoners, and killing many. From there they proceeded to Tunis. The knights' fleet was at the vanguard of the expedition. The large carrack of Rhodes; the *St. Anne*, La Valette's flagship; and three large galleys with eighteen brigantines were all at the disposal of Andrea Doria. Within the next few days the fleet recaptured the port of *La Goletta* and the important strategic city of Tunis, thus forcing the Turkish admiral Barbarossa to escape to the Levant.

La Valette chased Barbarossa and caught up with his few galleys, but Barbarossa, knowing the knight's ships were faster and that eventually would catch up with him, beached his own galley and quickly disappeared overland, making his escape in the direction of Alexandria. They took Barbarossa's ship as well as a couple of galleys and several hundred prisoners. Barbarossa had slipped away once more.

It was not the end of Barbarossa. The younger Barbarossa lived to be an old man, and he rose to a position of great power, winning for himself high renown at sea and a name that is not forgotten to this day in the story of the Turkish Empire.

Dragut Reis—The Sword Of Islam

Since Barbarossa had eluded La Valette disappointed he headed back and joined Andrea Doria. When they saw that Tripoli had not been attacked, they met with knight de Vallier its commander. They noted de Vallier had only thirty knights and 630 Calabrian and Sicilian mercenaries. La Valette assured de Vallier that Grand Master de Homedes had told him that he was sending reinforcements to soon. However, La Valette suggested they leave behind a token of two knights and a dozen soldiers.

With much apprehension and foreboding, they sailed east.

However everyone had missed a vital piece of intelligence, namely that the Ottomans had at Tajur, a city only twenty miles east or one day's, a force of several thousand soldiers. This army marched on Tripoli and established three batteries of twelve guns each on the high ground, encircling the fort.

Meanwhile Dragut's fleet approached from the north and stationed itself at sea, blockading the city.

The French Ambassador to the Ottoman Empire, Gabriel d'Araman, had sailed with Andrea Doria. He was in the port at the time. He bravely presented himself to Dragut. His mission was to dissuade the corsairs from attacking. He had been instructed to say that Malta was not a declared enemy of the Franco-Ottoman alliance. Dragut and Sinan Pasha, the general commanding the land forces refused to listen on grounds that they were under strict orders to eradicate the Knights of Malta from the African continent. D'Araman stomped away and threatened to sail to Constantinople to see the Sultan himself, but Dragut barred d'Araman from leaving the city until the siege ended.

The city was bombarded for six days, but de Vallier's soldiers, mainly mercenaries mutinied, demanding from their commander to enter into negotiations for surrender. The city was captured on the fifteenth of August. Upon the intervention of the French Ambassador, D'Araman, the knights, many of them French, were returned to Malta, and shipped on board his own galleys.

The Ottoman Turks recognized the cowardice of the mercenaries and enslaved them all. Commander de Vallier and Nicolas de Villegaignon were dispatched with the vanquished knights returning to Malta.

Villegaignon took advantage his trip back to Malta and wrote a day-to-day record of the events of this siege. This would become very useful in the days to come.

Importantly he also wrote to King Henry II and noted that D'Araman participated actively in the Ottomans' victory banquet; raising further suspicion of his role in the siege, leading to claims that France had participated in the siege's success to undermine Spain's and the order's influence in North Africa. It was not known whether he profited personally from this situation, but the doubt remained.

Upon his return to Malta, de Vallier was faced a tribunal, this stripped him of his habit and Cross of the Order, the severest humiliation a Knight of the Order could possibly endure, even worse than death itself. Even though Nicolas de Villegaignon tried to expose the duplicity of de Homedes and staunchly defended Vallier he was imprisoned.

La Valette, better than anyone else, knew that de Homedes had been slow to respond to his proposals for the reinforcement of the fortifications, with promises of more troops, which he never kept. He swore to vindicate his old friend de Vallier at the first possible opportunity.

As he sailed away searching for his enemy La Valette pondered on what history he knew about his second most dangerous enemy, Dragut Reis, the Muslim corsair.

Dragut Reis was known by the faithful as "the Drawn Sword of Islam", he loved Christians as the fox loves geese. But in that summer of 1550, his feelings acquired a far deeper malignancy; they developed into a direct and personal hatred that for intensity was second only to the hatred that La Valette bore for Dragut.

Earlier the allied Christian forces under La Valette had smoked him out of his stronghold of Mehedia; they had seized that splendid city and razed it to the ground as the neighbouring Carthage had been razed of old.

Dragut reckoned his losses with a gloomy, vengeful mind. He had lost his city and had been cast down once more to be a wanderer upon the seas.

He lost three thousand men, amongst them the very flower of his fiery corsairs.

He had also lost some twelve thousand Christian prisoner slaves—the fruit of many desperate raids.

He was furious he had lost his lieutenant and nephew Hisar, who was now a captive of his other inveterate enemy, Andrea Doria. But he was not the man to waste his days in brooding over what was done he recovered quickly.

He thought, *yesterday and today are but as pledges in the hands of destiny. Thanks to Allah, the Compassionate, the Merciful, he was still alive and free upon the seas.*

He still had three galleasses, twelve galleys, and five brigantines. He bent his energetic, resourceful, knavish mind to making good his losses.

The Sultan of Constantinople, the Exalted of Allah, warned him that Emperor Charles had, in letters, avowed his intent to pursue to the death *"the pirate Dragut, a corsair odious to both God and man"*. He knew that the Emperor had entrusted the task to the greatest seamen of the day—admiral of Genoa, Andrea Doria, and the terrible knight La Valette; both were already at sea upon his quest.

Dragut recalled with disgust that he had once been captured by the Genoese, whereupon he had toiled aboard a galley on the oars of the admiral's nephew, Gianettino Doria. He had known exposure to heat and cold; naked he been broiled by the sun and frozen by the rain; he had known aching muscles, hunger, and thirst; filthy crawling things over his body; the festering sores begotten of the oarsman's bench; and his shoulders were still a criss-cross of scars where the bo'suns' whips had lashed him to revive his flagging energies.

Barbarossa had ransomed him for a mere three thousand crowns. It was a bad bargain for Christendom. Dragut had not forgotten any of this. It was his duty, therefore to avenge himself.

This is why Charles V of Spain made up his mind to destroy that nest of pirates in Algiers, and put an end to them once and for all but luckily for Dragut, Emperor Charles miscalculated his offensive and started too late in the year. Autumn was upon him, and the dreaded early winter storms were at hand.

Gales buffeted them on the way to Algiers. The weather fought for Dragut as no army could have done. The sea had been so rough that few stores could be landed. The soldiers had neither tents nor cloaks to shelter them from the furious blast of the bitter wind and the cold, driving rain. The waterlogged soil became a sea of mud in which the men floundered miserably. Their powder was wet; they had little food; they were wet and cold and hungry; and had little heart to fight when the Turks and Moors sallied upon them.

Then one winter's morning a terrible hurricane sprang up, remembered to this day as *"Charles's Gale"*. This hurricane burst upon the great fleet and broke. Ship crashed into ship. Many were hurled ashore. In six hours one hundred and fifty vessels went to the bottom. Andrea Doria saved some of them by taking them out to sea, where they rode the storm in safety.

The losses were so great that Charles could not maintain his position before the city. The retreat began. But at length, the unhappy and reduced army gained the shelter of the remaining ships.

However there was no room to embark the horses. The chivalry of Spain had followed Charles and brought their finest chargers with them, animals of priceless value, the pride of the Spanish breed. Charles reluctantly had them all destroyed, a fatal blow to the great Spanish breed.

Once again, in the open seas, the ships were assailed by another dreadful storm, blown hither and thither by the gale. Wrecked ships ended on the shores of Algiers, and their crews seized by the pirates, leaving many of the soldiers and sailors in the hands of the enemy. Algiers teemed with Christian captives and it became a common saying that a Christian slave was scarce a fair barter for an onion.

The Harbour of Algiers

But that unhappy event was behind them and the new Christian expedition of Doria and La Valette planned an assault upon Tunis.

Dragut had now established himself there, and a strong army was sent to drive him out, with Andrea Doria attacking from the sea and La Valette, of his own free will, was in command of the land troops. This time La Valette's company scored a success. He assaulted and took over the city, and searched for Dragut, but found that the cunning pirate had taken flight.

Doria and La Valette scoured the coasts and the seas in pursuit of Dragut, in the hope once more of seizing him and chaining him to a rowing bench.

A wonderful stroke of luck came their way.

They heard that Dragut was near the island of Djerba, so they set sail there and took the corsair utterly by surprise. They found him there with a few galleys. They blocked his way of escape. Behind Djerba lay a vast inland lake, a favourite resort of the corsairs, reached only from the north by a narrow passage, down which Dragut had sailed. Here he lay in the lake, busily engaged in scraping the keels of his galleys and greasing them that they might slide more swiftly through the water. To Dragut's dismay, the powerful Christian fleet came in sight, which planted their ships squarely across the mouth of the northern channel, and chuckled to think they had enclosed Dragut in a trap.

Doria did not come into the lake—for excellent reasons. His heavy vessels would find it dangerous to attempt the narrow channel whose shoals and sandbanks the lighter pirate galleys had passed with ease. The old admiral was a very cautious man; he never risked seamen or ship except at urgent need, and here he had only to wait till the corsair was forced to come out. He sent word to Europe that he had safely trapped the corsair fleet, for though there was a southern channel, it was so shallow, so filled with mud and sand, that no one had ever heard of a vessel passing that way to the open sea.

At first Dragut knew not what to do. It was hopeless to think of venturing out of his refuge. He could not hope to pit his galleys against a fleet not only vastly more powerful, but under the command of the two most famous leaders of Christendom. His nimble wits went to work to find a way out of the trap.

First he landed his cannons, placed them in an earthwork, and fired briskly on the enemy. He did them little damage, but he knew that; he wished only to keep them at bay, making the Christians hesitate before attacking. In this way his objective could be achieved. Meanwhile, his men worked like ants at the other end of the lake, not visible from the sea. Thousands of native labourers called from the country roundabout were ordered to cut a channel and prepare a way of escape. On a moonless night, as soon as darkness fell, all hands turned to the task. They put rollers under the keels of the galleys, and hauled them across the shallows by thousands of willing hands. Next the galleys were worked and floated along the canal that had been cut, and long before dawn, oars were dipped in the deep water on the other end of the island, and Dragut, and his men, were off at full speed for Turkish-friendly waters and safety.

At daybreak Doria and La Valette rubbed their eyes in amazement. The pirate ships had disappeared. Only lst night they had seen the pirate galleys lying in the lake, and now at dawn they were gone. Where had they gone? Never had the famous old admirals endured a more bitter disappointment, the mouth had slipped the trap.

But La Valette knew that his cunning adversary would somehow show himself soon with new ships and fresh crews.

Dragut returned to Anatolia, and Sultan Suleiman the Magnificent nominated him as commander of Tripoli, making the city the capital of the Ottoman province of Tripolitania, and a practical centre for piratical raids.

La Valette heard of his return and once again set his mind to chase him down. One of his scout ships reported that Dragut had, from Tripoli, attacked Reggio in Italy and had taken all its inhabitants as slaves back to Tripoli.

La Valette was astonished at the speed at which Dragut moved around the Mediterranean; the man seemed to be everywhere at the same time.

Once again the powerful Christian naval force was sent to recapture Tripoli, and once again, ironically, thanks to the work previously done by the knights to the defenses and fortifications of Tripoli, the Christian force was defeated again.

La Valette had proposed to the Viceroy of Sicily, the Duke of Medina-Coeli, to reconquer Tripoli.

A combined fleet of Spanish, French, and the Knights Hospitallers had been put together by Phillip II. La Valette had cautioned that Dragut would be regrouping and improving the fortifications of Tripoli.

To La Valette's great consternation and annoyance, the Spanish Fleet unwisely diverted its course and sailed towards the island of Djerba (Spanish for "of grass" or "grassy island") in an attempt to vindicate their last defeat.

The result of this diversion was that instead of attacking Tripoli across the bay, the Spanish squadron attacked Djerba, a non-strategic small island. The planned attack on Tripoli was not carried through. La Valette sent a message to the Spanish commander telling him that he was forced to return to Malta. An annoyed La Valette wrote. *"My Excellencies, I find no reason to delay my return to my base if your Excellencies refuse to bid my advice. I consider your decision not to proceed with our original plan a serious mistake. I therefore bid you Excellencies farewell and wish you success and fair winds."*

The Spanish forces' stay in Djerba was short lived and tragic. In a short time the Turks regrouped, attacked the island, and retook it, forcing of what remained of the Christian armada to leave.

Dragut's fleet of corsairs secretly followed this fleet all the way to Malta where Dragut attacked and sacked the smaller island of Gozo to the east.

When word of this reached La Valette, who was by now in Birgu, at the other extreme end of the main island, he set his fleet about and sailed overnight with oars and full sails to rescue the sister island of Gozo. He reached the north side of the main island while it was still dark, but waited till first light. Then, in a pre-dawn attack, he surprised the Turkish fleet that was anchored for the night in a bay off the smaller island of Comino. Caught unawares, Dragut's fleet suffered heavy punishment at the hands of La Valette's galleys. The whole channel between the islands was strewn with ships' debris and floating humanity. Several of Dragut's galleys were sunk at their moorings a couple were so destroyed that they were set on fire; and others boarded and taken as booty. Several hundred

Christian prisoners from Gozo were set free, in all half a dozen galleys were taken captive.

When Dragut, who had been moored further down the coast, was awakened by the noise of the attack, he decided that his best course of action was to take advantage of a favourable wind and headed off home with what remained of his fleet.

La Valette's reaction to this escalation was to increase the Hospitaller's fleet activity at sea. Corsair-chasing was becoming increasingly successful for the knight's fleet. Their most important triumph was the engagement with a Turkish vessel carrying the governor of Cairo and a respected female dignitary, thought to be the wet-nurse of Suleiman the Magnificent's daughter.

Captain General Francesco St. Clement of the order had set out, with four ill-prepared and undermanned galleys to chase Dragut in the direction of the African coast. On encountering an enemy flotilla commanded by "renegade" Luciali, he took flight. When he returned to Malta, he was court-martialed and was sentenced to strangling for cowardice in the face of the enemy. After strangulation his body was tossed over the wall of the fort to the sea below. Some in the order had been showing signs of weakness, and a lesson had to be taught; it befell Knight Francesco St. Clement to serve as an example.

One of La Valette's new challenges was trying to run down "renegade" Christians.

One such individual was Hassan Pasha, formerly Vitorio Como, a fat, pompous, and perfumed Venetian renegade who dressed in the most traditional Arabic silk costumes and wore flamboyant headdresses studded with pearls and precious stones. He was always accompanied by young Moorish fan-boys. His cruelty to prisoners who tried to escape was legendary. Hassan Pasha had been a successful merchant in spice, ivory, and silk, between Alexandria and Venice. He later found a more lucrative business trading in "slaves"—there was the spice market, the silk market the tea market and the flesh market, he was very successful in the latter. As time progressed he discovered there were more riches as a corsair.

Reports had come in to La Valette that Hassan Pasha would burn Christian prisoners alive or that he beat others to death with his own hand or cut off noses.

There was a second special renegade one called El Louch Aly Fortex. Formerly a Dominican friar, he had served the Sultan and was elevated to become the governor of Alexandria. La Valette made a mental note to someday attack the port of Alexandria just to capture or kill this one-time man of the cloth.

La Valette had a further list of other renegades he dearly wanted to get rid of. For instance, Mam Arnaut, an Albanian renegade; then there was Morat Rais, a French renegade; Gaucho, a Venetian turncoat; Youssef, another turncoat, this one from Naples; also Daourdi Magmi, and Dali Mauri, all Greeks now serving the Sultan with Muslim names. All together, La Valette had listed thirty captains commanding Algerian galleys. "God help them when I get my hands on them."

La Valette's fleet took advantage of a Westerly wind, changed tack, and veered towards a mass of white sails. Friend or foe?

The fast brigantine scout sailed closer to the African coast to view and promptly raised flags signaling *"Enemy in Sight"*.

Next to La Valette stood his nephew Francois. La Valette turned to him and said, "It looks, Brother Francois, as if we have a battle on our hands. Get your sharpshooters aloft. Order them to aim for the oarsmen. We need to disable their ability to get away or move about; then we can position our vessel to fire."

La Valette's desire would soon come true. As his fleet sailed close to the Straits of Gibraltar, they spotted another mass of white sails close to the African coast in the vicinity of Ceuta, a Spanish possession formerly a Portuguese fortress.

One of Giovanni's Andrea Doria's scout galleys came alongside with news that a bigger combined Christian force from Spain had joined them. The messenger handed La Valette orders from the admiral.

The Christian fleet was to form up in four divisions, approaching two from the north, east and west.

One division was lead by ~Admiral Agostino Barbarigo, another by Sebasiano Venier and Marcantonio Colonna, the other by La Valette the other by Andrea Doria and all under John of Austria, the illegitimate son of Emperor Charles V and half brother to King Philip of Spain.

The despatch that La Valette received outlined the battle plan. It ordered him to stay in the western coastal region and to engage the enemy as he saw convenient. La Valette estimated that the new combined Christian fleet consisted of 206 galleys and four Venetian galleasses.

La Valette estimated that the composition of such a gigantic fleet was on the order of 22,800 soldiers, forty thousand sailors and oarsmen, and a total of 1,800 guns. This operation was to be the largest and most daring attempt ever to eliminate the Ottoman presence in the Mediterranean and the significant threat it presented to the total security of continental Europe. It now remained to be seen what combined force had the Ottoman Turks and Saracen corsairs had put together.

The battle plan was set out in the *Mandata*, the dispatch.

As Doria's right division slowly approached the enemy, La Valette's fleet remained on the western offshore side.

La Valette's observers counted the Ottoman fleet. It consisted of fifty-seven galleys and two *galliots* on its right under Hassan Pasha, formerly Vitorio Como, the Ventian "renegade"; sixty-one galleys and thirty-two *galliots* in the centre under El Louch Aly Fontex, the former Dominican friar; about sixty-three galleys; and thirty *galliots* in the south off-shore; with a small reserve of eight galleys, twenty-two *galliots* and sixty-four *fustas,* behind the centre body. Close to 400 vessels!

La Valette had heard enough. This was the Ottomans' south fleet, composed mainly of those renegades that he so much abhorred. Hassan Pasha was supposed to have told his Christian galley slaves: "If I win the battle, I promise you your liberty. If the day is yours, then God has given it to you." John of Austria, more laconically, warned his crew: "There is no paradise for cowards."

After a careful search he did not locate Dragut and Barbarossa's, larger vessels, they were not present for this battle. They must have remained in the north, close to the Anatolian coast; or perhaps they were waiting for the battle to start before making a surprise appearance.

When the fleet appeared in the western horizon the Turks mistook the galleasses to be merchant supply vessels and set out to attack them, not expecting that Christian fighting ships would be coming from the west. This proved to be a disastrous mistake for the Turks. La Valette's galleasses did not wait. La Valette had realized that Doria's fleet had delayed in attacking; therefore with this unexpected opportunity he set sail for the fight. When he finally engaged the enemy, with their many guns, they sunk about seventy Ottoman galleys in a matter of a few hours, before the others fled the scene of the battle. The flanking attack had another benefit: it disrupted the Ottoman formations. La Valette's greatest loss was of the Maltese grand carrack the *Capitana*, killing all but three men on board.

The Maltese squadron, as La Valette's fleet became known, gained a bloody victory and captured a Turkish galleon manned by two hundred janissaries and laden with precious merchandise. La Valette placed a price-crew on board the captured vessel and ordered it to set sail for Malta.

Doria found that Hassan Pasha's galleys extended farther to the south than his own, and so headed south to avoid being out-flanked instead of holding the Christian line. *I'll teach you a lesson, you turncoat pig*, Doria thought to himself. Doria was accused of having maneuvered his fleet away from the bulk of the battle to avoid taking damage and casualties.

La Valette's squadron took advantage of the big gap that Doria had left. La Valette nodded his head when he saw Doria's mistake, but smiled when he was told that the approaching enemy was none other than Hassan Pasha, his most hated renegade. "I'll get them one by one," said La Valette to young Francois.

In the north the French renegade Morat Rais had managed to get between the shore and the Christian north division. Commander Barbarigo, a very capable Christian captain, was killed by an arrow, but the Venetians, turning to face the threat, held their line.

On the south, offshore side, Doria was still engaged with some of Hassan Pasha's ships, taking the worst part of the battle. Dorea's commander, Pietro Giustiniani, the prior of the Order of St. John, was severely wounded by five arrows that had pierced him in various parts of his body, but he was found alive in his cabin.

The intervention of the Spaniards Álvaro de Bazán and Juan de Cardona with their reserve came just in time and turned the battle in the Christians' favour, both in the centre and in Doria's south wing. Hassan Pasha was forced to flee the battle with sixteen galleys and twenty-four *galliots*. But.

La Valette's grand carrack, the indomitable *St. Anne*, approached. His galleass got close to the port side of Hassan Pasha's ship, the *Sultana*, whilst he broadsided the other galleys from the starboard side. La Valette closed in, and in no time his men fearlessly boarded the deck of the *Sultana*. La Valette, dressed in full armour, with a hoard of troops, including six knights, boarded the Ottoman commander's ship and fiercely cut down the Ottoman janissaries who were putting up a strong resistance. A dozen sharpshooters perched on the yard-arms and rigging were scoring with each shot, as they had been trained to do. The company of knights fought in a spear formation, pushing the enemy into a corner in the stern of the vessel, a strategy initiated by La Valette. He assaulted two janissaries with his long battle sword in one hand and a shorter sword in the other and fought two-headedly as he had been taught since when he was a young trainee.

La Valette caught a glimpse of two individuals on the high stern of the *Sultana*, one of whom he recognized, with joyful surprise, to be Dragut. The other was the hated renegade Hassan Pasha.

"To me, knights! To me!" shouted La Valette as he cut another janissary across the shoulder and simultaneously pierced another through the armpit. With a savage leap, he came upon another. Using his right and left swords, he slashed the janissary across the face, scattering jaw and teeth to the deck. The Christian group rushed immediately towards La Valette. Five knights were with him as he stood a few paces away from the two Ottoman corsairs. He stood with his feet astride, resting his hands on his hips and holding his two swords, his armour covered in blood. Panting, he addressed the two leaders in the Turkish tongue: "Surrender your weapons and your fleet or you will die with all your men."

One of Dragut's personal guards jumped from nowhere and stood between them. La Valette swung his sword overhead at the intruder, and off flew his feathered turban, and with it a portion of his head.

"On what conditions are you calling for this armistice?" demanded a tremulous Hassan Pasha.

"Yes, on what terms do we negotiate this armistice?" repeated Dragut.

"I neither ask nor offer armistice!" shouted the furious La Valette. "I demand your immediate and unconditional surrender." As he spoke he took a step forward with his swords as if to strike. The other five knights and some other warriors, who had since joined them, followed his example.

"Will you spare our lives?" asked Hassan Pasha quickly.

"Indeed I will, you filthy renegade. I will spare your lives. Monsieur Dragut, it is the custom of war for me to condemn you below deck to work the oars with the whip, so that you can taste the same medicine that I and many others have tasted under your hand. You will learn what it is to be a slave. Do you accept or die?" said La Valette, placing the point of his sword on Dragut's chest.

Dragut wryly replied, looking at the sword on his heart, "It is indeed my change of fortune."

And so it came about that Dragut, the greatest of the corsairs, was taken prisoner for the second time in his lifetime.

True to his word La Valette did not kill Hassan Pasha. Instead, he transferred him to a smaller galley that was manned by a crew of recently liberated Christian slaves who had labored, for several years, under the cruelty of this renegade. La Valette refused to think of Hassan Pasha's fate in the hands of these recently liberated men, but whatever it was it would be well deserved.

In the meantime, in the other sphere of battle, the Spanish fleet was repelled twice with heavy casualties. But at the third attempt, with reinforcements from Álvaro de Bazán's galleys, they took the ship the *Müezzinzade*, and Ali Pasha was taken alive then killed, and beheaded, this was done against the expressed wishes of John of Austria. When the severed head was displayed on a pike from the Spanish flagship, it contributed greatly to the destruction of Turkish morale.

Even after the battle had clearly turned against the Turks, groups of janissaries still kept fighting with all their might. At some point the janissaries ran out of weapons and started throwing oranges and lemons at their Christian foes.

The battle concluded around 4:00 p.m. The Ottoman fleet suffered the loss of about 210 ships, of which 117 galleys, ten galliots, and three fustas were captured in fair condition.

On the Christian side, twenty galleys were destroyed and thirty were damaged so seriously that they had to be scuttled. One Maltese galley was the only prize the fleeing Turks took with them.

Admiral Uluç Ali, the one who had captured the Maltese knights' galley, succeeded in extricating most of his ships from the battle when defeat was certain. Since the Maltese vessel on tow was slowing him down, he decided to cut the tow rope and flee. He sailed to Constantinople, gathering up other Ottoman ships along the way, finally arriving there with eighty-seven vessels. He presented the huge Maltese black flag, with the eight pointed white cross, stolen from the Maltese vessel, to Sultan Suleiman, who thereupon bestowed upon him the honorary title of *Kılıç* (sword); Uluç thus became known as Kılıç Ali Pasha, but only for twenty-four hours. The Sultan, on reflection, after hearing the full story and realizing that he had been deceived, had him beheaded for the defeat of his precious fleet.

The Holy League had suffered the loss of around 7,500 soldiers, sailors, and rowers, but had freed about 10,000 Christian prisoners. The Ottoman casualties were around 15,000 dead and as many maimed, with a loss of 137 ships captured by the Christians and fifty sunk.

The engagement was a significant defeat for the Ottomans, who had not lost a major naval battle for a long time. They mourned the defeat as an act of Divine Will. Contemporary chronicles recorded that *"the Imperial Fleet encountered the fleet of the wretched infidels, and the will of God turned another way"*.

For Christendom, this event encouraged hope for the downfall of *los Turcos*, the Satan-like personification of the Ottoman Empire, who were regarded as the *"sempiternal enemies of the Christian"*.

News reached La Valette that Grand Master Sengle was gravely ill and expected to die at any time and he was expected to return forthwith to Malta. He bade farewell to the Spanish and the Genoese commanders Andrea Doria, and sailed north-east to the headquarters of the Order, Malta.

GREAT GARRACK

3 Mast Galley

MINOR GALLEY

MIRACULOUS HEAVENLY ARMY THAT WON THE FIRST SIEGE OF THE ISLAND OF RHODES 1522

ADMIRAL ANDREA DORIA—HEROE OF THE
BATTLE OF LEPANTO

**DESTRUCTION OF SACERAN GALLEY
BY CHRISTIAN GRAND GARRACK**

CONTEXTUS VII

THE BATTLE FOR SURVIVAL

THE GREATEST GRAND MASTER

La Valette sailed towards Malta, his mind occupied with the composition of the order's fearsome maritime fleet for which he was totally responsible. He also gave thought to their present distribution around various strategic areas of the Mediterranean where it was causing disruption in the Ottoman trade routes and its fleet.

La Valette estimated that he had engaged in no less than eighty-five sea battles, had been mortally wounded, taken prisoner as a slave and suffered other minor injuries in the course of his maritime and military career. He was convinced that God must be with him; Emmanuel, (God with us), was truly a faithful God.

The second development, unknown to La Valette as he sailed towards his destination, and whilst Grand Master Claudio de la Sengle was still in his deathbed, was that there had been an important meeting in Malta of the order's Supreme Council, the *Consiglio di la Comandancia*. They feared and anticipated that some great event was about to unfold, such as an invasion by the Ottoman Turks of the island. So they decided that the new grand master who would replace Sengle needed someone of extraordinary strength of character, both in battle and administrative capabilities.

It was important for the new leader to be a good strategist. The Supreme Council had decided unanimously that Jean Parisot de la Valette was the only man who met all these requirements. They recognized that in his military record the man had been a tower of strength and an inspiration to the order. Everyone was aware that the order needed transformation so it could recover its ancient authority. La Valette was considered by all the "man for the season". The only person who did not know this was La Valette himself.

A messenger was waiting at the dockside when his fleet sailed in and took shelter in the inner Grand Harbour, close to Birgu, where the order's headquarters was located. After the crew lowered the gangway, the messenger came aboard the *St. Anne,* paid his compliments to the captain, saluted the order's flag on board, and requested to see Commander La Valette. La Valette was promptly called and came on deck to meet the messenger, a recently commissioned young knight in shining new armour. The young knight saluted and offered a small parchment to La Valette saying "Knight Gustavo Bacarisa of the Italian Langue at your service sir." I have a Message for Commander Jean Parisot de la Valette, from the Supreme Council"

"What message do you bear? Has Grand Master Sengle died?"

"No sir. Grand Master Sengle is in a deep coma but still alive. I have been ordered to accompany you to the Supreme Council Chambers the moment your vessel berthed."

"Very well, young man, lead the way." Behind La Valette stood six of his fellow knights, also fully dressed in fresh uniforms. La Valette turned around and beckoned his knights to follow. One of his knights handed the Commander his cape, helmet and sword, which he deftly put on as he walked. The Supreme Council's chambers were not far away, just three minutes walk from the quayside.

La Valette stopped at the entrance to the chambers and made the sign of the cross then entered the chamber with his company of six knights who had donned their best surcoats, black capes, dress swords and daggers. He asked his men to stand easy in the shade. La Valette stopped at the entrance, his black cape drawn over his left shoulder with the white eight-pointed star to the right, feet astride, and hand on the pommel of his sword. He carried his shining silver and gold helmet under his left arm. At the entrance the sunshine coming through the door made his entrance even more dramatic. The young knight announced, in a very loud voice that bounced off the walls of the chamber: "Commander-in-Chief and Lieutenant to His Highness the Grand Master, Fra Jean Parisot de la Valette."

La Valette advanced towards the large, round table occupied by the most senior officers of the Council of the Hospitallers, the Order of St. John of Jerusalem and Rhodes. The whole gathering stood up simultaneously and advanced towards La Valette smiling and beaming. The chamber was packed with other knights who stood around waiting for the proceedings to begin. Amongst them was Oliver Starkey, who had not joined La Valette in this last expedition. Oliver stood by his lifelong friend Jean, elegant and smiling, an empty sleeve folded at the elbow, his sword on the other side. Over the years Oliver had learned to use his left hand equally as deadly as his right hand.

Greetings and comments were simultaneously directed at an amused La Valette: "Welcome, La Valette." "Good to see you, Jean." "You look well, my friend." "Come sit down good fellow, you must be glad to be on solid ground." "Here, have some refreshment." Someone proffered a goblet of wine thinned with fresh water, *a la romana*, and placed it in La Valette's hand.

La Valette lifted the goblet of wine, and as if making a toast he moved and pointed it at everyone in the room. "Well, well, it's nice to see you, too, my friends. To what do I owe this magnificent reception? Pray tell." He looked at Oliver Starkey his most trusted friend as if to read an answer in Starkey's face.

Oliver took La Valette's helmet and sword and handed them to the young knight. "Here, sir, take Sir La Valette's things and place them outside. You are dismissed," said a jovial Oliver. The young knight made a smart about turn and left the council chamber.

He took La Valette by the arm, showed him to the head of the table, precisely to the grand master's seat, then sat down next to him. Everyone else sat down as well, and slowly the commotion subsided until there was a pregnant silence.

"Well? For goodness sake will someone please tell me what this is all about and the urgency of your invitation for me to come? I was about to finish writing my report on board the *St. Anne* when your messenger interrupted me. How is the Grand Master, pray tell me?"

By popular consent, Oliver Starkey, as La Valette's closest friend and the most learned in the gathering, had been appointed spokesperson by the Supreme Council and charged to explain the situation to the new arrival.

Starkey cleared his throat and began. "We have collectively considered the order's present urgent situation. In view of Grand Master Sengle's condition who is in a deep coma from which he may not recover, we have decided to elect a new grand master immediately. We feel that our present situation is such that we cannot afford the tradition of waiting for Grand Master Sengle to die before appointing a new grand master. Our situation is far from satisfactory; in fact our situation is serious. Our enemy is getting more aggressive following several defeats at our hands, and we fear he may be planning on attacking our island. The situation calls for our order to appoint a new leader forthwith so that we can make decisive plans and carry out works in our defenses that, God knows, are well overdue."

La Valette interrupted. "Say no more, I agree with your thinking. We should delay no more in appointing a new leader. Have you thought as to when you will convene all the knights for the Grand Election vote to determine the new grand master? There are obviously a few excellent candidates that come to mind."

"We are glad that you, as one of the most senior officers in the order, agree with our proposition that we cannot afford to wait. We are not seeking to hold a Grand Election. Three days ago, in your absence, the Supreme Council met in a gathering with all the knights on the island, and it unanimously decided that you, Sir Jean Parisot de la Valette, should be named our next grand master of the Order of St. John of Jerusalem and Rhodes. We all agree that you alone have the experience and command the respect and confidence of all the knights. The Supreme Council and all the knights will pledge their loyalty to your person."

La Valette, in his customary humble way, sat there and looked around at all the familiar faces, who watched with affectionate and almost pleading smiles. He in turn looked directly at each of them, nodding his head gently. He knew them all, knew all their personal successes and trials, their hurts, and their joys. He had fought with most of them on many occasions in various theatres of war. With a knowing look, he searched their faces further for a hint of deception, joke even, but he found none. What he saw was simple trust and affection. He realized for the first time that he was indeed their senior not only in rank but also in age; he would in fact turn sixty four that same year. He raised his arm asking to be heard.

"Are you sure you want me to be grand master? You all know that I am not happy with the way the order and its members have been conducting themselves. You know my views; I have made them known to most of you on many occasions, and I warn you that if I become grand master I intend to make many changes.

"Those who have shown insubordination and have left the convent will be tracked down and punished. The order must be restored to its former standards. It will be put into shipshape, and all must work as a team. There is no room in the order for individualism, laziness or dishonesty. I expect my ship to perform like clockwork. But alas, I am greatly humbled and honoured that you put your trust in me. If it is God's will, I accept your valued nomination."

A thunderous applause and cheers filled the chamber. "Viva Grand Master La Valette! Three cheers for the new grand master!"

The grand master's installation ceremony took place on the following day. The Bishop of Malta, Monseigneur Carolus Caruana, Prior to the Order of St. John, and confessor to the new Grand Master performed the ceremonial appointment and the solemn mass that followed. The bishop sent a quick dispatch to His Holiness Pope John III in Rome, informing him of the circumstances and the reason for the order's appointment.

The day after the installation, Grand Master Emeritus Claudio Sengle died in his sleep. The great funeral took place, and the coffin was taken in procession from Birgu, across the bridge of boats to the church in the new city founded and built by Grand Master Sengle himself and named after him, Senglea, formerly L'Isle.

Order in the Order

La Valette was known for his organizational ability and meticulous planning, and he lost no time getting started. He called Sir Oliver Starkey, Pietro del Car, and the order's bishop, Carolus Caruana, to his chamber. "We need to act fast and efficiently. Sir Oliver Starkey, I appoint you as my senior advisor and my personal secretary. And you, Pietro del Car, I appoint you as Sir Oliver's lieutenant.

"We will create several advisory councils; I leave the appointments to these councils to your good judgment. The first council will be named to enforce the order's conventional rules and at the same time reform those rules of the order if necessary. Since the ancient rules have fallen in disarray and much insubordination and disrespect to rules have crept in, I appoint you, Bishop Carolus Caruana, to head this council. You in turn are free to name, at your own discretion, five other members to do this soon. Remember that five knights have recently deserted the order after creating a lot of internal strife; I want them found and brought back to recant.

"Knights must be prohibited from living outside the confines of their respective auberges. Dueling must be disallowed and drinking and dicing made illegal. These have crept in and have remained unchecked. It must be stopped. Bishop, I know you will restore the order's ancient reputation. I thank you for your cooperation. You may leave us now so you can start your work without delay."

La Valette then addressed himself to Sir Oliver Starkey. Oliver had sat down close to the grand master's chair and was taking brief notes with his good arm. His notes would later be expanded and written up by his religious clerk.

"Oliver, I wish you to prepare official papers for the immediate pardon and release of Marshal de Vallier from his home confinement, for as you know, grand master Juan de Homedes wrongfully imprisoned him after the fall of Tripoli. I want a full judicial letter of pardon and exoneration from all blame for the defeat of Tripoli wrongfully attributed to de Vallier. I also wish and order that de Vallier be appointed Grand Bailiff of Largo. He deserves a highly responsible position within the order that would set our old friend de Vallier close to us. I want him in my top advisory committee, as soon as he is able to take up the post, close to us, we must use his vast experience of warfare."

"Since funds and materials are required for a possible war, we must establish a diplomatic council whose responsibility will be to act as ambassadors for the order, and who will visit the various monarchs and princes in Europe demand fulfillment of their ancient obligations to the order to provide funds, men, and arms. Many of these have been in dereliction of their obligations to the defense of Christianity. I will not allow them to renege on their sacred oath," added the grand master with great determination.

"Grand Master, I have several excellent men in mind, selected from the different Langues, who will depart immediately, as soon as we dictate the official letters of introduction and instructions."

On the following day, these ambassadors were dispatched with letters to all the heads of state in Europe. The same ambassadors were given letters addressed to all those knights who had earlier returned to their estates or courts of their respective sovereigns saying, ***The Ottoman Turks intend to besiege Malta. Report to the convent, before spring, to Grand Master Jean Parisot de la Valette.***

The third advisory council which the grand master formed was the defense council. He asked Oliver to call all the engineers to a meeting.

Maps of the two islands of Malta and Gozo were laid out upon the large table. They had a preliminary discussion of their intended policy. And as was La Valette's custom, he would not be satisfied until he and his team of experts toured on horseback all the fortifications, whilst the engineers took notes and made observations and suggestions regarding the fortifications that required strengthening and what new fortifications required building. There was an air of excitement and expectancy amongst the group of engineers and commanders. There was an air of dynamic activity and or purpose in the island never seen before.

An army of stonemasons and carpenters from the local population was enrolled as builders, and many were employed as store clerks and clerks of works. A host of non-Muslim slaves were assigned to the quarries to handle the raw material, and were promised their freedom in four years time if they complied fully. Teams of oxen and mules with carts were soon appropriated by the order. However, the grand master insisted that everything that was commandeered would be paid for.

The task was ambitious. It was estimated that all the work that needed to be done had to be finished within two months before the good sailing weather set in. La Valette set out to correct the defects that had crept in during the construction of Fort St. Elmo at the time of Juan de Homedes. This required the building of an additional ravelin on the Marsamxett side to prevent an approach from that direction to the cavalier fort. Both ravelin and the cavalier were then connected with the main fort by a fixed bridge and a drawbridge respectively. The wood and earth used in this building had to be imported from Sicily, which was less than two days sailing in a north-westerly direction. The order's own big vessels undertook the transportation of building materials. The smaller galleys were employed to transport other forms of merchandise.

"Water, yes water!" emphasized the grand master, addressing the engineers. "You must appoint someone of your group to be the water engineer, whose task and responsibility will be primarily to find ingenious ways to find and conserve water. We must always have water. If we are to withstand a long siege, we must not run. We still have a few months when we can expect rain. Every drop that falls from heaven must be conserved. We must build large and small underground cellars for the storage of this heavenly commodity. If any house is found not to have its own underground water cistern then it must be made to provide one. An army cannot fight without bread or water."

La Valette's enthusiasm was contagious. An engineer eagerly offered suggestions to the grand master. The man appointed as the water engineer soon ordered deep water-storage tanks to be built under every building within the fortification walls. Any rain that fell on the roofs was directed to downpipes into the huge and small whitewashed underground cisterns. The engineer ordered that thousands of clay water bottles be filled from the natural water springs at Marsa and Mdina and be carried or ferried to their destinations and stored in special chambers in the various forts. Priority was given to this, as was the digging of new water wells. Even though some of them produced unsatisfactory-tasting water, they would be useful for purposes other than drinking.

Oliver said, "Grand Master, we also need to store plenty of grain. Grain and water will keep our army going; we must bring more grain from Sicily."

"Take note that we should triple the storage capacity for the grain that we intend to import. Ensure that this is within reach of our fortifications and that the stores are not easily accessible to the enemy should we be isolated." The grand master nodded his approval, and everyone knew that the quartermaster would immediately be instructed to order the grain.

The planning team visited several strategic locations within the forts where La Valette ordered man-made dry caves to be dug into the limestone and sandstone strata for the storage of the grain and the flour that was ground out of it. The same had to be done for the storage of ammunition and gunpowder, which had been arriving in great quantities from Venice. Round cannonballs and arms were also stored in magazines distributed around the fortifications. The powder was stored inside wooden barrels water-proofed with canvass in order to keep it dry.

The arsenal was busy producing swords and suits of mail, making new ones and repairing old ones. All of them were distributed as they came off the production line.

The armoury, with a team of pottery makers, was busy constructing round clay containers the size of ostrich eggs. The round container was a new invention by the knights. The clay sphere had one opening. An inflammable liquid, imported from Libya, was poured into the sphere, a piece of fuse was inserted into the top, and then the opening was sealed with wax. To throw this bomb at the enemy the ball was placed in a sling, a piece of fishing net, that acted as launcher. The fuse was lit, the container and net was swung around over the thrower's head. When enough speed had been gathered, one end of the net-sling was let go and the round container travelled a long distance in the direction of the enemy. The glow of the lit cordage increased as the sphere flew towards its target. On contact the clay container broke, the liquid spread about, the burning fuse would set the inflammable liquid on fire. When it came into contact with an object or person it would explode into flames, causing pandemonium amongst the enemy lines. Clothes and skin alike would be set ablaze. The liquid poured was a volatile mixture of a thin black liquid, the consistency of olive oil found in the interior of Libya or Algiers.

La Valette gave further instructions. "Our success depends upon our system of communications. We must have a system in place whereby we know precisely what is happening at any point on our island at any given time. The quickest way of sending messages, particularly announcing the landing of enemies, is by conventional signal fires. Therefore, for long distance signals, I want you to erect a system of warning beacons at several strategic points such as at Mdina, St. Angelo, St. Elmo, and in several guard posts along the coast. There has to be a warning post erected at the top of Gozo's castle that relays signals all the way to the mount at Sciberras peninsula. I want no less than fourteen signal-towers built. Here, here, here and here." He indicated on the map with the tip of his finger." The engineers were quick to take notes. "Reliable men must be posted at these places to give the signal. There must be piled stocks of fagots and brushwood, and the black liquid, this must only be used for sending signals at short notice. They must not be used, even when it gets cold at night, for warming the troops. Anyone who breaks this order will be severely punished. Our lives depend on a good and reliable signaling system. We must also have teams of mounted messengers assigned to each of these lookout spots to report to headquarters the detailed nature of the original beacon's signal, particularly when the enemy is sighted. I also think that one of you young engineers must have full responsibility for organizing this signal system. A large team of young runners is to be formed and trained at each of the fortresses to carry inter-fortress messages from one commander to the other.

"We must instruct farmers to collect their harvest quickly and take it, together with their animals, either to Birgu or Mdina. If and when the Turks land and the harvest is not completed the ground must be set on fire and the crops burnt so that when the enemy goes foraging the land, they will find it barren. The Turks will be forced to bring all their supplies by ship and they have a long way to travel to do this. Instruct the inhabitants of Gozo to do likewise and to take refuge inside the citadel as soon as an attack begins.

"All men who can bear arms and have not joined the militia are to rally to the standard of the order. All must be supplied with arms. Orders must be given to the population that when the retreat is called, all water wells are to be poisoned to deprive the enemy of water."

A recount of his manpower revealed a count of six hundred knights and their servants-at-arms. There were counted two thousand various troops from Spain, France and Italy. His original force of Maltese irregulars had increased to between eight and nine thousand men to virtually all the male population of Malta.

Following La Valettes efforts to improve relations between the order and the local Maltese population, this force was driven by a genuine desire for revenge against the Barbary corsairs who in the past had often pillaged the island and had taken many Maltese people as slaves—men, women, and children alike. There was neither scope nor hope for increasing the number of soldiers from within the island, so unless reinforcements came from abroad, what he had was all he had to confront the Ottoman Turks with.

"Grand Master, your presence is required above at the ramparts," a servant reported to La Valette. That day he happened to be in Fort St. Angelo. He climbed the steps and as he looked out to sea he saw a fleet of twenty-seven galleys approaching Malta. From their silhouette and the large pendants unfolded by the wind, he could see that the vessels belonged to the viceroy of Sicily. His first thoughts were that the viceroy had sent the reinforcements and assistance he had requested. His confidence increased when he learned that the viceroy himself, Don Garcia de Toledo, was with the fleet.

Regrettably, La Valette's hopes were crashed. The viceroy was only visiting the island to inform the grand master that he had asked King Phillip II of Spain to send 25,000 infantry troops to Malta, but La Valette knew that the king could not afford such a luxury. Don Toledo however said that the king had mentioned of sending about a thousand Spanish foot soldiers in the near future. He advised the grand master that he should personally avoid skirmishes and sorties. With great annoyance La Valette silently listened to Don Garcia de Toledo's unnecessary advice.

Toledo's most valuable advice was that he should evacuate women, children, and old people off the island because they could not contribute in a siege, and would consume valuable provisions. La Valette declared, "Now that we have improved the defenses of Fort St. Angelo and St. Elmo, we must apply ourselves untiringly to improving the defenses of Birgu."

They began to build make-shift houses within the forts to cater for the increasing incoming population.

Normally all cannons were placed in the high ramparts and bastions, but La Valette had a cunning idea. He ordered several embrasures to be opened at the base of the fortifications walls facing the entrance to the various harbours. Once these were built, cannons were placed inside the placements, and large sliding doors were constructed to hide the gun placements, which could be closed and opened at will making it possible for the guns to fire parallel to sea level and only few feet above the water. The idea was to assure accuracy and increase the chances of hitting moving vessels that dared to enter the harbour. Such a strategy would catch the enemy by surprise; much damage could be done before the enemy vessels escaped the trap.

La Valette needed the loyalty of all non-Islamic slaves; he did not want to allow slaves to waste away in dungeons, so he gave them an undertaking promising them that if they cooperated with him, and they were victorious against the Muslims, he would grant them their freedom. To support his promise he proceeded to have the slave dungeons converted into living quarters, the grand master was using more than 1,500 slaves for a useful purpose on the defenses.

One last item to be taken care of was the disposition of the order's galleys. La Valette concluded that a land battle was inevitable. Therefore, he had no option but to send the majority of the galleys to Sicily. A couple of them—the *St. Gabriel* and the *Royal Coronne*, which needed much work—were sunk off Birgu, where, if it became necessary, they could be raised later. At the same time, they could cause a serious hazard to any enemy ships that ventured to enter the harbour.

The Battle—The Cross and the Koran

Malta was no longer the barren island that the order had landed on in the year 1530. At first the order had not been favourable to residing in this island, which King Charles V had gifted them, together with the city of Tripoli, with full sovereignty. Most senior knights, including La Valette himself, would have preferred Tripoli as the order's centre of operations.

An inspection of the island in the early days revealed that it was totally unlike Rhodes—a disappointing, dreary, rocky, barren place with thin topsoil, where very few crops could be planted. Trees and scrubs were few and far between. However its most valuable asset was not lost on the knights. It had excellent natural harbours where military vessels could anchor and be protected from heavy storms.

It showed great potential as a fortress, Malta had no natural defenses against a landing from hostile forces. For years the island had been defenseless against the Barbary corsairs who would raid it, mainly for slaves and goats. The inhabitants of the coastal villages would find refuge in the only inland place of refuge that had defensive walls: Mdina, known as the "silent city". Mdina was the island's principal city and capital, where its few local and notable families lived in relative safety. Mdina had fine buildings and a fairly large church and was surrounded by a high wall—hence its Arab name, which means "walled city". But the order had not chosen Mdina as the centre of their activity. Instead, because of their expanding seafaring activities, they chose the areas of Birgu and L'Isle, rich in natural harbours and small beaches on which to land the galleys.

Much had been done in the previous thirty years by preceding grand masters. Because of Malta's irregular coastline, the task had not been easy. Various forts had been built at strategic points. Since the island was of hard-packed sedimentary sandstone and some limestone these raw materials served as quarries providing plentiful building materials. The packed sandstone was not as hard as limestone but its compactness lent itself as a building material and was easier to work with. Since the order had arrived on the island, thousands of slaves had been assigned to the task of quarrying the large, rectangular building blocks and carrying them on carts to the building sites. Wherever one looked one could see the countryside full of a steady stream of block-carrying carts and teams of sweaty men working the nearby quarries.

One building project was the defenses around the small peninsula called L'Isla (L'Isola) now called Senglea, it turned out to be a highly vulnerable place because of its proximity to the dockyard and stores. So without delay La Valette started to build a massive wall about 275 meters long around the seafront of Senglea, facing the heights of Corradino Hill to the east.

The order had developed its magnificent maritime fleet in Malta's natural safe-haven harbours. A dockyard had a built-in inlet between Birgu and L'Isla. The chief of the Maltese craftsmen was one Giuseppi Caruana, who had a team of excellent shipwrights. They imported wood from the Italian coast and built and repaired many galleys and other vessels in this dockyard.

For many years, relations between the knights of the order and the native Maltese population had been strained. The public relations attitude of the knights remained as it had been during their two-hundred-year stay in Rhodes; they viewed the locals as inferior and treated them with contempt.

La Valette changed that attitude. He ordered that the local population should be treated with respect and civility, with no verbal or physical abuse towards the Maltese people; any knight found breaking this order would be severely punished. He gave strict instructions that, where possible, the native population should be employed in all trades and at all levels. Many locals learned the art of stonemasonry, shipbuilding and arms building. Others soon learned the trades of clerks and store men.

Many others joined the order's navy and army in various capacities. In this way, La Valette gained the confidence of the local people and as the local people gained the confidence of the knights. Many improved their standard of living, while Valette's military and naval force acquired much-needed manpower with the addition of the non-Muslim slaves and the local militia. The whole island had become a beehive of activity with a purpose, namely to confront the Muslim forces should they attempt to invade the island. Above all, the devout Maltese Christians respected the grand master for his exemplary religiosity.

La Valette wrote to all the chapters of the order in Europe to re-establish his rightful authority over the order, particularly in the provinces of Germany and of Venice, which had hitherto refused to pay the taxes levied by the general chapters. He reminded them that if Malta fell to the Muslims, Venice and Germany would be next on the list for invasion by the Sultan, so it would be in their best interests to pay it, or pay a worse price later. His argument prevailed, and they paid the money.

La Valette's handling of affairs was producing much cooperation. Even the local population began to see him as the only one who could liberate them from the threat of the island's occupation by Islam. The island that the apostle St. Paul had converted to Christianity could not fall into the hands of the Muslim.

The grand master even tried hard to convince the queen of England, Elizabeth I, to lift the suppression of the English Order of St. John to allow nobles to enroll once again into the English Langue. Hopes were raised for a while, but nothing materialized. Only two English knights were left in Malta: Oliver Starkey and James Shelley, who arrived at a later date than Starkey. With so few English members La Valette decised to sell off all the property the English Langue had in Malta. The grand master had great faith in the fighting spirit of the English knights, but it was not to be.

He wrote to the pope and the kings of Spain and France, pressuring them to come to his assistance in the interest of Christendom.

The Spies

La Valette asked James Shelly to personally oversee a strategy for an intelligence-gathering group. He suggested to the Englishman to appoint Peter of Rhodes, formerly Tafur-Ali, to be James Shelly's second in command because Peter of Rhodes knew the geography around Turkey and its language. It was of primary importance to know the enemy's strength and its plans. James Shelly dispatched Peter of Rhodes and his heads of espionage to Constantinople, Crete, Rhodes, and North African ports. From there the network of spies, with its planned strategy, infiltrated the Ottoman ranks. It was ordered to report on troop movements, concentrations of fighting vessels, and the transportation of essential provisions.

Those at a higher level of the espionage ladder needed to find out the plans and policies of the generals; there were plenty of generals around. The spies were instructed to gather information from prostitutes who sold their services to senior officers, and to pay highly those slaves who worked in the Sultan's palace and attended to assistants and aides-de-camp. So Peter of Rhodes and his spies sat in taverns, eating houses, and palaces, listening to conversations of soldiers, and watching them as they marched or patrolled the walls. He chatted to traders at their stalls, and to old men sitting around wells, talking of their days in the army.

In fact, Sir James Shelly left no stone unturned, no keyhole left unattended.

Soon, news reached Malta of the ongoing Ottoman preparation for war. European diplomats, Venetians in particular, reported on the assembly of a large fleet at Constantinople. Sensitive information began to leak out from Constantinople to Grand Master La Valette about the extraordinarily busy work at the Ottoman shipyards. An urgent message from a spy in the port of Algiers gave the vital information that Dragut the Barbary corsair was setting sail north to Crete to meet with the Ottoman fleet there after it left Constantinople now renamed Istanbul by the Muslim.

La Valette calculated that this rendezvous would take place at least a month later, which gave him an idea as to when the much-expected attack on the island would take place.

La Valette calmly took in all information as it came. His cool demeanour conveyed to his advisors that he knew exactly what had to be done. He never relaxed in improving the fortifications or practising defensive maneuvers.

What he did not know was that the Turks had sent their own spies to Malta, two of whom came disguised as fishermen, a Sclavonian and a Greek, two renegade engineers who had visited Malta before and who had reported to the Sultan all that was going on in Malta. They had drawn sketches of the fortifications pointing out all the weak spots. Their report gave the Turks the impression that the island could not resist a Turkish attack for long.

Reports from the Christian spy network were now frequent and urgent. The Ottoman fleet and the army had embarked the vessels and were now leaving the Bosphorus on their way to Istanbul and then on to the Mediterranean. The coordination of all the information coming in from the spy network led to the conclusion that the army that had been put together was in the order of 40,000 men, composed of 6,300 janissaries of the finest troops; about nine thousand Spahis from Anatolia and Rumania; four thousand Layalers, religious fanatics who welcomed death in battle; the rest slaves and volunteers. The fleet consisted of 130 galleys and forty galliots. Eleven other big ships were loaded with gunpowder, each carrying five hundred men and over a thousand cannonballs. Above all, they carried monstrously large siege cannons. The command of the troops was in the hands of General Mustapha Pasha, and the naval force in the command of Admiral Reis Pasha Piali. The Sultan knew that these two were always at loggerheads, so he told them to wait for the arrival of Dragut, the notorious corsair, who had an excellent knowledge of Malta and had fought La Valette on several occasions.

A further report from his principal spymaster, Peter of Rhodes, gathered from merchants and fishermen, said that the Ottoman fleet had left the Grande Porte with the large sailing ships in tow behind the galleys. He heard during a calm, some of the ships had been carried onto a sandbank, and how one of them had sunk and a thousand men drowned. Another vessel with several cannons and eight thousand barrels of gunpowder overturned and all cargo was also lost. These losses however did not interfere with the fleet's inexorable progress. He had no doubt that the Sultan would immediately make good on all those losses. As a tactician, La Valette knew that an invasion of this sort would not be launched in winter, and galleys were notorious in bad weather. Moreover, an invasion in spring would carry the advantage of a whole summer ahead for an army to consolidate its gains. So he revised his previous idea and concluded that the Turks would attack sometime in April or May. This gave him a little over six months to make his final preparations. He doubled his efforts deepening ditches on the landward sides of Birgu and Senglea while providing larger cannons for Fort St. Michael. All beautiful Arab-style civilian houses, outside these two fortifications, were razed to the ground.

With the arrival of each vessel came the arrival of new knights and mercenaries to join the Christian forces. Regrettably, the number of arrivals was not impressive and did not meet with La Valette's expectations, never-the-less he was grateful to them. It was obvious that many of the pledges he had received were not being kept. Messengers arrived with moneybags, but these contained a fraction of what had been promised. Close to four thousand Maltese irregulars, from the other islands, joined his army. The Maltese people did not lack courage;

they were a hard-working, fearless people, accustomed, for centuries, to aggressive invasions by foreign powers. They had experience in skirmishing with corsairs and others, but had never had leadership and did not have experience in long-drawn formal war. La Valette took care of that. He started a crash programme of military training, square-bashing, arms training, musketry, gunnery, bowman-ship with crossbows, and sword handling. Because of the need to conserve gunpowder they were allowed only three live shots at a target, with a premium given for the best shot. Gunnery practice with real ammunition, however small, always raised the morale of the men.

But La Valette knew that this was not enough; he knew that unless he received reinforcements from elsewhere, they would have a very rough time. La Valette's only hope was King Phillip II of Spain. After all, Malta was still considered a Spanish dependency.

However, La Valette's enthusiasm for a confrontation was not in any way diminished, one quality that distinguished La Valette from previous grand masters was his sense of foresight, based not as much on his philosophical way of thinking as on his long military experience. He had an unshakeable faith that God would be at his side. He knew, too, that if the order were to be defeated, it would finish them forever, as the Ottoman Turks would certainly not repeat their chivalrous gesture of Rhodes. This reasoning gave La Valette his strong sense of purpose.

His principal spies, Sir James Shelly and Peter of Rhodes, returned to the island to join in its defense. Besides, La Valette had another plan for Peter of Rhodes, when the Turks landed he would assign him to personally infiltrate the Turkish camp surreptitiously in order to gather intelligence from behind the lines he was to take with him a group of hand-picked men.

The arrival of spring brought with it the arrival of the sailing season. It was highly possible that the enemy could appear on the horizon at any time.

The grand master called a general assembly of all the knights regarding the impending battle; he was a great believer in inspiring and informing his troops of their purpose. He reckoned that this might be the last general assembly that the knights could hold before taking their defensive positions.

"Ours is the great battle of the Cross against the Koran. A formidable army of infidels is getting ready to invade our island. We, for our part, are the chosen soldiers of the Cross, and if heaven requires the sacrifice of our lives, there can be no better occasion than the one that is to come. Let us hasten then, my brothers, to the sacred altar. There we will renew our vows, and will strengthen by our faith in the sacred sacraments and our cause and that contempt for death will alone render us invincible."

With these last words from their leader, all the knights rose from their seats and cheered, exulting and united in spirit. Then they all marched in procession to the church where they sang the Mass and received Holy Communion, which went further to dissolve any traces of weakness that might have remained. Afterwards, they were detailed to their various defensive positions.

La Valette speculated that the enemy would attack near the bay of Marsaxlokk, but did not rule out the northern bay of Marsamxett, adjacent to the Grand Harbour. Therefore Fort St. Elmo, which covered both harbours, needed to be well manned. But so far its complement had been six knights and six hundred men under the command of Knight Luigi Broglia, with an assistant knight named Juan de Guaras as his aide-de-camp. Seeing that St. Elmo would be a strategic target, he assigned another forty-six knights, all of whom had volunteered from the various Langues. A couple of days later, of the thousand promised by the viceroy, only two hundred Spanish infantry soldiers arrived from Sicily. These too were sent to swell the garrison of St. Elmo with their commander Don Juan de la Cerda.

Most of the order's cavalry were sent to Mdina to reinforce the garrison there; horses were impractical within the confines of small forts and many others were stabled in the various fortresses. Some more soldiers were sent to the castle at Gozo. The rest of the knights and Maltese infantry units were to remain in the complex of Birgu, Fort St. Angelo, and Fort St. Michael, because these could interchange their troops according to circumstances and the vagaries of the enemy. With all his dispositions in place, La Valette it was time decided to wait for the enemy to take the initiative.

Arrival of the Turks

The island awoke to a calm and warm sunny morning. There was a low mist that covered the horizon like a curtain, which kept visibility to a minimum. Within an hour a cool breeze dispersed the mist, and those on watch on the ramparts of forts of St. Elmo and St. Angelo stood gazing in amazement at the mass of tiny masts looming in the horizon. Spread along the distance, where the haze had been, sailed the Turkish Armada, slowly making its way towards the island.

The prearranged signal on sighting the enemy was set into motion. Three gun-shots were fired from Fort St. Angelo. The fort at Mdina and the castle in Gozo soon repeated the signal. The whole population was now on full alert. The military personnel immediately went to their stations and prepared for war.

No one had counted on the disruption that the populace would cause as they moved from the surrounding countryside inside the fortifications, as they had agreed to do when the time came. That time was now. Farmers arrived with horses and donkeys loaded with stores and provisions, their families carrying household goods on their backs and life animals of all kinds. Instead of hearing the noise of an army getting ready for war, what was heard was the predominant bleating of several hundreds of goats, the neighing of horses, and braying of donkeys, the squawking of geese and chickens, plus the excited shouting of their owners. It took all the patience of the commanders to organize this influx of humanity and beasts. On the other hand, Mdina, with its noble population, was relatively orderly; they had done this move many times before.

Fortunately, the enemy did not decide to land on that first day of the pandemonium. Instead, the never-ending line of ships continued sailing up the coastline, taunting the residents as they passed close to the fortifications. The army on land exercised much restraint in firing their cannons upon the passing ships.

La Valette sent a detachment of cavalry to follow the enemy fleet round the coast so they could observe and report if and when they landed. Since he expected them to land close to Marsasirroco, he gave orders for the water wells, from there to the Marsa district, to be poisoned. A giant iron chain, which could be raised and lowered, had been built and laid across the entrance between Castel Sant'Angelo and the Sciberras peninsula. Its purpose was to impede the entrance of vessels should a seaborne attack take place at that point.

La Valette immediately sent a fast, small sailing boat to Sicily with an urgent message to the viceroy informing him that the Ottoman attack had started and he needed help more than ever before.

The knights and Maltese militia were prepared and waited for the imminent assault. The chevalier Melchior d'Eguaras was dispatched to Mdina with the remaining body of cavalry. On the way they intended to intercept and harass the Turkish forces and foraging parties when they landed.

The guards were at their posts. The three Langues of Provence, Auvergne, and France held the landward side of Birgu. Aragon, which included Catalonia and Navarre, stood to arms along the westward side up to Fort St. Angelo. Castile defended the great bastion next to soldiers of Provence. The Germanic Langues held the rest of the line. The English Langue claimed only two knights, though for nostalgic reasons and out of respect for Sir Oliver Starkey, La Valette assigned to them detachments of various races to defend that part of the fortifications.

Some of the Ottoman fleet made a turnaround. They sailed back on the same route they had come and started to disembark at various points. Word started to come in during the day from farmers who had not heeded the earlier instructions and who were now fleeing before a vast, dark, tide of men and machines that had landed further south down the coast in Marsasirocco. The Ottoman Turks were coming.

But La Valette had already received the news from his cavalry scouts. The rest of the population was woken to the frenetic clanging of bells. They watched in dread as the Ottoman force spilled out from the vessels like swarms of ants and covered the whole countryside with men dressed in colourful uniforms and equipment. Three thousand men had landed at this point. Thousand others were getting ready to land a short distance away. They marched in precise order of formation, approaching the village of Zeitun, one mile and a half from the sea. Lances held high with flattering colourful pendants gave the whole area an unreal image.

A cavalry detachment sent by Marshal de Copier descended upon an advance patrol of Turks. Outnumbered and surrounded by the advancing janissaries and light infantry, the knights' cavalry patrol made a hit-and-run attack and withdrew. From Zeitun the Ottoman army advanced to the hamlet of Zabbar and then proceeded on open ground to the walls of Castile at Birgu.

By now all the water wells in the plains of Marsa had been poisoned, and all crops had been gathered or burned. The Ottomans had invaded a desolate countryside. Soon the enemy would be outside the walls and setting up camp.

That afternoon the siege began.

Again Marshal de Copier dispatched another surprise attack to confront the oncoming Turks. A fierce battle took place outside the wall, with heavy casualties on both sides, Marshal de Copier, after disrupting the enemy and killing many retreated under cover of the land-side guns from Birgu and Senglea.

La Valette again ordered a general assembly in all the forts. He gave them a short, encouraging speech.

"Brothers in Christ, the enemy approaches, but our order is ready to meet any and all challenges from those who wish to destroy our faith. But our faith is unbreakable, unshakeable; our faith in Christ will overcome the enemy. We shall be victorious; the Cross and St. John will prevail! Give the order! All our military and holy banners are to be flown from our ramparts and towers!"

In an attempt to confuse the enemy, La Valette sent another cavalry attack to confront a party of Turks farther inland, in the area of Marsa. A mounted messenger was sent to Mdina with the order. The Mdina cavalry was dispatched and descended from the slopes at the rear of the unsuspecting enemy. It was a hit-and-run attack, leaving many dead, wounded, and damaged stores and equipment. Except for these skirmishes by the cavalry, the Turkish army spread unopposed over the whole south of the island. They took their losses in their stride.

Overnight the country was dressed in multicoloured tents and banners; they arose from the ground like crocuses in early spring.

La Valette stuck to his original strategy of meeting the overwhelming enemy from behind the fortresses rather than in the open, a strategy that had worked before in sieges in the Holy Land and in Rhodes. The order had become highly specialized in defensive warfare. It had to be the same in Malta.

According to Ottoman intelligence, the Castile fortification walls, on the inland side of Fort St. Angelo, in proximity to the dockyard, was the weakest part of the fortifications, and it was here that the Ottomans were concentrating their efforts. La Valette's companies knew their drill well; troops were positioned accordingly with a prearranged plan. The Spanish, Italian, French, Germans, Portuguese, and Maltase contingents were now ready.

La Valette recognized that the physical defenses were not his main concern. The question lay in his soldiers or weaknesses. Wars were won and lost on four vital elements: morale, discipline, organization, and courage. This type of defense tactics raised morale.

He studied his soldiers on the walls—their alertness and their demeanor. Were they careless or slack? Were their officers decisive and disciplined? Were they confident of their strength, or merely arrogant? These were the questions that he sought answers to. He continually preached the heroic code set down by Heracles: *"Glory and service to God. Courage and love of homeland. Strength without cruelty."* This should be each man's creed.

In preparation, huge sacks of sand had been hauled from the beach to counter the spread of fires should the Turks shoot naphtha balls over the walls, which would crash down on rooftops that lined the walls bursting into flames. Lots of water barrels and buckets were stacked against protective walls in readiness for the same purpose.

Early in the morning, two days after the enemy's landing, troops on the walls of the Castile fortifications were getting impatient waiting and hiding under the parapets, against the volleys of shots, from the accurate, long-barreled muskets strafing them from the orderly skirmishing lines of the disciplined janissaries.

La Valette faced a lifelong enemy whom he had fought on many occasions. His opponent was General Mustapha Pasha, who came from one of the oldest and most distinguished families in Turkey, from an ancient dynasty that claimed descent from Ben Welid, the standard-bearer of the Prophet Mohammed at the time of the conquest of Arabia. La Valette knew that he was highly devoted to the Sultan and was considered a religious fanatic, known for his violence and brutality.

La Valette's orders were clear and strict: no knight must venture outside the walls; the strategy was to fight from a defensive position, it was their only hope of success against such an overwhelming force.

However, a company of young knights thought differently. Eager to engage the enemy, they disobeyed orders, and in their eagerness they opened the gates and charged the enemy in an unexpected but brave attack on the yet unprepared and unsuspecting Muslim troops.

When La Valette saw this he was furious, though at the same time he realized that he too, as a young knight, had done something similar in the battle of Rhodes. Realizing that the young knights might get into trouble and a beating, he immediately ordered three detachments of knights and Maltese militia to join the young knights in the spontaneous sortie. La Valette was hugely surprised and happy that the Maltese soldiers had turned out to be extremely brave and disciplined warriors, he began to rely on them more and more as the fighting went on.

The surprise attack was most successful, with musketry and steel-to-steel fighting. Over one hundred Ottoman soldiers in the front line were killed; the artillery from the bastions above fired over their heads and hit the rear enemy lines with much success. But La Valette could see from his vantage point that the knights would soon be surrounded and outflanked by the enormous and superior Ottoman force, so he ordered the trumpeter to signal the retreat call. With the trumpet call sounding above them, the knights withdrew in fighting order and managed to enter the safety of the fortification with much exultation and celebration. Their first taste of combat had luckily been successful; the action lasted six hours. The young knights had been "blooded".

Twenty-one Christian soldiers were killed and over 150 wounded. But from where La Valette stood he could see that several hundred Turks lay dead on the battlefield. As a victory this action served to raise the morale of the knights and Maltese militia who had fought with them.

As soon as they entered the fortress and the gates were closed La Valette stomped down from the ramparts and ordered the knights to fall in. He stood in front of them, feet apart and hands on hips, and shouted at them. "Idiots! What in heaven's name do you think you were doing? You disobeyed a direct order and placed, not just yourselves, but also the entire fort in peril by leaving the gate open. I repeat myself: our only chance of survival against this huge army is to fight them from the safety of the forts! Get that into your empty heads! Any attempt at an open confrontation with the enemy is a losing game. That does not mean that General Command may not, from time to time, order specific sorties to harass the enemy. Anyone who disobeys orders again will be punished."

He paused to turn, but then faced them again and added, "By the way . . . in passing, I might add that you fought well. That is all, dismissed and to your posts."

In the distance, huge, brightly coloured banners swirled in the hot air, making them appear distorted. The different multi-coloured squares and the uniforms distinguished divisions. The Ottoman generals had erected large coloured tents, with gigantic pendants flying from the tents' masts, and hundreds of smaller pendants of all colours carried at the point of the lances.

In front lay the Ottoman army, a formation nearly half a mile across, their appearance distorted by the haze. Thousands of men on horseback and thousands more foot soldiers waited patiently for their orders to march against the knights.

To the annoyance of the Turkish scouts, they found no food or provisions in the area between Birgu and Senglea and discovered that all the drinking wells were poisoned. Nothing but derelict houses, barren, rocky ground stood between them and the fortifications.

The beating of Muslim drums and clanging bells reached the knights behind the fortress walls and bounced off them like distant thunder. The horn trumpets relayed messages in a confusing sounds. After the trumpet sounds came the ululating battle cries from the enemy ranks, which spontaneously broke into a charge towards the fortress. The sight of this swarm of humanity, cloaks floating in the air, scimitars and lances flashing in the sunlight, and hundreds of banners at the end of long lances fluttering as they rushed with bestial shouts, was impressive.

Not to be outdone, La Valette had ordered that all the order's large flags and pendants, some black, some red, and others white, with their respective contrasting crosses, including the huge array of flags with religious images, was to fly high from the battlements and towers. As if by magic, a colourful and impressive sight emerged. In an instant the fortification walls transformed the fort's appearance, not for war, but for some great festive occasion. La Valette had planned this since he knew well how the Christian symbol of the cross and the religious images would disconcert his Muslim enemy. Similarly to drown out the musical sounds coming from the Ottoman lines, all the knights, sergeants, and militia men, women, and children, broke out into loud religious songs—Christian songs in Latin: *"Christus vivid, Christus exsulta, Christus vencid."* "Christ lives, Christ is exalted, and Christ conquers." La Valette knew that he was playing a psychological war game.

As soon as the enemy came into firing range a tremendous cacophony of gun noises filled the air as the battlement of Castile exploded into action. The oncoming mass of the Ottoman army was halted as if they had come into contact with an invincible wall.

True to his word General Command ordered night sorties to harass the Muslims. One of them was an attack by the knights' cavalry detachment. A skirmish ensued, but the mounted detachment had to withdraw under cover of the guns from Birgu and Senglea. Knights were first killed in this skirmish.

To their sorrow, the Portuguese knight Bartolomeo Faraone and the French knight Adrien de la Riviere were taken prisoner and interrogated by Mustapha Pasha himself. Under torture they revealed nothing, but later, when they could no longer resist the severe torture and interrogation, they confessed that the weakest point in the fortifications was the walls of Castile at Birgu, where they had been captured. This information confirmed the earlier intelligence that two of the Sultan's spies had reported. The truth was, in fact, that this fortification was indeed the strongest point, so even under torture the knights had played a dirty trick on Mustapha Pasha.

It was clear to La Valette from the enemy's position that the initial battle would centre on Castile, so he ordered all the foot soldiers from Mdina to be brought to the Birgu fortress, leaving behind only the cavalry in Mdina. He continued his effective quick hit-and-run surprise skirmishes on the Ottomans, taking several hundred prisoners.

That night a furious Mustapha ordered a heavy attack on the fortifications of Castile. La Valette raised his head and peered through the darkness over the gap in the crenulations of the ramparts. Ottoman Turks were gathering in the shadows and darkness of the rubble of the Arab-like dwellings that had been demolished ahead of the invasion. The Turks assaulted the walls with long ladders, while their cannons pounded overhead. Many managed to enter the fortification at various points. Ladders were pushed over when the defenders saw that two or more attackers were climbing the ladders. The night swelled with the sounds of battle, men screaming in pain or fury, swords ringing, shields clashing, cannonballs bouncing off walls. Smoke from hand guns, clouds of dense black smoke from cannons.

The order was given. "Fire bombs, throw firebombs!" Immediately dozens of firebombs exploded below among the attacking Turks whose flowing capes soon caught fire and set them ablaze, causing severe burns to the victims. Screams were heard everywhere around the fortifications. Illuminated figures frantically dashed below the walls. In spite of these awful deterrents several Muslim warriors clambered over the battlement wall and rushed towards La Valette and the company of his closest knights, whose assignment was to defend him. Aet La Valette took the initiative and rushed the assailants with furious screams of a battle cry that intimidated his attackers. "To me men! For the Cross! For St. John the Baptist!"

For a while it seemed that the Ottoman Turks were gaining a foothold along the wall. The knights did not break, but fought on with relentless courage. La Valette looked around to assess the situation and saw Pietro del Car and Emanuel Viale running to his aid with a company of thirty Maltese soldiers. They advanced in running formation, shields up, lances and swords swinging, and shouting their war cry, "*A Madonna!*" "For Our Lady!" The battlement was soon covered with the corpses of the attackers.

The night was full with the sounds of battle. The enemy had come to the wall as a single, solid mass. Many had fallen, crushed by the stones slung from above the city walls. Others, at the base of the walls, were burned alive in boiling oil, or blasted to bits and burned by the hand—bombs thrown from the walls above; many were hit by lead balls thrown by slingers. Those who actually reached the battlement faced such fierce resistance that they either surrendered or threw themselves over the walls, preferring broken bones to sure death. The Ottoman army's casualties were heavy.

A knight brought forward a captured Turkish standard and gave it to La Valette for his inspection. According to the report, a knight from Navarre, Jean de Morgut, had killed a richly dressed Turkish officer. The knight took the officer's gold bracelet and handed this to La Valette.

There was an inscription in Arabic on the inside of the bracelet. La Valette read this aloud. *"I do not come to Malta for wealth or honour, but to save my soul."*

"This, gentlemen, is the kind of enemy that we are facing." For the enemy's benefit he took the Turkish standard and waved it over his head. "Here, see come and get it, if you dare".

Mustapha Pasha soon realized that the two Christian prisoners had lied in their confession, that the information from the two early spies was intentionally misleading. These fortifications were not easy to take. On the contrary, they were strongly defended, and the walls were resisting the heavy shots from the large culverin guns. Castile would not be an easy nut to crack.

Mustapha gave explicit orders sentencing Adrian de la Riviere and Bartolomeo Faraone to be beheaded forthwith and Mustapha proceeded to make other plans.

When word of this reached La Valette he ordered a Muslim prisoner to be brought out of the cells. The carpenters quickly constructed a scaffold on the edge of the wall facing the enemy and the prisoner was soon hanged and left dangling from the scaffold. "Tell the Sultan that we will hang one of your own every day for as long as this siege lasts." It was not the hanging that displeased and upset the Muslim soldiers but the defilement of seeing a faithful follower of Allah not receive a decent burial.

Peter of Rhodes went about in his disguise penetrating the enemy camp as far as the lines of tents erected to treat the wounded and the rows of stall of war-followers who traded with the soldiers. He sat down with some soldiers who were resting and there he made contact with two Christian renegades who had been converted to Islam but who now had second thoughts and had decided to desert the Turkish army and join the Christian side. The truth was, they confessed that the Turkish soldiers were very despondent and discouraged with the resistance the army was facing.

Under darkness Peter of Rhodes took them into Birgu to see the grand master. "These fellows have something interesting to tell you, Excellency."

"Bring them to me at once." Said La Valette

"Grand Master, Mustapha Pasha plans not to continue his attack on the forts of Birgu, Senglea or St. Angelo. Instead, he intends to attack only Fort St. Elmo. Logistically, his troops will move into position much easier by taking his ships to Marsamuscetto. He intends to take the high ground on Mount Sciberras and place his guns there so his troops will descend downhill upon what he considers to be the easy prey of Fort St. Elmo." After cross-examination, the grand master was satisfied that they were genuine deserters.

La Valette responded, "Peter of Rhodes, take these fellows and have them change their uniforms. Then take them to the German Langue placement."

With this intelligence, La Valette pushed his men to strengthen the defenses of St. Elmo and provided it with adequate ammunition and provisions. The question was: For how long could this garrison withstand the impressive assault by the Turkish forces?

La Valette addressed both Knight Luigi and Colonel Mas. "We are grateful that you volunteered for this impossible mission. We are very aware that within days you may be isolated and I may not be able to support you, for such is our enemy's intention. We cannot give them an easy victory. We all expect you to hold on to the end. There is no question of surrender or armistice for St. Elmo. Your mission is to hold the fort for at least three weeks. In three weeks your brave action will demoralize the vain General Mustafa Pasha, whose plan is to take the fort in a matter of a day or two. The Pasha is not known for his perseverance or staying power. With our Lord's help I know you will hold, and your resistance will be a victory in itself that we will celebrate."

"I bless you in the name of the Father, the Son and the Holy Spirit. Go and do your duty." With that La Valette went forward and embraced the two men, kissing them, in the knight's tradition, on both cheeks. "God be with you, my noble friends."

BLESSING BEFORE BATTLE

Turkish Sipahis during the time of the Great Siege

SIPAHIS DURING THE TIME OF THE GREAT SIEGE

CONTEXTUS VIII

SHIELD OF EUROPE

THE FIGHT FOR ST. ELMO

True to the information reported by the two deserters, Mustapha ordered his divisions at Marsasirocco to sail to Marsamuscetto Bay and from there to high ground overlooking Mount Sciberras, closer to Fort St. Elmo. Dragut's contingent also formed part of this advance. La Valetta feared this move because he could not defend both the fort and the high ground. He had already decided that the best strategy against such great odds was to keep the enemy outside the fortifications. Skirmishers made lightning attacks on the Turks as they moved, and this delayed their advance as they pulled ten huge siege guns from the landing location known as Dragut Point to the high ground on Mount Sciberras. The ground was rocky, bumpy, and full of obstacles previously laid by the Maltese militia.

It was said that a lighthouse or beacon had existed in the vicinity of Mount Sciberras since Phoenician times, when the Punic traders had used the Grand Harbour.

Sciberras-ras meant literally "the light on the point". It was they who had given the island the name *Maleth*, "a haven". The Greeks corrupted the word to *Melita*, meaning "honey", from which the modern name of Malta derives.

At the extreme point of Mount Sciberras, on the water's edge, a fort had been built. The advantage of this fort was that it not only commanded the entrance to the Grand Harbour to the right, but also the entrance to Marsamuscetto, to the left. The latter was an important harbour on the northern side of Mount Sciberras. The fort was named Fort St. Elmo. It was shaped like a star with four points, and it had high sandstone and limestone walls. It was built on solid rock, so no attacker could undermine it. Another advantage, in time of war, was that it had no populated area in front or behind.

The one problem was that it had been built in a hurry. The sand-stone blocks were of poor quality, and there had been no time to build causeways or dikes within the wall to protect defenders once an enemy began bombarding the interior. At the time, deep ditches facing Mount Sciberras were dug around it. A counterscarp or ravelin was built, to stop an advancing enemy and delay them sufficiently to enable the defenders to retreat into the fort if necessary. The recently constructed fortifications were about 2500 feet long. But it was clear to all that Fort St. Elmo's weakness was in that it was built in a depression and dominated from the heights of Mount Sciberras.

There was much fighting on the rough and rocky route to Mount Sciberras as Dragut's forces advanced. Finding the opposition too strong, Dragut re-embarked and sailed north to Gozo, where he pillaged the island and carried away inhabitants as slaves. He left the Ottoman army and artillery to advance towards the siege of Fort St. Elmo. Dragut was merely testing the ground of the developing battle. After Gozo, his corsair fleet sailed round the island again and decided to anticipate the Ottomans' own fleet by sailing into the Grand Harbour.

The Sultan was very proud of his new fleet with its large galleys, and he had given strict instructions to Admiral Piali that he would view gravely the loss of any of his new vessels. This was tantamount to a death threat should the admiral lose a ship, so Admiral Piali remained prudent and held his ships well off the coast to avoid the loss of any of the Sultan's expensive vessels.

Piali was of Christian parents and had been found as a child abandoned on a ploughshare outside the city of Belgrade but now he sailed the largest and most beautiful ship that was ever seen on the Bosphorus. Over the carved and gilded poop deck, an awning of pure silk brocade gave shelter against the Mediterranean sun. Above the high admiral's stern quarters was set the personal standard of the Grand Turk—a beaten silver plaque, ten feet square, surmounted by the crescent moon and a golden ball from which floated a long horsehair plume. This denoted that Suleiman the Magnificent was represented aboard in the person of his janissaries. The Sultan himself was a janissary, holding the rank of a private.

They came well prepared for a siege; the Sultan's spies had informed him *"the siege should only take a few days"*. They knew that at Malta *"they would find neither houses for shelter, nor earth, nor wood"*. They had loaded in the merchantmen sacks of wool, cotton, cables, tents, and horses for the Spahis and sails, as well as provisions.

La Valette was becoming increasingly concerned about the future of Fort St. Elmo as the key to Malta. Why would the Turks put so much extraordinary effort into attacking St. Elmo? Did they, too, have the same opinion as La Valette, that St. Elmo was the key to victory?

Having placed the ten siege guns on the high ground at Mount Sciberras, the Ottoman artillery ceaselessly pounded Fort St. Elmo. These guns were so huge that it took the artillery men a long time to load the spherical rock missiles, so there was a long delay between one shot and the other. But the gunners knew their business well, and the six guns fired in sequence so that the firing was a continuous chain of shots. The knights had great confidence in themselves but had lost confidence in the material that had been used to construct the fort. Slowly, with each shot, the walls of St. Elmo were disappearing, and though the slaves and Maltese stonemasons worked at night to repair the damage, the destruction was so consistent that the repair teams could not keep up with the pace of enemy fire. Over and above this, whenever any of the construction workers exposed themselves, strategically placed snipers quickly fired upon them.

To counter this onslaught La Valette mounted two large cannons on a quickly built rampart at Fort St. Angelo across the bay, which fired directly at the Turkish emplacement across the harbour. The enemy responded by constructing yet another cannon site that, in turn, could fire upon Fort St. Angelo itself. The battle became a triangular action.

While the attack on St. Elmo continued, La Valette kept sending fast sloops to Sicily with messages pleading for help.

The Muslim troops comprised a mass of moving humanity and beasts. It looked as if an army of killer ants had descended upon the island, and unable to enter their nest, it formed the most unruly formation ever seen and it appeared as if the whole island of Malta was covered with a mantle of colours.

Truly, thought La Valette, *only an act of God, a miracle, could save us now.*

He commanded Knight Pierre de Massurez, known as "Colonel Mas", as second in command to Luigi Broglia. Colonel Mas had recently arrived with a company of soldiers and had pleaded with the grand master to place him in the battle-of-honour position. He was immediately ferried by boat to St. Elmo together with sixty-four extra knights who had volunteered for this post of honour.

After a long period of bombardment Commander Luigi Broglia, was concerned about the number of casualties they were suffering. Broglia sent an urgent message to La Valette through a Spanish knight called La Cerda asking for reinforcements. La Cerda's message painted a worse picture than was actually the case. La Valette realized that this man was scared.

"For how long Brother La Cerda do you think Fort St. Elmo can resist the enemy's assault?"

"No more than eight days, Grand Master," replied La Cerda.

"Eight days only? Is that all? You mean to say that they can only hold on for eight days? I can't believe the situation to be that bad after only three days of bombardment."

Silently enraged with the messenger's tone, La Valette asked for volunteers to go to defend St. Elmo. Fifty knights stepped forward. La Valette was impressed and told them, "You are a true example of the spirit of our order, for you have knowingly chosen to go forth to certain death in defense of the Cross." He also sent two hundred Spanish soldiers under the command of Chevalier de Medran.

"You too go with them Brother La Cerda, and tell Brother Luigi they must resist for another two weeks."

For the moment they *"depended only upon God and their own swords"*.

El Louck Aly, the governor of Alexandria, joined the besiegers with two thousand Algerian warriors; the attack upon St. Elmo became more intense. El Louck had arrived with four ships full of stores and ammunition.

A Surprise Counter-Attack

La Valette was watching the situation from his observation post in Fort St. Angelo. He turned suddenly to his aid and ordered his barge to transport him to Fort St. Elmo, along with several other boats and a company of his closest knights, including one-armed Oliver Starkey; the giant Emanuel Viale; Lionelli Bochetti; Joanni Caviglia; and Pietro de Car, with their respective sergeants and guards. In all a company of over fifty warriors armed to the teeth. He said to his knights, "My old tutor always told me, 'If all else fails, take the battle to an unsuspecting enemy.' So friends, we are about to give our enemy the second surprise of the week. And, at the same time we will fortify our defending comrades defending St. Elmo."

They arrived at St. Elmo fifteen minutes ahead of the Algerian troops. All six knights and the rest were dressed in full amour prepared for battle, but the grand master cut the most imposing figure. Over his armour he wore his white knee-length hauberk with the red frontal cross and on his black mantle the white eight-pointed cross on the right shoulder. His mantle, drawn in tightly over the hauberk, flowed out around the chausses that covered his legs. Chain mail gauntlets shielded his hands; a hood of mail protected his head and neck. Under one arm he carried his grand master's helmet. A medium wide broadsword hung from his belt. No thought of death was in his mind, no thought of anything, save a savage, reckless desire to visit vengeance on his treacherous enemies. To see their blood flow, to hear their anguished cries. It was a question of victory for the Cross or death under the Crescent.

When morning came, to the utter surprise of El Louck and the other Turks, there appeared a band of knights with flowing black capes and a company of warriors. Led by La Valette and his companions. Colonel Mas and Chevalier de Medran they dashed out of St. Elmo on this sortie, and after a brisk and bloody fight, captured the advance company of Muslim troops.

The firing and shouting of the fighters could be heard at St. Angelo. They were overjoyed by the audacity and bravery of their men, and congratulated themselves on the wisdom of sending the last batch of reinforcements under Colonel Mas. It appeared that the defenders of St. Elmo were capable of turning a defense into an attack.

When Mustapha Pasha heard the commotion, he went out of his tent, saw what was happening, and could not believe his eyes; he saw his troops recoil and retreat across the barren heights of Mount Sciberras. He immediately ordered his elite corps of janissaries forward.

Some janissaries hurled themselves against the attacking knights but with La Valette at the head, forcing them back they were repulsed. There was no option but to make a stand. Another twenty knights joined the fight. The melee of fighting men had built up in front of the fort. La Valette darted between the yawning gap of the enemy, slashing his blade through the throat of a black curly-haired warrior, and then lancing his left-hand short-sword into the neck of a second. His assault was sudden, his swords slashing, cutting, and cleaving. Those who confronted him recoiled at his courage and fighting skill. His movements were economical and deadly, it was difficult to penetrate his fast swinging swords that appeared not to stop. It was a combination of movements that dazzled any attacker who, if he dared, found himself struck dead or mortally wounded. "To me men! To me! Kill the swines. For Cross and the Baptist!"

A few Ottoman Turks tried to rush him; others sought to pull back from the fray, dismayed by the deadly speed of his strokes. Swords and spears clattered against his breastplate and bounced off, and a thrusting spear struck against his helm. La Valette was in their midst. Bodies lay at his feet, and his swords flittered as they rose, striking full flesh and bone. In the midst of his battle fury he realized he had advanced too far. His companions were with him and around him, protecting him, but by now the enemy had encircled them. La Valette thought that it would not be long before they would be over powered, hamstrung and dragged from their feet, lanced through and then beheaded, their heads held high at the point of a lance. Even as the thought came to him, a huge Ottoman Turk leapt at him, his shoulder cannoning into La Valette's breastplate. As he fell back he plunged a blade through the man's cheek. A hand grabbed him, steadying him. He saw Oliver alongside him thrusting the spear he held in his only hand into the assailant's face. Oliver, who had some movement at the elbow, had been fitted with a prosthesis to the stump of his right arm, it held a permanent small shield with a protruding stiletto-like spike in the centre, a tool he used for defense and for deadly attack. The giant Emanuel Viale swung his sword double handed at another's head with a ferocious cut that split his skull in two like a ripe watermelon and on the backward stroke tore another attacker's arm at the shoulder. The attacking Christian company was now surrounded and about to be overwhelmed by the superior numbers of the enemy.

Suddenly they felt the blast of explosions ahead of them. Two well aimed cannonballs, from St. Elmo, had flattened the whole line of wild janissaries immediately in front of the knights. It was a miracle that the flying cannonballs had not smashed into them as they flew through the air into the enemy lines; the credit for such precision belonged to either good marksmanship or God's providence.

"Vive le Croix!" shouted La Valette raising his sword and stepping over the heap of corpses in front of him.

"Long live the Cross!" repeated Oliver, lifting his spear and his small, round shield, which he used with great ease.

Several hundred Muslims lay dead or maimed and mutilated in front of them. Cries for help filled the air. When they saw the Muslims retreating, the knights withdrew in an orderly manner. As they stepped over the injured enemies they ended their misery.

Thinking that they had won a reprieve, La Valette, retreated back to St. Elmo and then onto to St. Angelo. Confidence returned, once again, to the brave defenders of St. Elmo.

An enraged Mustapha Pasha regrouped his forces and proceeded to make further bombardments before venturing into another head-on attack on the crumbling fortifications. Mustapha was known to throw his men mercilessly against all odds regardless of the cost to life. This was most evident in these battles taking place in St. Elmo.

Only hours later, the janissaries, in white flowing robes, some with scimitars in hand, others with their nine-palm long rifles in the firing position, climbed up to the great hole that had been breached in the fortification wall, they run screaming their war-cry of "Allahu Akbar! Allahu Akbar!"

It did not take long for the knights to split their ranks once again. The defenders bravely fought back and contested every inch of the fortress, forcing the Turks to retreat. La Valette watched this from St. Angelo and from there he said, "Well done Mas. Well done!"

Incredibly that same night, the defenders of St. Elmo loaded all the wounded on boats and carried them unmolested to the hospital in Birgu across the bay, returning immediately to their posts to defend St. Elmo the following day. Wounded men were a hindrance to the defenders; to remain there meant having to care for them, feed them, and share with them their precious reserve of water.

The Turks continued their attack, continually bombarding and reducing the walls of St. Elmo into fine dust. The blind night bombardment was the worst ever.

The janissaries, or *Yeni-Cheri*, the new soldiers, were an elite regiment that included sons of Ottoman Christians recruited when they were young and who showed physical and mental abilities. They received indoctrination in Islam, trained harshly in warfare, and were prohibited from marrying. Their only allegiance was to the Sultan himself. They always undertook very dangerous and difficult tasks, and were regarded as a commando unit—highly respected and feared by ordinary soldiers.

The following morning, after the night's silence, the fort was awakened again to the abrupt sound of gunfire. The difference was that the sound did not come from the heights of Mount Sciberras; rather it came from the direction of the sea.

They looked closely and saw Piali's vessels firing seaward. Piali's fleet was saluting the arrival of fifteen galleys, recognized by their large ensign as belonging to the squadron of Dragut, the corsair.

As agreed to with the Sultan, the notorious corsair had arrived to join Mustapha Pasha and Admiral Piali in the siege of Malta.

Dragut landed at Tigne at a location that in time became known as Dragut's Point, across the bay from Fort St. Elmo. From there he made the long march overland to meet Mustapha's army on the Sciberras Heights, overlooking the fortifications of St. Elmo, which so far, had relentlessly repelled all the Ottoman attacks.

Dragut, in a spirit of bravado, ordered his second in command to sail his massive fleet into the Grand Harbour irrespective of the gun emplacements up on the fortress.

He planned to storm his way into this secure inlet and fire right and left, first at the new Fort St. Elmo, and second at Fort of St. Angelo. Little did he know that he was sailing into a trap.

No sooner had Dragut's line of warships shown signs of sailing straight towards the mouth of Grand Harbour that La Valette, who was watching this maneuvers with glee, said, "Open all lower gun emplacements at the base of the fortifications! Wait for the order before firing." His order was quickly relayed to the artillery commanders located at sea level.

"Open the gun doors! Hold fire," like lightening the order down the chain of command to the battery. Immediately, the huge sandstone sliding doors covering the embrasures were slid to one side on wooden rollers, and the cannons were pushed forward into position. They had allowed the fleet to penetrate deeply into the harbour so that they could maximize the number of targets.

Dragut's captains were occupied and busy with their own maneuver of targeting the upper bastions. They fired a couple of salvos at the higher gun employments, not noticing the sudden opening of a gallery of guns at the base of the fortification walls aimed at them at sea level.

Finally the order went out. "Fire!" A tremendous barrage of grapeshot exploded from the lower walls, covering the fortification walls with smoke. The grape shots and round shot hit the enemy ships, dismantling rigging, and killing anyone on deck. The trained knights' gun crews opened a continuous barrage of fire hitting their targets at close range. The corsair hulls were destroyed, and several vessels sank on the spot, while other vessels broke into splinters. Dragut's fleet could not turn about and leave the harbour. Within an hour of the commencement of the firing, half of Dragut's fleet was beyond recovery. Only those few that had not yet fully entered the Grand Harbour managed to escape with slight damage. The whole harbour was littered with masts, debris, oars, and corpses. It was a scene of monstrous proportion, like a horrendous nightmare. Pirates who could not swim to shore drowned, and those who did reach the shores were slaughtered on the beaches.

La Valette knew that no other Ottoman vessel would now dare to enter either of the harbours and that they would maintain a prudent distance from the fortress from now on. Therefore, with this certainty in mind he ordered most of the ground cannons moved to the upper levels and placed them facing the enemy, in Fort St. Angelo, facing Mount Sciberras.

The Fall of St. Elmo

In the face of this disaster Dragut remained calm and continued to discuss the situation of St. Elmo with General Mustapha. As was his custom, he went personally to the front line and crept forward to inspect the fortifications at close quarters. This was one of Dragut's great qualities—he did not take what was told to him at face value, instead he personally double-checked things. On his return he informed the general that the reason St. Elmo was able to resist was because it was receiving continuous reinforcements by boat from St. Angelo across the bay. He told the general that this had to stop. He also told him that their gun battery at Mount Sciberras had to be strengthened.

The general ordered another fifty guns from Piali's vessels be transported to the high ground and placed at Gallows Point (thus called because it was there that the knights hanged pirates and criminals). This placement would not only cover St. Elmo, but also be used to fire at boats attempting to ferry reinforcements across to St. Elmo.

The general suggested building a new battery at Tigne Point to cross-fire upon St. Elmo from the north side. With this strategy the artillery attack on St. Elmo would come from three directions. The general knew that Dragut had the ear of the Sultan, so he made sure to comply.

As the Turk's plans developed, La Valette viewed these new arrangements with much concern; his fears for the future of St. Elmo increased. It meant that supplies and reinforcements to the fort would suffer. The defenders had to ration their provisions and supplies. The only means of sending messages back and forth from the harbour was at night, carried by strong Maltese swimmers.

When word of the disaster reached the Sultan he was annoyed at Dragut stupidity, though he was glad that he had lost none of his own precious and that Dragut's contribution in the planning and in the land battles was paying dividends.

The firing against St. Elmo had doubled in the two days since Dragut had arrived. But the defenders also increased their firing, so much so that St. Elmo looked like a volcano erupting, spouting fire and smoke. One night the Turks sent two engineers to spy the land. They crept very close and were able to peek over one of the downed walls. To their amazement they saw the defending guards asleep. They returned without delay and urged that janissaries be sent to make a surprise attack, where most of the guards were killed but a knight called Lanfreducci, who had the courage to hold the janissaries back, raised the alarm and continued firing at them as they stormed the walls using ladders and a plank bridge. Lanfreducci did this until the survivors were able to retreat to safety.

The janissaries continued their persistent attacks, and the defenders replied with musket fire, firebomb-hoops, and incendiary hand-bombs used for close-up combat. In this case, the St. Elmo defenders were successful against the Turks at a time when everything seemed lost. The janissaries in their flowing white robes, screaming *Allahu Akbar! Allahu Akbar!* became human torches when their robes caught fire. Since the defense trenches had been filled in by the Turks with wood and straw and earth to cross the trenches, this now turned into a fire trap when a firebomb set it on fire, creating a formidable obstacle to the enemy.

General Mustapha calculated that in the previous few days he had lost a further two thousand men. He stopped the assault and withdrew his men to regroup once again. Miraculously, only ten knights and seventy soldiers had been lost.

Even though they expected certain death, the knights and Maltese soldiers fought on, without rest. Since the situation seemed hopeless the remaining fifty-three knights sent the grand master a petition, asking him to allow them to withdraw so they could fight another day. La Valette considered their plight. He sent three knights to appraise the situation and report. Knight Commander Medina, Antoine de la Roche, and Constantino Castriola went over in a small boat on a moonless night. They made the return trip on the same night.

Two of the knights reported that the situation was hopeless; St. Elmo would fall soon. The third knight, Castriola, reported that the fort could be held and personally volunteered with six hundred of his men to defend fort St. Elmo.

La Valette's reply to the petitioners was that he had volunteers ready to replace them. These volunteers 'would take their place, as brave knights, and they would do their duty in defending the fort, as true Knights of the Order of St. John should do. Brothers our fortunes are writ in steel and sinew, not skulking in shadows and waiting for the end'. This was rather unfair on the defenders but it worked.

La Valette's reverse-psychological ploy paid out, and the fifty-three knights and their soldiers, not wishing to lose their honour, remained to defend St. Elmo.

Even under such excruciating circumstances, to withdraw was anathema to any knight. To do so was not in the code of the order. La Valette forgave them and instead sent ten knights and a few score soldiers.

Mustapha Pasha and Dragut were frustrated by the resistance and marvel at the courage of the defenders.

To top it all, a detachment of cavalry lead by Marshal de Copier surreptitiously circumvented the Muslim lines and attacked the Gallows Point gun battery destroying it and killing the gunnery detachment there. This now made it possible for boats to cross with reinforcements to St. Elmo.

Mustapha's fears were on the increase because he had received intelligence from Sicily that a large force was preparing to board and he expected a large fleet to arrive from Sicily any day now. His fears were compounded when two Maltese galleys appeared off the north of Gozo, and he wrongly assumed this to be the advance party of the Sicilian fleet. In fact, these galleys were the two that La Valette had sent away earlier to Sicily, they were now back with a mere five hundred soldiers who had no place to land.

Again the janissaries prepared to attack at night with orders to take the fort once and for all, and to kill all the infidels who were there. Once they reached the walls, they lit their torches and threw themselves into the attack. "Allahu Akbar! Allahu Akbar!" they screamed as they attacked.

There were so many torches that night looked as if it had turned into day, and the whole scene could be witnessed from Fort St. Angelo. It was another terrific battle, and the knights and Maltese soldiers, with incendiary bombs and pre-set traps, pushed the janissaries back time and again. When dawn broke and the fighting stopped, the Turks had lost over 1,500 men, and the defenders lost sixty valuable men. Any loss on the Christian side was disastrous, because unlike the Turks, they could not replace them. The Turks were so enraged and frustrated that they continued to bombard the fort for three more successive days. Gradually the fortification's walls were no more.

Mustapha sent a messenger offering the defenders a truce of unmolested passage and a few galleys for the Christians to leave on. The Turkish messenger was sent away with a volley of muskets.

Mustapha's desperation, on seeing his great losses, led him to throw the fanatical Layalars to attack. Drugged wild, after smoking hashish, they faced musket, cannons and firebombs with shields and scimitars shouting *"Allahu Akbar! Allahu Akbar!"*

The heroic knights and Maltese soldiers met them head-on and another fierce and deadly hand-to-hand battle evolved. The solid, well-trained knights and the equally fearless Maltese were outnumbered three to one. They needed no mind-altering substance to give them courage; their courage came with the Cross. Confronted by such savage and resolute armoured warriors, most of the Layalars stopped, panicked, and retreated. It was another unbelievable and unexpected victory; many Christian soldiers believed it to be miraculous. Surely their island was blessed; Christ and his blessed Mother must have been protecting them. But this victory was not the end.

A livid Mustapha ordered the open execution of ten of the Layalars as an example against cowardice. He then ordered another company of fresh janissary troops. These too met fierce resistance; they did not advance beyond the breached wall. When night-time came they were exhausted and had to call it a day.

The Christian defenders couldn't believe they had actually pushed back such a formidable force. The defenders had lost only 150 men, and the Turkish dead amounted to about a thousand.

Mustafa was tallying the totality of his losses and was concerned with what the Sultan would say about this. He dreaded the thought.

On the battlement across the bay in Castel San'Angelo, a large group of men stood around the grand master, pleading, some with tears in their eyes, to allow them to join the fight in St. Elmo. Thirty knights and three hundred soldiers were pleading with him to give them permission to cross over. The grand master considered. "Gentlemen no one more than I would wish that possibility. I myself feel as you do, and I would gladly join you, but lamentably, look yonder." He turned and pointed south. "The Muslim Dragut has repaired the battery at Gallows Point, and it would not be possible, even at night, since we have a full moon this next few nights, I cannot send you safely across the bay. You will be sitting ducks in the open. You will all be killed. Regrettably my answer has to be no! Enough! Get back to your posts!"

Dragut Is Killed

In the colourful command tent Mustapha Pasha and Dragut planned a final assault, a plan that should have meant the death blow to Fort St. Elmo.

The guns at St. Angelo had not stopped firing in their direction and causing havoc in their lines. Mustapha and Dragut discussed their plan in detail. As Dragut diligently pointed on the map before them, a shot from St. Angelo fell close by breaking a rock into fragments. Large pieces of the rock ricocheted and violently thrusting a large piece of the rock through the tent's covering. This hit Dragut behind the ear. He was thrown forward to the ground, and Mustapha thought he must surely be dead. A dreadful amount of blood came out of his mouth, ear and nose. Mustapha had the body covered and secretly taken away to his private tent by his personal guards; he feared that news of Dragut's death would demoralize an already desperate army. The last of the notorious corsairs, the infamous Dragut, La Valette's arch enemy, died a couple of days later.

A similar shot killed the Aga, leader of the janissaries. It appeared as if the gunners from St. Angelo were being ordered to aim at anyone with a colourful uniform.

News of Dragut's death reached La Valette through a deserter from the Turkish army. Sir Oliver Starkey was by the grand master's side when the news reached them.

"Praise be; this will now weaken Mustapha's resolve. Without Dragut's moral strength the General will crumble," said Oliver Starkey to the grand master.

"Indeed, Brother Oliver; today is a black day for the Sultan, as it is for our few brave men at Fort St. Elmo."

As La Valette uttered these words, he looked across to the distance towards the walls of Castile, attracted by the fury of noise coming from that direction. A merciless battle was taking place at the Castile fortification. Mustapha Pasha had opened a second front and had placed his large siege cannons opposite the walls and continued to fire against the walls incessantly with little serious effect. Luckily the walls were double width and made with much better material than St. Elmo's.

He ordered the St. Angelo's cannons to commence firing. From the advantage of their height, they opened fire incessantly upon the Muslim artillery on the plains with much success. Being the strategist that he was, La Valette calculated that by fighting a defensive battle from behind the fortifications, for every Christian warrior that died, ten or more Muslims died the kind of ratio that he was counting upon. He also hoped that the Ottomans' reserve of cannon shot, powder, and provisions would soon be depleting to a critical level. As the sun started to set, and expecting the enemy to ease their attack during the night, La Valette turned to Sir Oliver and said, "Brother Oliver, command a sharp lookout for the night. In the meantime, I shall do my customary evening round of the infirmary. Send for me if you have need. In the meantime prepare a team of Maltese saboteurs to attack, in the dead of night, and destroy those cannons."

Reports reached La Valette of an attack by two detachments of Maltese cavalry from Mdina on a body of Turkish troops near the village of Digli. Close to two hundred Turks had been killed, with the rest put to flight. This came as a surprise to La Valette who was not aware that the Maltese had a cavalry unit, so he suspected that such a unit had been formed and trained by his own knights.

The battleground in front of the fortress was not a nice sight. Hundreds, even thousands of Turks lay dead between the fort and the general's headquarters. The unburied corpses were rotting creating great peril for the enemy camp. The stench of rotting flesh in the open fields was overpowering; buzzards, crows, and seagulls had their fill. Even then, some daring Maltese peasants set out in the darkness to pillage the dead for valuable belongings.

Many of the invaders had drank from the poisoned wells in Marsa, and hundreds were now suffering from dysentery. The risk of an epidemic hitting the enemy forces was imminent.

In St. Elmo all form of order and discipline had disappeared. The situation was precarious for both sides. In the various attacks on the fort, the Ottoman army had suffered heavy losses, many thousands killed and an equal if not greater number, badly injured. Yet it appeared that the Ottomans' army seemed to have limitless reserves. For the defenders of St. Elmo, every single loss was a severe and irreplaceable blow to its strength.

Meanwhile the Christian guns in St. Elmo continued to fire at point-blank range at the oncoming Ottoman attackers, janissaries,

Layalars, Levies, and Spahis, who rushed forward in a huge mass of screaming humanity.

The reality was that no more than one hundred Christian soldiers remained, including two chaplains, who heard the men's confessions as the opportunity arose. The other practical reality was that in spite of the destruction, the attackers' route funneled into a tight passage where only a score or so could pass at a time, a veritable trap that required the minimum of defenders. Defenders also hid behind the broken remains of the defenses, half-parapets, and mounds of rubble, made use of every device that the Knights of St. John had learned in four centuries of warfare. Their most effective weapons were the firework-hoop invention attributed to one called Vertot, who had passed this directly on to La Valette himself, who in turn, passed it on to another brother of the order, Ramon Fortunii.

The following morning the Turkish artillery continued firing relentlessly from the guns at Gallows Point and Tigne and Mount Sciberras onto St. Elmo.

In a skirmishing attack, one of St. Elmo's heroes, Abel de Bridiers de la Gardampe, was shot and mortally wounded. His companions rushed to assist him, but he turned to them and shouted, "Count me no more among the living. Your time will be better spent looking after our other brothers. Go!" And so he was left to die.

That night after the fighting, when the knights made their way to the chapel for prayers they were amazed to find the knight of Gardampe stretched out on the floor, prostrated at the foot of the altar, reaching forward with both arms as if attempting to touch it. Half dead La Gardampe had dragged himself to the chapel while the fighting was going on.

The Fort's commander, Luigi Broglia, was badly injured as well, so Mechior de Monserrat, a knight of Aragon, took over command. But by a great misfortune, he too was shot dead soon after. Three other heroes of St. Elmo: Colonel Mas, Juan de Guaras, and Miranda were badly wounded, but even then they continued fighting. When they could no longer stand on account of multiple wounds to their legs, they sat down on chairs in the breaches and continued to fight, swinging their two-handed swords overhead. On hearing this news, La Valette cried. In frustration, he banged his fist upon the stone parapet. He felt helpless because he had dared not send reinforcements to them, even though there was no lack of volunteers, the cross-fire from Gallows Point was deadly. With a helpless gesture La Valette screamed "Lord, why have you forsaken these brave men? I should have withdrawn them earlier."

But the men of St. Elmo had no intention of surrendering. So far they had defended the fort for close to seventeen days.

The following day was the eve of the order's patron saint John the Baptist's and on this memorable day the fort was taken over by the Ottoman army.

In fact, strange as it may seem, while the fight had been going on in St. Elmo, the knights across the other side of the bay prepared to celebrate the feast of St. John. Huge bonfires were lit that night, and holy mass celebrated in the open square, Spanish, French, Italian, German, and the two English knights, plus thousands of Maltese and Spanish *tercios* participated and received communion. It was amazing that this solemn Eucharistic service boosted everyone's morale in spite of the lamentable loss of St. Elmo.

As the Turks cautiously entered the devastated fort of St. Elmo, they came upon six badly wounded knights sitting on chairs, swords in hand, prepared to continue fighting. The sight was the most heroic sight a warrior could see. They were encircled, De Guaras had his head struck off by a scimitar, and Colonel Mas was cut to pieces. Miranda was also dead, as were a number of other knights. There seemed to remain no further hope of saving Fort St. Elmo. Every single brave-heart had fallen.

The two surviving chaplains hid precious and sacred objects whilst burning everything within the chapel rather than allow desecration of these by the Muslim soldiers. Then the two, crying and praying, began to ring the chapel's bell. This was the final signal to the rest of the knights across the harbour: St. Elmo had finally fallen!

To weaken the resolve of the remaining knights in the other fortresses, Mustapha Pasha ordered the knights' headless bodies be set upon rafts in the form of crosses, and the rafts towed below the walls of Fort St. Angelo. The rafts slowly drifted past the walls, and from above the Christian soldiers looked down with revulsion, making the sign of the cross as they passed by. One raft snagged on a rock just below the battlement. The grand master recognized two of the corpses as those of Jacomo Mortelli and Alessandro San Giorgio. He was enraged at this barbarity, a satanic act of intimidation. Mustapha's other bizarre act was that of sticking the severed heads of Colonel Mas, Miranda, and de Guaras on stakes facing St. Angelo. "This is what awaits you" the message conveyed.

The grand master had seen much cruelty in his time, but none like this. He was furious. Brave men should not be treated in such a cowardly fashion, especially since these men were a credit to the Order of St. John. He screamed and banged on the parapet shouting, "Go and behead two hundred Muslim prisoners and then bring the heads to the gun emplacements up here. Quick!" Those present looked at each other in amazement. What would he want two hundred heads for? What was the grand master thinking of?

They soon found out. Two hundred decapitated Muslim heads were brought up in heavy wicker baskets and placed by the guns. To the amazement of his troops he ordered the heads loaded in the cannons facing St. Elmo. Gun powder bags were rammed home and about five severed heads loaded in place of a single round shot in each cannon! Guns were primed and then . . . the grand master lifted his sword, and said, "Ready!" And bringing the sword down in a swift stroke, said, shouted, "Fire!"

Heads landed on the Ottomans' lines, and frantic panic spread amongst the Turkish troops as the heads were seen looping towards them and smashing into pieces amongst them. The grand master shouted again, "Load and prepare to fire at will." His message, too, was clear: "This is what awaits you".

His rage subsided, and so he left the battlement in the direction of the chapel—no one knew if to pray for his fallen comrades or in repentance for his cruel application of the maxim "an eye for an eye".

On the other side of the harbour, Mustapha Pasha and his retinue entered St. Elmo amazed at the devastation and saw how few defenders there had been. He looked across to Fort St. Angelo and said, "Allah, if the daughter has cost us so much, how much will we have to pay to get the mother?"

The grand master's mood improved when he learned that reinforcements of seven hundred men had landed secretly in Malta. The naval commander had given strict and specific instructions to land the men only if Fort St. Elmo was still in the knights' possession. A scout was unable to verify this, but when the newly arrived knight saw the grand master's predicament, he lied to the naval commander sending him a messenger saying that St. Elmo was still in the Order's hands. The knight, guided by local Maltese scouts, instead of directing the seven hundred troops to St. Elmo, marched directly to Kalkara Creek, and from there took boats to nearby Birgu to join the main force.

CONFUSION AND REINFORCEMENTS FROM SICILY?

The information that reached the Turks was that the number of reinforcements was much greater. Mustapha's concern grew with this news. How would he explain to the Sultan that reinforcements had been able to land and get through his lines, and, add to this the fact that thousands of Ottoman troops who died at St. Elmo? He wondered if it would be a good idea to offer the knights a safe conduct off the island, in the same way that the Sultan had done to the knights at the island of Rhodes?

He sent a renegade Greek messenger to the grand master. "*Grand Master, the Sultan's General, His Excellency Mustapha Pasha, sends you this gracious message. He conveys that he values the bravery of your soldiers and that he does not wish for further blood to be shed. He begs you to consider withdrawing from Malta with all your men, weapons, and ships. He assures that every life will be spared in the merciful name of Allah."*

Hands behind his back the grand master listened intently without looking at the messenger. Instead, when the man had finished, he said to his commanding officer, "Hang this man from the flagpole!" The scared messenger pleaded for mercy.

To impress the messenger, the grand master instead ordered that he be given a tour around Fort of St. Angelo, showing the guns and the soldiers and knights in full armour at their stations. The amazed messenger cried out, "Allah have mercy on us, these people are really prepared for us!" Then La Valette showed the messenger a ditch, he pointed at it told him, "You see that hole? You tell Your Excellency Mustapha Pasha that that hole is the only place I will give him and his janissaries as their resting place! Go to your master before I change my mind and hang you. Off with you!"

The messenger delivered an account of what he had seen and a full verbatim report of the grand master's message. Having anticipated such a reply, the Ottoman commander-in-chief screamed, "If that is the infidel pig's answer to my generous offer, we will attack Senglea, St. Michaels, and Birgu positions forthwith. Give the order for the guns to commence firing."

If he first, conquered these three places then Fort St. Angelo, the strongest fortification would, in turn, fall like a ripe fig. With this hope in mind, Mustapha ordered sailors and deckhands off Piali's ships and assigned them to join and bolster the land fighting forces to make up for the thousands of janissaries lost earlier at St. Elmo. This move sapped the Ottoman navy of its fighting effectiveness.

Mustapha was in conference with his war council and engineers. "We must find a way of attacking these two targets heavily. These challenges are different from the Fort of Elmo. We no longer have the heights of Mount Sciberras to place our heavy siege guns and hit from above. Instead we have the Corradino Heights, but those hills are not high enough. The ideal strategy would be to get our ships close to the targets and bombard them at close quarters from the sea and from the land sides. But our problem will be to get our ships past the deadly heavy guns of St. Angelo. The question is how do we get our warships into the Grand Harbour to bombard Senglea, St. Michael, Fort St. Angelo, and at the same time attack from the land side, and still be out of range of the killer guns of St. Angelo?"

One of his Egyptian engineers coughed as the general studied the maps spread in front of him. Mustapha looked up at the engineer and nodded for him to continue. "Sire, I know that what I am about to suggest sounds ridiculous, but there is a way to get our vessels to the Marsa end of the Grand Harbour without the threat from the guns at Fort St. Angelo or any of the other forts."

"By the beard of the Holy Prophet how can this miracle take place? You must be hallucinating, Ibra Benkar. Don't talk nonsense and waste our time with foolish ideas."

The young engineer did not relent in the face of such a rebuttal from his commander. He continued, "Sire, allow me to explain. I have studied the terrain and the geography of the land, and I have determined that it is possible. Please hear me out. Let me explain. First, we sail our ships up the bay of Marsamuscetto to Pieta Creek. There is a sandy beach there where we can beach the ships. Then we pull and push the vessels up the beach by fitting wooden rollers under the keels of the ships, then we build wooden cradles to support the vessels. With our slaves and oxen we pull and tow the ships overland by interchanging the wooden rollers one in front of the other. I have calculated that about one hundred slaves can pull each ship. We will need another team of several hundred slaves to clear the path ahead of boulders and shrubs so that the rollers slide forward without hindrance. With Allah's help it should take us no more than five days to transport the ten vessels all the way from Pieta Creek to Marsa bay, where the ships can be slipped into the water and refloated there."

Mustapha stood erect, obviously impressed, hands on his hips, looking in total amazement, drawing lines on the map in front of him with his index finger. "Do you really think this will work?" he asked incredulously, looking at the rest of the assembly for approval or otherwise.

One of the senior commanding officers raised his hand, requesting permission to speak. "Sire, I do believe that such a plan is practical and achievable. When we beach the ships at Pieta Creek we need to unload the heavy guns to lighten the hulks. The guns can be towed independently on carriages driven by beasts, and once there, stowed back on board."

The general turned to the young engineer, "Ibra Benkar, I congratulate you on an ingenious idea, and I shall not forget this valuable contribution of yours. Gentlemen, we proceed with Ibra Benkar's plan. Inform your commanders."

The Turkish Defector

A stroke of good luck fell upon La Valette. A sentry on the Senglea bastion reported that there was a single man, across the bay on the shore of Mount Sciberras, waving a white piece of cloth. The man seemed to be well dressed, so they deducted that he must be an important personage. "Send a boat over quickly; we may have a deserter wanting our protection," said La Valette knowing the value of an enemy deserter at this point in the war.

The boat speedily set off to cross the bay and was seen by Ottoman soldiers in the distance. They ran downhill to stop the man from being picked up. The man, who could not swim, nevertheless dove in and struggled and splashed towards the approaching boat. "Help me. I can't swim. Please help me," cried the man in the water. On seeing his predicament, three crew members, a Syracusan named Ciano; Piron, a Provencal; and a Maltese called Giulio, dove in the water to get the man before the Muslim soldiers reached him first. The other crew members shot at the oncoming Turks.

Once safely in the fort he was taken directly to the grand master, they found out that the man's name was Lascaris, a Greek. Lascaris was so full of admiration for the way the Christians were defending themselves against the barbarians that he had decided to change sides and fight alongside the brave Christians.

"Sir, I have some important news for you. I have overheard Mustapha's new plans."

"What plan is this man? Explain!" Shouted the inpatient grand master.

The Greek continued, "He is preparing to sail his vessels to Pieta Creek and then transport his ships overland in order to attack the peninsula and fortifications of Senglea and Birgu from the Marsa end."

Unmoved, the grand master listened to this unbelievable news. The Greek continued. "Your Excellency, I overheard the General say that your defenses are weak on the southern side and that he can invade you from there. It would be wise to strengthen your defenses along the southern side of the Senglea peninsula."

La Valette thanked the man and told his assistant to provide clothes and food for the man but he should be watched closely, just in case. The grand master glanced at Sir Oliver Starkey and Peter of Rhodes and moved to confer with them.

No sooner had the Ottoman ships sailed from Marsasirocco into Marsamuscetto, than Christian scouts observed from hidden positions the Muslims' strange movements. They sent a Maltese messenger boy with a full report to the grand master in Fort St. Angelo.

When the full report from the scout from Marsamuscetto reached La Valette, it confirmed what the Greek Lascaris had said. La Valette nodded in understanding and considered the Muslims' move to be an audacious and brilliant maneuver. It was a repetition of what Dragut Reis had done years earlier at the island of Djerba.

He had no way of stopping the overland transportation of those vessels. He sent out various detachments of cavalry from Mdina to harass and slow down the operation. Mustapha countered by sending a large company of his cavalry to protect the long land-convoy of hulks, creeping along the countryside of Malta, pulled by a host of slaves and slave masters cracking their whips. It was a weird and unusual procession of timber, beasts, and sweating humanity that loomed in the distance. The Grand Master and his knights watched as the cavalcade of wooden hulks moved in the horizon like an army of worker-ants carrying their grub home.

La Valette conferred with his advisors and engineers: How could they neutralize Mustapha's plan?

One of his Italian engineers in this conference came up with a practical idea. "Sir, we may not be able to stop the ships from approaching and firing at us, even if they are vulnerable to our fixed battery guns, but we can avoid the landing of their troops on our shores, which is their intention—to bombard from a distance and land their army on the shores of Senglea."

"Please be quick and get to the point. What exactly is your idea young man?"

"Grand Master, we could build a high barricade, a palisade, a *palizzata* in fact, maybe about eight feet in height all around the shore line. We received a large store of pine logs from Sicily, and they are presently in the dockyard. If these can be piled into place in the seabed around the *isola* of Senglea so as to form a barrier, we can stop the intended invasion by infantry troops."

La Valette tilted his head slightly and looked at the young engineer, the whole proposed plan unfolding in his mind. "A *palizzata*, hey? A stockade—not to keep the cows in but rather to keep the bulls out? Yes, indeed, that just might do the trick. With a *palizzata* built at the water's edge there will be no place for the enemy to land. An impassable sheer wall of timber. Yes, yes, I like the idea, I like it very much. Commander, get every available man on the island onto the job. We need to work from sunrise till sunset and beyond, before the Turks have had time to refloat their ships and made ready for an attack."

The Attack on Senglea and Fort St. Michael

"It has taken us one hour to fix the first ten logs into place," Sir Oliver told the grand master.

"At this rate it will take us forty hours to place the rest of the four hundred logs in the arsenal," replied La Valette.

"This is not good enough I want every able-bodied man in the area: knights, sergeants, soldiers, militia, and civilians set to the task." Ordered La Valette and proceeded to walk down to the beach and with the help of another man picked up and loaded onto his shoulder one of the logs and carried it down to the working area. He believed in setting the example. Promptly a long line of men trudged in a loop carrying thirty-foot poles on their shoulders, two men per pole walking at double pace. An army of shipwrights and carpenters set to hacking points at one end of each pole, while blacksmiths set about building iron ties to hold the logs together in pairs as they were piled into the soft sea bottom. They worked all day and night under the flares of numerous torches. It was a task of pharaonic proportion, yet the palisade was finished in two days, long before the Ottoman ships were ready to sail towards Senglea.

When the Turks finally attacked, they came against a great obstacle a sheer wall of wood. They immediately sent scores of swimmers with axes and knives to cut and break down the barrier that was stopping them from landing their troops. Seeing this threat, the garrison commander, Admiral de Monte, turned to the native Maltese militiamen, mostly fishermen and men of the sea, who had learned to swim at an early age, and were perfect candidates to intercept the Turks.

Several boatloads of Maltese men, armed to the teeth, rowed round the new *palizzata* surrounding the peninsula to the other side of the palisade. They dived into the water where the Muslim swimmers were hacking away at the logs, bearing short-swords and daggers between their teeth, fierce hand-to-hand fight, one of the strangest of the whole siege, took place along the palisade. The aggressive and fearless Maltese, far better swimmers than the Turks, got the upper hand. The remaining Turks swam for their lives, several were killed, and many others injured, leaving the water around the palisade stained red with their gore and blood.

"I want to talk personally to these brave men who have fought today," ordered the grand master. The names of some of them were given to the grand master, pronounced by the Spanish commander as Pietro Bola as, Martin, Joanes del Pont, and Francesco Saltaron. When they came before the grand master, he told them "You have attacked the Turks with such spirit that I do not just say brave Maltese; but for men of any other nation, it would have been impossible to be more courageous."

With this failure, Mustapha Pasha attempted to tie the ropes to the poles of the palisade with the idea of pulling them from the opposite shore and bringing them down. No sooner had the Turks done this that another wave of Maltese swimmers went forth and scared the Muslim swimmers off. They sat astride the thick ropes, hacked away at them with sharp knives until they cut the ropes through. Once again Mustapha's plan was frustrated and was forced to abandon the scheme.

He decided then to employ sheer force. He ordered the newly arrived and eager Commander Hassem, son-in-law of Dragut, and viceroy of Algiers, to lead the attack on the landward side of Fort St. Michael with his Algerian troops. His Admiral, Candelissa, would lead the seaborne attack and invasion and try to get around to the other unprotected side of the palisade.

Masses of small boats loaded with troops set off from the shores of Sciberras peninsula opposite. It was an impressive and intimidating sight to behold from the ramparts of Fort St. Michael. Three boats containing imams dressed in black robes went ahead of the invading fleet shouting to the faithful, "Forward, faithful of Allah, you are fighting a jihad, a holy war. Paradise awaits you. *Allahu Akbar*!"

Behind the imams came several other boats loaded with the Muslim commanders—Turks and Algerians dressed in colourful garments ornamented with gold, silver, and jewels. On their heads they wore huge, fancy turbans decorated with pearls and jewels. In their hands were scimitars made in Alexandria and Damascus. Their fine nine-palm muskets from Fez were as decorative as they were deadly.

As the first of the boats neared the palisade, they ploughed at full speed into the stakes and chain. The Maltese workmen had done their job well. The boats laden with soldiers bounced about in the water not making any progress facing the obstacles. The defenders had built wooden-plank walkways on the inside of the palisade, so they were able to open a deadly barrage of fire with their muskets and crossbows from above. Admiral Candelissa had no other option but to throw himself into the water. His surviving men did the same. They waded and swam ashore holding their shields above their heads as protection from the musket shots and incendiaries that followed their path shoreward. Fortunately for them, two of the mortars above them were inoperative since their crew had been hit one of the cannons on the Sciberras shore opposite. When Candelissa reached the shore and looked back, he was horrified to see his men being annihilated, and survivors were being executed on the spot, so he quickly retreated.

Further along and simultaneously, Hassem and his Algerian force attacked in a wild rush, trying to set ladders to climb the strong fortifications of St. Michael on the land side. Newly arrived, they underestimated the preparedness of the knights. It was impossible to describe the wanton slaughter at those walls. The fort's cannons blew great holes in the ranks of the advancing army. But still they came forward with such ardour and resolution that soon one saw their banners waving along the parapets. Many Algerian soldiers managed to reach the battlements and stood to fight on them, but Chevalier de Robles ordered extra knights with Maltese soldiers to go forward to meet them. Soon Christians and Algerians were engaged in hand-to-hand battle like maddened scorpions.

When it seemed like the seaborne attack was about to be repulsed, a powder magazine blew up on the Senglea fortification just above the palisade. The blast was so great that it opened a large breach in the walls. Admiral Candelissa's troops regrouped and quickly took advantage of this, crossing the narrow strip of water from the shore of Sciberra's peninsula and scaling the smoldering breach of logs. The Christian forces had to withdraw because of the big explosion. They were aghast to see the Turkish banners lifted above them on the breach. Commander Zanoguerra, a Spanish knight, ordered a counter-attack. At his side stood the friar, Fra Roberto, a cross in one hand, and a sword in the other, his cassock pulled up and belted round his waist. He was a religious brother of the order, and was forbidden to bear arms, but seeing the perilous situation, and remembering the fate of the two chaplains at St. Elmo, he went to the enemy crying out *"to die like men, and perish for their faith, for the Cross."*

Both Zanoguerr in his shining armour, and the religious Fra. Roberto became a rallying point for the defenders a host of knights and Maltese militia. Their war cry "For the Cross and the Baptist!" slowly drove the attackers back through the debris, dust, and gun smoke down the breach. Regrettably, Zanoguerra's armour did not help him. As he put his sword through an attacking Turk, a lucky musket shot hit his face, blowing it apart. The death of their leader created confusion in the lines.

The Turks saw this, and with a cheer they took advantage and once again advanced to take the bastion. La Valette saw this from his vantage point in Fort St. Angelo. He also saw the Turkish standard flying. He turned to Oliver Starkey and said, "Brother Zanoguerra is in trouble. He needs our help. Dispatch a full company of knights to his aid."

Starkey repeated the order by shouting it to the knight commandant below. When the defenders at Senglea saw their comrades coming from Fort St. Angelo, they took heart, and the knights once again bravely re-took full possession of Senglea.

Mustapha Pasha also watched the battle from his own position in the Corrodino hills. Ten large boats with a thousand janissaries in them were waiting to go forward to attack any critical point of the battle. Thinking that the underbelly of Senglea fort had been softened, he smelled victory in the air, and played his trump card. A signal was sent for the thousand janissaries to take off. The boats shoved off at full speed and rounded the peninsular, taking them to where the giant chain blocked entry to the dockyard basin that had not been covered by the construction of the palisade.

Two days earlier, seeing the Muslim plan to attack Senglea, knight Chevalier De Guiral, stationed at Fort St. Angelo had moved guns back to the special gun emplacements at sea level. He saw the vessels approaching Senglea and could not believe his eyes. The enemy came directly to a point precisely opposite two of his hidden cannons at sea level.

La Valette was at his post, watching this development with a smile on his face. He turned to the knight and said, "Chevalier De Guiral, the fly—it has entered the spider's web again. Go and get them."

"Yes sir, I have given orders for the sliding doors to be opened and the guns loaded. No doubt they can see the guns and the danger now, but it is too late."

The Muslim vessels bunched together at their planned landing place below the fortification walls where there was no palisade. Chevalier De Guiral ordered the gun-sergeants to take aim and fire. At a range of about three hundred yards, the five guns fired simultaneously. Shot, shrapnel, and chain-shot flew through the air. The water around the janissaries' boats erupted like a spontaneous cascade. Foaming water, wood, human limbs, blood, and weapons flew violently into the air. Screams, shouts, and supplications to Allah came from the crumbling and disintegrating boats. The artillery crew quickly reloaded the cannons in strict precision, as they had been trained to do. Within one minute a second salvo pulverized what little remained of the janissary expedition. Only one boat, the last of ten, managed to reach the opposite shore, but with most of its occupants severely injured.

A few survivors swam to Senglea shore, and these met with a merciless reception by soldiers and civilians alike, who could not forget the atrocities done to their own men at St. Elmo. A local Maltese saying calls such retribution *"St. Elmo's payment"*. Eight hundred janissaries perished in this assault alone. La Valette was heard to say, "The battery of Commander Guiral was, in our judgment, the salvation of the island of Senglea. There is no doubt that, if these boats had managed to land their troops, we should not have been able to hold out any longer."

La Valette, from his vantage point, directed the fighting that was spread out in other parts of the island, sending messengers to the commanders; every spot close to a fort became a theatre of war.

On the land side Hassem's Algerian troops continued to attack the wall of St. Michael, where hand-to-hand fighting was intense. Chevalier de Quinay was creating carnage of the attacking troops, but one brave Muslim soldier, finding himself close, jumped at [de Quinay] and shot him in the head. Simultaneously, another knight, a second too late, pierced the Muslim soldier through the stomach with his sword. Meanwhile, the Maltese inhabitants, both women and children, hurled stones and artificial fire down upon their attackers and poured upon them large quantities of boiling water. The battle raged on relentlessly during the hottest hours of the day; about six hours. Then, without prompting, water-boys distributed skins full of fresh water and pieces of bread to the defenders within the forts.

Soon Hassem's Algerian troops, having suffered great losses, refused to attack. The Turkish toll in this sphere of battle was almost three thousand dead, whilst the Christians had lost about 250.

La Valette lamented the death of the knight Chevalier Quinay, and during a lull in the fighting, he asked the priest to celebrate Mass for the souls of all the dead, amongst which was the young son of the viceroy of Sicily, Federico de Toledo, who had recently been accepted into the order. Also dead was a well-known Portuguese knight, Simon de Sousa. A report on him said, "... *whilst, regardless of his own safety, being busy repairing the breach, he was killed by a cannonball which took off his head*".

After Holy Mass, and seeing that the Algerians were disorganized and demoralized, La Valette ordered, "Bring out the horses. Open the gates of St. Michael. I want two companies of knights to accompany me in an attack to chase the retreating enemy."

Hassem, a seasoned soldier, realized—as Mustapha Pasha had done during the battle of St. Elmo—that they were fighting a well-organized and intrepid opponent and that the notorious Christian knights were full of surprises. Although he had participated in many battles around the Mediterranean, he had never faced such a formidable and courageous enemy.

Mustapha Pasha was again enraged. His two objectives had turned out to be two major military disasters. The number of casualties was immense and became a great concern for the Pasha. His ammunition and provisions was getting low. He still had superiority in cannons and manpower, so he ordered all the guns to fire ceaselessly upon St. Michael and Senglea. The cannons got red-hot from non-stop firing; continued use would make them inoperable. The site of the Grand Harbour looked like an erupting volcano, but regardless of the bombardment of the smoke and fires, groups of Maltese swimmers continued to rob the corpses of richly dressed Muslims who had been the first casualties of the aborted landing on Senglea. They severed fingers to pick off rings golden and silver rings and retrieved ornamental weapons, jewels, and even leather purses full of gold coins. For days after, the bodies of the killed floated on the water. Expert Maltese swimmers seized them, and reaped a rich harvest.

Mustapha Pasha realized the important part that the Maltese population was playing. He did not blame them, for they had been invaded many times by Muslim Barbary corsairs. He decided to send them a message of *"friendship and peace"*.

The message went, *"The mighty Sultan Suleiman the Great appreciates your great devotion to your religion and your faith. He also understands that for the moment you prefer to be ruled by the knights rather than the Turks on account of past events. But the mighty Sultan will change all of that. Henceforth he will fully respect your customs and beliefs. You will never be invaded again by any Muslim. Instead, you will come under his mighty protection, and he will provide the island inhabitants with all their needs, including provisions, vessels, trade, weapons, and a yearly stipend for all the population. The only requirement is that you leave the island now, to return when hostilities have finished; and also that you promise to pay allegiance to the Sultan."*

The Junta of senior Maltese men met to consider the Sultan's proposal. One man, an Italian, expressed the opinion that the offer sounded good, and that it would be a good idea to accept the Turkish terms. The Maltese men took him to the ramparts and hanged him.

The attack on the forts resumed. The firing was so fierce that it could be heard, like thunder, from a hundred miles away, as far as Sicily.

Realising that Mustapha would next turn his attack on Birgu, La Valette put his slaves to work on building extra barriers inside the town. Slaves were scared of working in the open, fearing the constant bombardment. La Valette's determination was such that he executed or had the ears cut off those who showed cowardice. In the event of a breakthrough, the barriers would serve as obstacles and hold up a direct charge, giving the defenders time to wear down the enemy.

Mustapha Pasha mounted his white charger and led the attack himself against Senglea and St. Michael, while Admiral Piali set up a heavy battery in the area of Bighi Bay, opposite Birgu. Candelissa was given command of the fleet cruising off the entrance of Grand Harbour to attack from the seaside flank.

A few dozen of La Valette's messengers ran frantically back and forth, carrying orders and messages to commanders on the fronts. Companies of knights and militiamen responded quickly to the grand master's orders. Morale was high, and their faith unwavering but they were exhausted. Constant prayers went up to the heavens from their lips, not only from the knights but also from their adversaries the Muslims.

It was an impressive three-pronged attack as the *"Lions of Islam"* advanced like hungry preditors against the walls of the three garrisons. The war music continued; trumpets, drums, and cymbals filled the air as the armies attacked drowning the screams from the front lines.

On several occasions Mustapha's troops scaled the walls of St. Michael, and on one particular occasion they actually entered the fort. The defenders held fast for five hours, and to Mustapha's chagrin, in spite of all his efforts and overwhelming numbers, the flag with the Cross of St. John still flew high from the ramparts of Birgu. St. Michael, and Senglea, and the whole Maltese population in one way or another participated in the defense of the forts, climbing up ramparts and joining in the defense of Malta, every able-bodied Maltese in Birgu and Senglea had become part of the garrison. Every pair of hands was valuable. There was a different dynamic in place, the civilian population was not cowering and fearful it was now part of the resistance and fighting garrison. On seeing that his army was making no headway, Mustapha reluctantly stopped the infantry attacks, but continued with the bombardment.

From his vantage point Mustapha kept glancing constantly at the flag-poles inpatient to see the flags change from the black and white to the red and yellow, but this did not happen.

ATTACK ON THE CASTILE FORTIFICATION

A few days later, the Muslim infantry attack resumed against the fortifications of Castile at Birgu. "*Allahu Akbar!*" they screamed, "*Allahu Akbar!*" The massive Muslim cannons blasted a breach in one of the walls of Castile. Piali's land forces attacked the breach and managed to enter, only to find that there was a new wall, on the other side of the Castile fortification wall, blocking their advance.

La Valette's strategy had worked. The attackers were now caught in a trap, they were concentrated in a big mass in an enclosed area with nowhere to go and fired upon from three sides. Hundreds of Piali's men died in that attack, their bodies piled high one upon the other. It was so dense that Piali's troops could not move neither back nor forward.

"To me, Christian soldiers, for the Cross and the Baptist!" shouted La Valette, leading his men onto the defensive walls, with swords, lances, and pikes onto the attacking Turks. La Valette in his armour cut into the enemy troops and with nimble strokes swung his sword and blocked one thrust after another with his shield. A gap soon formed in the Turkish advancing lines, and the screaming knights and Maltese militia continued to cut through climbing over the heaps of corpses and gore. Eventually, after a couple of hours of fierce fighting, the Christians routed the Turkish forces. Piali watched in great astonishment as his men died on the spot, and those that survived turned tail and ran to safety.

Now Mustapha Pasha joined the battle, sword in hand, he led the forces once again into Fort St. Michael's. He gave orders for his elite janissaries to attack St. Michael. This he thought or hoped would be the final blow towards victory. The Turkish troops pushed until they were finally able to raise the Sultan's pennant on the bastion. The defenders, knights, soldiers, and civilians with their backs pressed to the wall and swords in hand were ready to engage the deadly janissaries. They prayed for a miracle, for only divine intervention could save them from sure slaughter.

La Valette could not send immediate reinforcements to St. Michael's because Birgu was still under attack. He hoped they would be able to hold their ground, though in his heart he felt this was doubtful.

Suddenly, from above the noise of the raging battle, they heard the Turkish retreat signal. In disbelief, they looked at each other. What was the reason for a retreat? Surely they were all dead men?

Mustapha, with victory finally within his grasp, turned his back on the defenders and walked away; giving away the ground they had recently and bravely won at the cost of so much blood.

Surprise Attack from Mdina

"Starkey," said an amazed La Valette. "Are my eyes and ears deceiving me, or am I seeing the Turks withdrawing, and have I heard a retreat call?"

"Yes, Grand Master, you are correct, they are indeed retreating, and I did hear the faint trumpet calls from the Turkish lines."

"Holy Mother of God, what could have caused such a turn of events? Didn't they have the battle won? Why did they retreat?"

When the Turks had fully withdrawn and had left the fort, the defenders at St. Michael fell to their knees, many wept with relief. They had prayed for divine intervention, surely this was the grandest providential answer and salvation from sure slaughter.

A messenger from Mdina arrived at the grand master's quarters. "Sire, I have been instructed to inform you that Chevalier Mesquita, Governor of Mdina, has advanced with his full cavalry under Chevalier Lugny and has attacked the Turkish camp in Marsa. Your valiant knights have destroyed the camp and killed everyone within. Only one man escaped on horseback, possibly to inform his general that a large Christian force had devastated the camp at Marsa."

"Excellent diversionary strategy by Governor Mesquita and Chevalier Lugn,." said La Valette. "Go back and inform them of our great gratitude, and tell them that with their action they have saved Fort St. Michael and hundreds of lives from capture by the Turks. Their action will give us time to regroup and strengthen the fort."

Mustapha Pasha assumed that reinforcements from Sicily had finally arrived and were attacking him from the rear; the attack on the Marsa camp was the proof. He knew, of course, that all Christian forces in Malta were concentrated in Birgu, Senglea, and St. Michael; he had decided to made a tactical retreat from the fortresses to protect his rear and avoid being outflanked.

La Valette addressed Starkey. "Which reminds me—when in heaven's name will Don Toledo send the reinforcements that he promised me? I have sent him no less than five requests for help, and I have informed him of our precarious situation, and still we get no reply."

As if Don Toledo had heard La Valette's complaint, at that precise moment, a soldier came up to the watchtower with a disheveled sailor.

"What is the meaning of this? Explain!" asked Oliver Starkey, sword in hand, standing between the sailor and La Valette.

"Sir, this man was picked up from the sea, floating on a piece of wreckage. He says he has something important to tell the Grand Master."

"Well, man, what have you to say? Speak up quickly, and speak the truth, or I shall cut your nose off."

"Sir, I was a crew member of a fleet of twenty-five galleys that left Sicily on the instructions of Viceroy Don Toledo. The fleet carried eight thousand soldiers that were supposed to land on this island to reinforce your army. A devil of a deadly storm broke as soon as we left Sicily. We rode the storm for two days and two nights. It caused grave damage to the fleet, and all the soldiers were as sick as dogs."

"What happened to the fleet? Was it sunk?"

"Master, I was swept overboard by a huge wave. Luckily, with God's help I got hold of some wreckage, and the currents must have brought me here."

"But the fleet, where did it go?" asked Sir Oliver impatiently whilst La Valette watched the man. Was he a spy sent to demoralize him?

"Tell me sailor, what was your destination to be when you arrived in this island? Surely you know that; all sailors get to know what their destination will be."

"Master, I did hear someone say that we were to land in Malta."

"Yes, I know that, stupid. But where in Malta did they say they were heading for?"

"Sorry Master, please don't get angry with me. I misunderstood your question. Yes, yes, wait a moment sir, I remember now, I did hear one of the crew members say that we were unloading the soldiers at a place called Mellieha Bay."

"Starkey, this man is genuine. Only Don Toledo knew that I advised him to land the relief force at Mellieha—St. Paul's Bay. Our only hope is that Don Toledo does not abandon us and that he will set sail as soon as he completes repairs and his soldiers have recovered from the unpleasant sea malice."

"Commander," ordered La Valette to the other officer standing close by. "Take this sailor to the hospital below, treat his cuts and bruises, and make sure he is fed and given a little wine."

He turned to the sailor and asked him. "Providence has brought you to our safe shores. Is there anything else? Have you any additional information that may be useful to us?"

"Yes, Master. I have seen more than two hundred knights board the vessels, they came from all over the world, from their garments, I think, they belong to your order. I know because they were giving the viceroy a headache on account of the length of time he was taking to find them transport to ship them to your garrison. Eight thousand soldiers accompanied them."

"Heaven be praised!" shouted La Valette. "Wonderful two hundred eager knights; that is indeed good news. One of our knights is worth five thousand Muslim soldiers. But I can't believe that the viceroy has only been able to raise eight thousand soldiers. That is not sufficient to hold back the Ottoman forces. But we will see. With Christ on our side, we have an overwhelming majority."

In a heated council meeting with his top commanders, Mustapha Pasha screamed, "Who was responsible for watching over the fortress at Mdina?" A member of the staff stood stiffly forward, not daring to look at the general. The general looked up at the man and screamed at him. "Why did you not inform me that there was an important detachment of cavalry stationed in Mdina? And how come this detachment left Mdina, and you did not report its movement so that we could have intercepted them?"

"Your Highness, the cavalry detachment has been in Mdina since we landed on this island. That information was part of the original intelligence. I thought you knew. As for not informing you of their movement, they must have left the fortress in the darkness of the night, since there was no moon on the night of their attack on Marsa."

"No moon on that night, is that it?" Pointing to his commander he shouted. "Off with his head! I will not tolerate any dereliction of duty. This man's unprofessional conduct has caused many lives and robbed us of our legitimate victory." Mustapha pointed to the entrance of his tent and directing himself to the sergeant of his personal guard, repeated, "Off with his head!" The man was roughly manhandled and taken out to the back of the tent and made to kneel. With a swift downward swoop the sergeant's scimitar took off the man's head.

"I want you to start tunneling once again under the town of Birgu, and I want you to place heavy charges to create the greatest possible damage, if necessary, to bring the whole damn place down once and for all, and bury all the people in it. Have I made myself clear?" ordered Mustapha to his engineers and commanders.

"General, that is a great idea, but we will use up a lot of valuable gunpowder and we will not have enough to continue firing our guns," added one of his senior commanders.

"Commander, if we blow up the whole place, there will be no further need to use our cannons any more. We will just walk in and place our flag on whatever is left of the fortification," answered Mustapha.

Thereafter, thousands of slaves worked on tunneling the ground under Birgu, an old siege trick often employed by the Muslims, from time immemorial.

Once the tunnels had been completed, they set a large batch of gunpowder under the walls in a dug-out chamber and set the charge off, creating a gigantic explosion that brought down a large part of the bastion wall of Castile, but not all. Piali's remaining troops were ready, and once the wall went tumbling down, they rushed in and gained a foothold in the town of Birgu, the grand master's and the order's headquarters.

La Valette Leads the Attack

The bells of the conventual church pealed with frantic alarm, signaling loudly to the town's people that the enemy had managed to enter the fortification. La Valette was at his observation and control position in the clock tower in Birgu's main square when he was shaken by the explosion. This serious situation required his personal attention.

He took a spike and a shield from a soldier standing nearby, called his men to him, ordering his squire to bring his armoured horse and his full-armoured dress. In a few minutes he was helped onto his horse, he put on his full-helmet and then led the company to the area of the fallen bastion of Castile. Unsolicited, a company of knights ordered their mounts dressed in armour and quickly joined the grand master.

The sight of the grand master, together with a company of knights in full armour riding purposely in company order down the street, soon attracted the townsfolk, and they started to follow the grand master as the children had followed the Pied Piper of Hamelin. The only difference being that this particular mass of people meant business. Along the way they picked whatever weapons they found: iron bars, wooden planks, hayforks, picks, shovels, and rocks.

La Valette climbed the still-smoldering slopes of Castile bastion and waved his spike in the air. He screamed, "To me men! For the Cross and the Baptist!"

His companions tried to form a circle around him and constantly and urgently urged him to take cover behind them; but La Valette refused to listen. Instead he challenged the Turks, in their own tongue, to come forward. "Come forward, you child killers. Come and face some real Christian men!"

The mass of townspeople climbed the torn-down walls and blocked the breach, screaming at the oncoming Turkish troops in their neo-Arabic tongue. The Turks understood them pretty well. A huge avalanche of bodies—knights, soldiers, had formed pushing back the civilians but the crowd pressed forward. They soon ran down the rubble and attacked the enemy, were dumbfounded, not knowing what was coming at them. Where were the soldiers? This appeared to be a mass of women and children? La Valette screamed at the top of his voice, "To me, people, to me, for the Cross!"

The people followed and shouted, "For the Cross! For the Cross!"

A split second later a grenade from the enemy's side exploded close to La Valette. Several civilians were killed, and La Valette was wounded in the leg. His comrades came to him and wanted to carry him away from the front line of the battle. He shook them off and stubbornly carried on, wielding his spike into whoever came his way. "We will not stop until we bring that Muslim banner down from our ramparts."

On seeing the courage of this mass of people fighting and rushing towards them, the Turkish troops stopped in their tracks, looked at each other, turned tail and ran. Witnessing this withdrawal, the grand master raised his arms and called a halt to the advance. "Well done, my people. Today you can be proud of yourselves; you have beaten those barbarians." The people turned around, rejoicing and praising God and the Blessed Virgin. "Bring down that enemy banner, I wish to hang it in my chambers." Having driven the enemy back he pivoted his stallion on its haunches. The mass of civilians continued their jeers and challenges at the retreating enemy. "You knights hunt down the fleeing enemy but turn around at the top of that hill yonder." Pointing ahead.

The engineers got down to repairing the breach, but advised the grand master that Birgu should be abandoned because no doubt the Turks had placed further charges underneath the rest of Birgu. For all they knew the whole town was mined and in danger of blowing up.

The grand master promptly rejected the idea. "If Birgu is left undefended, the enemy will take it, and then we face a double danger, not only at Senglea, but also at St. Michaels and St. Angelo. No, my brothers, it is here where we must stand and fight! We either perish together here or, with the help of God, succeed in driving our enemy off!"

The grand master was resolute in his decision because he witnessed the courage of the Maltese people. If he and his soldiers withdrew from Birgu, the civilian population would of necessity have to be left behind since there was no room for so many people in the other fortresses. He could not bear to think of abandoning them. He would not desert them. He was heard to have said, "If knights, soldiers, and Maltese men and women have to die, we will die fighting together." To enforce this, he moved most of his men from Fort St. Angelo to Birgu, and he burned the bridge that joined the two forts so there was no question of deserting Birgu.

That night the Candelissa's ships started another fierce bombardment on the fort to soften the sea defenses and to make it easier for the Turks to attack the walls on the other side of Castile. In spite of his frustrations Mustapha and his commanders were hoping that the Christian defenders could not possibly stand up to further attacks.

The Resistance of Fort St. Angelo

The grand master's losses had been heavy, and there was no reinforcement to call upon. Ammunition and supplies were also running crucially low. The hospital overflowed with casualties, and doctors worked overtime amputating and stitching monstrous wounds. All able bodied persons were ordered to stand guard. Most were in a pathetic state, injured, and covered in gore and dust. Others had one arm in a sling and a sword in the other ready to fight.

Mustapha's engineers had constructed several siege engines on wheels to scale the remaining walls, and were now ready for use.

That night, anticipating the Muslims' move, two knights, Claramont and Guevarez de Pereira, led two teams of Maltese militiamen through an opening in the wall; their task was to destroy the siege engines. The Maltese saboteurs crept on their bellies and quietly slithered forward in the darkness, on reaching the target they silently cut the throats of the unsuspecting guards. But instead of destroying the contraptions, they decided to steal the siege towers and wheeled them into the fort.

The defenders of Birgu were desperate, but Mustapha was more so, all his plans had been frustrated. Even the destruction of Fort St. Angelo had failed! Some fuses underground had not gone off.

Mustapha dreaded the thought of facing Sultan Suleiman. When his many failures and defeats reached the Sultan's ears, he would be furious and probably order his execution. His frustration grew when he learned that one of his ships, carrying fresh provisions and arms, had been taken by a Sicilian galley. It included a herd of goats and a supply of flour and gunpowder. The thought of this booty going to the Christian defenders was unbearable. It meant that his men would be deprived of these provisions. It also meant that he would have to curtail the bombardment by his cannons to conserve cannonballs. At the same time, Mustapha's military opposite number, Admiral Piali, was talking about withdrawing.

Mustapha resorted to commence tunneling again since a few tunnels were still intact, and he hoped to further undermine the remaining fortifications of Birgu. From interrogation of prisoners, the grand master found out about this. Maltese militia and the stonemasons started digging their own tunnels, attempting to meet up with the Turkish miners. They listened carefully for sounds of underground digging and went to meet the moles. When they finally met underground, there was hand-to-hand fighting with picks and shovels. In the commotion some tunnels caved in and buried men from both sides. The charges once again did not go off and so the Maltese militia either killed or drove the Turkish moles off, and carried the powder away to the fort.

For three long months the Christian forces resisted the best of the Ottoman Empire, and everyone in the forts questioned whether they could resist another day more. Their strength was at its lowest. They were exhausted, weak, and hungry. A wounded knight was heard to pray, "Dear God, let your will be done, but I know that only your divine intervention will save us from sure defeat. Father in heaven, we plead you come to our help."

Simultaneously, all the defenders—knights, soldiers, civilians, men, women, and children began to pray: *"Pater noster qui es in caelis . . ."*

"Our Father who art in heaven, hallowed be thy name, thy kingdom come thy will be done on earth as it is in heaven. Give us this day our daily bread, and forgive us our wrongs as we forgive those who wrong us. Lead us not into temptation but deliver us from evil. Amen." They prayed their last rite as if it were their last day on earth; a couple of chaplains moved around and distributed Holy Communion to all the community in the fortifications.

Providentially, it was Mustapha himself who provided the miracle the defenders of Senglea, Birgu, and Fort St. Angelo had prayed for. Mustapha changed his strategy in a way that would result in his downfall.

"We know that our enemy is at the end, so we will come back and attack these fortresses later, but first we will go up and capture the capital city of Mdina. The Sultan will no doubt be pleased if we at least capture the capital," the general pontificated hopefully at this possible symbolic victory of the capital city.

The Portuguese governor of Mdina was very aware that his city was poorly manned. Spies had brought him news of the impending attack on his city. What could he do to defend his precious citadel against overwhelming odds? He decided on a bluff. Since he did not have enough soldiers, he would invent them. He gathered all the civilians in the city, young and old men, old women and children and dressed them up and armed them to look like soldiers, some with sticks that from a distance appeared to be rifles. He made the children stand on raised planks so they would appear taller. He placed this huge multitude on the parapets and ramparts of the city.

So great were the numbers that when the Muslim forces approached, they halted and looked in amazement. Where had this army come from? Having been scalded several times before, Mustapha ordered a halt. The cunning Christian knights, whom he had considered easy targets, turned out to be a tough enemy to beat. This citadel appeared to be so hugely garrisoned that he ordered a full retreat. Then decided to resume his attack on the softer fortresses of Senglea, Birgu, and St. Angelo.

This useless round trip took the Muslim forces over a week to accomplish, long enough to give La Valette's men time to recover their strength and for La Valette to send another desperate message to Don Toledo in Sicily.

Arrival of Troops from Sicily

The Sicilian fleet of twenty-four galleys, carrying eight thousand soldiers and two hundred knights, who had converged in Sicily, from all over Europe, had already set sail towards Mellieha Bay.

Finally the troops and knights disembarked. News immediately reached La Valette. He was disappointed at the small number of soldiers because the remaining Turkish forces still outnumbered his own.

He estimated that about fifteen thousand Turks had been killed and maybe five thousand were injured or incapacitated, but he did not know whether the Sultan had sent further reinforcements in the course of the last three months, a high possibility.

Instead of cowering, the grand master sent a knight, under a white flag, with a message for General Mustapha, *"Give up your immoral invasion of our island. Sixteen thousand fresh Christian troops with cavalry have landed in Malta this day. If you do not withdraw, I will order these troops to chase you and your army and slaughter you all."* Signed, Jean Parisot de la Valette, Grand Master of the Order of St. John of Jerusalem.

The bombardments on the forts stopped.

Don Garcia Toledo having unloaded the troops further up the coast decided to make the return trip of his fleet by sailing close to the coast and round the peninsula of the Grand Harbour, he fired a three-gun salute at Fort Angelo, to give them courage and as he rounded Gallows Point he saw the Muslim fleet anchored close by, so he formed a line of battle with his ships and fired at what appeared to be a helpless Muslim fleet that, although in much greater numbers to his own, could not chase or return fire, since they were badly undermanned.

Mustapha Pasha Withdraws His Forces

Mustapha withdrew from the Grand Harbour area with the idea of embarking his troops and heading out.

When the early morning mist lifted there was no sign of the enemy. Instead, what was heard, was the sound of cannon fire from the forts and the pealing of bells coming from every chapel, church, and convent in the island, the loudest of which came from the order's conventual church of St. Lawrence, transmitting the sound of victory.

The day coincided with the feast of the birth of the Blessed Virgin Mary, to whom the Maltese attributed their deliverance. Malta was devastated it was a shamble of rubble, cannonballs, smoke and fire, smudged with the unpalatable signs of war, blood, and body parts everywhere.

All the town's people and soldiers gathered in the great square at Birgu to the ringing of the bells and to sing the *Te Deum* in thanksgiving to God. After the *Te Deum* there came a silence over the entire place. Even the birds in the air stopped their flight. The silence overcame those present with a sigh of anticlimax. People embraced each other, many broke into tears and cried unashamedly, both for joy and for the thought of those who had perished in these three months of struggle against overwhelming odds.

Once again the chanting of thousands of voices took up singing and with uplifted arms to heaven; they praised God: "*Deus gratias! Gratiarum accion, Deus Omnipotens!*" "Blessed be to God. Blessed be His Holy name. We give thanks to God for He is powerful and merciful. Praise Madonna, Mother of Christ! Praise St. John".

The people once again could go out beyond the wall of the fortifications and visit their torn-down homes. They found nothing but destruction and ruin. Everywhere was the grotesque signs of battle and desolation. The enemy had cleaned up in true Islamic fashion; enemy corpse had been duly buried and those that had not were meticulously searched for booty.

La Valette did not rest on his laurels. He ordered the cannons to be placed in more strategic positions to fire upon the Turkish fleet fleeing from Marsa, Grand Harbour, and Marsamuscetto, even though many of those had been abandoned since the chances of successfully escaping the deadly cannons at the base of the fortifications were minimal.

As the celebrations progressed in towns and villages, La Valette was consulting with his battery commanders when Oliver Starkey called him. "Grand Master! Messages are coming in from our lookouts along the coast. They report that the Turkish Fleet has anchored in Mellieha Bay and are landing soldiers there."

"What? That is strange," replied La Valette hastily. "I was of the impression that they were heading off to Constantinople. What could have induced them to such a reversal of action?"

Oliver explained, "One report said that some Turkish soldiers, who had been left stranded when their main corps withdrew, had spied the unloading of the incoming reinforcements from Sicily. They figured that the Christian forces they saw were not an army of sixteen thousand, but much less, perhaps about half that number. They decided to relay this information to General Mustapha immediately. The general was enraged that the grand master had fooled him once again. He reckoned that his present force of over twenty thousand could still take revenge by attacking the new relief force.

When the grand master heard of Mustapha's change of plans, he reacted fast and sent a mounted messenger, Ascanio de Corna, to inform the commander of the Sicilian forces of this development. When the Sicilian commander received the message, he soon looked for high ground near Naxxar and positioned his men to await the Turkish advance from Mellieha Bay. Soon they got sight of the advancing Turkish army. He gave orders for his men to lay low and wait for them to be within musket fire.

"Prepare all mounts. All knights and militia cavalry, to me! Bring me my war-horse and my armour," ordered the grand master. He was helped into his armour and then he mounted his fully armoured horse. All his knights did likewise. When they were all ready he raised his sword overhead pointing forward, he yelled. "Forward! We join our Sicilian friends. Company . . . advance!" Close to three hundred warhorses, belonging to the knights that had been stabled in the three fortresses of St. Michael, Birgu, and Fort St. Angelo clattered out of the battle area in anticipation of a final victory. Now the company, lead by the grand master with sword raised above his head, set off at a canter towards the interior to rendezvous with their comrades. "To victory for the Cross and the Baptist!" Chnated the knights in unison.

The Sicilian Commander Corna watched his men and bade them to hold their fire and position. But the impatient two hundred knights that accompanied him, who as yet had found no enemy, were itching for a fight. To Corna's consternation and dismay the company of knights took off galloping down the hill to meet the Turks yelling, "for the Cross and the Baptist!" Seeing this some of Corna's foot soldiers, caught in the excitement and euphoria of the battle cry, followed the knights. Soon all eight thousand Sicilian troops, including Corna himself, attacked the disorganized and unprepared Turkish army.

When the two forces met there was an explosive clash. Rifles fired away, cross-bows twanged their arrows, and slingers let go lead balls. Fierce hand-to-hand fighting took place. Even Mustapha Pasha himself joined the battle to encourage his men forward. He lost two mounts in the fray, but once again he was astonished that his greater number of soldiers faced a fearless and well-trained army. His side was once again taking a good licking. He was being outflanked and overwhelmed, his lines were breaking up and withdrawing with no sense of order.

Then, to his horror La Valette's company of cavalry appeared at the crest of the hill and with trumpets blaring they galloped downhill screaming and joined the battle, his cavalry broke through the Turkish lines slaughtering the enemy that dared to stand in their way.

Mustapha insisted and ordered his janissaries to form a rear guard with their harquebuses. They made a fair attempt at fighting, but Mustapha, cursing with impatience again, seeing his army overpowered by a smaller but powerful force, finally gave the order to withdraw and once again headed in haste towards St. Paul's Bay where Piali's vessels were anchored.

The Sicilian force and the knights relentlessly followed them every foot of the way, inflicting heavy casualties and killing stragglers.

They drove the Turks into the sea as they attempted to board the waiting boats. But some of the troops did not wait for boats those who could swim threw away their armour and weapons and tried to swim to the vessels. Mustapha had never experienced the likes of this defeat and regretted having made the decision to re-land his troops.

Over three thousand died in this encounter and on the way to the shores of St. Paul's Bay, the sands of that saintly place were covered as if with a mantle of red coral; but the mantel was blood—Turkish blood.

La Valette and his followers stood on the cliff top above the beach, cheering and waving their swords over their heads. A jubilant cry filled the air "*Vive le Croix!* Long live the Cross! Viva la Cruz!"

Once again the Turkish armada and the Ottoman army had been duly humbled by an inferior force. The defeated Turkish fleet humbly sailed away, never to return to the shores of Malta.

To the glory of Christianity the Siege of Malta had ended.

Invicta—Vittoriosa—Island of Heroes

Messengers were sent in fast sloops to carry the victorious news to the world.

Europe had been saved from the clutches of the fearful and mighty Ottoman Empire.

All churches throughout Europe celebrated in thanksgiving; bells rang incessantly day and night. Great victory parades and religious processions abounded through the main thoroughfares of large and small cities.

Festivals celebrated what was declared to be the salvation of Europe from Muslim dominance.

The line had been drawn at Malta, drawn by a few courageous men of faith and an even braver and faithful Maltese population. Malta became known as the **"bulwark of the faith"** and the **"island of heroes."**

The name of Grand Master Chevalier Jean Parisot de la Valette was on everyone's lips, undoubtedly the **"greatest of the Grand Masters"** in the history of the Order of St. John of Jerusalem and Rhodes, to be known thenceforth as the **Order of St. John of Jerusalem, Rhodes, and Malta**, and later **the Order of Malta**. Honours came to La Valette from all kingdoms and principalities. King Phillip II of Spain presented La Valette with a ceremonial sword bejeweled and inlaid with gold.

His Holiness the Pope offered the grand master a cardinal's hat, which La Valette refused. Instead he asked for money.

Funds started to come in for the restoration of the devastated cities and towns of Malta. The grand master took to the job of restoration. The town of Senglea would be known as **Invicta**, meaning **"Unconquered"**, and Birgu as **Vittoriosa**, meaning **"Victorious."**

A ceremony for the laying down of the cornerstone for the new city was held. A grand parade of all the knights, soldiers and militiamen stood to attention, with flags and banners flying, while a band played military music.

At the front was the group of senior knights in full ceremonial dress, black capes flowing in the light breeze, shining silver helms, ceremonial swords, and daggers at their waist. Sir Oliver Starkey, Peter of Rhodes (formerly Tafur-Ali), Emanuel Viale the Giant, Lionelli Bochetti, Joanni Caviglia of Genoa, and Pietro del Car stood around the grand master, a veritable group of giants and heroes amongst men: proud crusaders, defenders of the faith and warriors of the Cross.

La Valette's plans were to rebuild a new city on Mount Sciberras, the site of the great battle of St. Elmo. The Fort of St. Elmo was the first to be reconstructed, and the 'new' city would become co-capital with Mdina. It would be called Valletta. La Valette stood up from applying a layer of mortar to the corner stone's topside, as the crowd cheered in unison, calling out, **"For the Cross and La Valette! The Cross and La Valette!"**

La Valette waved at "his Maltese people". ***"We are victorious today because we had faith in Christ yesterday. The glory of this victory belongs to you all, the people of Malta and to our Order, who I declare this day to be called henceforth, The Order of Malta, and our eight-pointed cross will be called The Cross of Malta."***

Throughout the last five centuries the order had lost its home in the Holy Land, had been short-changed in Cyprus, thrown out of the island of Rhodes, finally it had found its new home: **Invicta and Vittoriosa,** the island of Malta.

In 1566, at Our Lady of Victories, La Valette himself laid the foundation stone for the building of the new city of Valetta.

In the final *De Profundis* Mass, Sir Oliver Starkey, La Valette's lifelong friend and companion, gave an eloquent account of the life of his friend Jean Parisot de la Valette, starting with the time in their youth when they had prepared to become young Knights of the Order of Hospitallers, at Valette's own family chateau in Provence, and how Starkey's own uncle, the chivalrous knight, Lord Williams Starkey, had been La Valette's military tutor.

Sir Oliver Starkey, wrote the worthy epitaph, in Latin, on La Valette's tomb.

HERE LIES LA VALETTE, WORTHY OF ETERNAL HONOUR.

HE WAS ONCE THE SCOURGE OF AFRICA AND ASIA, THE SHIELD OF EUROPE, WHENCE HE EXPELLED THE BARBARIANS BY HIS HOLY ARMS, IS THE FIRST TO BE BURIED IN THIS BELOVED CITY, WHOSE FOUNDER HE WAS.

Sir Oliver Starkey was, other than a grand master, the only man to be buried in that same crypt.

DEBELLATUM EST. (THE WAR HAS COME TO AN END).

Voltaire is quoted as having said, "Nothing is better known than the Siege of Malta."

LATTER COAT OF ARMS OF JOHN LA VALETTE

FIRING OF SARACENS DECAPITATED HEADS ON MUSLIM CAMP

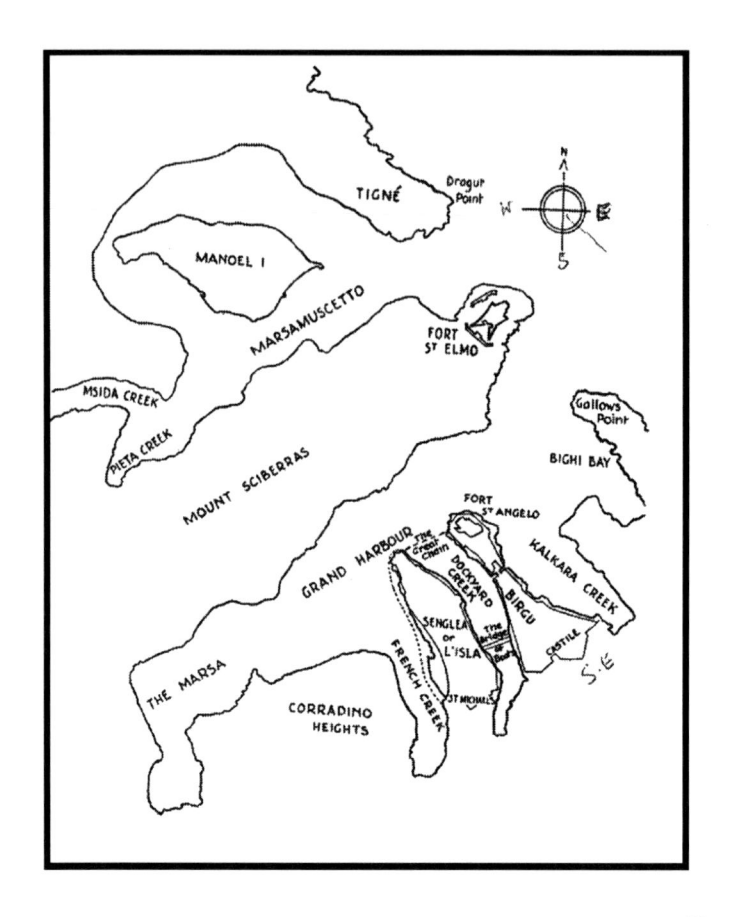

AREA WHERE MAIN BATTLES TOOK PLACE AROUND THE GRAND HARBOUR. 1565

GRAND MASTER FIGHTING OF SARACENS

Appendix A

Tradition of the Holy Lance

The lance (Greek: λογχη, *longche*) is mentioned in the gospel of John (19:31-37). To ensure that Jesus was dead, a Roman soldier (named in extra-Biblical tradition as Longinus) pierced his side. ". . . but one of the soldiers pierced his side with a lance (λογχη), and immediately there came out blood and water."—John 19:34

Saint Longinus

In the apocryphal gospel of Nicodemus, appended to late manuscripts of Acts of Pilate of the fourth century, the soldier is identified as a centurion called Longinus, making the spear's correct Latin name *lancea longini*.

No actual lance is known until the pilgrim Antoninus of Piacenza (AD 570), describing the holy places of Jerusalem, said that he saw in the basilica of Mount Zion "the crown of thorns with which Our Lord was crowned and the lance with which He was struck in the side." A mention of the lance occurs in the so-called *Breviarius* at the Church of the Holy Sepulchre.

In AD 615, the Persian forces of King Khosrau II (Chosroes II) captured Jerusalem and its relics. According to some accounts the point of the lance had been broken off.

Appendix B

Traditional Story of the Holy Relic of the Cross

Small pieces of the Holy Cross abound. In the tradition of the Church it is said that it was Empress Helena, mother of the Holy Roman Emperor Constantine who uncovered the Holy Cross. According to Socates Scholasticus (AD 380), Empress Helena (AD 250-330), visited Jerusalem to establish relief agencies for the poor and started building churches. It was during this period, as Theodoret (died c. 457) writes, in Ecclesiastical History: "Three crosses were seen buried near the Lord's sepulchre. All held it . . . was that of our Lord Jesus Christ and the other two those of the two thieves . . . . Yet they could not discern to which of the three the body of the Lord had been brought nigh . . . But the wise and holy Macarius . . . caused a lady of rank, who had been long suffering from disease, to be touched by each of the crosses, with earnest prayer, and thus discerned the virtue residing in that of the Saviour. For the instant this cross was brought near the lady, it expelled the sore disease, and made her whole."

"She (Empress Helena) had part of the Cross of our Saviour conveyed to the palace. The rest was enclosed in a covering of silver, and committed to the care of the bishop of the city, whom she exhorted to preserve it carefully, in order that it might be transmitted uninjured to posterity."

The presence of the Holy Cross featured heavily during the early Crusades.

It is believed that sometime in the sixteenth century the Holy Father sent a small, wooden cross made from the wood of the holy relic to Mary Queen of Scots.

The author visited the Church of the Holy Cross in Leicester, UK, which is run by the Dominican Friars, whose order started in Cologne in the 1500s. A piece of the relic of the Holy Cross, believed to have come from Cologne, is kept there. I talked to one of the friars, hoping I could see it for myself, but the relic is kept in a safe and is brought out only on special occasions.

Appendix C

Prince Phillip, Duke of Edinburgh investing Bishop Charles Caruana CBE as Prior to the local Chapter of the Order of St. John of Jerusalem.

Appendix D

*Ordo Militaris et
Hospitalaris Sancti Lazari
Hierosolymitani*

Magister Magnus his litteris declarat

Joseph Louis Caruana

*admissum esse ad Ordinem Militarem et Hospitalarem
Sancti Lazari Hierosolymitani*

ut munere **Officer**

fungatur in Iurisdictione

Grand Priory of England and Wales

Numero ordinali **93-166**, datum Brisaci, die **XXIII**
mensis **Augusti** anni **MCMXCI**

**CERTIFICATE OF THE AUTHOR WHEN HE JOINED THE
ORDER OF HOSPITALLERS OF ST. LAZARUS, A SISTER
ANCIENT ORDER OF ST. JOHN OF JERUSALEM.**

Author's Notes

True and Fictional Events

Little is written on Jean de la Valette's youth. In this work, the author has assumed some events as "logical possibilities," and has exercised much artistic license based on historical remarks.

Non-dialogue paragraphs in quotes, to the best of the author's knowledge, are direct historical quotes from other narratives.

- In the year 1558, a year after Valette's election as grand master, a baptismal record at a parish church in Birgu records the registration of a baptism of a child as the grandson of Jean Parisot de la Valette—an interesting note because La Valette must have had a son when he was bound to the vows chastity. Although this situation was not uncommon.
- However this note needs to be substantiated.
- The encounter of the Forbidden Romance comes from the author's imagination, based on the alleged baptismal registration in Birgu.
- The Heavenly Vision during the Siege of Rhodes is as reported by a Flemish historian of the time.
- It is not clear that La Valette was General of the Fleet or in fact present when Andrea Doria attacked of Tunis. But I transposed La Valette into this action though the sea battle is as recorded.

- La Valette's last words, "Jerusalem, Jerusalem," were originally attributed to King Louis IX of France, Saint Louis the Crusader, who died of dysentery in 1270 A.D.
- The Children's Crusade, which inspired the legend of the Pied Piper of Hamelin, forms part of a historical legend.
- The story of Longinus's Lance and the Holy Cross form part of recorded tradition, though La Valette played no part in its movements. (See appendices A and B.)
- The manuscripts and scrolls recovered from the island of Rhodes exist to this day, but at the time of this story they were located in other locations such as Antioch and Jerusalem.
- Valette was indeed wounded by two arrows in the Siege of Rhodes and left the island with the arrowheads still in his body.
- Valette did spend one year as a slave in a galley. The author's story of the mutiny and escape is another piece of embellishment. The order paid a heavy ransom for Valette's release.
- Valette's two early imprisonments in Rhodes for "youthful pranks" are true, as recorded.
- Oliver Starkey's loss of his arm is a purely fictional addition. He continued to serve the order with his two arms.
- The incendiary hand-bomb as used by the order during the siege is true.
- For easy flow of the story, La Valette's arrival and nomination as grand master appear in the story to have happened in the same year, but his appointment took place six years <u>before</u> the siege.
- Most of the references of the attacks and the battle for St. Elmo reflect the true historical accounts, although La Valette is not known physically to have participated in the defense of St. Elmo. My account of the battle is but a poor reflection of the true historical incredible accounts of the siege.
- The sea battle off Ceuta in North Africa did not take place there. It is in fact an account of the famous Battle of Lepanto, in 1571, six years after the victory of the siege of Malta. I include it here because it was the second victorious defeat of the Ottoman Empire's fleet and its final humiliation: The account of the battle is factual, and took place three years after Jean de la Valette's death. The Lepanto battle was the kind of battle that La Valette

would have cherished to have been in. Naturally, I repositioned La Valette in this battle and moved its location.

- The story of Miguel Cervantes and his quotes, as well as being a Muslim slave and his various escapes, appear to be true, although perhaps slightly embellished by someone obsessed with the chivalric period. I am not aware that the paths of Cervantes and La Valette ever crossed.
- Both Dragut and Hassan Pasha were enslaved and employed in Christian galleys. Dragut was ransomed by the Sultan, which was a great tactical mistake by the Christian forces, since Dragut became the order's greatest antagonist and La Valette's greatest foe during the Great Siege.

About the Author
Joe Louis Caruana, MBE

Joe Caruana was born in Gibraltar on 13 November 1937. He attended Gibraltar Technical College. He worked as a draughtsman at the Air Ministry in Gibraltar and the UK and studied Engineering at the London Polytechnic. He became a specialist in industrial diamonds.

Joe's public life started in 1966 when he became founding secretary of the Gibraltar Junior Chamber of Commerce. In 1967 he entered politics and joined the executive of the Integration with Britain Party in Gibraltar. The IWBP won the 1969 general elections, and he served as Minister for Medical Services from 1969-70, and from 1970-72 as Minister for Public Works). He served as a member of the Gibraltar Council and was chairman of several important committees including the Development and Planning Commission.

In 1975 Joe and his family went to Canada and stayed there for twelve years, starting a successful business in his old profession in the industrial diamond drilling industry.

Around 1984 Joe volunteered to help at a home that helped teenage prostitutes and drug addicts called Exodus House in Calgary Alberta, run by lay Franciscan brothers, an order he joined at the time.

In 1987 Joe sold his business and with his Franciscan spirit moved back to Gibraltar. With him he brought the idea of starting a rehabilitation centre, which he called Camp Emmanuel. Camp Emmanuel became very well known from 1987 till 1998. In 1991 Joe pioneered the Narcotics Anonymous group in Gibraltar and also assisted in starting another NA group in nearby Spain. That same year Joe started two other vital groups, 'The Family Group Meetings,' known today as 'Family Anonymous,' and the 'Drug Advisory Service,' a place where people could make contact and get support.

In 1999 he revived the Integration With Britain Movement, continuing the political ideal of making Gibraltar a region of the UK.

Joe is an accomplished painter, and his paintings have sold worldwide.

To this day, Joe continues to give valuable counselling to those who seek help and is a director of Nazareth House, that houses 'The Soup Kitchen' and where several self-help groups meet on a daily basis.

His first book, *'Spirit Of The Phoenician'*, is his own autobiography that starts with what he considers the roots of his family, the vastly travelled and ingenious Phoenicians—no doubt a reflection of his own life.

In 2010 on the occasion of Her Majesty Queen Elizabeth II's birthday Her Majesty made Joe a Member of the Most Excellent Order of the British Empire and awarded Joe the MBE.

Lightning Source UK Ltd.
Milton Keynes UK
UKOW05f1942221213

223525UK00001B/70/P